DANA GIOIA

Poet and Critic

MERCER UNIVERSITY PRESS

Endowed by

TOM WATSON BROWN
and
THE WATSON-BROWN FOUNDATION, INC.

DANA GIOIA

Poet and Critic

Edited by

John Zheng and *Jon Parrish Peede*

MERCER UNIVERSITY PRESS

MACON, GEORGIA

MUP/ P705

© 2024 by Mercer University Press
Published by Mercer University Press
1501 Mercer University Drive
Macon, Georgia 31207
All rights reserved. This book may not be reproduced in whole or in part, including illustrations, in any form (beyond that copying permitted by Sections 107 and 108 of the U.S. Copyright Law and except by reviewers for the public press), without written permission from the publisher.

This publication is made possible in part with support of Fieldstead and Company to whom we offer heartfelt thanks.

28 27 26 25 24   5 4 3 2 1

Books published by Mercer University Press are printed on acid-free paper that meets the requirements of the American National Standard for Information Sciences—Permanence of Paper for Printed Library Materials.

Printed and bound in the United States.

This book is set in Adobe Caslon.

Cover design by Burt&Burt.

Cover photograph ©2023 John Burgess / *The Press Democrat*

ISBN 978-0-88146-956-1 Print
978-0-88146-957-8 eBook

Cataloging-in-Publication Data is available from the Library of Congress

CONTENTS

ABBREVIATIONS

Poetry

DH *Daily Horoscope*

GW *The Gods of Winter*

IN *Interrogations at Noon*

PB *Pity the Beautiful*

99P *99 Poems: New and Selected*

MML *Meet Me at the Lighthouse*

Criticism

CPM *Can Poetry Matter?*

CPM10 *Can Poetry Matter? Tenth Anniversary Edition*

DI *Disappearing Ink: Poetry at the End of Print Culture*

CW *The Catholic Writer Today*

DANA GIOIA

A CHRONOLOGY

April Lindner and John Zheng

1950 Born December 24 at California Lutheran Hospital in Los Angeles to Michael Gioia, a cab driver, and Dorothy Ortiz Gioia, a telephone operator. Given the name of Michael Dana Gioia.

1955 Family moves into a triplex apartment in Hawthorne, California, next door to Gioia's Sicilian grandparents, aunt, uncle, and cousins. Gioia's maternal uncle, Theodore Ortiz, a Merchant Marine, who has been living with the family while not at sea, dies in November in a plane crash. A working-class intellectual devoted to classical music and involved in radical politics, Ortiz leaves behind a library of books in six languages, recordings, and musical scores that fill the Gioia apartment and garage. These books and records will play a profound role in Dana's intellectual and artistic development.

1957 Brother Ted is born in Los Angeles.

1957–1965 Attends St. Joseph's, a parochial school run by the Sisters of Providence, in Hawthorne.

1958 Begins piano and music theory lessons at St. Joseph's. Will continue music lessons until college, eventually learning alto clarinet, bass clarinet, and tenor saxophone in addition to piano.

1959 Father opens a children's shoe store two blocks from the family home. Dana begins to work in the store on weekends and babysits his brother Ted while their parents work.

1965–1969	Attends Junipero Serra High School, a Marianist Catholic boys' school, in Gardena, California. Studies Latin. Is valedictorian, editor of school paper, and president of the speech club. Wins a statewide essay contest. Expelled or suspended for conduct three times.
1969	Enters Stanford University in the fall with the plan of becoming a composer.
1970	In May, brother Gregory is born in Los Angeles.
1970–1971	Studies German and music in the Stanford-in-Austria program in Vienna. Develops love of opera. Decides to be a poet.
1971	In July, sister Cara is born in Los Angeles.
1971–1973	Majors in English with German minor. Learns French. Mentored by Herbert Lindenberger and Diane Middlebrook. Edits *Sequoia*, Stanford's literary magazine. Wins department prize for best English honors essay (on Edgar Allan Poe's short stories).
1973	Graduates Stanford with highest honors and receives a fellowship to Harvard University, where he studies comparative literature.
1974–1975	Works with Robert Fitzgerald, Elizabeth Bishop, and Northrop Frye. Becomes resident tutor at North House. Completes all course work for PhD but decides not to complete degree. Parents leave Los Angeles to move to Sebastopol, California.
1975	Returns to California in the fall to attend Stanford Graduate School of Business. Becomes poetry editor of *Sequoia*. Starts reviewing regularly for *Stanford Daily* and other Bay Area journals. Audits eighteenth-century English poetry with Donald Davie. Decides to stop publishing poetry but continues writing. Meets Mary Hiecke, fellow MBA student.

1976	Works for the summer as a marketing intern at General Mills in Minneapolis, Minnesota. Discovers the poetry of Weldon Kees.
1976–1977	Enrolls in Davie's graduate poetry writer's seminar with the reluctant permission of the business school dean. His fellow students in Davie's class include Vikram Seth, John Gery, and Vickie Hearne. After class is finished, they create informal writing group.
1977	Graduates in June with MBA. Spends summer in Rome, writing and reading. In September begins work as assistant product manager in the Beverage Division of General Foods in White Plains, New York. Keeps literary career secret from fellow employees.
1980	Marries Mary Hiecke (born in Los Angeles on May 26, 1953). They move to an apartment in Bronxville, New York. Promoted to product manager on new product development. Meets Michael Peich, a fellow Kees enthusiast, who is planning to start a private press in West Chester, Pennsylvania.
1981	Becomes product manager in General Foods Beverage Division. Continues to write on nights and weekends. Resumes publishing verse after seven-year hiatus but conceals his identity as a poet from co-workers.
1982	Fine press publication of *Two Poems* from Bowery Press and *Daily Horoscope* from Windhover Press. Poems appear in the *New Yorker*, the *Hudson Review*, and *Poetry*.
1983	Moves to Hastings-on-Hudson, New York. Abbatoir Editions publishes *The Ceremony and Other Stories* by Weldon Kees, edited with introduction by Gioia. Abbatoir also publishes Gioia's *Letter to the Bahamas*. Michael Peich's newly established Aralia Press issues *Summer* in a fine press edition as its first poetry publication.

1984	Graywolf Press publishes expanded edition of Kees's *The Ceremony and Other Stories*. Gioia is included in *Esquire*'s first list of "The Best of the New Generation: Men and Women Under Forty Who Are Changing America." The *Esquire* article inspires a series of magazine and newspaper profiles about "the businessman-poet." Literary career becomes known to co-workers at General Foods.
1985	New Rivers Press publishes *Poems from Italy*, an anthology of Italian poems in translation, co-edited by William Jay Smith. Co-edits with Alastair Reid *The Printed Poem / The Poem as Print*, a series of twenty-four broadsides published by the Press at Colorado College, which becomes a touring exhibition in libraries and art galleries. Invited to teach poetry at the Wesleyan Writers Conference in Middletown, Connecticut—his first teaching position. He will teach or speak at the conference each summer for the next twelve years.
1986	Graywolf Press publishes first full-length poetry collection, *Daily Horoscope*. Fine Press publication of *Journeys in Sunlight* from Ex Ophidia. Joins the Board of Governors of Poetry Society of America.
1987	One of fifteen young poets selected by former Library of Congress Consultants in Poetry to read at Library of Congress. Fine Press Publication of *Words for Music* from Parallel Editions. First son, Michael Jasper Gioia, born in August. In December, the boy dies from sudden infant death syndrome. Stops writing for a year.
1988	Promoted to marketing manager of Desserts Division. Second son, Theodore Jasper Gioia, is born in November. Becomes contributing editor to the *Hudson Review*.
1989	Produces and performs with his brother, pianist Ted Gioia, in "An Evening of Jazz and Poetry" in New York City. Translates work by Mario Luzi, Bartolo Cattafi, and Valerio Magrelli for special Italian issue of *Poetry*.

1990	Graywolf Press publishes translation of Eugenio Montale's *Mottetti: Poems of Love*. Promoted to vice president of marketing at General Foods. Delivers the first "Poets on Poetry" lecture at the New York Public Library. This lecture, "The Subculture of Poetry," becomes revised and expanded into the essay "Can Poetry Matter?"
1991	Publication of second poetry collection, *The Gods of Winter*, from Graywolf Press. The book is published in England by Peterloo Press and is chosen as the main selection by the Poetry Book Society. Fine Press publication of *Planting a Sequoia* from Aralia Press. Publication of *New Italian Poets*, a bilingual anthology co-edited by Michael Palma. Appointed as elector for the US Poets' Corner. Joins board of directors of Story Line Press and is elected president. In May *Atlantic* publishes "Can Poetry Matter?," sparking heated public debate on the role of poetry in contemporary American intellectual life. Gioia is featured in television, radio, and print interviews.
1992	Leaves General Foods for career as full-time writer. First critical collection, *Can Poetry Matter?: Essays on Poetry and American Culture*, published by Graywolf Press. *The Gods of Winter* shares Poets' Prize with Adrienne Rich's *An Atlas of the Difficult World*. Teaches a graduate course in poetic form at Johns Hopkins but declines invitation to teach again. Becomes commentator for BBC Radio. Elected vice president of Poetry Society of America. Tours extensively giving readings and lectures.
1993	Birth of third son, Michael Frederick Gioia, in January. Fine Press Publication of *Juno Plots Her Revenge* from Aralia Press. Becomes poetry editor of *Italian Americana*.
1994	Aralia Press publishes *Formal Introductions: An Investigative Anthology*, the first anthology of New Formalist poetry. *Counting the Children* staged as a dance performance by Mark Ruhala Performance Ensemble, Hastings-on-Hudson, New York. Successful production is extended for

fourteen performances. Delivers the Fales Lecture, "Poetry at the End of Print Culture," at New York University. HarperCollins publishes *An Introduction to Poetry*, eighth edition, co-edited with X. J. Kennedy. Helps Scottish poet Gerry Cambridge create *The Dark Horse*, a transatlantic journal of poetry and opinion, for which Gioia becomes US advisory editor.

1995 Premiere of staged reading of *The Madness of Hercules*, Gioia's translation of Seneca, by Presence Productions, with Angelica Torn and Rodney Charles, in New York City. HarperCollins publishes *Literature: An Introduction to Fiction, Poetry, and Drama*, sixth edition, and *An Introduction to Fiction*, sixth edition, both co-edited with X. J. Kennedy. Co-founds, with Michael Peich, West Chester Poetry Conference on Form and Narrative. First annual conference held June with Richard Wilbur as keynote speaker. Translation of *The Madness of Hercules* appears in *Seneca: The Tragedies*, vol. 2, from Johns Hopkins, which also features a long introduction by Gioia. The Berg Collection of the New York Public Library opens the first half of its two-part centenary exhibition, *The Hand of the Poet: Original Manuscripts by 100 Masters*, co-curated by Gioia and Rodney Phillips.

1996 Moves to Sonoma County, California, outside Santa Rosa, to be near his parents. Accepts Ferrol Sams Visiting Chair in Writing at Mercer University. First showcase of music from the opera-in-progress, *Nosferatu*, performed at Mercer in May.

1997 University of Arkansas Press publishes *Certain Solitudes: Essays on the Poetry of Donald Justice*, co-edited with William Logan. Becomes classical music critic for *San Francisco* magazine. Serves as John Ebey Distinguished Visiting Writer at Colorado College.

1998 Addison Wesley Longman brings out the ninth edition of *An Introduction to Poetry*. *Nosferatu* presented as a work-in-progress in a full-evening concert showcase at Western Slope Music Festival in Colorado.

1999 The seventh editions of *Literature: An Introduction to Fiction, Poetry, and Drama* and *An Introduction to Fiction* are published by Addison Wesley Longman. Fine press publication of *The Litany* from Aralia Press. The essay "Fallen Western Star: The Decline of San Francisco as a Literary Region" is published in *Hungry Mind Review*, igniting a heated controversy in the Bay Area. Final scene of *Nosferatu* premiered at Derriere Guard Arts Festival in San Francisco.

2000 Publication of *Dana Gioia & Fine Press Printing* by Michael Peich from Kelly/Winterton Press. Publication of *Dana Gioia* by April Lindner in the Western Writers Series of Boise State University.

2001 Graywolf Press publishes third collection of poetry, *Interrogations at Noon*, and opera libretto, *Nosferatu*. Publication of *Longman Anthology of Short Fiction: Stories and Authors in Context*, co-edited with R. S. Gwynn, from Addison Wesley Longman. In January, the *Hudson Review* hosts a fiftieth birthday party for Gioia at the Knickerbocker Club in New York City. Starts first Teaching Poetry Conference at the Sonoma Country Day School in Santa Rosa. *The "Fallen Western Star" Wars*, edited by Jack Foley, is published to chronicle the debate over Gioia's *Hungry Mind* essay. Gioia is approached by White House to be the chairman of the National Endowment for the Arts, but he declines nomination. Father dies.

2002 *Interrogations at Noon* is awarded the American Book Award. University of Michigan publishes *Barrier of a Common Language: Essays on Contemporary British Poetry*. Graywolf publishes tenth anniversary edition of *Can Poetry Matter?* Newly appointed chairman of NEA dies suddenly, so White House approaches Gioia a second time. Nominated as chairman by President George W. Bush in

	October. Moves to Washington, DC, to serve as "nominee designate" at the head of the Arts Endowment. Meets with members of Congress.
2003	Unanimously confirmed by US Senate in January. Launches the NEA's first national initiative, Shakespeare in American Communities, a fifty-state tour by six regional theater companies to bring live theater to small towns and schools. Obtains additional funds from Department of Defense to tour military bases. The program will become the largest Shakespeare tour in history, involving seventy-seven theater companies reaching millions. Appointed to lead the US Cultural Affairs delegation to UNESCO. Appointed to Federal Council on the Arts.
2004	Expands agency jazz programs to create NEA Jazz Masters with national touring, radio and television broadcasts, increased fellowships, and new school education programs. Launches Operation Homecoming: Writing the Wartime Experience, a program that invited US troops and their families to document their experiences. Writing workshops are set up at bases across the US and abroad. Launches American Masterpieces to bring exhibitions, performances, and broadcasts of art, dance, and music to large and small communities. Publishes *Reading at Risk: A Survey of Literary Reading in America*, which documents the national decline of reading and its consequences. NEA publishes *How the United States Funds the Arts* (co-authored with Tyler Cowen). McGraw-Hill publishes anthologies *Twentieth-Century American Poetry* and *Twentieth-Century American Poetics*, co-edited with David Mason and Meg Schoerke. Heyday publishes anthology *California Poetry: From the Gold Rush to the Present*, co-edited with Chryss Yost and Jack Hicks. Graywolf publishes *Disappearing Ink: Poetry at the End of Print Culture*.
2005	Initiates Poetry Out Loud, a high school recitation competition, in partnership with the Poetry Foundation. Program is piloted in the District of Columbia and

	Chicago. Pearson publishes *100 Great Poets of the English Language*, co-edited with Dan Stone. Albany Records releases *Nosferatu*. Wins the John Ciardi Award for lifetime achievement in poetry. Mother dies.
2006	Launches The Big Read in ten cities in partnership with Arts Midwest and the Institute of Museum and Library Services. Expands Poetry Out Loud nationally. Random House publishes *Operation Homecoming: Iraq, Afghanistan, and the Home Front in the Words of US Troops and Their Families*. Nominated for a second term as NEA chairman. Unanimously confirmed by US Senate.
2007	Expands The Big Read to all fifty states and creates international exchanges with Russia, Egypt, and Mexico. Expands the Federal Council on the Arts indemnity budget to $10 billion to support museum loans and exhibitions. Documentary *Operation Homecoming* broadcasts on PBS and wins two Emmys. NEA publishes *To Read or Not to Read: A Question of National Importance*. Arts Endowment receives largest funding increase in twenty-nine years. Delivers the Stanford commencement address.
2008	Expands Shakespeare, Big Read, and Operation Homecoming programs. NEA publishes *The Artist in the Workforce: 1990–2005*. *Tony Caruso's Final Broadcast* wins the National Opera Association Award and premieres in Los Angeles. University of South Carolina republishes *This Man's Army: A War in Fifty-Odd Sonnets* by John Allan Wyeth, edited by Gioia and Matthew Bruccoli. Gioia awarded Jazz Journalist Association Award, John Conyers Jr. Jazz Advocacy Award, and Presidential Citizens Medal. Gioia announces his intention to resign his federal office and return to writing.
2009	Leaves public office. Becomes the Harman-Eisner Director of Arts Programs at the Aspen Institute in Washington and Colorado. Appointed to the Citizens' Stamp Advisory Committee by US Postal Service to supervise the subjects

and designs of US postage. Wins John Houseman Award and *Christianity & Literature*'s lifetime achievement award. NEA publishes *Reading on the Rise*, demonstrating large positive impact of Big Read programs.

2010 Wins the Laetare Medal from Notre Dame. Trinity Forum publishes *Sacred and Profane Love: The Poetry of John Donne*. Ediciones el Tucán in Mexico publishes a bilingual selected poems, *La Escala Ardiente / The Burning Ladder*.

2011 Returns to California after his younger son graduates from high school in Washington. Appointed Judge Widney Professor of Poetry and Public Culture at the University of Southern California to teach each fall semester. Wins John Carroll Society Medal.

2012 Graywolf Press publishes his fourth collection of poems, *Pity the Beautiful*. Aralia Press publishes *The Living and the Dead: Translations of Mario Luzi*. Organizes and hosts national conference on Robinson Jeffers at USC.

2013 Pearson publishes anthology *Literature for Life*, co-edited by X. J. Kennedy and Nina Revoyr. Delivers keynote lecture "Poetry as Enchantment" for the International Association of University Professors of English at Tsinghua University in Beijing, China.

2014 Wiseblood Books publishes *The Catholic Writer Today*. Wins Aiken-Taylor Award in Modern American Poetry. Lori Laitman's opera, *The Three Feathers* with his libretto, premieres with Opera Roanoke in Virginia.

2015 Creates and hosts "The Future of the Catholic Literary Imagination," a three-day national conference at USC, which gains national attention. Delivers lecture "Poetry as Enchantment" at Library of Congress. Appointed California State Poet Laureate by Governor Jerry Brown.

2016 Graywolf Press publishes *99 Poems: New & Selected*. Wiseblood Books publishes critical monograph *Poetry as*

	Enchantment. Wins Denise Levertov Award. Morten Lauridsen releases *Prayer: Songs of Morten Lauridsen* with liner notes by Gioia and a setting of his poem "Prayer." Albany Records releases Paul Salerni's *Speaking of Love* with liner notes by Gioia and musical settings of nine poems. Gioia begins project to be the first state laureate to visit all fifty-eight counties of California.
2017	Wins Walt Whitman Champion of Literacy Award, Mercury Award in the arts, and *CASE Magazine* Award for best opinion piece published in a college magazine. BBC Radio 3 broadcasts documentary "radio road movie," *Every County in the State of California*, about Gioia's laureate travels. Second "Future of Catholic Imagination" Conference meets at Fordham University. BBC World Service features Gioia on *In the Studio* to discuss "The Ballad of Jesús Ortiz."
2018	Wins Poets' Prize for *99 Poems* as the best book of 2016. Scribner's publishes anthology, *Best American Poetry 2018*, edited by Gioia. Providence Press publishes *The Ballad of Jesús Ortiz*. Hosts statewide gathering of California's local, county, and regional laureates. Completes statewide tour with 124 events across all fifty-eight counties. Deutsche Gramophone releases *Light Eternal: Choral Music of Morten Lauridsen* with choral version of "Prayer." Jazz pianist Helen Sung releases album titled *Sung with Words: A Collaboration with Dana Gioia*.
2019	Premiere of dance opera *Haunted* (music by Paul Salerni). Wins Cinequest Creative Vision award. *Planting a Sequoia and Other Poems* (selected poems in Greek) appears in Athens. Third "Future of Catholic Literary Imagination" Conference at Loyola Chicago. Donates literary archive to Huntington Library. Resigns from USC to write full-time. Kincade Fire damages Santa Rosa home and studio.
2020	Spends pandemic year in Sonoma County clearing, cleaning, and repairing his property from fire damage. Pre-

Textos publishes *La oscuridad intacta: Poemas escogidos* (*The Unbroken Dark: Selected Poems*) in Madrid and Buenos Aires. *The Colosseum Critical Introduction to Dana Gioia* edited by Matthew Brennan appears from Franciscan Press.

2021 Paul Dry Books publishes *Studying with Miss Bishop: Memoirs from a Young Writer's Life*. University Press of Mississippi publishes *Conversations with Dana Gioia*, edited by John Zheng. *Éditions Allia* of Paris publishes *Que reste-t-il de la poésie?* ("Can Poetry Matter?"). Undergoes hip replacement surgery at Stanford. Providence Press publishes *Psalms and Lament for Los Angeles*.

2022 Elected to Board of Governors of the Huntington Library, Art Museum, and Botanical Gardens. Delivers "Christianity and Poetry" lecture at the dedication of the St. Michael's Abbey library. Awarded lifetime achievement award at the Athens International Poetry Festival. Performs with Helen Sung at the fourth Catholic Literary Imagination Conference at the University of Dallas. Sonoma County studio severely damaged by flood.

2023 Graywolf publishes *Meet Me at the Lighthouse*. Wiseblood publishes revised and expanded *Seneca: The Madness of Hercules*. Premiere of Lori Laitman's "Becoming a Redwood" symphonic song cycle. Premiere of James MacMillan's *Fiat Lux*, a symphonic choral work with text by Gioia. Trinity Forum publishes *Stoic Wisdom: Sentences from Seneca*. Laitman's *The Three Feathers* has first California production from Solo Opera.

2024 Wiseblood publishes *Christianity and Poetry*. It also appears in an Italian translation from Graphe.it Edizioni. Paul Dry Books simultaneously publishes *Poetry as Enchantment*, a critical collection, and *Weep, Shudder, Die*, a study of opera and poetry. Book Club of California publishes *From California*, a letterpress edition of twenty-six Gioia poems with engravings by Richard Wagener.

INTRODUCTION

DANA GIOIA: A VOICE FOR OUR TIME

Jon Parrish Peede

During the past forty years, Dana Gioia has had as transformative an impact on American literature as any living poet. We make this bold claim based on the breadth and depth of his achievements as a poet, critic, anthologist, arts leader, and public intellectual. It is easy to argue against such a conclusion in the abstract; it is harder to do so after considering the totality of his impact in interlocking roles over decades. Though the sales of Gioia's poetry collections are in the tens of thousands, commercial popularity is an inadequate lens to evaluate artistic excellence in any field. In *Conversations with Dana Gioia*, my co-editor, John Zheng, makes a compelling case for Gioia's significance as a poet and critic:

> A creative visionary, forthright critic, and pioneering poet, Gioia has played a pivotal role in contemporary American poetry similar in some ways to that of Ezra Pound in early Modernism. Like Pound, Gioia's goal has been to change literary opinion and expand the possibilities for poetry. He recognized the end of Modernism and the moribundity of the institutionalized avant-garde; he argued for more honest and intelligent reviewing; he questioned the isolated state of American poetry; he advocated the return to form and narrative.[1]

Zheng hits the mark with his historical comparison. But, as we will discuss, expanding the readership for contemporary poetry does not necessarily garner the appreciation of literary critics and university-

---

[1] John Zheng, ed., *Conversations with Dana Gioia* (Jackson: University Press of Mississippi, 2021), xv.

based poets—especially when one's approach is as unabashedly non-conformist as Gioia's has been. It is time for a wholistic assessment of this cultural figure.

This essay collection is the first multi-author critical effort to explore the extent of Gioia's influential presence as a poet and critic. While our admiration for his work and career is clear, we have no interest in offering a *festschrift* or hagiography. We left out dozens of reviews praising each new book release. We also decided against including mere tirades opposed to rhyme and meter. Having stated our aesthetic tastes, we hope you will find this essay collection to be a nuanced and perceptive scholarly undertaking.

Dana Gioia: Poet and Critic brings together more than thirty years of academic scholarship, book reviews, and journalistic articles to illuminate the scope of Gioia's artistic achievement and cultural impact. It includes the most significant critical responses to his poetry, varying in length from concise commentaries by Hilton Kramer and Anne Stevenson to extended scholarly considerations by Shirley Geok-lin Lim, James Matthew Wilson, and others. Collectively, these essays provide a foundation for understanding his literary influences, preoccupations, and intentions. Several essayists focus on the same celebrated poems, such as "The Burning Ladder," "Planting a Sequoia," and "Summer Storm," but locate different meanings within the works; yet, these findings are in harmony with one another. Where one critic sees subtle allusions to Dante and Catholic thought, another traces the same work back to Gioia's lifelong attachment to California and its terrain. Both arguments show that his overall commitment is to what T. S. Eliot called "the permanent things."

Indeed, this essay collection serves as a reminder of how consistent Gioia has been as a poet. "Although he writes in both free and metrical verse," my co-editor has noted, "Gioia sees form as essential to all poetry. Some formal principle—traditional or innovative—is necessary to shape and thereby intensify ordinary language into poetry."[2] He explains his approach as trying "to combine the intensity and integrity of modernist poetry with the sensual appeal and musical power of meter

---

[2] Zheng, *Conversations*, xx-xxi.

and rhyme."[3] He never attempted to reinvent himself to match the fashion of the times, following the example of two masters of form—Anthony Hecht and Richard Wilbur—who endured "poetry wars" of their own during a time when *vers libre* was the industry standard among creative writing programs and literary presses. Gioia was the leading figure in bringing down this barrier. He found public support for his efforts. But it did not endear him to the gatekeepers.

This essay collection provides insights into the politics of the poetry world but does not dwell on such topics. Instead, the focus is on Gioia's poetry and the overarching themes of his work, such as his religious faith, love of California, and engagement with the Western intellectual tradition. The book is divided into three sections covering Gioia's early career (*Daily Horoscope*, *The Gods of Winter*, and *Can Poetry Matter?*), mid-career (*Interrogations at Noon* and *Nosferatu*), and later career (*Pity the Beautiful*, *99 Poems*, and *Meet Me at the Lighthouse*).

Because these essays were written over decades, there will be numerous statements that were correct originally but are now out of date, such as referring to a particular book as Gioia's "latest collection" or references to his then-current professional position. With a few exceptions, such as standardizing the titles of specific poems—"Cruising with the Beach Boys," for example—to their revised titles, there has been no effort to update this information. Most of the essays are reprinted as published except for correcting typographical errors and adjusting to follow our publisher's house style. We have provided the year of original publication after each essay title. If the essay has been extensively updated, then we have provided the date of the revision.

ᴓ

Born in 1950, Gioia started publishing poetry in national journals in 1979. He wrote for leading publications, including the *New Yorker* and the *Hudson Review*, but also brought out poems and reviews in new ventures such as Scotland's *Dark Horse*, a journal he helped found. From the early 1980s on, he also collaborated with fine press printers such as

---

[3] Qtd. in Zheng, *Conversations*, xvi.

Michael Peich of Aralia Press to issue individual poems and sequences.

His first full-length collection, *Daily Horoscope*, came out from Graywolf Press in 1986. (The press had published his edition of Weldon Kees's short stories in 1984.) The nonprofit press has remained his main publisher for more than forty years, growing from a three-person operation into an esteemed literary publisher. Graywolf issued an initial run of 750 hardback and 3,000 paperback copies. The book received both stellar reviews and heated denunciations. It also sold well. As Gioia's reputation grew, the book had a second paperback printing, of which 200 were used for a UK edition issued by Peterloo Poets.[4] It is now in its third printing. Gioia's reputation and readership has grown with each volume of poems.

His second collection, *The Gods of Winter*, came out in 1991 with the same initial print run as his first book. Again, the printing did not meet the demand. Six weeks later, a second paperback printing was rushed to booksellers. To satisfy overseas readers, Peterloo printed 2,112 copies, of which 1,800 went to the Poetry Book Society. By 1994, a fourth US printing was needed. It, too, sold out.[5] Co-winner of the Poets' Prize with Adrienne Rich's *An Atlas of the Difficult World*, the collection is in its eighth printing.

In 2001, his third collection, *Interrogations at Noon*, was issued as a paperback with a first printing of 4,000 copies. Three months later, Graywolf reprinted the volume.[6] The book won the American Book Award and has gone through seven printings to date.

Gioia followed with three more collections: *Pity the Beautiful* (2012); *99 Poems: New & Selected* (2016), winner of the Poets' Prize; and *Meet Me at the Lighthouse* (2023). In a testament to the quality of his poetry and to his publisher's loyalty, every Gioia poetry collection remains in print. Throughout his career, he found an eager audience—but one that largely resided outside of the academy.

Through his own poetry and by championing others, Gioia became the most visible (and vilified) member of the New Formalist movement,

---

[4] Jack W. C. Hagstrom and Bill Morgan, *Dana Gioia: A Descriptive Bibliography with Critical Essays* (Jackson, MS: Parrish House, 2002), 21–22.

[5] Ibid., 41–45.

[6] Ibid., 65–67.

which worked to revive formal and narrative poetry. After much controversy, the movement won gradual acceptance for meter, rhyme, and other traditional devices within the literary world. Gioia argued that formalism "connected literary poetry to the energy of the popular culture—which had remained rooted in auditory forms like song and storytelling. In this sense the revival was both populist and democratic, though deeply informed by literary tradition. It also helped reconcile modernist poetic practice with the possibilities of traditional techniques. It moved poetry forward while also reconnecting it to its primal roots in orality and performance."[7] When we refer to Gioia's transformational impact, we have this role in mind. It is hard to overstate how much opposition existed three decades ago to formal verse such as the sonnet, sestina, villanelle, and other traditional forms.

Gioia returned poetry criticism to public prominence with his 1991 *Atlantic* essay "Can Poetry Matter?" Never known to be shy in person or print, he opens the piece boldly:

> American poetry now belongs to a subculture. No longer part of the mainstream of artistic and intellectual life, it has become the specialized occupation of a relatively small and isolated group. Little of the frenetic activity it generates ever reaches outside that closed group. As a class, poets are not without cultural status. Like priests in a town of agnostics, they still command a certain residual prestige. But as individual artists they are almost invisible. (*CPM* 1)

This provocative essay generated more letters to the editor than the renowned magazine had received for any article in its history.

Capitalizing on the media attention, Graywolf brought out *Can Poetry Matter? Essays on Poetry and American Culture* the next year with simultaneous 1,000-copy hardback and 4,000-copy paperback printings. The book went through numerous reprintings, and, after ten years, was issued with a new introduction. Rather than focus his energy on broad cultural criticism, Gioia offered reconsiderations of derided nineteenth-century poets such as Longfellow, resurrected the reputation of

---

[7] Qtd. in Zheng, *Conversations*, xvii.

Weldon Kees, and brought national attention to underappreciated contemporaries such as Kay Ryan and Ted Kooser, both of whom would be named US Poets Laureate after he championed their work. In many ways, *Can Poetry Matter?* made his public reputation by introducing his poetry and ideas to an audience that had little interaction with the works of contemporary American poets after Robert Frost and Langston Hughes. In other ways, the essay collection damaged his literary standing. MFA program directors, tenured poets, and their acolytes were outraged by his claim that the academy had narrowed the subject matter of modern poetry, robbing it of its appeal to everyday readers beyond the campus gates.

If one wishes to find a comfortable university position, calling out creative writing programs is a poor career decision. Gioia supported his family in successive roles as a corporate marketing executive, freelance journalist, cultural critic, and government official. Though he spoke on hundreds of campuses and received eleven honorary degrees, Gioia never taught full-time or occupied a tenured position. After concluding his NEA chairmanship, he taught one semester each year as the Judge Widney Professor of Poetry and Public Culture at the University of Southern California from 2011 to 2019. Gioia chose not to join the English department but served as a university-wide professor across several schools. He declined to teach creative writing but taught courses in literature, music, and arts leadership.

While universities serve as the most visible anchors, contemporary poetry could not exist without the efforts of hundreds of large and small literary organizations. Gioia served on the board of leading poetry nonprofits for much of his career, including Story Line Press and the Poetry Society of America. Story Line became the foremost publisher of critical works by New Formalists, including *Expansive Poetry: Essays on the New Narrative and the New Formalism* edited by Frederick Feirstein and Frederick Turner (1989) and *Rebel Angels: 25 Poets of the New Formalism* edited by Mark Jarman and David Mason (1996). After Story Line closed, Gioia facilitated the transfer of the press's correspondence and manuscripts for Rita Dove's verse play *The Darker Face of Earth* to the University of Virginia library. Since Dove lost numerous manuscripts and records in a house fire, this small Story Line archive of her dramatic work has particular significance.

In 1995, Gioia co-founded the West Chester Poetry Conference with Michael Peich, and for nearly a quarter of a century it became a joyful home for formal poets at all skill levels to study and socialize, share current work, and learn more about their craft. The daily workshops focused on specific aspects of poetic craft, such as scansion and translation. Rejecting the practice of some prominent writing conferences, West Chester faculty and students sat together for meals and other gatherings. Gioia, Peich, Rhina Espaillat, B. H. Fairchild, Mark Jarman, David Mason, Marilyn Nelson, and the other faculty mixed freely among friends and strangers alike. A social person by nature, Gioia eagerly mentored younger writers who attended the annual conference. (I was one such attendee.) This book includes an extensive chronology that highlights his additional service to the field.

For thirty years, Gioia edited a series of influential and best-selling literary anthologies. In 1992, he took over X. J. Kennedy's popular college textbook series. *Introduction to Poetry* published its eighth edition in 1994, followed by *Literature: An Introduction to Fiction, Poetry, and Drama*, sixth edition, and *An Introduction to Fiction*, sixth edition. Under Gioia's direction, the anthology series became more notably inclusive featuring writers from diverse cultures with expanded international coverage. (It was the first college textbook to include hip hop lyrics.) The production list grew as the publishers changed from HarperCollins to Longman to Pearson. To date, he has edited or co-edited more than twenty literary textbooks. The Kennedy-Gioia *Literature* anthology has been the best-selling college textbook in the nation for two decades, rivaling Cleanth Brooks and Robert Penn Warren's New Critical anthologies of the mid-twentieth century in terms of popularity, literary quality, and aesthetic diversity. Millions of students came to know American and world literature through their literary selections and editorial commentary.

In October 2002, President George W. Bush nominated Gioia as Chairman of the National Endowment for the Arts. Gioia accepted the challenging position reluctantly. He knew that it would bring his focus on writing poetry to an end for many years. He accepted because the agency was endangered due to partisan politics over past grants.

Speaking of the importance of the arts to his immigrant family, Gioia announced a populist approach as chairman, and he was confirmed by the US Senate by unanimous consent in the following January. As NEA chairman for six years, Gioia gained the trust of a talented but wary agency staff, a wartime US president, a divided Congress, suspicious national media, and a balkanized cultural sector. He was able to increase the agency's budget each year and widen its geographic reach.

As Mark Bauerlein discusses in detail in *National Endowment for the Arts: A History 1965–2008*, Gioia expanded funding for the literary field and created major literary programs, including Shakespeare in America, the Big Read, Poetry Out Loud, and Operation Homecoming: Writing the Wartime Experience. The Shakespeare initiative brought back the touring of serious dramatic works by supporting performances by seventy-seven theater companies in more than 2,300 cities and towns. It also provided free educational materials to more than 24 million students.[8] Following the "City Reads" model, the NEA then created a national book program that provided competitive grants and educational resources for communities to unite around discussing a single book, including Harper Lee's *To Kill a Mockingbird* and Ray Bradbury's *Fahrenheit 451*. The project has proven so popular that every NEA chairperson since Gioia has funded its continuation. To date, some 6 million Americans have attended a Big Read event through the efforts of some 40,000 community organizations.[9]

In 2004, Gioia created Operation Homecoming to help US troops and their families chronicle their wartime experiences through writing workshops on military installations. I served as its director for five years. With a distinguished faculty that included Richard Bausch, Andrew Hudgins, Bobbie Ann Mason, Marilyn Nelson, and Tobias Wolff, we taught therapeutic writing workshops on military bases and medical centers domestically and in Afghanistan and other locations abroad.

---

[8] Mark Bauerlein, *National Endowment for the Arts: A History 1965–2008* (Washington, DC: National Endowment for the Arts, 2009), 150–51.

[9] "Announcing the 2023–2024 National Endowment for the Arts Big Read Communities." National Endowment for the Arts, 14 June 2023, www.arts.gov/news/press-releases/2023/announcing-2023-2024-national-endowment-arts-big-read-communities.

The project resulted in the largest literary archive available of Iraq and Afghanistan veterans (now housed at the National Archives and Library of Congress), the award-winning documentaries *Muse of Fire* and *Operation Homecoming*, and an acclaimed anthology edited by Andrew Carroll. The educational CD includes interviews with Richard Wilbur and other WWII poets who discuss how writing helped them overcome the trauma of war.

Gioia brought the love of poetry to millions of high school students through Poetry Out Loud. Since 2005, 4.2 million students in 18,000 schools have memorized and recited poems as part of the national competition. "This was easily one of the greatest experiences of my teaching career," a high school teacher raved about the program. "It was the level of intellectual confidence and enthusiasm that we as teachers usually only fantasize about."[10] The annual contest has become a national news story, reminding a wide public audience of poetry's oral, performative roots.

During his tenure, Gioia awarded approximately $600 million to artists and arts organizations. For the first time in its history, the agency reached every congressional district in the nation, including small towns whose local cultural celebrations help to keep the arts available to school children. He increased the funding of nonprofit literary presses, created international literary exchanges, expanded support for translators, revitalized regional touring for Shakespeare plays, and launched a series of bilingual poetry anthologies with cultural partners in Mexico, Northern Ireland, Pakistan, and Russia. He strengthened the NEA's relationships with other federal agencies, which led to him being appointed to the Citizens' Stamp Advisory Committee of the US Postal Service, where he advocated for the depiction of notable American artists, musicians, writers, and other creators on new stamps. Gioia saved the Literary Arts stamp series, which had been cancelled when he arrived at the committee. The Post Office subsequently honored Ralph Ellison, Henry James, Ursula K. Le Guin, and Flannery O'Connor, among others.

Gioia worked hard to bring poetry into public life. For example,

[10] Bauerlein, *National Endowment for the Arts*, 161.

after Librarian of Congress James Billington established the annual National Book Festival with First Lady Laura Bush in 2001, Gioia convinced the Library of Congress two years later to include a poetry pavilion in the festival under the NEA's management. Over the next seven years, the pavilion presented a broad range of voices across diverse poetic styles, including Elizabeth Alexander, Rhina Espaillat, Donald Hall, Mary Karr, David Lehman, Li-Young Lee, N. Scott Momaday, Kay Ryan, William Jay Smith, Natasha Trethewey, and Kevin Young. Gioia also selected talented poets who at the time seldom spoke at nationally televised events.

After his chairmanship, Gioia and his wife, Mary, returned to California, where he continues to write. In 2015, he was appointed California State Poet Laureate by Governor Jerry Brown. No laureate had ever celebrated poetry in person in every county of the large and diverse state. Gioia set out to do so. By the end of his two-year appointment, he had completed the task, reaching tomorrow's readers. He returned to his poetry and other writings.

Nearly forty years passed between the release of Gioia's debut collection, *Daily Horoscope*, which opened with the biblical tale of Jacob and the burning ladder to heaven, and that of his latest collection, *Meet Me at the Lighthouse*, which ends with a journey to the Underworld. Rereading "The Burning Ladder" in middle age, I understand the story of Jacob differently than I did as a younger man. I feel the somber truth of the simple line that concludes the poem: "Gravity always greater than desire" (*DH* 3). In failing to climb, Jacob remained earthbound. But he still had his community. In "The Underworld," Gioia's speaker addresses the reader directly: "you" are invited to a different eternal place where there is "No sun, no moon, no stars, no sky, no end" (*MML* 54). Gioia's poetry is, in many ways, about what we experience in our private and public passages between heaven and hell. In the fractious, distracted twenty-first century, we are in desperate need of cultural leaders who can remind us, through their art and advocacy, that our journey has a destination, and where we go and with whom we go and what we do with our lives along the way matter. Dana Gioia is such a figure.

I

Early Career

Daily Horoscope, *The Gods of Winter*, and *Can Poetry Matter?*

1

DANA GIOIA AND VISIONARY REALISM (2002)

Robert McPhillips

In the past quarter century, Dana Gioia has established himself as the leading poet-critic of his generation. He has done so, moreover, in an unusual fashion and, in the process, has stirred more than a little controversy. Most poets during the post-World War II baby boom earned their credentials by attaining an MFA degree in creative writing at an institution like the Iowa Writers' Workshop where they absorbed—whether passively or passionately—the free-verse orthodoxy of an older generation of modernists like Ezra Pound and William Carlos Williams. These poets equated "making it new" with eschewing traditional poetic techniques such as meter and rhyme and came to consider free verse a peculiarly American form of poetic democracy. Most critics, on the other hand, were products of doctoral programs in English or comparative literature of universities where literary theory in its various manifestations—structuralism, deconstruction, Marxism, feminism, cultural studies—reigned as the predominant form of literary discourse. Although by 1980 poets and critics had largely stopped speaking a common language, they both, ironically, were united and legitimized by their uneasy coexistence within the groves of the American academy.

Gioia found both forms of institutionalized legitimacy imaginatively stifling. Instead of completing his doctoral degree, he walked away from the Harvard program in comparative literature to pursue, instead, an MBA at Stanford. Armed with this peculiar degree for a poet, Gioia launched his literary career from the unlikely campus of the General Foods Corporation in suburban Westchester County, New York. Free from the constraints to publish or perish, Gioia placed his highly polished poems in such prestigious journals as *Poetry*, the *New*

Yorker, and the *Hudson Review*. In these same journals, as well as in the *New York Times Book Review* and the *Nation*, Gioia established himself as a discriminating critic of contemporary poetry; a champion of critically forgotten or overlooked poets like Weldon Kees, Robinson Jeffers, and Ted Kooser; and as a memoirist of writers who strongly influenced him as a young man like Elizabeth Bishop, John Cheever, and Robert Fitzgerald. The culmination of Gioia's early career came with the publication of his first collection of poems in 1986, *Daily Horoscope*, an unusually strong debut volume focusing on the dichotomy between the poet's youth in California and his young adulthood in the East, as well as the tension arising from his dual career as poet and businessman.

In an ideal world, *Daily Horoscope* would have established Gioia as a major poet. Instead, Gioia had by this time become identified with a poetic movement, the New Formalism, a group of young poets who in the late 1970s and early 1980s had revived traditional poetic techniques such as meter, rhyme, and fixed forms. Although this group had been originally noted and named by its free-verse detractors, Gioia nonetheless chose to align himself publicly with this movement, in a major way, with his spirited and cogent defense of its aesthetic, "Notes on the New Formalism," first published in the *Hudson Review* in 1987. This widely noted essay left Gioia, along with other poets like Brad Leithauser, Vikram Seth, Mary Jo Salter, Gjertrud Schnackenberg, and Timothy Steele, open to generic attacks for their allegedly politically retrograde politics and aesthetics—"yuppie poets" was a typical phrase—rather than to careful readings of his individual poems.

But it was the publication of his essay "Can Poetry Matter?" in the *Atlantic Monthly* in 1991 that typecast Gioia first and foremost as a poetic polemicist in the minds of the American literary establishment—a fame that overshadowed his poetry. In his *Atlantic* piece, Gioia had the audacity to propose that poetry was no longer an art that spoke directly to a wide public audience—as had, say, the poetry of Longfellow and Frost—but had become relegated to a poetic subculture centered in the university creative writing programs and producing work of interest, at best, to a limited group of readers within that subculture. While highlighting Gioia's reputation as a critic, the critical debate his essay raised in publications ranging from the *Village Voice* to the *New*

Criterion to the *Times Literary Supplement* to the *Washington Post* had the unfortunate effect, as well, of virtually muting him as a poet.

The publication of Gioia's second volume of poems, *The Gods of Winter* (1991), published almost simultaneously with the essay, went largely ignored in this country. By contrast, in Great Britain, where poetic form has never been equated with a political agenda and where the tempests of the American poetry world don't have a serious influence on the local literary climate, *Gods* became the main selection of the prestigious Poetry Book Society, an honor seldom bestowed upon an American, and Gioia is recognized as a serious American poet. The truth is that as distinguished a critic as Gioia is his first claim to our attention is as a poet of the first rank. In addition to his own poetry, Gioia has devoted much energy to translating verse from the Italian, German, Latin, and Romanian. His interest in narrative poetry is reflected in his translation of Seneca's verse drama, *The Madness of Hercules* (1995), and his libretto for Alva Henderson's opera, *Nosferatu* (2001), based on the silent film by F. W. Murnau. The publication of his third collection of poems, *Interrogations at Noon* (2001), moreover, presents Gioia writing at the height of his powers in mid-career.

Gioia was born in Los Angeles, California, in 1950 and grew up in the working-class town of Hawthorne. Raised in "a tightly-knit Sicilian community," he attended a local Catholic high school, where he received what he describes as "a sectarian but nonetheless broadening and oddly international education." Later at Stanford, he majored in English as an undergraduate and edited the university's literary magazine, *Sequoia*. After graduating in 1973, he spent two years doing graduate work in comparative literature at Harvard, receiving his MA in 1975. At Harvard, Gioia studied epic poetry and English versification with Robert Fitzgerald and modern poetry with Elizabeth Bishop as well as literary theory with Edward Said and Northrop Frye. He subsequently returned to Stanford to work on an MBA, though he continued to write poetry as well as publish critical reviews and essays in the *Stanford Daily*, *Sequoia*, and *San Francisco Review of Books*. It was ironically as a business student that Gioia took his only poetry workshop, with the British poet-critic Donald Davie, in a class including such poets as Vikram Seth, Vickie Hearne, and John Gery. After graduating from business school in 1977, Gioia took a job with General Foods in White Plains, New York, where he worked for fifteen years, eventually becoming a vice president. In 1992 he resigned to pursue writing full time. Gioia now lives with his wife, Mary Hiecke, and two sons in Sonoma County, California.

Gioia, like Timothy Steele, was at Stanford University during the 1970s, and he was somewhat influenced by the laconic, classical plain style of Yvor Winters, the attendant poetic spirit at Stanford, though he never studied with Winters or any of his disciples. Gioia's aesthetic, however, was mostly shaped by such diverse modernists as Ezra Pound, T. S. Eliot, Wallace Stevens, Robert Frost, and Robinson Jeffers, and his range is wider than that of the lyric and epigrammatic forms most favored by the "Stanford School" of formalists. Though his lyrics concern universal themes such as love and mortality, they are more concrete in specific autobiographical detail and more colloquial and overtly emotional—without eschewing linguistic elegance—than the abstractly logical lyrics of the Wintersians. Similarly, if Frost's lyric poetry influenced both Steele and Gioia (as well as numerous other New Formalists like David Mason, Robert McDowell, and Mary Jo Salter), Frost's blank verse narratives and dramatic monologues also influenced Gioia. In fact, in both his lyric and narrative poems, Gioia often writes with a novelist's instinct for plot and significant detail.

The impact of the more experimental modernists is also evident in Gioia's ongoing interest in free verse. About one-third of his published poetry is written in free verse—a significant percentage, especially compared to his Stanford contemporaries such as Steele and Seth, who work exclusively in formal meters. More importantly, whether written in metrically formal or in free verse, Gioia's poems are marked by a distinctive poetic style of visionary realism in which memory imbues details of the ordinary world with a sensuous luminosity, making them at once seemingly tangible yet tantalizingly elusive, as if existing in a border region between time and eternity.

In his first collection of poetry, *Daily Horoscope* (1986), Gioia explores themes of the poet's dislocation in the modern world, drawing on his own experiences as a Californian living in New York and a poet earning a living as a businessman. *Daily Horoscope*, with its meditations on the interplay between the ideal and the real, heaven and earth, business and poetry, seems, on some level, to come out of the difficult choice Gioia made in his early twenties to leave the academic world of Harvard for a career in business. For fifteen years his life in poetry was confined to evenings and weekends.

The first of *Daily Horoscope*'s five sections constitutes an informal autobiography of the poet as a man in his early thirties who has achieved some worldly success and some moments, usually tantalizingly brief, of spiritual fulfillment. The first poem, "The Burning Ladder," announces the spiritual significance of Gioia's poetic undertaking. The poem is a retelling of the biblical story of Jacob's ladder. The biblical Jacob dreams, from his pillow of stone, of "a ladder set up on earth, and the top of it reached to heaven: and behold the angels of God ascending and descending on it" (Genesis 28:12). From heaven, God declares Jacob's divine election, his position as a descendent of Abraham in the Hebrew race that will inherit the Promised Land. For Gioia, this episode from Genesis is a cautionary tale as well. Gioia's Jacob "never climbed the ladder / burning in his dream." Instead, he is too tired to rise from sleep to "mount the brilliant / ladder" with the choir of angels ascending into heaven. "Gravity," the poet concludes, is "always greater than desire" (*DH* 3). Gioia clearly identifies himself with the Jacob of the poem, which thus becomes, on the surface, a parable of his struggle between the "desire" to become a poet, to join "that choir" of "Seraphim / ascending" the ladder into heaven, and the "gravity" of everyday life—the responsibilities, say, of a businessman—with gravity apparently defeating desire.

Gioia follows "The Burning Ladder" with three poems commemorating his native California—"California Hills in August," "Cruising with the Beach Boys," and "In Chandler Country."[1] "California Hills in August," Gioia's most anthologized poem, is a portrait of the parched, summer landscape of California presented from a double perspective, that of the "Easterner" that Gioia had become and that of the

[1] In *Daily Horoscope*, this poem was titled "Cruising with the Beachboys," but Gioia changed the title to "Cruising with the Beach Boys" in *99 Poems*. We have standardized all references to the poem to the latter title, which reflects the band's spelling.

native Californian that he remains, "someone / raised in a landscape short of rain." The "Easterner," whose perspective dominates the first four of the poem's five stanzas is an observer:

> who would scorn
> the meagerness of summer, the dry
> twisted shapes of black elm,
> scrub oak, and chaparral, a landscape
> August has already drained of green. (*DH* 4)

By contrast, there is a turn in the final stanza in which the native Californian perceives this same landscape as "gentle"—"the skyline of a hill broken by no more / trees than one can count, the grass, / the empty sky, the wish for water"—implicitly asking the reader to perceive this unique gentleness, much in the way that Robert Frost so often celebrates beauty in "diminished thing[s]," like the "midsummer song" of the oven bird or the dried-out Hyla Brook.

"Cruising with the Beach Boys," looking back nostalgically on the poet's adolescence in Los Angeles in the late 1960s (the Beach Boys, like Gioia, hail from Hawthorne), is perhaps the poet's most disarming lyric. It is also a poem that most pointedly distinguishes New Formalist personal lyrics from both the more emotionally distanced lyrics of the academic formalists who emerged after World War II in the wake of the New Criticism and the more turbulently emotional lyrics of the Beats and the Confessionals. A poem like "Cruising" seems to walk a middle path between these aesthetics, drawing on the formal reserve of the first and the colloquialism of the second. The lyric "I" in "Cruising" can perhaps be identified with Gioia as the young businessman-poet that he was in the 1980s:

> So strange to hear that song again tonight
> Travelling on business in a rented car
> Miles from anywhere I've been before.
> And now a tune I haven't heard for years
> Probably not since it last left the charts
> Back in L.A. in 1969.

I can't believe I know the words by heart
And can't think of a girl to blame them on. (*DH* 5)

The first line of the poem immediately establishes how naturally the cadences of ordinary American speech align themselves with iambic pentameter, to which they conform without any strain or any strong metrical substitutions. The voice of the poem is intimate without making embarrassing claims on the reader—indeed, the whole notion of a song heard repeatedly on a car's AM radio during a summer's "cruising" that becomes inextricably associated with a particular part of one's youth, is certainly an archetypal contemporary experience, especially for the post-World War II generation coming of age in the 1960s and early 1970s.

For Gioia, the unnamed Beach Boys tune becomes the occasion for a Wordsworthian spot of time, the past momentarily replacing the present vividly and movingly in the mind. The would-be sophisticated speaker admits to a secret fondness for pop culture unimaginable in poets like Anthony Hecht, John Hollander, and James Merrill. He admits:

Every lovesick summer has its song,
And this one I pretended to despise,
But if I was alone when it came on,
I turned it up full-blast to sing along—
A primal scream in croaky baritone,
The notes all flat, the lyrics mostly slurred.
No wonder I spent so much time alone
Making the rounds in Dad's old Thunderbird. (*DH* 5)

The speaker confesses that his youthful lovesickness was overly dramatic, that he was "The Cecil B. DeMille of my self-pity." Nonetheless, this doesn't stop the flow of memories from "Tumbling like boxes from a dusty shelf"—memories he "thought by now [he'd] left … behind," of unrequited crushes and his junked "old T-Bird"—which he finds, unexpectedly, "Tightening my throat for no reason at all / Bringing on tears shed only for myself" (*DH* 5, 6). Gioia risks bathos, but instead makes his unabashed self-pity moving, to a large extent because his use of meter and rhyme provides just enough formality to objectify the speaker's emotions.

The final California poem in this section, "In Chandler Country," incorporates snippets from Raymond Chandler's atmospheric Southern California detective novels, providing a harsher vision of the state than Gioia's other California poems. As in Chandler's fiction and in Joan Didion's essays on California, the hot, dry Santa Ana wind is seen as mechanistically provoking human despair and violence. This West Coast poem is balanced, later in the book, by the more substantial "In Cheever Country," which draws in a similar manner from John Cheever's mythologization of Westchester County, New York, in which Gioia spent most of his early adult life, a poem about the idea of place and home as a serenely paradisal landscape that gives the section a satisfying closure.

In between these two literary homages are a series of poems dealing with the pleasures and frustrations of a business life. "Eastern Standard Time," for instance, is a poignant meditation on a suburban corporate parking lot on a fall evening just after "the clocks went back an hour." It deals with the speaker's initial alienation from this environment and his ultimate acceptance of it—poet and businessman, Westerner and Easterner momentarily, at least, reconciled. This reconciliation foreshadows the strong sense of having found a psychic home in "In Cheever Country." Preceding that resolution come moments of frustration with life as a businessman in "Men after Work" and "The Man in the Open Doorway," the latter written in a modified Sapphic stanza with a fixed *abcb* rhyme scheme that emphasizes the stultifying routine and spiritual barrenness attendant on a life devoted entirely to a career. "Insomnia" attests to the anxieties that can accompany the material possessions that a steady job makes possible. By contrast, "Flying over Clouds," a kind of Stevensian counterpart to the more mundane "Waiting in the Airport," describes the extravagant beauty that can be encountered on what the poem's context in the book suggests is a business trip:

> O paradise beyond the glass,
> beyond our touch, cast and recast,
> shifting in wind. Delicate world
> of air too thin to breathe, of cold
> beyond endurance. (*DH* 14)

This is one of Gioia's many paradoxical visions of a paradise that seems at hand but is in fact tantalizingly unrealizable—except in the imagination.

Gioia's final vision of "paradise" in this first section of *Daily Horoscope* is far less extravagant, in keeping with the diminished but "gentle"—an ethical as well as aesthetic category for this poet—beauty discernible in the California hills in August. "In Cheever Country" is a celebration of Gioia's adopted home in Westchester County. Indeed, Gioia's suburban New York seems far more of an ideal paradise than we usually encounter in John Cheever's fiction, where descriptions of paradisal suburban gardens are often undercut by bitter irony. What Cheever and Gioia have in common, however, is that the Edens in which they live differ from the traditional Romantic lost paradises of literature—the lost paradise of childhood. If it was a shorter journey to Westchester County from Cheever's Yankee boyhood in Quincy, Massachusetts, than it was from Gioia's Hawthorne, California, the psychic journeys are similar. Both Cheever and Gioia share the experience of creating their own fragile domestic paradises, their own careers and marriages, their own "homes," as adults.

Gioia presents his vision of an earthly paradise by describing a Metro North train ride along the Hudson River, the Hudson line that passes through Gioia's adult hometown of Hastings-on-Hudson just as it does through Cheever's Ossining. In this poem, written in five-line stanzas of loose blank verse, the speaker advises that the best way "to know this country" is to:

> see it from a train—even this crowded local
> jogging home half an hour before dark
>
> smelling of smoke and rain-damp shoes
> on an afternoon of dodging sun and showers.

One trip without a book or paper
will show enough to understand
this landscape no one takes too seriously. (*DH* 19)

Gioia's goal here, as it was in "California Hills in August," is to make the reader reconsider a landscape he finds either too foreign or too familiar to perceive its inherent beauty. Commuters who travel daily to and from their jobs in Manhattan are so entrenched by habit that they overlook the beauty of the Hudson Valley they are moving through; they are unaware of the potential beatitude that bathes them, as are the travelers Gioia describes:

The sunset broadens for a moment, and the passengers
standing on the platform turn strangely luminous
in the light streaming from the palisades across the river.
Some board the train. Others greet their arrivals
shaking hands and embracing in the dusk.

If there is an afterlife, let it be a small town
gentle as this spot at just this instant.
But the car doors close, and the bright crowd,
unaware of its election, disperses to the small
pleasures of the evening. (*DH* 20)

Gioia perceives, in the luminosity shining forth from the Jersey Palisades on the western shore of the Hudson, the potential "election" to paradise that most commuters are too rushed to realize. The "after-life" Gioia nominates as paradise is the suburban community he has chosen to settle in; paradise is "home," the quotidian transformed:

And this at last is home, this ordinary town
where the lights on the hill gleaming in the rain
are the lights that children bathe by, and it is time
to go home now—to drinks, to love, to supper,
to the modest places which contain our lives. (*DH* 21)

The remainder of *Daily Horoscope* is hardly content with sunnily reaffirming this hard-won vision of home. "Daily Horoscope," the six-poem sequence that follows "In Cheever Country," reflects upon the complex, troubling interrelation between the imagination and reality in a style more elevated than the directly accessible voice established in the book's earlier poems. The title sequence is dedicated to the memory of Gioia's Harvard mentor, Robert Fitzgerald, whom, in an epigraph from Dante's *Inferno*, the author credits with passing on to him "*lo bello stile*." The six poems trace a typical day in the life of the unnamed person addressed—whose horoscope they constitute—from his reluctant awakening out of dreams by the morning's alarm clock to the insomnia prompted by a late-night, abortive phone call.

The language of "Daily Horoscope" combines the diction and rhetoric of a newspaper horoscope with the intricate imagery and richly evocative phrasing of the modernist lyrics of Wallace Stevens and Eugenio Montale. The first poem opens with the announcement that "Today will be like any other day," an ordinary day in which "any change would be an argosy— / an hour's sleep, an unexpected visit." Yet even such modest diversions will be denied: "they are lost to you—the dreams, the sleep, / the faceless lovers you desire" (*DH* 25). The sequence's second poem suggests that the cost of living daily is that one must forego fulfilling one's most extravagant desires, "And realize / that you must choose again but over less" (*DH* 26). But the third, "Do Not Expect," presents the possibility that resigning oneself to less offers an unforeseen, if minor consolation: "And only briefly then / you touch, you see, you press against / the surface of impenetrable things" (*DH* 27). But even here, genuine transcendence, though palpably present, remains out of reach. "Beware of Things in Duplicate," set in the early evening, evokes the ominous eeriness that arises from such mundane doublings as the hands of a clock "fixed on the same hour / you noticed at your morning coffee."

The final two poems in "Daily Horoscope," set in the early evening and in the middle of the night, once again emphasize the tantalizing sense of the imminence—yet frustratingly elusive sense of transcendence—of the quotidian. "The Stars Now Rearrange Themselves" instructs one that "you must look toward earth," toward this paradoxical end:

> Look for smaller signs instead, the fine
> disturbances of ordered things when suddenly
> the rhythms of your expectation break
> and in a moment's pause another world
> reveals itself behind the ordinary. (*DH* 29)

In his role as a poet, this is what Gioia, like Stevens, is in constant quest of: "another world / ... behind the ordinary."

"News Will Arrive from Far Away," the last poem in the sequence, reminds us that as a poet, Gioia, unlike Stevens, always remains grounded in the real world. The phone call that promises so much—"names you haven't heard for years, / names of another place, another time," ends in "silence. / A dial tone. An intervening voice. / Or nothing." The listener is left finally with "the cold disorder of the bed" (*DH* 30). This is the opposite of the consolation of "home" experienced by the autobiographical persona in "In Cheever Country," though one senses that "Daily Horoscope," despite the absence of a first-person speaker, is no less than a spiritual autobiography of the poet.

The lyrics that make up the third and central section of *Daily Horoscope* focus on Gioia's cultural interests—jazz, classical music, history, religion, and painting. One of the most notable of this section's erudite poems is "Lives of the Great Composers," in which Gioia adapts the musical form of the fugue to poetry. Gioia has described his poetic figure as one in which:

> The continual repetition of a small group of facts and images dictated that the poem have some progressive narrative or thematic structure. In this way statements could be repeated for a cumulative musical effect without exhausting their significance, since the words would take on a slightly different meaning each time. Without the "plotting" the poem would have become more arbitrary and less interesting with each stanza.[2]

---

[2] Dana Gioia, "A Tune in the Back of My Head," in *Ecstatic Occasions, Expedient Forms: 61 Leading and Contemporary Poets Select and Comment on their Poems*, ed. David Lehman (New York: Macmillan, 1987), 66–67.

The narrative armature underlying the poem is a person listening to the radio during an electrical storm that causes the music to fade in and out. This disturbance leads to the speaker's meditation on fragmentary anecdotes recalled, with much verve, from the biographies of classical composers—Bruckner, Berlioz, Schumann, Holst, Mendelssohn, Paganini, and Liszt. What emerges is a patchwork illustration of the sometimes painfully comic circumstances in which sublime music is created.

"Journeys in Sunlight," a sequence of five poems that originally appeared in a luxurious boxed, limited edition illustrated by the Italian artist Fulvio Testa, is similar in its didactic tone and its sublime language to *Daily Horoscope*'s title sequence. Its epigraph, "an Italy of the mind," is taken from Stevens, and the sequence itself can be seen as a poetic Baedeker to this metaphysical but simultaneously sensuous Italy. In "Instructions for the Afternoon,"[3] we are advised to "Leave the museums, the comfortable rooms, / the safe distractions of the masterpiece," and to "Consider what you've come for." The speaker continues:

For this
is how it must be seen to understand:
by walking from the sunlight into darkness,
by groping down the aisle
as your wet skin cools and your eyes adjust,
by finding what you've come for thoughtlessly,
shoved off into a corner, almost lost
among the spectacle of gold and purple. (*DH* 57)

Yet this is, finally, a cautionary guidebook; for all of the beauty of its description, the poem warns that travel can't be depended upon to yield up eternal epiphanies, for "vision fails," and ultimately the regretted "insufficiencies make up the world" the speaker must inhabit. Having begun as a quest for transcendence, the poem concludes: "Strange how all journeys come to this: the sun / bright on the unfamiliar hills,

[3] Gioia revised and retitled this poem as "Most Journeys Come to This" in *99 Poems*.

new vistas / dazzling the eye, the stubborn heart unchanged" (*DH* 58).

The fifth and final section of *Daily Horoscope* also concerns itself with "the stubborn heart," its lyrics and the volume's one major narrative poem mostly dealing with "Love and the imminence of love and the intolerable remembering," as the section's epigraph, taken from Jorge Luis Borges, suggests. Gioia is an exquisite love poet, as one can see in such varied lyrics as the complexly compelling "His Three Women" and the straightforward "Parts of Summer Weather," "The End of the Season," and "The Sunday News." They all focus on the beauty and fragility of love and the pain that is often associated with it.

Among *Daily Horoscope*'s most memorable achievements is the narrative poem "The Room Upstairs," an expansive and eerie tale of love lost, or love evaded—perhaps both. Gioia's narrative poems occupy a distinctive place in contemporary poetry: their lyric intensity—their defining characteristic—is such that one may categorize them as "lyric narratives." The narrative instinct that is so strong in his shorter lyrics, and even in his more complicated poetic sequences, is developed to its logical conclusion in "The Room Upstairs" and in "Counting the Children" and "Homecoming,"[4] the two longer narratives in his second collection of poetry, *The Gods of Winter*.

"The Room Upstairs" is spoken in the voice of an aging college professor who rents a room in his home to students. The poem's structure is that of a Chinese box, the staid professor moving by increments from a calm, though only seemingly objective, description of a Western landscape to deeper and deeper revelations of his inner life, culminating in an otherworldly vision of love. The dramatic monologue opens with the professor, speaking in tightly decorous blank verse, inviting a young man who has come to inquire about the room for rent to view the landscape from his window: "Come over to the window for a moment— / I want to show you something." By the second verse paragraph, the professor, realizing the emotional significance this view of the California hills has for him, asks the student: "How did I get started on this

---

[4] Gioia titled this poem "The Homecoming" in *Gods of Winter*. When he included it in *99 Poems*, he revised the poem and changed the title to "Homecoming." We have made the editorial decision to follow the final title and revised text.

subject? / I'm really not as morbid as I sound." And slowly the poem shifts into a deeper examination of the professor's psyche when he answers an implied question from the student:

> No.
> I never married, never had the time
> Or inclination to. Still, getting older,
> One wonders ... not so much about a wife—
> No mystery there—but about a son. (*DH* 81–82)

Here, the speaker's false bravado concerning his mastery of the "mystery" of women not only exposes his perhaps unconscious misogyny but also leads to a revelation of his homoerotic disposition.

The latter becomes more explicit in the next verse paragraph, which begins the professor's story about David, "a boy who lived here years ago— / ... a clever, handsome boy / Who thought he was a poet" (*DH* 82). At first, David is presented as the professor's younger mirror image—"That was back / When I still dreamed of writing.... / How sure I felt that he / Would spur me on"—the son he never had (*DH* 82). But as his narrative continues, the professor, as if hypnotized by his narrative, becomes more explicit about the sexual component of his memory. This subtle revelation is achieved in two brilliantly juxtaposed passages, themselves mirror images. The first describes the injuries covering David's body, incurred during a climbing accident, which he displays to the professor; the second—the poem's emotional core—comprises four verse paragraphs in which David, who has now died in a similar accident while traveling in Europe after his graduation, again appears to the professor, this time as a ghostly figure in a dream.

In the first of these scenes, David seems to offer his body to the professor, who describes the action in extremely lyrical and erotic terms:

> When he called me in,
> I watched him standing in the steamy bathroom—
> His naked body shining from the water—
> Carefully drying himself with a towel.
> Then suddenly he threw it down and showed me

Where the ropes had cut into his skin.
It looked as if he had been branded,
Wounds deep enough to hide your fingers in. (*DH* 83)

The lyricism of this passage is heightened by the end rhymes—in/skin/in—that are unexpectedly added to the blank verse. And yet, faced with David's frank eroticism, his seemingly Christ-like offering of himself to the professor to provide both physical and spiritual salvation, the professor is too reserved to respond as he would like:

I felt like holding him but couldn't bear it.
I helped him into bed and spent the night
Sitting in this room, too upset to sleep.
And on the morning after he drove home. (*DH* 83)

The poem achieves both its narrative and its lyric climax in four verse paragraphs describing the professor's dream the night he hears of David's death. This dream is an eerie mirror image—at once chilling and beautiful—of David's previous offering of himself to the narrator, now visible but ironically incorporeal. David's appearance is preceded by a halo-like glow:

I dreamt
That suddenly the room was filled with light,
Not blinding but the soft whiteness that you see
When heavy snow is falling in the morning,
And I awoke to see him standing here,
Waiting in the doorway, his arms outstretched.
"I've come back to you," he said. "Look at me.
Let me show you what I've done for you." (*DH* 84)

The language setting the scene for this final, ghostly encounter between professor and student achieves the same synesthetic effect as the previous one, the repetition of the sibilants, languorous *l*'s, and long *i*'s presenting a visual and aural sense of the color and sound associated with "snow … falling in the morning." This lyric description blends seamlessly into the dramatic element of the poem, the conversation between David and the professor.

After David's death, in the middle of the night, he appears as a quite literal embodiment of an epiphany, a shining forth, once again offering the psychically and physically repressed professor a chance for salvation—of sorts. At first, the professor resists: "'Why are you doing this to me?' I asked. / 'Please, go away.'" But David implores him: "'But I've come back to you. / I'm cold. Just hold me. I'm so very cold'" (*DH* 84). Once again, Gioia masterfully combines the lyric and the dreamlike in this narrative climax, as the professor yields to David's request:

> What else could I have done but hold him there?
> I took him in my arms—he was so light—
> And held him in the doorway, listening.
> Nothing else was said or lost it seemed.
> I waited there while it grew dark again,
> And he grew lighter, slipping silently away
> Like snow between my fingers, and was gone. (*DH* 84–85)

In "The Gods of Winter," the title lyric of Gioia's subsequent collection, the image of snow on a March night stands for the jeweled perfection of love—whether that between a husband and wife or a parent and child—which will necessarily melt in the light of the coming noon. Within the narrative of "The Room Upstairs," snow functions similarly to emphasize that the consummation of the professor's erotic desire for David is at once achieved and elusive, occurring only in a dream after the physical body has melted away. In both his conventional lyrics, then, and in his lyric narratives, Gioia illustrates, in more accessible forms, the philosophical paradoxes he explores in more complexly modernist-influenced poems like "Daily Horoscope": that however "briefly then / you touch, you see, you press against / the surface of impenetrable things," we ultimately remain on the surface; within the limitations of the quotidian world we have no choice but to live in, transcendence into a more permanent realm of ideal love and beauty remains "impenetrable" (*DH* 27). But it remains imperative that we continue to "press against" them, or life would indeed devolve into the "waste land" of Eliot's early modernist vision.

In the final brief verse paragraph of "The Room Upstairs," its denouement, the professor awakens from his reverie on the past to the present business of renting his room to the new student he has been addressing throughout. Or almost, for Gioia has one more revelation for us—that the structure of the poem is in fact Wordsworthian, that the professor's narrative was inspired by his confusing of this student with David:

> That's all there is to say. I can't explain it.
> And now I'm sorry to have bored you so.
> It's getting late. You know the way upstairs.
> But no, of course not. Let me show you to your room. (*DH* 85)

So, the ordinary world remains penetrated by the extraordinary. The narrative poem's brief conclusion leaves us speculating about the professor's feelings for the new tenant—and the student's response to the narrative he's just heard.

In December 1987, Gioia's first son, Michael Jasper, who was only four months old, died of sudden infant death syndrome. The grief suffered by Gioia and his wife underlies the profound lyric melancholy of *The Gods of Winter* (1991), which appeared five years after *Daily Horoscope* and four years after the death of his son, to whom the book is dedicated. The themes of death and mortality dominate the first two sections of *The Gods of Winter*. The epigraph to the book and to the first group of lyrics both refer, in puns used poignantly rather than wittily, to the poet's son, "gioia" meaning, of course, "joy" in Italian. The first is a line from the "Gods of Winter": "Briefest of joys, our life together." Although that poem was completed before Michael Jasper's death, in proximity to the dedication, the line invites reinterpretation. The other epigraph, beginning the first group of poems, is from Ben Jonson's "On My First Son"— "Farewell, thou child of my right hand, and joy."

Except for "Night Watch," an elegy to Gioia's maternal uncle, a Mexican American Merchant Marine who died in a plane crash shortly before he was to return to civilian life, the remaining six poems in the opening section of *The Gods of Winter* are all concerned with the poet's lost first son. The section opens with "Prayer," a litany to an unnamed god—"Seducer, healer, deity or thief"—who the poet asks to "watch over him / as a mountain guards its covert ore // and the harsh falcon its flightless young" (*GW* 3).

Two of the lyrics in this section, "All Souls'" and "Veterans' Cemetery," formalize Gioia's emotions using iambic pentameter quatrains with *abab* rhyme schemes. "All Souls'" uses the feast of All Souls' Day (November 2) to meditate upon the afterlife of souls. Gioia opens the poem with this somber speculation:

> Suppose there is no heaven and no hell,
> And that the dead can never leave the earth,
> That, as the body rots, the soul breaks free,
> Weak and disabled in its second birth. (*GW* 4)

He goes on to paint an eerie portrait of the earth perceived without the physical senses, concluding with the soul's recognition that "The pallor of the rose is their despair." "Veterans' Cemetery" uses a description of the cemetery in which the poet's son is buried to symbolize the child's death. The observations on nature here emphasize that death is always immanent in it:

> The afternoon's a single thread of light
> Sewn through the tatters of a leafless willow,
> As one by one the branches fade from sight,
> And time curls up like paper turning yellow. (*GW* 7)

In "Planting a Sequoia," Gioia addresses his son's death most explicitly, in long, free-verse lines that come closest to any in his work to the overtly confessional, albeit with supreme dignity. The poem describes a winter afternoon at his parents' home in Northern California shortly after his son's death, "the sky above us … the dull gray / Of an old year coming to an end." He and his two younger brothers have gathered in their parents' orchard to modify the Sicilian custom of a father planting a fruit tree "to celebrate his first son's birth." "Defying the practical custom of our fathers," they plant a sequoia, "our native giant," instead of one of the traditional trees like a fig or olive. "Wrapping in your roots a lock of hair, a piece of an infant's birth cord, / All that remains above earth of a first-born son, / A few stray atoms brought back to the elements" (*GW* 10). The sequoia, like the poem itself, is meant to symbolize the son's enduring existence beyond his parents' lives:

> And when our family is no more, all of his unborn brothers dead,
> Every niece and nephew scattered, the house torn down,
> His mother's beauty ashes in the air,
> I want you to stand among strangers, all young and ephemeral to
>   you,
> Silently keeping the secret of your birth. (*GW* 10)

If "All Souls'" and "Veterans' Cemetery" commemorate Gioia's son's actual burial in New York, then "Planting a Sequoia" rehearses the symbolic reinternment of him in the California homeland to which his family was to return a few years after his death.

"Counting the Children," the first of the two narrative poems in *The Gods of Winter*, with its concern for familial love, deals with the most ordinary material of the mid-length narratives. It also strikes the reader as the one closest to Gioia's heart. Although some critics believe that it was written in direct response to the death of Gioia's son, the poem had been composed before then; it was, however, substantially revised and expanded after December 1987. While the personal loss is not addressed directly, its influence on the poem is clear.

Mr. Choi, an accountant who is more comfortable with numbers than with emotions, is nonetheless led to a visionary experience of the nightmarish responsibilities and transcendent joys of parenthood. The poem—written in the pentameter tercets, if not the rhyme scheme, of Dante's *Commedia*—begins with Mr. Choi being presented with a vision of hell in the form of a menagerie of dolls: "Some battered, others missing arms and legs, / Shelf after shelf of the same dusty stare / As if despair could be assuaged by order." He has found them in the bedroom of a woman recently dead, whose estate he has been asked to assess. The horrific image of the doll collection, which summons visions of abused and abandoned children, leads to Mr. Choi's own nightmare, in which he dreams his daughter will die unless he can successfully balance the thousands of figures contained in a ledger. He witnesses as well generations of his Chinese ancestors pressuring him to solve the sum, to save his daughter, only to see the numbers as they, as well as the dolls, catch ablaze.

In the next section of the poem, the accountant admits how much he has always worried about his daughter, often looking in on her in her sleep. Aware of the tenuousness of life, he observes: "How delicate this vessel in our care, / This gentle soul we summoned to the world, / A life we treasured but could not protect" (*GW* 17). The accountant reflects upon the "terror" that this helplessness evokes as well as the uncanny "joy," emotions he can't fully understand or communicate to his wife or daughter, instead experiencing, like the professor in "The Room Upstairs," "the loneliness that we call love."

The poem's final section occurs several years after Mr. Choi's nightmare about the dolls, recounting a vision he has while once again watching over his sleeping daughter. The very fact "that an accountant / Can have a vision" underlines the visionary realism that so characterizes Gioia's narrative poems. Here, Mr. Choi's domestic vigil leads to a moment of Platonic insight:

> What if completion comes only in beginnings?
> The naked tree exploding into flower?
> And all our prim assumptions about time
>
> Prove wrong? What if we cannot read the future
> Because our destiny moves back in time,
> And only memory speaks prophetically?
>
> We long for immortality, a soul
> To rise up flaming from the body's dust.
> I know that it exists. I felt it there,
>
> Perfect and eternal in the way
> That only numbers are, intangible but real,
> Infinitely divisible yet whole. (*GW* 18)

Mr. Choi locates paradise, eternity, in beginnings, not endings, in the state of childhood which is perfect because, in it, all life is unrealized potential. This paradoxical immortality, then,—"intangible but real, / Infinitely divisible yet whole"—is achieved not in ourselves but in our children:

We die, and it abides, and we are one
With all our ancestors, while it divides

Over and over, common to us all,
The ancient face returning in the child,
The distant arms embracing us, the salt

Of our blind origins filling our veins. (*GW* 18)

Despite this connection, the speaker finally recognizes both his interrelatedness with and his separation from his daughter, now protected in sleep by her own shelf of dolls, eyeing the father suspiciously:

I felt like holding them tight in my arms,
Promising I would never let them go,
But they would trust no promises of mine.

I feared that if I touched one, it would scream. (*GW* 19)

Once again, Gioia's narrative is resolved in a complex lyric vision. The imminence of renewed terror balances the earlier experience of the transcendence of temporal flux.

"Homecoming," the second dramatic monologue in *The Gods of Winter*, represents a departure for Gioia, presenting both a psychologically astute and luridly compelling narrative dramatizing incidents of torture, the horrors of prison life, and, in the poem's central dramatic incident, an escaped prisoner's murder of his foster mother, for whom his hatred has become a kind of demonic religion. The most interesting moments of this poem involve the narrator's mystical rebirth into evil. Abandoned by a beautiful young mother, raised by a Calvinistic harridan, the narrator seeks his identity first in fantasy novels and then in a well in a field where another local boy was reputedly killed. This well becomes his secret place, a refuge from his foster mother. Here, he invokes the spirit of the dead boy, whom he sacrilegiously equates with the body of the risen Christ:

> One night I started whispering down the well.
> What was it like, I asked him, to be dead?
> . . .
> Of course he didn't answer me. The dead
> never do. Not him. Not even Jesus.
> Only a razor's edge of moonlight gleaming,
> silent at the bottom of the well. (*GW* 45)

At one point in the poem, the narrator declares: "Madness makes storytellers of us all." And the stories his madness produces lead him to an act that he sees as inevitable: the murder of his foster mother. The narrative of this act and of the events that provoked it is recounted after the fact, as the speaker waits in the foster mother's house. He has attained his negative transcendence and is content to return to prison and live off its memory.

The remaining lyrics in *The Gods of Winter*, which occupy the volume's third and fifth sections, are more eclectic thematically and stylistically than the poems that relate to Gioia's son's death. Some, it is true, use the harshness of the Western landscape of his childhood (no longer presented as ultimately "gentle," as in "California Hills in August") to reflect the poet's stoicism, as in "Rough Country" and "Becoming a Redwood." "Redwood" can be seen as connecting the middle-aged poet with the son he buried in "Planting a Sequoia," flourishing in a landscape where

> Coyotes hunt
> these hills and packs of feral dogs.
> But standing here at night accepts all that.

You are your own pale shadow in the quarter moon,
moving more slowly than the crippled stars,
part of the moonlight as the moonlight falls,

Part of the grass that answers the wind,
part of the midnight's watchfulness that knows
there is no silence but when danger comes. (*GW* 55–56)

This poem echoes the darker voice that Gioia deploys in "Homecoming" while extending the darker vision of California first encountered in "In Chandler Country." In the aftermath of his son's death, California increasingly becomes for Gioia a *paysage moralisé* of stoic endurance in the face of life's inescapable "danger."

By contrast, the lyrics in *The Gods of Winter* extend the more quietly elegiac autobiographical voice from *Daily Horoscope*. Two particularly resonant lyrics are translations. "On Approaching Forty," from the contemporary Italian poet Mario Luzi, clearly reflects Gioia's feelings on the subject—"So soon come forty years of restlessness, / of tedium, of unexpected joy" (*GW* 25). Here, the teenage self brought into focus in "Cruising with the Beach Boys" is seemingly glimpsed in early middle age. "Orchestra," from the Romanian of Nina Cassian, beautifully employs musical imagery to write of the depth of love and the sorrow that follows its loss. "Orchestra" is one of four love poems with which *The Gods of Winter* concludes, the others being "Los Angeles after the Rain," "Speaking of Love," and "Equations of the Light." The last, the book's final poem, about a luminous but only putative affair, suggests that the encounter between poet and reader that *The Gods of Winter* provides is an analogous experience, leaving both sides with the recognition that "at the end what else could we have done / but turn the corner back into our life?" (*GW* 62).

For Gioia's readers, the decade between *The Gods of Winter* (1991) and his third collection, *Interrogations at Noon* (2001), seemed a painfully long separation. Part of that time Gioia devoted to the translation of Seneca's verse tragedy, *The Madness of Hercules* (1995), and the writing of the libretto for Alva Henderson's opera *Nosferatu* (2001). Both works are represented by excerpts in *Interrogations at Noon*. Three arias from

Nosferatu appear in "Words for Music," a group of songs that occupies the central position in the volume. The songs—which, Gioia explained, are written for the ear rather than for the eye—also include some of Gioia's light verse. Notable among these is "Alley Cat Love Song," a playful parody of Tennyson's "Maud" and "The Archbishop," a satiric puncturing of "a famous poetry critic." *The Madness of Hercules* is represented by "Juno Plots Her Revenge," a reworking of the play's long opening monologue in which the outraged goddess outlines her sinister plan to trick Hercules into murdering his wife and two sons. This dramatic monologue, which functions as Gioia's main narrative piece in the volume, bears a family likeness to "Homecoming," the matricidal monologue from *The Gods of Winter*. Likewise, "Descent to the Underworld," a vision of hell also adapted from Seneca, extends Gioia's focus on the darker themes he has explored since the death of his son. The original lyrics in the volume are rather evenly divided among those that continue the meditation on death, those that consolidate his status as an elegiac love poet, and those that speculate upon metaphysical (including metapoetic) themes.

At the center of all these poetic enterprises lies the central paradox that has concerned Gioia since *Daily Horoscope*, stated in *Interrogations at Noon*'s first poem, "Words": "The world does not need words" and "Yet the stones remain less real to those who cannot / name them, or read the mute syllables graven in silica." Moreover, just as "The Burning Ladder," the first poem in *Daily Horoscope*, dramatizes Gioia's entry into "that choir" of "Seraphim / ascending" representing the poetic canon even as it seemingly asserts that "Jacob / never climbed the ladder / burning in his dream," "Gravity" being "always greater than desire," so too does "Words," through its *sound*, assert that poetry contributes something extra to the visual world: "The daylight needs no praise, and so we praise it always— / greater than ourselves and all the airy words we summon" (*IN* 3). In musically "summon"[ing] words, the poet exists in a magical and necessary position between experience and the ineffable.

In one form this idea surfaced in "The Next Poem" from *The Gods of Winter*, where the poet, in the process of writing *this* poem recognizes "How much better it seems now / than when it is finally written" (*GW*

35). What is realized, the poem asserts, is always inferior to what can be imagined. This theme surfaces in another form in "Interrogations at Noon" where the poet is made aware of his human—as opposed to merely poetic—inadequacies, by the "voice" of "the better man I might have been, / Who chronicles the life I've never led" (*IN* 5). And it finally surfaces in his elegies to his son as well as those addressed to elusive lovers and friends. "The Litany" is one of the poems in *Interrogations at Noon*—"Metamorphosis," "Pentecost," and "A California Requiem" are others—that continues the poet's impossible but necessary dialogue with his deceased son, being "a prayer, inchoate and unfinished, / for you, my love, my loss, my lesion." "After a Line by Cavafy" contemplates the poet's unique but circumscribed friendship with another poet whom he met only once before his death from AIDS.

The love poems all focus on similar situations. "Corner Table" dramatizes the dinner conversation during which the speaker's former lover declares her intention to marry another man. "Long Distance" presents the phone conversation of a couple uncharacteristically separated for a few weeks faced with the daunting challenge of communicating with words a love that had, until then, always been conveyed through touch. "Summer Storm" evokes a brief, erotically charged encounter between a young man and a woman at a wedding reception, brought to mind years later by a summer storm. These lyrics all elucidate the paradoxical evanescence of love, the coincidence of intimacy and separateness, speech and silence, past possession and present loss. In "Corner Table," the lovers "understand / This last mute touch that lingers is farewell" (*IN* 51). In "Long Distance," the speaker wonders "Why is a lover's touch most keenly felt / The moment it is first withheld?" recognizing that, while "words are never as precise as touch. / Now words that have no body ask her love" (*IN* 52). "Summer Storm" leads the speaker to muse upon a question that has been important to Gioia since it was implicitly dramatized in "The Room Upstairs": how would life have been different if a frustrated relationship from the past had only been consummated?

And memory insists on pining
For places it never went,

As if life would be happier
Just by being different. (*IN* 67)

This Jamesian scenario of the unlived life is addressed from a different perspective in the penultimate poem of *Interrogations at Noon*, "The Lost Garden." With its obvious reference to Eden, this poem recalls not only a shared past that no longer exists but also the life "lost" by not taking a different direction. It concludes, however, with a description of memory as redemptive, transformative:

The trick is making memory a blessing,
To learn by loss subtraction of desire,
Of wanting nothing more than what has been,
To know the past forever lost, yet seeing
Behind the wall a garden still in blossom. (*IN* 68)

This, for Gioia, has always been the magical paradox of poetic language: it is able to affirm what logic insists should be beyond words, to "say," even what one is describing is, to use the title of the final poem in *Interrogations at Noon*, the "Unsaid." This short poem echoes the volume's first, "Words," by returning to the idea that the profoundest emotions "are no less real / For having passed unsaid." And so *Interrogations at Noon* ends with the observation that:

So much of what we live goes on inside—
The diaries of grief, the tongue-tied aches
Of unacknowledged love are no less real
For having passed unsaid. What we conceal
Is always more than what we dare confide.
Think of the letters that we write our dead. (*IN* 69)

Gioia's language here not only points as accurately as is possible to the subject of this poem—the many important things that usually remain unsaid—but also gestures toward what so many of his poems in all three volumes have been, "The letters we write our dead"—a landscape; a lover; a first-born son. In composing such letters, such poems,

Gioia has fashioned a unique style of visionary realism poised upon paradox, in both his lyric and narrative poems, that distinguishes him as one of the most vital American poets writing at the beginning of the twenty-first century.

2

POEMS OF EXILE AND LOSS: *DAILY HOROSCOPE* (2003)

April Lindner

Daily Horoscope, Dana Gioia's first collection of poetry, received sharply divided reviews, stirring up an unusual degree of controversy. Reviewers either loved the book or hated it. Two years after the book's publication, the anti-formalist critic Greg Kuzma assailed it in the *Northwest Review*. He wrote, "The fault I find with Dana Gioia is that his poetry is the poetry of leisure, or ease, or idle pleasures. I have called it the poetry of money because what it values most are material things and what it promotes is an aesthetic based on what one can afford."[1] Kuzma points to the poem "In Cheever Country," in which the poem's speaker, a businessman who may well have stepped out from a Cheever story, rides through suburbs on his nightly commute, observing the convents and orphanages that "Robber Barons gave to God" in the name of charity and atonement (*DH* 20). He observes the formerly grand estates:

> And some are merely left to rot where now
> broken stone lions guard a roofless colonnade,
> a half-collapsed gazebo bursts with tires,
> and each detail warns it is not so difficult
> to make a fortune as to pass it on. (*DH* 20)

Of this passage, Kuzma writes, "Ruined splendor, lost wealth, obsess this poet. Perhaps he fears bankruptcy most of all things."[2] Kuzma fails to notice that these gently chiding lines are less concerned with

---

[1] Greg Kuzma, "Dana Gioia and the Poetry of Money," *Northwest Review* 26/33 (November 1988): 114.

[2] Ibid., 118.

wealth than with loss itself, whether due to bad business sense or the passage of time.

While we find regret for squandered fortunes in "In Cheever Country" and elsewhere in *Daily Horoscope*, that regret is part of a larger thematic pattern of regret for places and states of mind that can be achieved, if at all, only ephemerally. As the volume's opening poem, "The Burning Ladder," warns, no matter how strong desire is, gravity is always more powerful. This principle undergirds the poems in *Daily Horoscope*, many of which revolve around a sense of loss. In these poems, fields are paved to make way for parking lots, and the things that matter most—innocence, dreams, fortunes, home, the past and one's memory of it—are always on the verge of slipping away.

When looked at as part of this larger pattern of loss, Gioia's poems of place take on an added significance. As a displaced Westerner, Gioia is acutely interested in geography and questions of travel, just as Elizabeth Bishop—his former teacher—was. The first section of *Daily Horoscope* is made up of poems that either analyze and contrast the East and West Coasts, or in which the poem's speaker is in limbo, caught somewhere between two destinations.

Los Angeles and its piers and mist feature prominently in "Cruising with the Beach Boys." Here Gioia writes ironically about nostalgia. The poem's speaker, a businessman in a rented car, is surprised by the power of an old hit song to trigger strong memories of teenage lovesickness. To his chagrin, he finds the song can still move him to tears, despite his understanding of the adolescent posing and self-dramatization that originally led him to choose the song as a kind of private theme-song:

> Every lovesick summer has its song,
> And this one I pretended to despise,
> But if I was alone when it came on,
> I turned it up full-blast to sing along—
> A primal scream in croaky baritone,
> The notes all flat, the lyrics mostly slurred.
> No wonder I spent so much time alone
> Making the rounds in Dad's old Thunderbird.

Just as the unnamed song is inextricably tied to memory, both are tied to place:

> Some nights I drove down to the beach to park
> And walk along the railings of the pier.
> The water down below was cold and dark,
> The waves monotonous against the shore.
> The darkness and the mist, the midnight sea,
> The flickering lights reflected from the city—
> A perfect setting for a boy like me,
> The Cecil B. DeMille of my self-pity. (*DH* 5)

Although the adult speaker critiques nostalgia by recognizing that his current tears are as self-pitying as the ones he shed as a teenager, he is nonetheless unable to resist the urge to wallow. The old song brings on tears "for no reason at all," except for the powerful memories popular music can summon. Against his better judgment, nostalgia swamps the speaker, and his homesickness for the past is inextricably bound to the place where he lived out his early dramas, a seascape he now describes in loving particulars.

A similar note is sounded in the poem "California Hills in August." Initially, Gioia presents the landscape in unappealing terms: hot and dusty, dotted with "sparse brown bushes" and weeds. By the poem's end, however, the hills and their environs are revealed as a test of sensibilities. The speaker hypothesizes that an Easterner in this landscape would be disdainful of

> the meagerness of summer, the dry
> twisted shapes of black elm,
> scrub oak, and chaparral, a landscape
> August has already drained of green.

A native, however, could understand and appreciate the California landscape. In the last stanza, the poem's tone modulates, and criticism of the landscape turns into affection for it:

And yet how gentle it seems to someone
raised in a landscape short of rain—
the skyline of a hill broken by no more
trees than one can count, the grass,
the empty sky, the wish for water. (*DH* 4)

The poet values these dry California hills precisely because they can only be appreciated by the initiated.

While *Daily Horoscope* also contains numerous poems about East Coast life, Gioia consistently writes as a displaced Californian. The rugged West Coast landscape described in "California Hills in August" hides like a pentimento beneath the surface of all Gioia's poems about Westchester County. "Eastern Standard Time," for example, is a poem of displacement, spoken by a recently arrived Californian who has only just learned to recognize:

the changes that prefigure storms:

the heavy air, the circling wind
and graduate darkness, but still

each time the air goes through even these
accustomed changes, I grow uneasy.

Sudden storms, shifts in temperature, even snow
in midwinter still surprise me,

unable to feel at home in a landscape
so suddenly transformed. (*DH* 9–10)

The speaker's discomfort with unfamiliar weather patterns proves to be a symptom of something larger, a discomfort with suburban life in general: "Sometimes the saddest places in the world / are just the ordinary ones seen after hours" (*DH* 10). The only thing that can reconcile the speaker to his lack of connection with the barren landscape he walks through—a parking lot—is his abrupt realization that once it was a part of nature. This fact—that a dramatic change has taken place in the landscape—somehow reconciles the speaker to what he refers to, in a tone of ironically self-conscious melodrama, as the "Suburbs of Despair / where nothing but the weather ever changes!" (*DH* 10). The poem's modulation in tone and its ironic exclamation point reveal the speaker's annoyance with his own inability to appreciate such safe and relatively comfortable surroundings. A poorer or more beleaguered man might long for the calm and affluent suburbs; for the poem's narrator, however, the static, paved-over nature of the suburbs of New York is their most alien feature, particularly in contrast to the untrammeled and therefore ever-changing California hills.

Two other poems in the volume's first section offer contrasting views of the West and East Coasts. "In Chandler Country" is spoken in the voice of the hard-boiled Philip Marlowe, hero of Raymond Chandler's popular detective novels. Gioia's appropriated narrator says things like:

> Another sleepless night,
> when every wrinkle in the bedsheet scratches
> like a dry razor on a sunburned cheek,
> when even ten-year whiskey tastes like sand,
> and quiet women in the kitchen run
> their fingers on the edges of a knife
> and eye their husbands' necks. I wish them luck. (*DH* 7)

This highly stylized voice is a product of the rough cityscape that spawned it. In fact, the poem's shadow subject is the ways in which a particular environment gives rise to a particular type of art, in this case Chandler's novels. Atmosphere and content are inseparable from one another. Ironically, though, in the poem's most atmospheric—and therefore most lyrical—moments, the voice seems farthest from Marlowe and closest to the speakers of Gioia's other poems:

> Tonight it seems that if I took the coins
> out of my pocket and tossed them in the air
> they'd stay a moment glistening like a net
> slowly falling through dark water. (*DH* 7)

The heat and the peculiar liquid quality of air are more than a backdrop to violence. They function, in the world of the poem, as a motive for the crime. And the two-dimensional men and women who populate the landscape of the poem are no less driven by their animal urges than the coyotes who close in at the poem's end.

In contrast, the violence Gioia depicts in "In Cheever Country" is more subtle, a trespass against the sensibilities and the souls of those who live in New York's Westchester County. What once was a landscape of wealth and privilege has been disfigured by time and the bad business sense of those who allowed their estates to fall into ruin. On the other hand, good business sense can also bring about crimes against good taste. The speaker observes the fabricated posture of the suburban towns:

> The town names stenciled on the platform signs—
> Clear Haven, Bullet Park, and Shady Hill—
> show that developers at least believe in poetry
> if only as a talisman against the commonplace. (*DH* 19)

In these lines, a mild sense of despair over the cheapening of language and landscape mingles with an understanding of the motives and methods of developers.

Paradoxically, while "In Cheever Country" coolly laments the change inflicted on the land by decaying mansions and mushrooming apartment complexes, the poem's speaker is further dismayed by a certain eerie timelessness of the landscape. His view that "here so little happens that is obvious" hearkens back to "Eastern Standard Time." In both poems, aspects of Westchester County are depicted as soul-deadeningly static. In both poems, however, Gioia achieves a reconciliation with the landscape. The narrator of "In Cheever Country" finds beauty in a static domestic tableau, a beauty the reader may contrast with the wild and dangerous beauty of California. Of a particular train station, Gioia writes: "If there is an afterlife, let it be a small town / gentle as this spot at just this instant" (*DH* 20). The poem concludes with a vision of family life as a source of consolation:

> And this at last is home, this ordinary town
> where the lights on the hill gleaming in the rain
> are the lights that children bathe by, and it is time
> to go home now—to drinks, to love, to supper,
> to the modest places which contain our lives. (*DH* 21)

The comfort the speaker finds in his safe homelife is a momentary stay against the larger East Coast world of decaying grandeur, ruined landscapes, and potential financial ruin.

This vision of the suburban household as a refuge nonetheless proves false in the small hours of the morning. In "Insomnia," a sleepless character addressed in the second person hears his own failures and disappointments in the various nighttime noises of his house. The poem is quoted in full:

> Now you hear what the house has to say.
> Pipes clanking, water running in the dark,
> the mortgaged walls shifting in discomfort,
> and voices mounting in an endless drone
> of small complaints like the sounds of a family
> that year by year you've learned how to ignore.
>
> But now you must listen to the things you own,
> all that you've worked for these past years,
> the murmur of property, of things in disrepair,
> the moving parts about to come undone,
> and twisting in the sheets remember all
> the faces you could not bring yourself to love.
>
> How many voices have escaped you until now,
> the venting furnace, the floorboards underfoot,
> the steady accusations of the clock
> numbering the minutes no one will mark.
> The terrible clarity this moment brings,
> the useless insight, the unbroken dark. (*DH* 18)

In "Insomnia," the demands of property—getting it and keeping it from falling apart—resemble the demands of loved ones, whom despite our best efforts we can never love enough. The middle-class haven money can buy proves a trap, and the "you" in this poem is haunted by the ways in which his possessions have come to own him. Gioia's use of the second person serves a dual purpose by momentarily implicating the reader and by enabling Gioia to avoid the appearance of Confessionalism.

Another trapping and/or trap of middle-class success—air travel—is addressed by Gioia in "Waiting in the Airport." In this poem, he explores the anonymity of the airport terminal, that placeless place leading to so many destinations. The poem's meter mimics the relentless nature of frequent job-imposed travel:

> But nothing ever happens here,
> This terminal that narrows to
> A single unattended gate,
> One entrance to so many worlds. (*DH* 13)

The poet chooses once again to substitute an "eye" for an "I," coolly observing the interactions—and the lack thereof—of his fellow travelers:

> On the same journey each of them
> Is going somewhere else. A goose-necked
> Woman in a flowered dress
> Stares gravely at two businessmen.
> They turn away but carry on
> Their argument on real estate.
>
> Lost in a mist of aftershave,
> A salesman in a brown toupée
> Is scribbling on his *Racing Form*
> While a fat man stares down at his hands
> As if there should be something there.
>
> The soldiers stand in line for sex—

With wives or girlfriends, whoever
They hope is waiting for them at
The other end. The wrapped perfume,
The bright, stuffed animals they clutch
Tremble under so much heat. (*DH* 13)

The people observed here are reduced to stereotypes—salesmen in toupées and goose-necked women. The soldiers' pending reunions with their respective wives or girlfriends are boiled down to one bad word: sex. If the poem provided more of the speaker's identity, we might be tempted to see him as a jaded or insensitive character. The poem's refusal to do so instead denies even the speaker his full humanity, hinting that air travel dehumanizes us all by whisking us out of context. When they arrive home, the poem's characters will again be fully human, but in the airport, each is reduced to a type.

A thematically related poem, "Flying over Clouds," is markedly less detached emotionally. In this poem, the seeming purity of a cloudscape glimpsed from an airplane window triggers an intense nostalgia for

an innocence one may have felt
on earth—but only for a moment,
. . .
O paradise beyond the glass,
beyond our touch, cast and recast,
shifting in wind. Delicate world
of air too thin to breathe, of cold
beyond endurance. (*DH* 14)

Interestingly, even in childhood the feeling of innocence is as elusive and mutable as a cloud. The mood here is nostalgia for an innocence that existed, if it existed at all, only fleetingly. Moreover, as in "Waiting in the Airport," there is a sense of suspension between places. The commuter, of course, is neither here nor there, and his plight is therefore "cold beyond endurance," like the air through which he moves. Nevertheless, something seductive remains about the "fluent oblivion" of the clouds and of travel itself. The desire for freedom, like the nostalgia for childhood innocence, outweighs, in this poem at least, the longing for any particular place. The poem's heightened rhetoric is much more self-consciously poetic than that of "Waiting in the Airport," hinting at the impracticality of the speaker's longing to remain suspended in air.

In contrast, the brief poem titled "Cuckoos" is expressly about homesickness. While reading of cuckoos, the speaker remembers climbing in unidentified mountains, and hearing the cries of cuckoos,

> back and forth from trees across the valley,
> invisible in pinetops but bright and clear
> like the ring of crystal against crystal.
> . . .
> So now, reading how the Chinese took their call
> to mean *Pu ju kuei, pu ju kuei—*
> *Come home again, you must come home again—*
> I understand at last what they were telling me
> not then, back in that high, green valley,
> but here, this evening, in the memory of it,
> returned by these birds that I have never seen. (*DH* 70)

Although the speaker is returned to those mountains by memory, the difference between return to memory and an actual homecoming looms large. Moreover, the speaker of "Cuckoos" is exiled from the longed-for landscape not only by distance but also by the passage of time.

Of all the poems in *Daily Horoscope*, the one with the strongest sense of longing for the ephemeral is also the most cryptic and complex. The volume's title sequence takes the daily newspaper horoscope column as a jumping-off point, employing an oracular speaker who doles out advice. In the first section of this long poem, the reader is advised that no matter how much she might want to return to the dream from which she's just been awakened, she can't. Dreams are presented as more attractive and more real than reality—but nevertheless just out of reach:

> These walls, these streets,
> this day can never be your home, and yet
> there is no other world where you could live,
> and so you will accept it. (*DH* 25)

Section two is more consoling, advising that even if we can't choose to remain in our dreams, when we awaken they aren't really lost. Nothing is truly lost, the poem's all-knowing speaker insists, although it may be diminished. We are advised to accept each thing—no matter how small—when it returns to us, and to see its importance.

In section three, however, the advice grows more ominous as the speaker warns us against presuming we can have any true understanding of the world around us:

> One
> more summer gone,
> and one way or another you survive,
> dull or regretful, never learning that
> nothing is hidden in the obvious
> changes of the world, that even the dim
> reflection of the sun on tall, dry grass
> is more than you will ever understand.
>
> Any only briefly then
> you touch, you see, you press against
> the surface of impenetrable things. (*DH* 27)

Only in realizing that we will never fathom any of life's mysteries will we achieve moments of understanding, and these visions will be fleeting, the oracle warns.

However, even the advice against searching for meaning proves ephemeral. The poem's fifth section advises that meaning may be found not in the stars—the usual source of astrological wisdom—but on earth, in the humblest of natural details. We should

> Look for smaller signs instead, the fine
> disturbances of ordered things when suddenly
> the rhythms of your expectation break
> and in a moment's pause another world
> reveals itself behind the ordinary. (*DH* 29)

It's this hidden world—the world of dreams, epiphanies, and sudden but ephemeral visions of the ordinary world—from which we are usually exiled. The rare and brief moments in which we again glimpse that other world are, ironically, the only times in which we feel truly at home. This sense of exile from essential things is underlined by the poem's last section, where a late-night phone call momentarily transports us to "the lost geography of childhood," a landscape in which we cannot remain (*DH* 30). A state of mind is envisioned as a place—interestingly, an Edenic landscape in which one's childhood was spent. By the poem's end we are thrust back into the fallen world of adulthood, where we must face such harsh details as "the ticking of the clock / the cold disorder of the bed" (*DH* 30). Once again, we are in exile from what matters.

Though the volume's title sequence is its most adamant crystallization of the poetics of exile, the themes of loss and displacement run through much of the rest of the volume. In "The Memory," for example, Gioia again employs the second person to warn us that memories are seductive and tricky:

> Don't listen to it. This memory
> is like a snatch of an old song
> in the back of your head: something
> you heard years ago. Pay
> attention to it now, and it
> sticks forever, just out of reach,
> getting louder all the time
> until you swear you know the words.
> Don't fool yourself. You know by now
> you can't remember where it's from,
> and all you'll ever get for searching

is just the sense of having left
something important in a place
you can't get back to. (*DH* 46)

In railing against the attractions of memory, the poem's narrator gives away his own obsession with random bits of the past, fragments that resurface when we're not expecting them, only to submerge again as quickly as they appeared. The speaker's admonitions are a cover-up of his own disappointing inability to experience the past fully.

If the past is a place we can't get back to, then the place in which we spent our past, "the lost geography of childhood," is the most emotionally potent place of all. In contrast, a visited landscape and the cultural artifacts it contains can never have the power to shape and change us in the way that a lived-in place can. This idea is touched upon in "Instructions for the Afternoon."[3] Here an omniscient speaker advises a tourist on how best to find what she's looking for—the art object that will change the way she sees the world. The reader/tourist is advised to forsake popular tourist attractions in favor of

Sad hamlets at the end of silted waterways,
dry mountain villages where time
is the thin shadow of an ancient tower
that moves across the sundazed pavement of the square
and disappears each evening without trace. (*DH* 56)

Only by trying to blend into her surroundings will the traveler find the desired object "shoved off into a corner, almost lost / among the spectacle of gold and purple" (*DH* 57). But even if a tourist can, with effort, achieve moments of understanding and transcendence, she should not expect these moments to have a lasting impact on her life: "Strange how all journeys come to this: the sun / bright on the unfamiliar hills, new vistas / dazzling the eye, the stubborn heart unchanged" (*DH* 58).

[3] As noted earlier, Gioia revised and retitled this poem "Most Journeys Come to This" in *99 Poems*.

In order really to be changed by a landscape, we have to live in it long enough to be transformed by it, especially by its hardships. In "Song from a Courtyard Window," the longed-for epiphany is figured as imaginary music:

> This was the only music we had hoped for:
> something to make us close our eyes and lose
> the courtyard full of people, silence all
> the conversations at the other tables
> and stop us from believing that we heard
> the sunlight burning in the open sky.
> Yes, and for a moment we heard nothing
> but the rush of cool water underground
> moving from the mountains to the hills
> into these fountains splashing in the sun.
>
> And listening we did not wonder
> that all the buildings melted to a field,
> off in some high country—a landscape we
> had never seen before, nor had imagined,
> a bitter landscape that two thousand years
> of pastoral could not obscure or soften:
> a wide dry field under the sun at noon
> where tall brown grass was bending in a wind
> filled with the sharp smell of a single weed
> that had marked this season here for centuries. (*DH* 60)

The music heard by the poem's speaker and his fellow traveler is a product of the harsh landscape, just as in "California Hills in August," the driest and seemingly least welcoming places test the speaker's sensibilities, and his ability to appreciate his surroundings yields satisfaction. In this small and limited way, the speaker relives a tourist's version of the reward reaped by those who live in the landscape and triumph over its hardships. Ultimately the music comes from "a thirsty man / singing praises to the heat, a song / to celebrate the dust, the weeds, the weather, / the misery of living here alone" (*DH* 60–61). Because the speaker and his implied companion can appreciate the landscape, they are able to hear the music for a while. The music soon fades, however, as it must for the traveler. Presumably, only the native, who sings the song celebrating his home, is allowed unlimited access to the music. The tourists enjoy only a momentary epiphany. The poem ends on a not entirely pessimistic note, as the travelers are left wondering whether or not they carry their recent epiphany within them.

It is significant that Gioia's protagonists experience their short-lived epiphanies in Italy. Gioia finds an affinity between the respective landscapes of southern Italy and California, the home of his childhood and adolescence:

> My Italian grandfather said he settled on the coast of California because it reminded him of Italy. When I went to Italy for the first time, I was immediately stuck by the similarity to California. Both are dry landscapes, full of light, with the sea as a presence. I wrote about the Italian landscape because I knew how to read it.[4]

Like Gioia, the protagonists of "Song from a Courtyard Window" know how to read the Italian landscape, which is why it yields up its song—however briefly—to them. Moreover, while most American poets who write about Italy focus on art and culture, Gioia writes about the landscape, seeing it in terms of the American West—harsh, dry, demanding, and austerely beautiful.

The speakers of Gioia's poems tend to prefer rugged countryside to picturesque vistas. Gioia's penchant for finding beauty in that which isn't normally considered beautiful corresponds with his interest in finding poetry where few if any have found it before. His commitment to exploring new subject matter leads him to write about the corporate office and the experience of the white-collar worker.

In his essay "Business and Poetry," Gioia notes the historical reluctance of American poets to write about business, even though our poetry celebrates all subject matter, from the high to the low. He writes:

---

[4] April Lindner, unpublished interview with Dana Gioia, no date.

> American poetry had defined business mainly by excluding it. Business does not exist in the world of poetry, and therefore by implication it has become everything that poetry is not—a world without imagination, enlightenment, or perception. It is the universe from which poetry is trying to escape. (*CPM10* 102)

Gioia defines the tradition of businessman poets in American literature, and observes a disconnect between the work and lives of the poets who wrote in this tradition. Although quite a few American poets—notably Wallace Stevens, A. R. Ammons, and James Dickey—have supported themselves in the world of business, their work contains no poems about business.

In poems like "Cheever Country," Gioia plays against this absence, contrasting the quiet suburbs with an imagined landscape in which the commercial activity is bustling and idealized: "Somewhere upstate huge factories melt ore, / mills weave fabric on enormous looms, / and sweeping combines glean the cash-green fields. / Fortunes are made" (*DH* 21). This description, which ironically portrays commerce in a manner of a Depression-era WPA mural, has prompted criticism from the critic Greg Kuzma, who sees this passage as sanguine, a chamber-of-commerce-like vision of industry. Kuzma writes, "I find it rather difficult to accept this vision as either valid or humane. My father worked in one of those 'huge factories' upstate from 'Cheever Country,' and was made deaf there, and spiritually damaged, and my brother killed himself in a car rather than accept that same fate."[5] This ideological critique misses the fact that the poem's idealized vision of production belongs to its persona, a character from a Cheever story, and his cheerful vision of industry contrasts ironically with the darker one set forth in Gioia's other poems. In "Men after Work," for example, Gioia depicts workers in coffeeshops or diners as, "always on the edge of words, almost without appetite, / knowing there is nothing on the menu that they want" (*DH* 12). These spiritually exhausted workers are faceless, their names, jobs, and social classes left unspecified. All we see of them is their weariness and alienation from their families and fellow writers. Clearly the

[5] Kuzma, "Dana Gioia and the Poetry of Money," 119.

vision of an idealized, hyper-productive economy imagined by the speaker of "In Cheever Country" comes with a human price-tag.

The malaise of the working man is figured in more explicitly white-collar terms in "The Man in the Open Doorway." Gioia's depiction of a typical corporate office illustrates how airless and distant from the natural world such workplaces can seem:

> This is the world in which he lives:
> Four walls, a desk, a swivel chair,
> A doorway with no door to close,
> Vents to bring in air. (*DH* 16)

Elsewhere in the poem, we learn that the movement of the clock's hands is the only movement within this artificial space. The poem's hypnotic meter and rhyme move it along as relentlessly as the hands of the clock. Ultimately, the businessman's longing for contact with other human beings and the natural world is revealed by a single gesture; even while he muses on the day's successes, the nameless man may find himself afterhours at the office,

> Then pause in a darkened stairway
> Until the sounds of his steps have ceased
> And stroke the wall as if it were
> Some attendant beast. (*DH* 17)

Gioia's relationship to the sphere of business is clearly a complex one. In describing the loneliness of the businessman, he presents a darker vision of the working life than one might expect. On the other hand, in overtly addressing the businessman's estrangement from nature and from other human beings, he attempts to speak about a world that other poets might see as not worth talking about. He has commented,

> It's the poet's job to redeem the ordinary world around us for the imagination and the spirit—even if that world is the suburbs and office life. But the poet cannot attempt this redemption at the price of simplifying or distorting it. One must see

> the world for what it is. One must present all of the burdens and miseries of this common life and still see the value in it.[6]

In making white-collar lives the subject of poetry, Gioia communicates to workers (who are, after all, members of his intended audience) that their daily life may be the stuff of poetry after all—albeit a poetry of vague discontent, into which fresh air is rationed by vents.

---

[6] Qtd. in Robert McPhillips, "Dana Gioia," *Verse* 9/2 (Summer 1992): 25.

3

DANA GIOIA: CRITIC AND POET OF THE NEW FORMALISM (2001)

Franz Link

In 1991, the *Atlantic* published Dana Gioia's essay "Can Poetry Matter?" According to Gioia, contemporary American poetry was nearly exclusively produced in creative writing workshops by professors and students and could, as such, no longer matter. He asked for poetry that could matter. It should take up subjects of general interest, should use argumentation as well as narration, prefer everyday language, and rehabilitate traditional poetic forms. The last of these demands qualified him as one of the leading figures of the group of poets that very soon became known as the New Formalists. Together with Frederick Feirstein and Frederick Turner's *Expansive Poetry: Essays on the New Narrative and the New Formalism* (1989) that reprinted his "Notes on the New Formalism" of 1987, Robert McDowell's *Poetry after Modernism* (1990), and Timothy Steele's *Missing Measures: Modern Poetry and the Revolt against Meter* (1990), his *Can Poetry Matter?: Essays on Poetry and American Culture* (1992) became central in New Formalist criticism. None of the other publications received as much attention as Gioia's original essay. Though damned and banned as reactionary by Marjorie Perloff, Helen Vendler, and other critics of the establishment,[1] his question has not yet been silenced, and Gioia is spending much of his time defending his conception of contemporary poetry in talks, essays, and interviews. Charles Altieri raised the question about the value of contemporary poetry already in his *Sense and Sensibility in Contemporary Poetry*

[1] Marjorie Perloff's criticism being the harshest: "Poetry Doesn't Matter," *American Book Review*, December 1992/January 1993. For Helen Vendler, see her *Soul Says: On Recent Poetry* (Cambridge: Harvard University Press, 1995).

(1984).[2] Vernon Shetley discussed the problem of workshop poetry in his *After the Death of Poetry: Poet and Audience in Contemporary America* (1993), locating the trouble with contemporary poetry in "the unexamined belief in the power of subjectivity to shape meaningful poetic forms."[3] Neither of the two led up to a new conception of poetry. It was Gioia's essay which opened the discussion on New Formalism and kept it going.

Called on to the scene, Gioia has become an engaged critic for the past seven years. He gave up a promising business career already in 1992 to have time for his poetry. During the nineties he has been trying to live from his writing. He wrote the chapter on Longfellow for Jay Parini's *Columbia History of American Poetry*, arguing that "narrative poetry was the prime source of [his] immense popularity"[4] and pleading for narrative poetry in his own time. He tried to reevaluate for his readers what he considered as some of the forgotten "masters" of our century, Weldon Kees and Barbara Howes; he espoused Donald Justice, Howard Moss, and X. J. Kennedy among his elders who wrote formal poetry in the time of modernism, wrote encouraging reviews on the poetry of Thomas Carper, R. S. Gwynn, and others among his contemporaries, and supported new periodicals and publishing enterprises. In 1994 he joined X. J. Kennedy as editor of *An Introduction to Poetry*, one of the leading textbooks on this subject in the tradition of *Understanding Poetry* (1938) by the "new critics" Cleanth Brooks and Robert Penn Warren.

Gioia tries to combine two concerns. One is to find a larger audience for poetry. For that purpose, poetry has to matter again and speak the language of that audience. This is the main thrust of his original essay. The other concern is, to use his own formulation, "to expand the available forms of contemporary poetry to include all the traditional forms and genres as well as the modernist mode." He "fought for

---

[2] See Dean Lance, review of *Can Poetry Matter?*, by Dana Gioia, *American Literature* 66/1 (1994): 193–94.

[3] Vernon Shetley, *After the Death of Poetry: Poet and Audience in Contemporary America* (Durham: Duke University Press, 1993), 20.

[4] Jay Parini, *The Columbia History of American Poetry* (New York: Columbia University Press, 1993), 79.

narrative and meter because they are so central to poetry and were so much discriminated against." He himself prefers to call the poetry of the "new formalism" "expansive poetry." In his own poetry, he says, he "always worked in both fixed and open form."[5] Actually, very few of his poems are written in fixed form. There are only one sestina, two triolets, one villanelle, and one unrhymed sonnet in his two poetry collections. "If you want to summarize my prosody versus other New Formalists," he wrote me in a March 3, 1998, letter, "you might say that I use rhyme the least but have the greatest metrical range." He usually writes stanzas with a regular number of lines to tighten and focus the poem, preferring quatrains and tercets. Among the variety of metrical forms, blank verse, as practiced by Robert Frost, dominates in his best poems.[6]

Unfortunately, little attention has been paid to Gioia's poetry. Critics were too much engaged with his critical opinions to pay attention to his poetry. He himself was too much occupied with "criticizing the critics" since the publication of his essay in the *Atlantic* to find the time to write much poetry in recent years. His second—and for the moment last—volume of poetry, *The Gods of Winter*, appeared in 1991, five years after his first volume, *Daily Horoscope*, in 1986. He also translated Italian poetry and Seneca's *Hercules Furens*. Since then, a number of poems were published in the *Hudson Review* and other journals. He is working on a libretto for an opera on Nosferatu, parts of which have been published already in *Sparrow* in 1996 and 1997.

Gioia's attack against workshop poetry and his plea for the rehabilitation of traditional forms in poetry join in "My Confessional Sestina" from *The Gods of Winter*, a kind of satiric companion piece to "Can Poetry Matter?" The first stanza already contains all his objections against workshop poetry:

---

[5] Frederick Feirstein and Frederick Turner, eds., *Expansive Poetry: Essays on the New Narrative and the New Formalism* (Santa Cruz: Story Line Press, 1989), 174.

[6] Together with E. A. Robinson and Robinson Jeffers, Robert Frost is one of the masters of narrative poetry in our century. For *The Dark Horse*, Gioia wrote a review essay "Fire and Ice: on Robert Frost," *Dark Horse* 3 ([July] 1996): 20.

> Let me confess. I'm sick of these sestinas
> written by youngsters in poetry workshops
> for the delectation of their fellow students,
> and then published in little magazines
> that no one reads, not even the contributors
> who at least in this omission show some taste. (*GW* 31)

Here one finds his argument against poetry written by students for their own delectation as well as for that of their fellow students, the flowering of little magazines not even read by its contributors. The subject is playfully repeated in variations in the next five stanzas to be summarized in the three-line stanza at the end.

It is in "My Confessional Sestina" that Gioia comes closest to a fixed form. He varies the line sequence from stanza to stanza and contracts the six lines to three in the concluding seventh stanza. As it is now customary in contemporary American poetry, he takes the liberty to use free rhythm. The lines vary from four to seven stressed syllables. Unusual is the distribution of the six rhyming words in the last stanza, four of which are crowded into its second line.

Using the form of a sestina for a poem against writing sestinas is, of course, parodying it. As a parody, "My Confessional Sestina" is a successful poem. It is fun to read this making fun of workshop poetry. Objections that may be raised would be 1) that the formalist poet makes fun of formalist poetry, and 2) that the dominant tendency in workshop poetry follows the "open" and not the "fixed" form of a sestina. Admittedly, the sestina is not a form often used by New Formalists. Their first comprehensive anthology, *Rebel Angels*, contains only two of them: Gioia's and Rachel Wetzsteon's "Dinner at Le Caprice," and that is a very "capricious" one. Despite our objections, Gioia's sestina was a success among its readers. It *was* and *is* read.

The forms preferred by Gioia are not the complex ones, certainly not the sestina. It is above all—as already mentioned—conversational blank verse which he masters and succeeds best when it is joined with his talent for telling stories. This is the case in the early "The Room Upstairs," the later "Counting the Children" and—the longest—"Homecoming." In "The Dilemma of the Long Poem," one of his contributions to Feirstein and Turner's *Expansive Poetry*, Gioia joins the advocates of the "new narrative," but, instead of the "long poem" as a modern counterpart of the traditional epic poem, he favors the shorter narrative poem such as the ballad or the dramatic monologue, and presents such a monologue, following the tradition developed by Robert Browning and Robert Frost, with "The Room Upstairs." It is introduced by the following thirteen lines:

> Come over to the window for a moment—
> I want to show you something. Do you see
> The one hill without trees? The dust-brown one
> Above the highway? That's how it all looked
> When I first came—no watered lawns or trees,
> Just open desert, pale green in the winter,
> Then brown and empty till the end of fall.
> I never look in mirrors any more,
> Or if I do, I just stare at the tie
> I'm knotting, and it's easy to pretend
> I haven't changed. But how can I ignore
> The way these hills were cut up into houses?
> I always thought the desert would outlive me. (*DH* 81)

Expertly Gioia fits the everyday language of his speaker into the pattern of his blank verse. He follows the example of Frost as far as his language is concerned and complies with Robert McDowell's call for a witness of the told events. The speaker of "The Room Upstairs"—not to be identified with the author—is present at the occasion. He is showing the new lodger of the room upstairs the surrounding neighborhood thereby introducing the reader to the place of action as well. In the continuation of the monologue, the description of the room and the neighborhood is followed by the story of a former lodger who had been badly wounded while rescuing a companion on a climbing tour in the nearby mountains and who was subsequently killed on a tour in the Alps. His death is bound to the house where the story is told insofar as the night he died the speaker dreamt of seeing him standing in the doorway. This turn in the story may, of course, demand too much credulity on behalf of the reader.

The proximity of Gioia's lines to those of Frost may very well be seen in line 9: "Or if I do." In Frost's "The Old Man's Winter Night" the penultimate line reads: "or if he can." In general, it's not the external features that remind the reader of Frost, but rather the stoic attitude toward life, accepting its limitations.

The speaker of "Counting the Children" is an accountant of Chinese descent sent by the State to take an inventory of the house of a woman who had died without a will. A neighbor is showing him the rooms filled with hundreds of dolls assembled on shelves. Her explanation does not develop into a dramatic monologue. The speaker tells his story without addressing somebody else. The essence of the story is—as it was in "The Room Upstairs"—a dream and a vision. Worried about not finding any meaning to the collection of discarded dolls, he dreams of his father who holds his daughter in his arms. He is confronted with all of his family:

> My family stood behind him in a row,
> Uncles and aunts, cousins I'd never seen,
> My grandparents from China and their parents,
>
> All of my family, living and dead,
> A line that stretched as far as I could see. (*GW* 15)

It becomes obvious that the family's dead are seen in analogy to the discarded dolls he has seen. The meaning of this escapes him in his dream. Waking up after the dream, he makes sure that his daughter is asleep and safe. A vision supplies him with an explanation:

> We long for immortality, a soul
> To rise up flaming from the body's dust.
> I know that it exists. I felt it there,
>
> Perfect and eternal in the way
> That only numbers are, intangible but real,
> Infinitely divisible yet whole.

> But we do not possess it in ourselves.
> We die, and it abides, and we are one
> With all our ancestors, while it divides
>
> Over and over, common to us all,
> The ancient face returning in the child,
> The distant arms embracing us, the salt
>
> Of our blind origins filling our veins. (*GW* 18–19)

The speaker finds an explanation for the ancestor worship of his forebears. In a way, he finds immortality in the constant regeneration of life. The dolls were discarded—his daughter will continue the family life.

Writing "Counting the Children" in *terza rima* stanzas, Gioia's aim is to allude to Dante's *Divine Comedy*. There are no rhymes but the pretty regular pentameter lines convey a certain authority to the phrases that fill them. Taking the allusion to Dante's epic into account, "Counting the Children" becomes a kind of palimpsest to his *Divina Comedia*: the collection of dolls in Part I representing the "Inferno," the dream in Part II the "Purgatorio," and the awakening in Part III the "Paradiso." Part IV, considered as a "vision," would fit with the "Paradiso," but it promotes—with its Chinese ancestor worship—quite a different conception of transcendence than Dante's.

"Homecoming" is a dramatic monologue again and written in the blank verse he had mastered so well already in "The Room Upstairs." This time there are no dreams or visions to rely on. The story—the murderer of his foster mother tells the police—convinces the reader with its psychological realism. Similar to Mark Jarman's longer narrative *Iris* (1992), it makes the reader feel the absolute desolation of the criminal's world. The speaker was raised by his foster mother, ran away, and turned criminal. Escaped from prison after seven years' detention, he comes back to his foster mother in order to murder her, holding her responsible for his failed life:

> I felt a sudden tremor of delight,

a happiness that went beyond my body
as if the walls around me had collapsed,
and a small dark room where I had been confined
had been amazingly transformed by light.
Radiant and invincible, I knew
I was the source of energy, and all
the jails and sheriffs could not hold me back.
I had been strong enough. And I was free.

But as I stood there gloating, gradually
the darkness and the walls closed in again.
Sensing the power melting from my arms,
I realized the energy I felt
was just adrenaline—the phoney high
that violence unleashes in your blood.
I saw her body lying on the floor
and knew that we would always be together.
All I could do was wait for the police.
I had come home, and there was no escape. (*GW* 51–52)

Gioia succeeds in his short narrative to make the life of his criminal believable and understandable. With his three narrative poems, particularly with the last one, he has achieved some of the best the "new narrative" has to offer.

"The Burning Ladder," the poem that introduces *Daily Horoscope*, may be considered as having programmatic value for Gioia's whole poetry. His poetry is the ladder which he wants to climb "to join that choir" of angels Jacob saw in his dream traveling up and down from heaven. Like Jacob, he does not succeed in climbing the ladder:

Jacob
never climbed the ladder
burning in his dream. Sleep
pressed him like a stone
in the dust (*DH* 3)

The remaining four stanzas follow the same pattern as the lines we quoted. The verse is shaped by the stanza form to such an extent that it no longer can be considered as "free verse." The stanzas form the emblem of the ladder he wants to climb in his poetry. He misses the ladder and—as Jacob—

> slept
> through it all, a stone
> upon a stone pillow,
> shivering. Gravity
> always greater than desire. (*DH* 3)

Gioia's poetry proves that he did not *sleep*. "Gravity" keeps him within the limits of his everyday world, yet his poetry tries to catch glances of the world Jacob saw in his dream.

Aware of his limits, Gioia is willing to arrange himself within them. Within these limits everybody has to go his own way and face his particular destiny. "On the same journey each of them / Is going somewhere else." "Waiting at the Airport" describes the people waiting for their next flight. There is nothing particular about the waiting:

> But nothing ever happens here,
> This terminal that narrows to
> A single unattended gate,
> One entrance to so many worlds. (*DH* 13)

Everybody has to find his own world: "divorces, birthdays, / Deaths and million-dollar deals" are mentioned as examples in the penultimate fourth stanza.

According to his six "daily horoscopes," there is no escape from this everyday world. The advice of the horoscope is to accept it, as in "Today Will Be," the first one:

> These walls, these streets,
> this day can never be your home, and yet
> there is no other world where you could live,
> and so you will accept it. (*DH* 25)

Man remains a stranger in the limited world he has to live in. He is warned not to expect any particular revelation that might change his life, as in the third "horoscope." Hearing children sing "*tolle lege*," Augustine opens the book with the letters of the apostles and finds the passage which finally makes him believe in Christ. Gioia does not expect "that if your book falls open / to a certain page, that any phrase / you read" or any sign in nature "will make a difference." Man is

never learning that
nothing is hidden in the obvious
changes of the world, that even the dim
reflection of the sun on tall, dry grass
is more than you will ever understand.

And only briefly then
you touch, you see, you press against
the surface of impenetrable things. (*DH* 27)

There is, of course, something under the surface, beyond the limits, and there are moments in which man becomes aware that there is this something. It does not make itself felt in cosmic events. The fifth "horoscope" opens with: "The stars now rearrange themselves above you / but to no effect." It is in the small things to which the door may temporarily open in a world beyond our ordinary limits:

Look for smaller signs instead, the fine
disturbances of ordered things when suddenly
the rhythms of your expectation break
and in a moment's pause another world
reveals itself behind the ordinary. (*DH* 29)

It is a dichotomy that determines Gioia's poetry, on the one side reflecting our limited and uninhabitable everyday world that nevertheless has to be accepted, on the other side a world beyond without these limitations. The medieval painters of the Last Judgment, Bosch, Van Eyck, Fra Angelico, and others, saw beyond "The End": "They knew, as we hardly do, that the world / is an uninhabitable place, temporary at best, / the delicate balance between eternities" (*DH* 51).

The limited world is a temporary world. Those who had no access to the world beyond are lost at the end. The temporary world gives dignity to their despair: "And, if there is no hope, there is at least / the dignity of their despair" (*DH* 51).

The second part of the poem transfers the situation of doomsday or a nuclear apocalypse into a contemporary dream: People notice "something unexpected in the air" but do not even try to read the signs:

> a pale face looking up against the light,
> then bending down again indifferently,
> only this dull reflex of acceptance,
> then nothing else, nothing ever again. (*DH* 52)

"The Journey, the Arrival and the Dream" elaborates man's basic situation in the image of a journey. The speaker of the poem, a woman, travels in foreign countries. Her destination is "an ancient house on a yellow hill" in "dry mountains." "Journeys are," for her, "the despair before discovery, / you hope, wondering if this one ends" (*DH* 64). In her room she finds "badly painted cherubs on the ceiling, / who ignore" her. She tries to tickle them with the lazy smoke of her cigarette:

> to no effect and realize you don't
> belong here in their world where everything
> is much too good for you, and though the angels
> will say nothing, they watch everything you do. (*DH* 64)

She hears "the murmuring / of swallows in the eaves," opens her window but cannot see them.

> There's only this blue patch
> of sky and endlessly empty afternoon,
> where the light is fading.
> Close your eyes. Accept
> that some things must remain invisible.

Somewhere in the valley a grey fox
is moving through the underbrush. Old men
are harvesting the grapes. And the dark swallows
you cannot see are circling in the sunlight
slowly gliding downward in the valley
as if the light would last forever. (*DH* 65)

The speaker talks of her "dying body." She dreams of writing a letter. After having sealed up the envelope she turns "to face / an old man in a dark-red uniform. / He nods. … / who is he? … / … / his footsteps fade into the murmuring / of swallows in the eaves" (*DH* 65). It is the footman opening the door and leading into the beyond. In this poem life is imagined as a journey to a destination never reached or never realized, but in certain moments surfacing in awareness. Life depends on something beyond itself.

The first two parts of the poem are written in free verse. It tightens up to pentameter or tetrameter in epigrammatical passages, as in the following lines: "Journeys are the despair before discovery, / you hope, wondering if this one ends" (*DH* 64).

The clarifying dream of Part III is written in blank verse (see the earlier quotation from *DH*, page 65) giving shape to the insight that was communicated. With his unrhymed blank verse Gioia has written a contemporary equivalent to the rhymed stanzas of William Cullen Bryant's "To a Waterfowl." Bryant's waterfowl turned into Gioia's unseen swallows.

In a number of Gioia's poems something beyond the ordinary is experienced in moods. A comparatively simple example for such a mood is described in "Parts of Summer Weather." On a warm night, the speaker of the poem is with his lover on their bed. The well-known songs they hear from the radio upstairs become part of the moment: "we lie in silence saying more / than anything we hoped to say" (*DH* 74).

That "more" is part of a mood that has its own reality. Ordinary reality appears differently as the concluding stanza reveals:

> And yet I wake an hour later,
> reach out and find myself alone.
> No words spoken, no message left,
> the room so quiet, and you gone. (*DH* 74)

The "having said more / than they hoped they could say" has vanished. Its existence was in imagination only. What actually cannot be spoken of is *love*. It is a "mood" that elevates the lover into a world beyond and does that only temporarily.[7]

This mood may also turn into jealousy as in "The Sunday News." In the *Local Weddings* section, the speaker finds the wedding announcement of a girl he formerly loved. He is stung by envy.

> And yet I clipped it out to put away
> Inside a book like something I might use,
> A scrap I knew I wouldn't read again
> But couldn't bear to lose. (*DH* 77)

He cannot bear to lose the memory of his past love, part of an experience of something "beyond" ordinary life.

Among Gioia's poems so far considered, "My Confessional Sestina" was the only one strictly written in a traditional fixed form and it was written as a parody. Two of the three narrative poems we interpreted were written in what we called "conversational" blank verse. It turns up in quite a number of his poems. Other poems are written in tetrameter or in free verse of varying length. Tercets, quartets, quintets, and stanzas of irregular length are used in other poems. The last two poems considered both rhyme *xaxa* though only an eye rhyme is achieved in the last stanza of "Parts of Summer Weather": "alone"—"gone." Both poems use iambic meter, varying the number of feet: 4444 and 5553 or 5552. Each line is formed by a syntactical unit. It might be said that Gioia comes closest to formalism in these two poems as well

---

[7] Glyn Pursglove speaks of his work as "a poetry of strong feeling" in "Dana Gioia," *Acumen* 27 (January 1997).

as in one of his recent ones: "Summer Storm."[8]

In "Summer Storm" the speaker describes his having met a girl on a patio watching the storm at a wedding party. He remembers the situation on the occasion of a similar storm twenty years later. This time he is telling the story in nine ballad meter stanzas: *xaxa*, 4343. The first stanza reads as an attempt to come as close to the form as possible:

> We stood on the rented patio
> While the party went on inside.
> You knew the groom from college.
> I was a friend of the bride. (*IN* 66)

The next stanzas are very regular. The last three stanzas ask why he remembers the short meeting of long ago.

> Why does that evening's memory
> Return with this night's storm—
> A party twenty years ago,
> Its disappointments warm?
>
> There are so many *might-have-beens*,
> *What-ifs* that won't stay buried,
> Other cities, other jobs,
> Strangers we might have married.
>
> And memory insists on pining
> For places it never went,
> As if life would be happier
> Just by being different. (*IN* 66–67)

What matters is not action but—as in many of Gioia's poems—mood. The something "beyond" are the "*might-have-beens*" this time. The last stanza shows irregularities again. Gioia doesn't, as he told me in a letter of July 28, 1996, usually scan his poems. He did it for me on this occasion.

---

[8] Link refers to this poem and later to "Corner Table" from their magazine appearances in 1996 and 1998. Both poems were included in *Interrogations at Noon.*

He scanned the last two lines as follows: "As if life would be happier / Just by being different."

The last syllable of the last line doesn't carry an accent and as an unstressed syllable cannot be considered as a rhyme to "went." While the irregularity of the first stanza does not make difficult reading, that in the last stanza does, as the reader has got used to the rhythms of the preceding stanzas.

In "Prayer," the opening poem of *The Gods of Winter*, Gioia successfully uses a flexible tercine pattern to express the urgency of his address to the one "beyond." The "one" or that "something beyond" is addressed as:

> Echo of the clocktower, footstep
> in the alleyway, sweep
> of the wind sifting the leaves.
>
> Jeweller of the spiderweb, connoisseur
> of autumn's opulence, blade of lightning
> harvesting the sky.
>
> Keeper of the small gate, choreographer
> of entrances and exits, midnight
> whisper travelling the wires. (*GW* 3)

The stanzas could be easily reshaped into syntactical units by setting the last words of the first two lines at the head of the following line. As they stand, the lines express the urgency of the address. The speaker doesn't wait with the next item of the address for the next line. Another aspect of the art of these lines is the imagistic quality of the items addressed. All the phenomena called up stand for what or who is revealing it—or himself in it. They are its or his epiphanies. This becomes obvious if Gioia's spiderweb image is compared with the one Pound uses in his "Canto LXXX." For Pound, the works the poet or the artist leaves behind, the spider's web, are witnesses and a transmitter of the light which the poet was able to see and which he has gathered: "Their works like cobwebs when the spider is gone / encrust them with sun-shot crystals."[9]

What is felt as revealing itself in the phenomena addressed is of ambiguous character but has power to destroy or to heal. The speaker prays that it may protect him whom he cares for, in the author's case: his firstborn son who died early.

> Seducer, healer, deity or thief,
> I will see you soon enough—
> in the shadow of the rainfall,
>
> in the brief violet darkening a sunset—
> but until then I pray watch over him
> as a mountain guards its covert ore
>
> and the harsh falcon its flightless young. (*GW* 3)

The mysterious something usually cannot be formulated in words. Or it is a groping for words to say what can only be felt. This is the case in "Speaking of Love":

> Speaking of love was difficult at first.
> We groped for those lost, untarnished words
> That parents never traded casually at home,
> The radio had not devalued.
> How little there seemed left to us.
>
> So, speaking of love, we chose
> The harsh and level language of denial
> Knowing only what we did not wish to say,
> Choosing silence in our terror of a lie.
> For surely love existed before words. (*GW* 60)

---

[9] Ezra Pound, *The Cantos of Ezra Pound* (New York: New Directions, 1996), 501. See Franz Link, "The Spider and Its Web in American Literature," *Literaturwissenschaftliches Jahrbuch* 36 (1995): 302.

At first sight, the only regularity of the poem seems to be the number of lines in each of the five stanzas. The exception is—as in other poems by Gioia—a single line as a conclusive statement. Following the rhythm of common speech, the single lines read as separate units carrying their one image or message, and thereby creating their own form.

As far as the message of the poem is concerned: the silence as expressing what language can no longer express "becomes its own cliché." Thus the lovers use speech again to express their love. But it never does what it is expected to do: "Our borrowed speech demanded love so pure / And so beyond our power that we saw / How words were only forms of our regret."

The love "beyond" our everyday reality remains a "memory," or something "desired": "Obsessed by memory, befriended by desire, / With no words left to summon back our love" (*GW* 60).

The "Unspeakable" remains a permanent subject of Gioia's poetry. His last poem so far, "Corner Table" continues in its use: "What matters most / Most often can't be said" (*IN* 51). The concluding poem of *Daily Horoscope*, "Sunday Night in Santa Rosa," describes the folding up of the booth tents, merry-go-rounds, and pleasure palaces at the fair and the return to everyday normality. The concluding lines—an equivalent to the final couplet of the Elizabethan sonnet—reveal the whole fair as an only temporary escape from the normal world, as an image for the world as a "vanity fair": "while a clown stares in a dressing mirror, / takes out a box, and peels away his face" (*DH* 87).

As in "Speaking of Love," Gioia finds his own form in "Sunday Night at Santa Rosa," this time a rhymeless sonnet. The enumeration of the different parts of the pleasure ground that are being dismantled stand for thesis and antithesis in the traditional sonnet, distributed among octet and sestet. The last two lines stand for synthesis of the final couplet in the sonnet. "Sunday Night at Santa Rosa" is another variant of Gioia's continual endeavor to catch something "beyond" in the form and imagery of his poem.

We agree with Kevin Walzer's observation in "Dana Gioia and Expansive Poetry" that "it would be premature to say that Gioia—or anyone else involved with Expansive Poetry—is a major poet." Is there any contemporary major American poet? Gioia certainly is already—quoting Walzer again—"one of the most influential poets and critics of his generation."

4

DANA GIOIA AND EXPANSIVE POETRY (1998)

Kevin Walzer

In his essay on the Expansive poets—the group dedicated to restoring rhyme, meter, and narrative to contemporary poetry, and to expanding poetry's audience—Robert McPhillips suggested that Dana Gioia "is the poet who most fully realizes the potential" of the movement.[1] (I use the term "Expansive" rather than the earlier label "New Formalism" that critics applied to this movement, because "Expansive" also encompasses the related resurgence of interest in narrative poetry by poets of the baby boom generation.) Given the range that Gioia covers in his two books of poetry, *Daily Horoscope* (1986) and *The Gods of Winter* (1991), as well as his essay collection, *Can Poetry Matter?: Essays on Poetry and American Culture* (1992), this judgment seems valid.

Gioia's range, in both style and subject, is unusually broad. In his lyric poems, he works equally well in free verse and traditional forms, and in fact merges them in many cases. He works hard to give his metrical poems the colloquial quality of the best free verse, while his classically trained ear gives his free verse a sure sense of rhythm that approaches a formal measure. Also, some of his most distinctive poems (such as "Lives of the Great Composers" from *Daily Horoscope)* are formal experiments of his own devising, based on neither a metrical form nor free verse, but on forms of music. Within the lyric form, his subjects range from short portraits of the world of work ("Men after Work") to historical poems ("A Short History of Tobacco," "My Secret Life") to music ("Bix Beiderbecke"). But Gioia is not limited to lyric: apart from

[1] Robert McPhillips, "Reading the New Formalists," in *Poetry after Modernism*, ed. Robert McDowell (Brownsville: Story Line Press, 1991), 327.

the mid-length narratives of *The Gods of Winter*, he has also written numerous shorter poems that make use of narrative elements and dramatic personae. And just as his free and traditional verse complement each other, so do Gioia's lyric and narrative poetry. He has the ability to sketch out character and story with great economy in short poems, while his longer poems—especially "Counting the Children"—develop deep and beautiful meditations on their subjects.

Though he works in a wide range of forms and modes, Gioia's work features a concern that spans its stylistic diversity: probing beneath the surface of middle-class life. By itself, of course, this is not a unique subject; it has been a staple of American poetry since Confessionalism, and practically became dogma in the first-person, free-verse workshop lyric. And Gioia, to be fair to his critics, does not always break the clichés of middle-class poetry; his widely praised "Cruising with the Beach Boys" is little different from hundreds of other workshop poems from the 1970s or 1980s, save for its use of rhyme and meter. Here are the concluding two stanzas:

> Some nights I drove down to the beach to park
> And walk along the railings of the pier.
> The water down below was cold and dark,
> The waves monotonous against the shore.
> The darkness and the mist, the midnight sea,
> The flickering lights reflected from the city—
> A perfect setting for a boy like me,
> The Cecil B. DeMille of my self-pity.
>
> I thought by now I'd left those nights behind,
> Lost like the girls that I could never get,
> Gone with the years, junked with the old T-Bird.
> But one old song, a stretch of empty road,
> Can open up a door and let them fall
> Tumbling like boxes from a dusty shelf,
> Tightening my throat for no reason at all
> Bringing on tears shed only for myself. (*DH* 5–6)

Gioia's admirers praise the ironic self-mockery of the first stanza, and it does effectively undercut the sentimentality of the poem's theme. The final stanza, however, opens the floodgates: the speaker's throat tightens for "no reason at all," the tears "shed only for myself," privately, some adolescent angst recalled but not clarified.

Gioia's most distinctive work is much better than "Cruising with the Beach Boys." He explores middle-class life from a broader range of perspectives than most contemporary poets. That diversity of perspectives, in fact, is a central feature of *Daily Horoscope*. It contains the majority of his poems on unusual subjects (the pornographic memoirs of a Victorian gentleman, the title sequence modeled after newspaper horoscopes, and the early history of tobacco in America), and Gioia carefully organizes this diversity into a nuanced exploration of his subject.

A central example of his technique is "In Cheever Country." Here is the second half of the poem:

> If there is an afterlife, let it be a small town
> gentle as this spot at just this instant.
> But the car doors close, and the bright crowd,
> unaware of its election, disperses to the small
> pleasures of the evening. The platform falls behind.
>
> The train gathers speed. Stations are farther apart.
> Marble staircases climb the hills where derelict estates
> glimmer in the river-brightened dusk.
> Some are convents now, some orphanages,
> these palaces the Robber Barons gave to God.
>
> And some are merely left to rot where now
> broken stone lions guard a roofless colonnade,
> a half-collapsed gazebo bursts with tires,
> and each detail warns it is not so difficult
> to make a fortune as to pass it on.
>
> But splendor in ruins is splendor still,
> even glimpsed from a passing train,

and it is wonderful to imagine standing
in the balustraded gardens above the river
where barges still ply their distant commerce.

Somewhere upstate huge factories melt ore,
mills weave fabric on enormous looms,
and sweeping combines glean the cash-green fields.
Fortunes are made. Careers advance like armies.
But here so little happens that is obvious.

Here in the odd light of a rainy afternoon
a ledger is balanced and put away,
a houseguest knots his tie beside a bed,
and a hermit thrush sings in the unsold lot
next to the tracks the train comes hurtling down.

Finally it's dark outside. Through the freight houses
and oil tanks the train begins to slow
approaching the station where rows of travel posters
and empty benches wait along the platform.
Outside a few cars idle in the sudden shower.

And this at last is home, this ordinary town
where the lights on the hill gleaming in the rain
are the lights that children bathe by, and it is time
to go home now—to drinks, to love, to supper,
to the modest places which contain our lives. (*DH* 20–21)

This is a lengthy quotation, but necessary because the poem exemplifies many aspects of Gioia's work. The poem's subject is consistent with Gioia's larger concern with middle-class life, but Gioia does not approach the subject from the standpoint of autobiography—even though the poem is spoken by a voice that identifies itself as "I." Instead, the poem, written in loose blank verse, incorporates material from John Cheever's fiction about the Hudson Valley bedroom communities that orbit, sometimes at a far distance, New York City.

The poem is set on the long train ride out of the city to the suburbs, sometimes an hour away or more. Its speaker, presumably a white-collar executive in the city, observes the countryside passing outside the train window. He notes the landscape's history, ruined shrines erected by the previous century's tycoons, and the landscape's beauty. He is also conscious of the darker side of this capitalist landscape, both the invisible physical work of business that executives in their offices sometimes miss ("Somewhere upstate huge factories melt ore, / mills weave fabrics on enormous looms") and the subtle toll that devotion to business exacts on its executives ("Careers advance like armies. / But here so little happens that is obvious"). Then the speaker observes the bright present, the reason he goes to work: "it is time / to go home now—to drinks, to love, to supper, / to the modest places which contain our lives" (*DH* 21). He has arrived in his own "modest place," where the love and comfort of family await.

This poem is distinctive for several reasons, most obviously for its tone of quiet celebration. It is more common for poets to attack the problems of middle-class life, either loudly (W. D. Snodgrass, Anne Sexton) or with a quiet whine (Stephen Dunn, Jonathan Holden). But Gioia's speaker arrives home to a quiet happiness, despite his consciousness of the costs—physical and spiritual—of the system in which he is employed. The poem is complicated, suggesting that modest happiness is possible even with knowledge of the middle class's dark side. The speaker seems to have found peace but has no illusions about the life he lives.

Also integral to the poem's distinctiveness is its form, both in terms of prosody and narrative. Its blank verse measure establishes a regular, but unobtrusive, background to let the poem's story and meditations unfold. The last stanza, especially, has a quiet epigrammatic quality that would be difficult to achieve in free verse. The poem's appropriation of a figure from prose fiction is also unusual in the history of recent American poetry and gives the poem a useful distancing from the personal to the general; though its setting is recognizably New York, the suburban landscape of houses on well-lit streets it describes could be found in any region of the country. The poem's use of a Cheeveresque speaker celebrates the work of that writer, who also explores the light and dark sides of middle-class suburban life—as Gioia's poem "In Chandler

Country," spoken by Philip Marlowe, that hard-boiled Los Angeles detective, explores the borders between prose and verse narrative. Elsewhere, Gioia has written affectionately about Cheever and pays him an homage through this poem.

Daily Horoscope, like many poets' first books, is relatively broad in the range of its subjects; though it coheres in its explorations of the economic and personal dimensions of middle-class life, it is in part a record of Gioia's development over a decade or more as he gradually experiments with different subjects and different forms. The book draws its strength partly from its careful organization, with Gioia's core vision emerging through the varied poems. Gioia's second book, *The Gods of Winter*, moves beyond *Daily Horoscope* in its unified focus, in subject as well as theme: it is a book obsessed with the subjects of mortality, generations, and love, especially as manifested in family.

The Gods of Winter is divided into five sections, which alternate between short lyrics and longer narratives. The book's first section is a sequence of elegies for Gioia's son who died in infancy; it sets the book's tone, dark but redemptive. The strongest poem of the sequence—which is full of strong poetry—is the concluding poem, "Planting a Sequoia":

> All afternoon my brothers and I have worked in the orchard,
> Digging this hole, laying you into it, carefully packing the soil.
> Rain blackened the horizon, but cold winds kept it over the Pacific,
> And the sky above us stayed the dull gray
> Of an old year coming to an end.
>
> In Sicily a father plants a tree to celebrate his first son's birth—
> An olive or a fig tree—a sign that the earth has one more life to
> bear.
> I would have done the same, proudly laying new stock into my
> father's orchard,
> A green sapling rising among the twisted apple boughs,
> A promise of new fruit in other autumns.
>
> But today we kneel in the cold planting you, our native giant,
> Defying the practical custom of our fathers,

Wrapping in your roots a lock of hair, a piece of an infant's birth cord,
All that remains above earth of a first-born son,
A few stray atoms brought back to the elements.

We will give you what we can—our labor and our soil,
Water drawn from the earth when the skies fail,
Nights scented with the ocean fog, days softened by the circuit of bees.
We plant you in the corner of the grove, bathed in western light,
A slender shoot against the sunset.

And when our family is no more, all of his unborn brothers dead,
Every niece and nephew scattered, the house torn down,
His mother's beauty ashes in the air,
I want you to stand among strangers, all young and ephemeral to you,
Silently keeping the secret of your birth. (*GW* 10)

This remarkable poem is a direct but dignified elegy for the lost son. Gioia's predilection for direct emotion, which sometimes goes astray in his lesser work, here finds a proper balance with the gravity of the subject. The poem depicts a dreary day, with its speaker adapting an old Sicilian ritual—planting a tree to celebrate birth—to a new country and a tragic occasion: to memorialize a child taken by death. The tree is a sequoia, or redwood, one of the grandest trees found in North America; they grow huge and ancient, as enduring a symbol of life as one could imagine. The redwood's use to memorialize a dead child, therefore, is especially poignant; as the speaker notes, once they nurture the tree from "a slender shoot against the sunset," it will long outlive its planters and those people who come afterward, "silently keeping the secret of [its] birth," a child's death, another slender shoot cut down before it could grow.

"Planting a Sequoia" is unusual in Gioia's work because of its prosody. Although he frequently writes in free verse, Gioia's line usually hovers around an iambic pentameter beat; this poem, however, adopts the long-lined, falling rhythm of Whitman or, more likely, Robinson Jeffers, whom Gioia has praised lavishly—and whose celebrations of the California landscape are an obvious precursor to this poem set in a California orchard. The Whitman/Jeffers line is entirely appropriate; the long line and oratorical rhythm counterpoint Gioia's simple, colloquial language, giving the poem its beauty. (Interestingly, a critic such as Thomas B. Byers—who has little good to say about Expansive Poetry—terms this poem "stunningly beautiful.")[2]

Although "Planting a Sequoia" and other poems in the first section of *The Gods of Winter* deal with the death of a child from a personal standpoint, Gioia also explores the subject and related themes—about adult aging, about family generations, about love—from other angles in this book, particularly from a narrative perspective. "Counting the Children" is one of two long narrative poems in *The Gods of Winter* (the other is "Homecoming," about a convicted murderer's return to the home where he grew up).

Divided into four parts, "Counting the Children" is an extended blank-verse meditation on relationships across family generations. The poem is narrated by Mr. Choi, a Chinese American accountant. In the first section, Mr. Choi is sent to examine the estate of a deceased wealthy woman. The woman, a bit unbalanced mentally, had liked to wander around and rifle through her neighbors' trash, and had amassed a large collection of discarded dolls. Mr. Choi sees the dolls and is stunned by them:

> They looked like sisters huddling in the dark,
> Forgotten brides abandoned at the altar,
> Their veils turned yellow, dresses stiff and soiled.
>
> Rows of discarded little girls and babies—
> Some naked, others dressed for play—they wore
> Whatever lives their owners left them in.

---

[2] Thomas B. Byers, "The Closing of the American Line: Expansive Poetry and Ideology," *Contemporary Literature* 33/2 (Summer 1992): 407.

Where were the children who promised them love?
The small, caressing hands, the lips which whispered
Secrets in the dark? Once they were woken,

Each by name. Now they have become each other—
Anonymous except for injury,
The beautiful and headless side by side. (*GW* 14)

Mr. Choi wonders if the dolls are emblems of childhood's end, relics forgotten in "dim / Abandoned rooms … staged / For settled dust and shadow, left to prove // That all affection is outgrown, or show / The uniformity of our desire" (*GW* 14). Shaking himself from his shock at the sight, he turns away and begins his work.

Mr. Choi cannot forget the sight of those broken, dusty dolls. Later, in the second section, they reappear in a nightmare. In his dream, Mr. Choi cannot get numbers in the ledger he is working on to add up—every accountant's nightmare—and then suddenly finds his family, stretching back for generations, watching him as his daughter's life hangs on his computational skill:

And then I saw my father there beside me.
He asked me why I couldn't find the sum.
He held my daughter crying in his arms.

My family stood behind him in a row,
Uncles and aunts, cousins I'd never seen,
My grandparents from China and their parents,

All of my family, living and dead,
A line that stretched as far as I could see.
Even the strangers called to me by name.

And now I saw I wasn't at my desk
But working on the coffin of my daughter,
And she would die unless I found the sum.

But I had lost too many of the numbers.
They tumbled to the floor and blazed on fire.
I saw the dolls then—screaming in the flames. (*GW* 15–16)

The broken dolls still haunt Mr. Choi's memory, arousing a parent's most profound fear: losing a child. Mr. Choi feels a sense of powerlessness, that he can do nothing to prevent his daughter's death, as nothing prevented the dolls themselves from decaying and breaking. He also feels the weight of generations of family, which in Chinese culture (as in Gioia's Sicilian culture) is elevated above the individual. His fear is one that extends through families for generations. Mr. Choi elaborates on this fear in the poem's third section when, after waking from his nightmare, he reenacts a nighttime ritual of checking on his daughter: "How delicate this vessel in our care, / This gentle soul we summoned to the world, / A life we treasured but could not protect" (*GW* 17). He came to accept this fear as part of parenthood: "So standing at my pointless watch each night / In the bare nursery we had improvised, / I learned the loneliness that we call love" (*GW* 17).

Watching his daughter, now seven years old, sleeping, Mr. Choi in the poem's final section relates a sudden vision about the nature of life and death in families:

We long for immortality, a soul
To rise up flaming from the body's dust.
I know that it exists. I felt it there,

Perfect and eternal in the way
That only numbers are, intangible but real,
Infinitely divisible yet whole.

But we do not possess it in ourselves.
We die, and it abides, and we are one
With all our ancestors, while it divides

Over and over, common to us all,

The ancient face returning in the child,
The distant arms embracing us, the salt

Of our blind origins filling our veins. (*GW* 18–19)

For Mr. Choi, his certainty of immortality—his daughter's and his own as they take their place in an extended familial lineage—provides no consolation for the parental fear he feels. In the mortal present, immortality is divided and diminished, each person entering and living the same path as their ancestors, and then dying. That the cycle repeats over each successive generation does not change the anguish one feels when facing the question of mortality. If anything, it heightens the fear, because it reinforces the sense of powerlessness that Mr. Choi depicts. This seems evident when Mr. Choi concludes the poem by noticing his daughter's dolls:

Their sharp glass eyes surveyed me with contempt.
They recognized me only as a rival,
The one whose world would keep no place for them.

I felt like holding them tight in my arms,
Promising I would never let them go,
But they would trust no promises of mine.

I feared that if I touched one, it would scream. (*GW* 19)

The dolls, forever children, again become emblems of his powerlessness. His daughter will not remain a child, will leave them behind, just as children left behind the discarded dolls of the wealthy woman's collection.

"Counting the Children" develops its meditation on the theme of mortality and family on a deep scale. Because of its narrative focus, it adds a dimension to *The Gods of Winter* that might be missing from a more personal poem. Of course, given its context in the book, it is impossible to separate the poem wholly from Gioia's autobiographical elegies; it clearly reflects many of the same concerns. Though Gioia bases the poem on Chinese culture, an emphasis on family across generations also runs deeply in Gioia's Sicilian heritage. In part, this accounts for William Walsh's criticism of this poem: "the reader can be excused for wondering whether it is Mr. Choi who is speaking, or Mr. Gioia."[3] David Mason is more on the mark when he observes that "Gioia may have felt that the … openly emotional lines … could not have been written without the protective mask of a dramatic monologue."[4] That mask allows Gioia to develop a philosophical meditation on mortality and family in another dramatic context, making the book's exploration of these issues more complex and substantial.

Fear is one of the two dominant emotional tones of "Counting the Children"; the other is love, inevitably intertwined with the subject of family. Elsewhere in *The Gods of Winter*, Gioia examines the subject of love more directly. Perhaps the most substantial exploration of it comes in "Speaking of Love," the book's penultimate poem:

> Speaking of love was difficult at first.
> We groped for those lost, untarnished words
> That parents never traded casually at home,
> The radio had not devalued.
> How little there seemed left to us.
>
> So, speaking of love, we chose
> The harsh and level language of denial
> Knowing only what we did not wish to say,
> Choosing silence in our terror of a lie.
> For surely love existed before words.
>
> But silence can become its own cliché,
> And bodies lie as skillfully as words,
> So one by one we spoke the easy lines

---

[3] William F. Walsh, "Loose Talk and Literary History: Language Poetry, New Formalism and the Construction of Taste in Contemporary American Poetry" (PhD diss., Miami University, 1994), 188.

[4] David Mason, "Other Lives: On Shorter Narrative Poems," *Verse* (Winter 1990): 19.

The other had resisted but desired,
Trusting that love renewed their innocence.

Was it then that words became unstuck?
That star no longer seemed enough for star?
Our borrowed speech demanded love so pure
And so beyond our power that we saw
How words were only forms of our regret.

And so at last we speak again of love,
Now that there is nothing left unsaid,
Surrendering our voices to the past,
Which has betrayed us. Each of us alone,
Obsessed by memory, befriended by desire,

With no words left to summon back our love. (*GW* 60)

This is a complex poem that, in certain ways, explores the same territory as Robert Hass's famous poem "Meditation at Lagunitas" ("a word is elegy to what it signifies").[5] The Gioia poem explores the connections between love and the language used to express that love. The couple in the poem fears to use the clichéd language of love, and so avoids articulating this love at first, leaving it unspoken, even taken for granted. But love demands articulation, and so the couple falls into the old, shopworn words—a language against which their actual love pales, since the human language for love inevitably idealizes it, removing love from daily experience. And so the couple seems to have found both their love and its language diminished: "no words left to summon back our love." The poem's philosophical, blank-verse investigation of its topic is reminiscent of Wallace Stevens and adds yet another dimension to *The Gods of Winter*.

Though it also features different subjects and styles, *The Gods of Winter* is ultimately a much more focused, unified book than *Daily Horoscope*. Gioia's careful organization is evident in this collection as well,

---

[5] Robert Hass, *Praise* (New York: Ecco Press, 1979).

which serves to make the book's explorations of its subjects even more precise. With its mixture of narrative and lyric, free verse and traditional form, the book could in fact serve as the paradigmatic Expansive collection. The book is among the finest yet to emerge from the Expansive movement—at once further solidifying Gioia's connection to the school and establishing the likelihood that his work will outlive its association with the group.

Gioia's poetry is not the only means by which his career has helped to define the Expansive movement. As noted, his criticism has played a central role as well. His most influential essays are collected in *Can Poetry Matter?: Essays on Poetry and American Culture* (1992). In this volume Gioia writes at length about the Expansive poets, but also about more general issues: poetry's place in American culture; the relationship between poetry and criticism; and neglected poets who deserve greater recognition. A unifying theme of the essays is the conviction that the university, which has become the dominant patron of poetry in the past half-century, is failing in its stewardship, and that significant changes are needed.

Gioia makes this case most pointedly in the book's title essay, its most famous (or notorious), which addresses the subject of poetry's relevance in contemporary culture. Gioia's conclusion: poetry has become enclosed in a professional subculture that has little relevance to the ordinary reader. Although there is more poetry published today than at any point in American history, Gioia argues that poetry has mainly become a self-enclosed subculture of American society associated with universities. He asserts that during the modernist period, contemporary poetry was an art form that literate people read often, in magazines and anthologies if not in books, but that today's average, educated person does not read poetry.

As both a symptom and a cause of poetry's isolation, Gioia cites the migration of poets to the university and the attendant pressure to publish or perish. This pressure, he suggests, shifts poets' attention from writing to be read toward writing to gain tenure, with an apparent unconcern whether anyone reads their work:

> The proliferation of literary journals and presses over the past thirty years has been a response less to an increased appetite

> for poetry among the public than to the desperate need of writing teachers for professional validation. Like subsidized farming that grows food no one wants, a poetry industry has been created to serve the interests of the producers and not the consumers. And in the process the integrity of the art has been betrayed. (*CPM* 10)

Gioia believes that rigorous criticism, in the form of selective anthologies and candid reviews, is essential for the transmission of poetry to a general audience, and he argues that poetry has traded honest criticism for networking and boosterism.

Additionally, Gioia calls for poetry readings that include the work of writers other than the reader, and which make use of other art forms, such as jazz, to attract a more varied audience; teaching methods that emphasize performance of poetry over critical analysis to show students the art's sensual pleasures; and greater use of radio for the performance of poetry. These changes, Gioia suggests, would help shake up the university's "stifling bureaucratic etiquette that enervates the art. These [academic] conventions may once have made sense, but today they imprison poetry in an intellectual ghetto. It is time to experiment, time to leave the well-ordered but stuffy classroom, time to restore a vulgar vitality to poetry and unleash the energy now trapped in the subculture" (*CPM* 24).

Much of the rest of *Can Poetry Matter?* and Gioia's uncollected critical prose is devoted to exploring related questions about the university's stewardship of poetry. Gioia's essays about Robinson Jeffers, Weldon Kees, Ted Kooser, and Henry Wadsworth Longfellow in *Can Poetry Matter?* and elsewhere show what can happen to strong poets whose achievements fall outside the avant-garde poetic lineage from modernism to postmodernism that university critics champion. (Helen Vendler, beginning with Stevens, represents the academic establishment's conservative wing while Marjorie Perloff, since her shift to the "poetics of indeterminacy," occupies the radical wing; Ashbery represents their common ground.) Without academic critics championing their work, such poets are mostly neglected and unread.

Gioia's discussion of Jeffers is characteristic: "No other American poet has been treated worse by posterity than Robinson Jeffers....

Academic interest in Jeffers remains negligible. No longer considered by critics prominent enough to attack, he is now ignored" (*CPM* 47). During his lifetime, Jeffers was at odds with modernist aesthetics in his insistence on fierce moral clarity and vivid narrative. As the New Critical consensus about the ideal poem hardened into an orthodoxy that still shadows readings of modernism, Jeffers's reputation simply withered. (Arguably, the only poet at odds with modernist orthodoxy to survive unscathed was Frost.) As Gioia notes:

> [Jeffers's verse] states its propositions so lucidly that the critic has no choice but to confront its content. The discussion can no longer be confined within the safe literary categories of formal analysis—internal structure, consistency, thematics, tone, and symbolism—that still constitute the overwhelming majority of all academic studies....
>
> But Jeffers's poetic independence came at the price of being banished from the academic canon, where the merits of a modernist are still mostly determined by distinctiveness of stylistic innovation and self-referential consistency of vision. (*CPM* 49, 51)

Jeffers does not go entirely unread, of course. As Vendler, writing about Jeffers at the same time as Gioia (the occasion was the publication of *Rock and Hawk*, a volume of Jeffers's selected poetry edited by Hass), notes, "Jeffers is periodically resurrected ... [but] remains, it seems to me, a finally unsatisfying poet—coarse, limited and defective in self-knowledge."[6] In short, Jeffers's status as a poet is not entirely settled. But Vendler, steeped as she is in Stevens and the modernist canon, is not likely to praise a poet such as Jeffers.

Instead, as Gioia notes, Jeffers "is the unchallenged laureate of environmentalists," with a significant non-academic readership. A similar status has come to Weldon Kees, whom Gioia discusses at length in *Can Poetry Matter?* and a recent uncollected essay, "The Cult of Weldon Kees." After disappearing in 1955, largely a neglected writer, Kees

---

[6] Helen Vendler, *Soul Says: On Recent Poetry* (Cambridge: Belknap/Harvard University Press, 1995), 52.

gained a significant readership among poets and artists who champion his work but remains unmentioned in most scholarly histories of American poetry. (A significant exception is *Unending Design: The Forms of Postmodern Poetry* by Joseph M. Conte, which includes discussion of Kees's modeling the form of some of his poems on the musical style of the fugue—a group of poems which has exerted significant influence on Gioia's own poetry, as "Lives of the Great Composers" from *Daily Horoscope* demonstrates.)[7] In "The Cult of Weldon Kees," Gioia discusses the large split between writers of poetry and the university-based critics who largely determine the poetic canon:

> The disparity between the legion of imaginative writers who admire Kees's work and paucity of academic interest demonstrates that there is now something out of joint between the worlds of poets and literary critics. One wonders how much real dialogue about modern poetry now goes on between writers and scholars—even those teaching in the same university departments. The administrative division between English and Creative Writing departments found in most large universities has become symbolic of a deeper schism in sensibility, taste, attitudes, and parlance in literary culture. Poets and theorists not only share no common sense of purpose; they increasingly lack a common language in which to discuss their differences.[8]

This discussion points to Gioia's deep sense of disappointment with the contemporary university's custodianship of poetry.

Expansive Poetry is itself a response to this sense of disillusionment about the university—a response that goes far beyond Gioia, and which he articulates in several essays, most notably "Notes on the New Formalism" and "The Poet in an Age of Prose." Because those essays form two of the central theoretical documents of Expansive Poetry, they

---

[7] Joseph M. Conte, *Unending Design: The Forms of Postmodern Poetry* (Cornell University Press, 1991).

[8] Dana Gioia, "The Cult of Weldon Kees," *AWP Chronicle* 28/3 (December 1995): 10. This essay was reprinted and expanded in *The Bibliography of Weldon Kees* (Jackson, MS: Parrish House, 1997), xv–xxxiv.

have both been discussed at length elsewhere, and there is little need to repeat their arguments here. However, they both extend Gioia's ideas about canon revision, the poet's place in contemporary culture, and the aesthetic possibilities for contemporary poetry.

It would be premature to suggest that Gioia—or anyone else involved with Expansive Poetry—is yet a major poet. Two books, even ones as accomplished as *Daily Horoscope* and *The Gods of Winter*, are simply insufficient. In his mid-forties, Gioia still has decades of productivity ahead of him, and final judgment about his career cannot come until much later. That said, it is also clear that Gioia has already had a measurable impact on contemporary poetry, both in his verse and in his criticism; he is already one of the most influential poets and critics of his generation. His work with form and narrative has been integral to restoring those modes to wider use, to exploring long-dormant aesthetic possibilities in contemporary poetry. Moreover, his essays on poetic form and poetry's place in American culture have been influential far beyond the contexts of the Expansive Poetry school. Gioia's achievement, then, is already substantial. Among the many poets associated with the school, Gioia has produced arguably the most coherent and strongest body of work. Final judgment must wait, but if any Expansive poets are still read in fifty years, then Gioia is likely to be among them.

5

ON *THE GODS OF WINTER* (1998)

Anne Stevenson

Seeking a precise adjective to describe Dana Gioia's poetry, I came up with *beautiful*—an epithet twentieth-century criticism has smeared with suspicion. To speak of "beautiful" poetry without sneering calls for explanation. Yet there was a period in the 1950s when American poetry seemed to be developing in a beautiful direction. In 1957, Meridian Books in the United States and Canada published an anthology edited by Donald Hall, Robert Pack, and Louis Simpson; it was called *New Poets of England and America*, and it brought to the public's attention a group of young lyricists who looked to be turning their backs on modernism. Robert Frost, their patron father or grandfather, provided an introduction that, today, will strike some people as heretical. "Overdevelop the social conscience and make us all social meddlers," he wrote, welcoming a resurgent, happy marriage between poetry and scholarship. "As I often say a thousand, two thousand, colleges, town and gown together in the little town they make, give us the best audiences poetry ever had in all this world."

In retrospect, those were the words of an old man whose influence on American poetry was running into the sands. Hall-Pack-Simpson's "formalist" anthology gave rise to a counter anthology edited by Donald Allen, that, by representing the work of the new left, sounded the trump for the radical 1960s. The camp war that resulted—university "orthodoxy" versus experimental extremism—raised a good deal of dust that during the 1970s and 1980s (ironically enough) settled down finally in the halls of academe—where most American poets of all camps now find employment. When the history of twentieth-century American poetry comes to be written, such ironies will not be lost upon our great-grandchildren.

Meanwhile, poetry in America, weakened by demotic correctness and critical blindness, stands in need of a thorough clean. Dana Gioia has appeared at a good moment to attack the job from two sides. His poetry, harkening back to Frost, Richard Wilbur, and Anthony Hecht, is usually constructed in lines and stanzas, or in blank verse with an unmistakably iambic pulse running through it. His criticism radically attacks the system of "creative-writing programs" and academic jobs for poets whose credentials rest on an overvalued reverence for "creativity." (See *Can Poetry Matter*?)

The Gods of Winter is an important book, if only because it exemplifies Gioia's courageously aesthetic approach to poetry—to its language and rhythms. Fortunately for those of us who agree with him, it is also a good book. His poems are limpid, mellifluous, quotable, and likely to be loved. Clearly, they are rooted in experience and compassion. Nor can their subject matter be dismissed as genteel. Two long poems, "Counting the Children" and "Homecoming," give weight to a volume that might otherwise concede too much to peaceable iambs. Employing dramatic monologue in a specifically American mode (Edgar Lee Masters, Robert Frost, Robert Lowell), "Counting the Children" meditates on "love's austere and lonely offices" in the person of a Chinese accountant called in to audit the estate of a woman whose life has been spent rifling through rubbish bins to save discarded dolls. At the end, Mr. Choi, viewing his sleeping daughter, has a vision of immortality as a destiny for human souls moving backward, not forward, into time.

> I saw beyond my daughter to all children,
> And, though elated, still I felt confused
> . . .
> What if completion comes only in beginnings?
> The naked tree exploding into flower?
> And all our prim assumptions about time
>
> Prove wrong? What if we cannot read the future
> Because our destiny moves back in time,

And only memory speaks prophetically? (*GW* 17, 18)

Moral or meditative philosophizing in poetry is often mockingly outlawed by the English intelligentsia, but it rings true in Gioia's vernacular American; "Counting the Children" has to be considered a triumph. Likewise, the psychological insight that plays through "Homecoming"—a monologue by a murderer who recounts the gruesome story of his childhood—seems a triumph of descriptive narrative.

Other poems are witty ("Money," "Orchestra") or ironical ("News from Nineteen Eighty-Four"), wry ("The Next Poem") or subtly, though effectively moving. "Planting a Sequoia," an almost impossible poem to write without sentimentality, only touches on the burial of the poet's "first born son ... brought back to the elements" with the planting of a sapling giant that will stand "when our family is no more, all of his unborn brothers dead ... / Silently keeping the secret of your birth" (*GW* 10).

In retrospect, the poetic civil wars of the American 1960s and 1970s look to have been fought with a good deal of blather over nothing very much. Today we read fine, formal poems like Gioia's or Hecht's, and then avant-garde high jinks, like the "art" poetry produced by Frank O'Hara or John Ashbery, conceding that, at their best, they are branches with a common root. I take it the root is Walt Whitman. Look hard enough at Eliot, Pound, and William Carlos Williams, and that honest common stock can be spotted there, too. Outward forms may violently disagree, but the heartwood of these poets is shared, together with their wryness and eagerness to branch out into speculation once a tangible or visible connection with the world has been established. Metaphysical rootedness in "things" is a quality Dana Gioia shares, too, with Sylvia Plath, Marianne Moore, Elizabeth Bishop, Amy Clampitt; there is nothing sexist about it; and nothing at all that rejects the reality of the world in the name of ideological, aesthetic, or political correctness.

A poem from the recently published *Selected Poems of Frank O'Hara* called "Ode on Causality" contains the lines "and there's the ugliness we seek in vain / through life and long for like a mortuarian Baudelaire." The pivotal word there is not "ugliness" but "seek." American poetry tends to be a poetry that seeks, and whether it seeks ugliness or beauty, the test of its success rests in the appropriate form of its expression. Where there is too much self-consciousness, piety, or strain for novel effect, it fails—as all copybook poetry ultimately fails. In Dana Gioia we have a poet who succeeds without strain. Almost every poem in *The Gods of Winter* fulfills the expectations raised by its form: a poetry of intuitive honesty that penetrates beyond appearances into possible aspects of the truth.

6

CULTURE AND THE SUBCULTURE: ON *CAN POETRY MATTER?* (1993)

Christopher Clausen

What audience still exists for poetry in contemporary America? Or, to put it less optimistically, why is poetry today largely confined to what Dana Gioia describes as a "subculture" in university English departments? Why does the educated public that reads serious magazines and continues to enjoy quality fiction no longer, on the whole, pay much attention to living poets? These questions have often been asked in recent years—including notably by Joseph Epstein in "Who Killed Poetry?" (*Commentary*, August 1988)—but seldom with as much penetration and knowledge of the literary world outside the university as Gioia brings to them here.

Since the appearance in 1986 of his first book of poems, *Daily Horoscope*, Dana Gioia has become something of a prodigy in American letters. His essays have appeared in the *New York Times Book Review*, the *Hudson Review*, and other magazines that reach well beyond the academic world that most contemporary poets inhabit. When "Can Poetry Matter?" appeared in the *Atlantic* in 1991, it inspired hundreds of letters, not only from infuriated members of the poetry "subculture" but also from those presumably mythical beings, general readers who would gladly read more poetry if there were more poets writing for a non-coterie audience.

Gioia assures us, there are such poets; part of the problem is that few people ever hear of them. The reviewing of poetry in most newspapers and general-circulation magazines is a thing of the past. Even the *Times Book Review* rarely deigns to notice new poetry, and when it does so the result is almost always a one-page omnibus review of volumes by three separate poets. Furthermore, the poets who get noticed are nearly always those whose work appeals to (and emanates from) the subculture of writing programs. Although Gioia does not make this point, the reviewing of poetry in nonacademic publications has become very much like the publication of poetry by commercial houses: an occasional activity carried on because it presumably still garners some prestige, not because anyone thinks there is an audience that really cares about the stuff.

Instead of an audience outside the universities, we have MFA programs inside them. In the decades since Randall Jarrell, himself a poet (and critic), ruefully observed that God had given the modern poet students to keep the wolf from the door but simultaneously taken away his readers, the whole operation has been put on an almost industrial footing. "The proliferation of literary journals and presses over the past 30 years," Gioia writes,

> has been a response less to an increased appetite for poetry among the public than to the desperate need of writing teachers for professional validation. Like subsidized farming that grows food no one wants, a poetry industry has been created to serve the interests of the producers and not the consumers. And in the process the integrity of the art has been betrayed. (*CPM* 10)

Gioia is himself that rare thing, an American poet who exists outside the university. Until recently he was a vice president of General Foods, and he writes feelingly about the careers of such businessmen-poets as T. S. Eliot, Wallace Stevens, L. E. Sissman, and Ted Kooser. "The campus," he points out, "is not a bad place for a poet to work. It's just a bad place for all poets to work."

Things were not always so. Before World War II, the university poet was a rarity. Particularly in New York, there was a world of letters—of publishing houses, magazines, literary journalism, theaters, and lecturing—where a poet was not wholly alien and could at least scrape by. Furthermore, poets as different as Robert Frost, Stephen Vincent Benét, Vachel Lindsay, and Edna St. Vincent Millay had large nonacademic audiences and were regularly discussed in the general-interest press. With the debatable exception of Frost, none of these poets is widely studied in universities today, or even much represented in recent anthologies.

What difference does it make how a poet pays his bills? For one thing, it means that the poetry itself grows out of a narrower range of experience than in the past. If nearly all poets were farmers or accountants or worked in the Social Security Administration, the limiting effect on their art would be obvious. As it is, the only thing that obscures the narrow boundaries of an art whose practitioners are too much alike is the fact that nearly all their readers are also faculty members or students in writing programs.

Then there's the McPoem effect, aptly named by Donald Hall to describe the kind of poem that university workshops often encourage. A minimalist free verse lyric aping the most currently fashionable models, it simply endorses the present state of the art and accredits its author as a member in good standing of the subculture, ready for a job teaching others to write the same thing. But as Gioia points out, free verse and minimalism are not themselves the problem. The similarity of effort, the imitativeness, the need to publish rapidly for tenure and promotion, the in-group reviewing and reading circuits—all these consequences of adapting an art to academic circumstances—have combined to reduce its range, power, and audience.

As anyone discovers who writes on these matters, however, another world of American poetry still survives outside the universities, even more invisible than the subculture Gioia anatomizes so well. A decade ago, I published a book titled *The Place of Poetry* that tried to analyze the decline of poetry's audience and cultural influence. I anticipated cries of outrage and denial from academic poets, and I was not disappointed. But a large volume of mail came from people far outside universities—men and women in every part of the country who had been writing poetry for years and hoped I could help them get it published, or at least confirm their belief that poems for a nonprofessional audience *should* be published.

Most of their poems were bad—but with a badness completely unlike the badness of so much of what does get published. Usually, though not invariably, they employed rhyme, meter, and traditional forms like the sonnet. Their subjects, too, were personal experiences that fell within the traditional matter of poetry—love, death, war (many of my correspondents were veterans), children. Usually, their poetry had something to say, even if often not well, and collectively it communicated a sense of tremendous human variety. Half a century ago the best of these poets would have found publishers.

Supposing they did find publishers, would they find an audience today? They might, but a more profitable question is whether poetry that was at the same time more sophisticated than theirs and more broadly based in experience than most of what comes out of universities could reclaim some of the audience and influence poets have lost in the twentieth century. The New Formalists, a movement with which Gioia has been identified and which he discusses in two of his chapters in *Can Poetry Matter?*, have been working for about fifteen years on the assumption that it can.

The infelicitous name implies that these poets write in traditional forms rather than free verse, which is not always true (Gioia himself has written both kinds of poems), but makes them controversial in writing programs. As he tells us in "The Poet in an Age of Prose":

> At odds with the small but established institutional audience for new poetry, these young writers imagined instead readers who loved literature and the arts but had either rejected or never studied contemporary poetry. This was not the mass audience of television or radio, for whom the written word was not a primary means of information. It was an audience of prose readers—intelligent, educated, and sophisticated individuals who, while no longer reading poetry, enjoyed serious novels, film, drama, jazz, dance, classical music, painting, and the other modern arts. (*CPM* 249)

Such diverse poets as Frederick Turner, Timothy Steele, Charles Martin, Wyatt Prunty, and Vikram Seth—some of them academics, others not—have experimented not only with form but with content, attempting, among other things, to revive narrative poetry. Their most ambitious goal is to reconnect poetry with a wider world. In 1986 Seth published *The Golden Gate*, a novel in verse that actually became a bestseller. Gioia's own second collection, *The Gods of Winter* (1991), contains briefer narratives and made a considerable splash in England.

Despite its author's affiliations, *Can Poetry Matter?* is not a manifesto. As a well-informed, undoctrinaire study of the present situation of American poetry, it makes its points with engaging modesty and bestows praise according to no ideological formula. It is not surprising to find that Gioia admires Elizabeth Bishop and Wallace Stevens, two poets who are almost universally acclaimed today. More pleasing, because more unexpected, are elegant essays commending Weldon Kees and Howard Moss.

"There is a type of criticism," Gioia writes in his preface, "that benefits from speaking in a public idiom to a mixed audience of both professional literati and general readers—groups that do not entirely share common assumptions. Such criticism has traditionally been at the center of literary culture" (*CPM* xi-xii).

Like poetry, in other words, criticism suffers when it becomes wholly academicized. The university is a great but limited institution, and one of the many virtues of this book is its reassertion of a literary world that continues to exist.

7

POETRY & THE SILENCING OF ART (1993)

Hilton Kramer

> Some claim the best stopped writing first.
> For the others, no one noted when or why.
> A few observers voiced their mild regret
> about another picturesque, unprofitable craft
> that progress had irrevocably doomed.
> —Dana Gioia, "The Silence of the Poets"

From time to time there appears a volume of criticism that, in the course of its attention to particular works of art, illuminates a good many more questions about our artistic and cultural affairs than are specifically addressed in its pages. Criticism tends to be at its best, of course, when it is most specific, when it derives its taste and standards from a particular artistic discipline and has something new and intelligent to say about the practice of the art from which it springs. Yet from Dr. Johnson's *Lives of the Poets* to T. S. Eliot's *The Sacred Wood* to Randall Jarrell's *Poetry and the Age*, the most important criticism has always done something more than this. It has brought us up to date on the condition of art, on the place it now occupies in the world at large, and on the historical imperatives that may imperil its very existence. Criticism of this kind follows the course of art itself in making vital connections between art and life.

The volume of criticism that Dana Gioia has recently published under the title *Can Poetry Matter?: Essays on Poetry and American Culture* is a book of this sort. While it has much to tell us about particular poets and about the condition of poetry at the present time, it also raises profound questions about the fate of art, which is to say high art, in a society now in turmoil over the definition of its cultural goals. To these questions Mr. Gioia brings the gifts and experience of a first-rate literary artist, the intellectual rigor of a rough-minded critic, and an outlook on the world that is the reverse of everything we associate with the word "academic." He also brings a generosity of spirit that lives on easy terms with the obligation to make distinctions, including distinctions of quality. There was a time—a distant time, alas—when it might have been enough to say of Mr. Gioia that he approaches the critical task as an accomplished poet. But as he and his readers are keenly aware, in our society at the present time the figure of the poet as a cultural spokesman is much diminished, if in fact it can still be said to exist. This loss of public status and influence, together with its causes and consequences, is indeed one of the central concerns of this book, which in its very first paragraph describes the fate that has overtaken the career of poetry in our cultural life.

> American poetry now belongs to a subculture. No longer part of the mainstream of artistic and intellectual life, it has become the specialized occupation of a relatively small and isolated group. Little of the frenetic activity it generates ever reaches outside that closed group. As a class, poets are not without cultural status. Like priests in a town of agnostics, they still command a certain residual prestige. But as individual artists they are almost invisible. (*CPM* 1)

This is the theme that serves as the foundation of every essay in this book. It informs Mr. Gioia's analyses of individual poets, it underlies his discussion of language and form in poetry, and it sets the terms within which his more general observations on the condition of poetry and the lives of our poets are largely formulated.

About the poetry that derives from this peculiar cultural situation Mr. Gioia writes with uncommon critical penetration. No one is likely to write a better essay on the poetry of Robert Bly, for example, than Mr. Gioia's. Here is a characteristic passage on Bly's verse:

> Is it possible for a stanza of poetry to be both unadorned and overwritten? Here [in Bly's poem "A Meditation on Philosophy"] every phrase contains at least one heavy-handed hint to the author's mood. (Excerpting these clues, one could easily compose a telegram version of the poem: "Restless gloom

> grieving leaves down dusk low abandons cold.") But despite its crude overstatement, the language remains weirdly inert for a lyric poem. Characteristically, Bly simply asserts his emotions. His utilitarian language does little to re-create them in the reader. Instead, in the manner of the New Sentimentality, he tries to bully the reader into an instant epiphany of alienation and self-pity. (*CPM* 177)

Here is an assessment of two of the many translations Bly has attempted, in this case of poems by Mallarmé and Rilke:

> As an impromptu translation in a French II oral exam, the Mallarmé might eke out a passing grade, but as poetry in English it fails the most rudimentary test. Not only does it not seem like the verse of an accomplished poet, it doesn't even sound like the language of a native speaker. Nor does the Rilke exhibit the virtues of a smooth literal translation. It transforms the tight, musical German into loose, pretentious doggerel....
>
> By propagating this minimal kind of translation Bly has done immense damage to American poetry. Translating quickly and superficially, he not only misrepresented the work of many great poets, he also distorted some of the basic standards of poetic excellence.... In promoting his new poetics (based on his specially chosen foreign models), he set standards so low that he helped to create a school of mediocrities largely ignorant of the premodern poetry in English and familiar with foreign poetry only through oversimplified translations. (*CPM* 171, 172–73)

It should be pointed out, in this connection, that Mr. Gioia is himself a superb translator of poetry; see, for example, his version of Eugenio Montale's *Mottetti*.[1]

He is equally good on the very different problem of John Ashbery's

[1] Eugenio Montale, *Mottetti: Poems of Love*, trans. Dana Gioia (St. Paul: Graywolf Press, 1990).

poetry.

> Ashbery is a discursive poet without a subject. Although he deals indirectly with several recurrent themes, themes that have become increasingly dark and personal as he has grown older, the poems are mainly the surface play of words and images. One never remembers ideas from an Ashbery poem, one recalls the tones and textures. If ideas are dealt with at all, they are present only as faint echoes heard remotely in some turn of phrase. Ideas in Ashbery are like the melodies in some jazz improvisation where the musicians have left out the original tune to avoid paying royalties. They are wild variations on a missing theme with only the original chord changes as a clue. This sort of music can be fun as long as someone doesn't try to analyze it like a Beethoven symphony. (*CPM* 185–86)

Some of Mr. Gioia's subjects are surprising—Robinson Jeffers, for instance, whose poetry he praises with such conviction that he almost persuades me to have another look at it, something I wouldn't have thought possible. One of the most appealing qualities of Mr. Gioia's criticism is, indeed, that it is neither sectarian nor ideological in its tastes and interests. And his critical method, if it can be called that, is anything but narrow. It ranges from excellent close readings, where poems seem to require that kind of focus because of their complexity or unfamiliarity, to the kind of biographical or autobiographical approach that can sometimes afford a fresh perspective on poetry already well known to us. Thus, the critic who makes such a strong case for Jeffers also writes with great insight and feeling about Wallace Stevens—about Stevens's limitations, too—while at the same time giving us the best overall introductions to the poetry of Donald Justice, Weldon Kees, and Howard Moss that I have read.

Mr. Gioia knows how to praise and illuminate what he most admires—a rarer thing in the contemporary criticism of poetry than you might imagine—and he brings to every subject a voice that is entirely his own, the voice of a poet who knows what he likes and dislikes and why. His account, in "The Example of Elizabeth Bishop," of how he came to that wonderful poet's work as a student and what it meant to him is a beautiful example of the way criticism, when intensely personal, can sometimes illuminate an important poetic achievement while also describing very accurately an entire literary period.

> I noticed that most of my teachers—professors and graduate students alike—talked most comfortably about contemporary poetry when they could reduce it to ideology. The Beats espoused political, moral, and social revolution; hence they deserved attention. The feminists demanded a fundamental revision of traditional sexual identities; therefore their poetry became important. This utilitarian aesthetic transformed poetry into a secular version of devotional verse. The reading lists covering contemporary poetry rarely seemed to originate from genuine love or excitement about the work itself but rather from some dutiful sense of its value in illustrating some theoretically important trend. This dreary moral and aesthetic didacticism had little to do with the "lonely impulse of delight" that had brought me to poetry.
>
> Likewise I found it hard to consider Ginsberg or Ferlinghetti revolutionary when I first encountered them as classroom texts in an elite private university. To me they represented the conventional values—most of which, incidentally, I accepted—of the establishment I had just entered. Moreover, its novel trappings aside, their work often appeared predictable, prolix, and sentimental. By contrast, Bishop seemed original without being ostentatious, conversational without becoming verbose, and emotional without seeming maudlin. Her childhood reminiscence "First Death in Nova Scotia" worked all the more powerfully by being restrained. Her short narrative poem "House Guest" explored the subtle psychology of class relations more convincingly by being so insistently personal. She explored moral dilemmas without having a predetermined destination. Despite its familiar feel, her poetry almost always surprised one. (*CPM* 241–42)

This single essay has more to tell us about the history of American poetry since the 1950s than most of the books that have been devoted to the subject.

The criticism in *Can Poetry Matter?* is also personal in other respects. It has a good deal to say, for example, about Mr. Gioia's own aesthetic outlook as a poet who has been much involved in the revival of formal and narrative verse. The subject of writing—and not writing—poetry in traditional metrical forms inevitably comes up in some of the essays on individual poets, but it is discussed more directly, along with the related issue of narrative poetry, in two essays, "'Notes on the New Formalism" and "The Dilemma of the Long Poem." In the first of these essays, originally published in the 1980s, Mr. Gioia gives us the recent history of this declining interest in poetic form with his characteristic clarity:

> Two generations now of younger writers have largely ignored rhyme and meter, and most of the older poets who worked originally in form (such as Louis Simpson and Adrienne Rich) have abandoned it entirely for more than a quarter of a century. Literary journalism has long declared it defunct, and most current anthologies present no work in traditional forms by Americans written after 1960. The British may have continued using rhyme and meter in their quaint, old-fashioned way and the Irish in their primitive, bardic manner, but for up-to-date Americans it became the province of the old, the eccentric, and the Anglophilic. It was a style that dared not speak its name, except in light verse.... By 1980 there had been such a decisive break with the literary past that in America for the first time in the history of modern English most published young poets could not write with minimal competence in traditional meters (not that this failing bothered anyone). Whether this was an unprecedented cultural catastrophe or a glorious revolution is immaterial to this discussion. What matters is that most of the craft of traditional English versification had been forgotten. (*CPM* 36–37)

There then follows an unexpected and devastating account of what Mr. Gioia calls "the emergence of pseudo-formal verse" in the 1980s—a development that, in his view, is only another measure of our cultural loss. About these matters Mr. Gioia writes more in sorrow than in anger, and always with an admirable absence of dogmatism, and his principal interest is never argument for its own sake but the vitality of poetic art and its need for an audience beyond the academy. It is precisely because he sees in the revival of formal and narrative verse a means of achieving these goals that he writes about them with so much enthusiasm and intelligence.

> All these revivals of traditional technique ... both reject the specialization and intellectualization of the arts in the academy over the past forty years and affirm the need for a broader popular audience. The modern movement, which began this century in bohemia, is now ending it in the university, an institution dedicated at least as much to the specialization of knowledge as to its propagation. Ultimately the mission of the university has little to do with the mission of the arts, and this long cohabitation has had an enervating effect on all the arts but especially on poetry and music. With the best of intentions the university has intellectualized the arts to a point where they have been cut off from the vulgar vitality of popular traditions and, as a result, their public has shrunk to groups of academic specialists and a captive audience of students, both of which refer to everything beyond the university as "the real world." (*CPM* 40)

This "real world" beyond the university is, as it happens, one that the author of this passage knows well at first hand. Last year Mr. Gioia, who is now in his early forties, resigned a vice presidency at Kraft General Foods to become a full-time writer. He had worked as a business executive in New York for some fifteen years, during which time he also published his first two volumes of poetry—*Daily Horoscope* (1986) and *The Gods of Winter* (1991)—his translations of Montale and other poets, and the essays that have been collected in *Can Poetry Matter?* (He holds masters' degrees in both business administration and comparative literature.) This experience has naturally kindled his interest in other American poets who chose careers in business rather than in the academy to sustain their literary endeavors, and about this phenomenon he has written a brilliant and unusual essay called "Business and Poetry." This is one of the most interesting essays about the relation of art to life that any American poet has ever written.

It is astonishing, first of all, in the sheer number and quality of poets cited for discussion. We all know about Wallace Stevens in the insurance business and William Carlos Williams as a pediatrician, but Mr. Gioia's roll call goes well beyond the famous cases. Richard Eberhart, L. E. Sissman, Archibald MacLeish, A. R. Ammons, James Dickey, Robert Phillips, Richard Hugo, Ted Kooser (about whose poetry Mr. Gioia writes a separate essay in this book), William Bronk, and a number of lesser-known names are more than enough to persuade us that this is a development in American cultural life that has remained largely invisible to the literary public. For Mr. Gioia, what is most striking about this group of poets is what he describes as "their aversion to using this part of their lives"—that is, their working life in the business world—as the raw material of their poetry. Whatever their involvement in business, they turn out to be no more likely than the poets in the academy to reach beyond the "subculture" of poetry in what they write or in the way they write.

> The inability of these businessmen-poets to write about their professional worlds is symptomatic of a larger failure in American verse—namely its difficulty in discussing most public concerns. If business is nonexistent as a poetic subject, there is also a surprising paucity of serious verse on political and social themes. Not only has our poetry been unable to create a meaningful public idiom, but it even lacks most of the elements out of which such an idiom might be formed. (*CPM* 126–27)

In the end, Mr. Gioia writes of the businessman-poet that "his job, like the academic's, has sheltered him from the economic consequences of writing without an audience. It even tutored him in surviving alienation" (*CPM* 127). His poetry, too, belongs "to the private world that is the poet's mind" (*CPM* 128). If, all the same, these businessmen-poets enjoyed a certain advantage, it was the advantage of remaining outsiders in the professional literary world.

> By refusing to simplify themselves into the conventional image of a poet, they affirmed their own spiritual individuality, and the daily friction of their jobs toughened the resolve. Ultimately the decisions they made forced them to choose between abandoning poetry and practicing it without illusions. Anyone who studies the lives and works of the men who combined careers in business and poetry finds this hard-won sense of maturity and realism at the center. Their lives may not always provide other poets with overtly inspiring examples, but their careers offer pragmatic and important lessons in spiritual survival. In a society that destroys or distracts most artists, they found a paradoxical means to prosper—both as men and writers. In American literature that is not a small accomplishment. (*CPM* 139)

No one, I think, has written with greater clarity or greater poignancy—or with a greater sense of urgency, either—about the "subculture" in which the art of poetry is still confined and about its need to find what Mr. Gioia calls a "rapprochement with the educated public." Yet I have to say that as I turned the pages of this very good book, I often felt the same sense of melancholy and despair that I felt in reading the last lines of Mr. Gioia's poem "The Silence of the Poets," in *The Gods of Winter*.

> And what was lost? No one now can judge.
> But we still have music, art, and film,
> diversions enough for a busy people.
> And even poetry for those who want it.
> The old books, those the young have not defaced,
> are still kept somewhere,
> stacked in their dusty rows.
>
> And a few old men may visit from time to time
> to run their hands across the spines
> and reminisce,
> but no one ever comes to read
> or would know how. (*GW* 30)

This poem is, in a sense, about "the educated public" that Mr. Gioia has in mind for the poetry of the future, and he knows as well as the rest of us what has happened to it. He speaks in the title essay of his book about "the decline of literacy, the proliferation of other media, the crisis in humanities education, the collapse of critical standards, and the sheer weight of past failures"; and even this melancholy inventory of our cultural woes does not tell the whole story (*CPM* 21). Poetry was once the exception in its lack of an "educated public," but that condition of loss and isolation is now becoming the norm for the entire realm of high culture. "The Silence of the Poets" now speaks for the silencing of art in many fields. This, too, is a subject of great concern in *Can Poetry Matter?* As Mr. Gioia writes in his title essay:

> If the audience for poetry has declined into a subculture of specialists, so too have the audiences for most contemporary art forms, from serious drama to jazz.... Contemporary classical music scarcely exists as a living art outside university departments and conservatories. Jazz, which once commanded a broad popular audience, has become the semi-private domain of aficionados and musicians.... Much serious drama is now confined to the margins of American theater, where it is seen only by actors, aspiring actors, playwrights, and a few diehard fans. Only the visual arts, perhaps because of their financial glamour and upper-class support, have largely escaped the decline in public attention. (*CPM* 21)

I am not at all sure myself that the "financial glamour" that surrounds the visual arts hasn't done them more harm than good, for public attention of this sort has a price, too; but otherwise Mr. Gioia's account of the way the other arts are rapidly being consigned to the status of subcultures is perfectly correct. I do not therefore see what hope there is in expanding the audience for serious poetry at the very moment when the audience for classical music, for example, is diminishing at so rapid a rate that the whole profession is in crisis.

In Mr. Gioia's discussion of these problems, something very important has been left out—the subject of popular culture. For as the silencing of high art proceeds at a rapid rate in our society, what is taking its place on a scale never seen before is the noise of the most noxious and degraded varieties of pop culture. High culture cannot compete with its lethal effects on the minds and bodies of the young—and not only the young, of course—and neither can serious education, not as it is now conducted, anyway. And as long as the juggernaut of pop culture continues to swamp everything in its path, not only will poetry remain confined "to the private world that is the poet's mind" but so will all of high art—whatever remains of it—be confined to the private world of its subculture. *And what was lost? No one can judge* will be a line applicable to many things we now cherish. *Can Poetry Matter?* is an important book, but it does not yet have an answer to the question posed in its title.

II

Mid-Career

Interrogations at Noon and *Nosferatu*

8

ON *INTERROGATIONS AT NOON* (2004)

Leslie Monsour

Poet, critic, and current NEA chair Dana Gioia has made a practice of subdividing his books into five sections, each headed by an elucidative quotation. It's an intriguing device and an example of how Gioia, a particularly hospitable poet, frequently lights the way for his readers as he leads them through the varied and various chambers of his art.

In *Interrogations at Noon*, his most recent book, he opens the first section with a quote from Flaubert: "Human speech is like a cracked kettle on which we beat crude rhythms for bears to dance to, while we long to make music that will melt the stars." Flaubert's comment serves to introduce the theme of human inadequacy—a persistent motif throughout this volume.

This theme is encountered head-on in the title poem, "Interrogations at Noon," which, for all its lyrical polish, is a harshly unforgiving piece. Noon is the hour when nothing can hide from the sun, and Gioia's noon, like Milton's, is "without all hope of day." The poem begins with the poet imagining the voice of "the better man I might have been." Through this persona, he berates himself with a startlingly acrimonious self-accusation. Socrates once observed that, "The unexamined life is not worth living," an admonition largely ignored in today's antidepressant-ridden, feel-good climate of irresponsible self-affirmation. "Interrogations at Noon" takes Socrates to heart with a vengeance. It turns the ancient philosopher's observation inside out by insisting the examined life is also not worth living, because all it reveals is falsity and unworthiness.

> "You cultivate confusion like a rose
> In watery lies too weak to be untrue,

And play the minor figures in the pageant,
Extravagant and empty, that is you." (*IN* 5)

This stark admission of failure escapes irony. Gioia delivers his disconcerting message in a terse, tense pentameter, shaped further by graceful pairs of rhymes, as he fashions an unusual poem that makes the annihilation of self-worth and self-importance seem almost elegant. However, despite its composed surface, "Interrogations at Noon" ultimately unsettles with its unexpected, contumelious outpouring.

Clearly by design, "Failure" is the title of the poem that follows "Interrogations at Noon." Unlike its predecessor, it brightens with irony. Gioia now celebrates failure in atypically plain, free-verse stanzas:

Why not consider it a sort of accomplishment?
Failure doesn't happen by itself. It takes time,
effort, and a certain undeniable gift.
Satisfaction comes from recognizing what you do best. (*IN* 6)

In its closing line, the sarcasm of "Failure" is almost comforting. "You only fail at what you really aim for," the poet shrugs, calling to mind the resonating irony of Bob Dylan's, "There's no success like failure." Failure, after all, is evidence that you've tried.

"Divination," which follows, unsettles the reader once again with its menacing glimpse of delusional romance. It is written as a pantoum, a French form in which lines are repeated in a pattern of refrains. In this poem, the repetition seems to mock the mounting tension from the beginning:

Always be ready for the unexpected.
Someone you have dreamed about may visit.
Better clean house to make the right impression.
There are some things you should not think about.

To the end:

Notice the cool appraisal of his eyes.

> Better clean house to make the right impression.
> You sometimes wonder what you're waiting for.
> Always be ready for the unexpected. (*IN* 7)

A strained yet fluent self-consciousness unites much of Gioia's poetry. In "The Voyeur," a scene of domestic bliss is rendered sensuously psychedelic and hauntingly weird when a husband falls prey to the notion that he is "missing" from his life. Imagining he is observing his existence from the branches of a tree outside his bedroom window, "He notices a cat curled on the bed. / He hears a woman singing in the shower. / The branches shake their dry leaves like alarms" (*IN* 4).

These and the last poem in this group, "The Litany," bring two poets—Robinson Jeffers and Weldon Kees—to mind. Indeed, their influence is felt throughout *Interrogations at Noon.* Gioia writes in *Can Poetry Matter?* that "Jeffers's central human obsessions emerge as the suffocating burden of the past on human freedom ... and the impossibility of human salvation" (*CPM* 55). Of Kees, he writes, "The mythic landscape of Kees's poetry is the wasteland, a fallen world where real time has stopped ... the vision of human destiny as an endless succession of heroes who try to redeem this fallen world and always fail" (*CPM* 76, 77).

In his poem "For My Daughter," Weldon Kees captures desolation with one line: "These speculations sour in the sun." But Gioia's viewpoint is more tempered. He writes of sorrow, not bitterness. Kees wrote about a child he never had, while Gioia writes from experience, having lost a four-month-old son to sudden infant death syndrome (SIDS). This immense and inconsolable sense of loss permeates much of his poetry. It is most notable in his previous book, *The Gods of Winter*, particularly in the title poem, as well in as the oft-referenced "Planting a Sequoia." In the current volume, "The Litany" addresses these complex emotions in anaphoric lamentation:

> This is a litany to earth and ashes,
> to the dust of roads and vacant rooms,
> to the fine silt circling in a shaft of sun,
> settling indifferently on books and beds.

> This is a prayer to praise what we become,
> "Dust thou art, to dust thou shalt return."
> Savor its taste—the bitterness of earth and ashes.
>
> This is a prayer, inchoate and unfinished,
> for you, my love, my loss, my lesion,
> a rosary of words to count out time's
> illusions, all the minutes, hours, days
> the calendar compounds as if the past
> existed somewhere—like an inheritance
> still waiting to be claimed. (*IN* 10–11)

These tearful explorations extend into Section II of *Interrogations at Noon*, which addresses the heaviest burdens of the poet's past and is announced by a quotation from Jeffers: "I have heard the summer dust crying to be born." At this point, we are likely to find ourselves hoping the poet will soon purge these sorrows from his system. The poems begin to blur with similarities. "The Litany" proclaims itself, "a benediction on the death of a young god, / brave and beautiful, rotting on a tree" (*IN* 10), while "Metamorphosis" ends:

> I'll never know, my changeling, where you've gone,
> And so I'll praise you—flower, bird, and tree—
> My nightingale awake among the thorns,
> My laurel tree that marks a god's defeat,
> My blossom bending on the water's edge,
> Forever lost within your inward gaze. (*IN* 17)

"Pentecost" opens by addressing "the sorrows of afternoon," reiterating with a biblical aura the sense of torment that afflicted "Interrogations at Noon." The poet relives sleepless nights, "when memory / Repeats its prosecution" (*IN* 18). Like Jeffers, Gioia often writes of flames and ash. Here they are like the mystical inspiration of the Holy Spirit in the New Testament, serving to intensify the spiritual anguish of the heart.

Jeffers, on the other hand, is all earthly fire and godless nature, the very things that give him solace. Upon the death of his wife, Una, Jeffers wrote in "Hungerfield":

> But the ashes have fallen
> And the flame has gone up; nothing human remains. You
> are earth and air; you are in the beauty of the ocean
> And the great streaming triumphs of sundown; you are
> alive and well in the tender young grass rejoicing
> When soft rain falls all night, and little rosy-fleeced clouds
> float on the dawn.—I shall be with you presently.[1]

For Gioia: "Nor the morning's ache for dream's illusion, nor any prayers / Improvised to an unknowable god / Can extinguish the flame" (*IN* 18).

While the Pentecostal tongues of fire revived and empowered the disciples of Christ, Gioia writes desolately, "Death has been our pentecost, / And our innocence consumed by these implacable / Tongues of fire" (*IN* 18). Ending in a sense of mournful resignation—"I offer you this scarred and guilty hand / Until others mix our ashes"—the poet's *je m'accuse* ethos persists throughout (*IN* 18). He leans hard on his "scarred and guilty hand," but it can never be hard enough, as in the spirit of Robert Frost, who also suffered the loss of children. Frost, we recall, wrote in his great poem, "To Earthward": "When stiff and sore and scarred / I take away my hand / From leaning on it hard / In grass and sand, // The hurt is not enough"; and, "Now no joy but lacks salt, / That is not dashed with pain / And weariness and fault."[2]

Gioia takes great risks with these poems as he grapples with the never-ending aftermath of loss. He succeeds because the poems are genuine, not forced. The poet elevates his personal grief to the universal by means of scriptural and allegorical allusion. Fragile and pure, these poems are elegant, miniature monuments to spiritual heartache.

---

[1] Robinson Jeffers, "Hungerfield," *Poetry* 80/2 (May 1952): 87.

[2] Robert Frost, *The Poetry of Robert Frost. The Collected Poems*, ed. Edward Connery Lathem (New York: Henry Holt, 1979), 227.

Section II closes with two of the strongest poems in the volume. "A California Requiem" harkens back to two poems in Gioia's first book, *Daily Horoscope*: "California Hills in August," his most widely anthologized poem, and "In Chandler Country." Both were instant hits upon their appearance in the *New Yorker* in the 1980s. "A California Requiem," once again keeping with the thematic unity of "Interrogations at Noon," opens its iambic pentameter quatrains amid graves "New planted in the irrigated lawn," as the "square, trim headstones quietly declared / The impotence of grief against the sun" (*IN* 20). Traversing the manicured landscape, the poet's tone becomes both elegiac and cynical:

> My blessed California, you are so wise.
> You render death abstract, efficient, clean.
> Your afterlife is only real estate,
> And in his kingdom Death must stay unseen. (*IN* 20)

Soon the beseeching chorus of the dead is heard, calling from a brand-new circle of the Inferno. "'Stay a moment longer, quiet stranger. / Your footsteps woke us from our lidded cells. / Now hear us whisper in the scorching wind, / Our single voice drawn from a thousand hells'" (*IN* 20). They agonize under the burden of the destructive past in which they hedonistically participated, hastening the ruin of the beloved places that were so generously good to them. "'We lived in places that we never knew. / We could not name the birds perched on our sill, / Or see the trees we cut down for our view. / What we possessed we always chose to kill'" (*IN* 20).

The poet then faces the realization that he won't resist their plea to "'Become the voice of our forgotten places. / Teach us the names of what we have destroyed. / We are like shadows the bright noon erases, / Weightlessly shrinking, bleached into the void'" (*IN* 21). Once again, noon dazzles mercilessly. The landscape, both interior and exterior, is a wasteland, and the poet is the hero who always fails. The melodrama nearly becomes oppressive before the poem concludes with one of Gioia's most memorable and quotable stanzas:

> "We offer you the landscape of your birth—
> Exquisite and despoiled. We all share blame.

We cannot ask forgiveness of the earth
For killing what we cannot even name." (*IN* 21)

The words, "Exquisite and despoiled" bring to mind Jeffers's "Shine, Perishing Republic." There is, however, a considerable attitudinal difference between these two poets. Jeffers shows no human sympathy. He crisply instructs his children: "And boys, be in nothing so moderate as in love of man." On the other hand, Gioia's sensibility bows to compassion. The voices of the guilt-ridden dead tell him, "We are your people, though you would deny it." But he never does.

"The End of the World" is an ominous title for a poem, and by now, we might expect something truly eschatological here. But this is not the case. The poem opens almost merrily: "'We're going,' they said, 'to the end of the world'" (*IN* 25). What follows is a literal excursion by car, on foot, over bridge and gravel, tracking a river to its spectacular waterfall.

The stanzas are energetic quatrains that fall easily into the regular rhythm of hiking. This poem is both simple and lush—its landscape is no wasteland. There are ospreys and green mountains and oak trees by the shore. The journey to view the void is conducted by "guides" who have the anonymity of angels. Their traveler is unafraid and accompanies them willingly. At a certain point along the way,

My guides moved back. I stood alone,
As the current streaked over smooth flat stone.

Shelf by stone shelf the river fell.
The white water goosetailed with eddying swell.
Faster and louder the current dropped
Till it reached a cliff, and the trail stopped. (*IN* 25)

The literal trek along the river may be interpreted as a metaphysical idealization of death. The beauty of the forest behind him, his trail spent, the traveler is left alone to face eternity:

I stood at the edge where the mist ascended,
My journey done where the world ended.
I looked downstream. There was nothing but sky,
The sound of the water, and the water's reply. (*IN* 25)

While *Interrogations at Noon* spends considerable time exploring the darker heart of existence, it is by no means a depressing volume. It contains in nearly equal measure a lyrical levity and wit, and what Gioia calls "the cool subtraction of desire" in "The Lost Garden," a poem that addresses the mature contentment that comes with "wanting nothing more than what has been" (*IN* 68).

"At the Waterfront Café"—almost a satirical response to "A California Requiem"—presents living hedonists, blithely consuming the planet's resources. They are contrasted in alternating stanzas with those who serve them. The poet is mildly derisive, but doesn't alienate himself as he watches the departure of the café's wealthy patrons:

But tonight I hope they prosper.
Are they shallow? I don't care.
Jealousy is all too common,
Style and beauty much too rare. (*IN* 38)

The last section of *Interrogations at Noon* features reflective serenades to lost love. These poems, some in free, some in metrical verse, are concerned with the superiority of touch over the inadequacy of words, circling back to the first poem in the book, "Words," which begins, "The world does not need words," asserting, "The kiss is still fully itself though no words were spoken" (*IN* 3). "But words are never as precise as touch," we are told in "Long Distance" (*IN* 52). In "Corner Table," a relationship comes to an end when one of the lovers announces her intention to marry someone else. "What matters most / Most often can't be said ... / ... We understand / This last mute touch that lingers is farewell" (*IN* 51). In "The Bargain," the poet reflects, "I had forgotten the sharp / exactitude of touch" (*IN* 62).

Again, these poems have the edginess of Weldon Kees without his bitterness. The slight discomfort of Gioia's confessional intimacy appeals to us, unlike the disturbing self-annihilation of "Interrogations at Noon." Gioia articulates the distance of time that shades old, quiet romantic yearnings, as he unaffectedly comes to terms with his own history of desire and the futility of questioning his choices, as in the last lines of "Summer Storm":

> And memory insists on pining
> For places it never went,
> As if life would be happier
> Just by being different. (*IN* 67)

Gioia relieves his autobiographical mood in such clever departures as, "Elegy with Surrealist Proverbs as Refrain," a crazy quilt of biographical fragments from the French Dadaist era of art. The note tells us, "All of the incidents and quotations in the poem are true." So, in this scattershot romp through suicidal love and worship of the absurd, we learn, "Dali dreamed of Hitler as a white-skinned girl—," and "Wounded Apollinaire wore a small steel plate / inserted in his skull. 'I so loved art,' he smiled, / 'I joined the artillery.'" The poem reaches hilarious heights with, "Wealthy Roussel taught his poodle to smoke a pipe. / 'When I write, I am surrounded by radiance. / My glory is like a great bomb waiting to explode'" (*IN* 8).

Subtitled "Words for Music," Section III of this volume also contains many delightful poems. An accomplished opera librettist, Gioia has included here "Three Songs from *Nosferatu*," a new opera by Alva Henderson for which he has written the book. These arias are a voluptuous fusion of melancholy and romance. They unite pleasure and pain in just the right measure for the high-gothic melodrama of vampire lore. "Alley Cat Love Song" follows these opera excerpts with playful wit and a nod to T. S. Eliot. But Old Possum's lines aren't quite in the same blue league as,

> Come into the garden, Fred,
> For the neighborhood tabby is gone.
> Come into the garden, Fred.
> I've nothing but my flea collar on,

And the scent of catnip has gone to my head.
I'll wait by the screen door till dawn. (*IN* 35)

The body of *Interrogations at Noon* owes much of its flesh to translations that pay homage to Cavafy, Seneca, Rilke, and the modern Italian poet Valerio Magrelli. It has been argued that the translations are too numerous in this collection, which, without them, would shrink to a chapbook. The complaint is somewhat valid, since some of the translations seem more gratuitous than relevant—in particular, "Juno Plots Her Revenge," which occupies the entire fourth section of the volume. The six Magrelli translations are four or five too many. They force a monotonous interlude into a section containing some of the most engaging pieces, Gioia's own poems of lost and failed love.

It is with these fine poems that *Interrogations at Noon* reaches its satisfying conclusion. The final six-line poem, "Unsaid," begins, "So much of what we live goes on inside" (*IN* 69). Five lines later, "inside" is end-rhymed with "confide." The connection summarizes the aim of Gioia's most memorable work. That his aim succeeds in this volume is the result of his profound and artful preoccupation with failure.

9

DANA GIOIA: A CONTEMPORARY METAPHYSICS (2009)

Janet McCann

Contemporary metaphysical poetry is the response to the dryness of the post-Christian world that many, including many Christians, believe we now inhabit. It is not Christian poetry *per se*, but it often dips between a luminous sadness and a sense of divine presence. Richard Wilbur writes it, also Mary Oliver, Annie Dillard, Marie Howe, and many others. This is not to say that many explicitly Christian poems are not being written, and that these poets do not write such poems. Rather, I would affirm that there is a kind of poetry that is metaphysical/non-sectarian and stops short of stated religious commitment—the religious content remains underneath. Dana Gioia is a contemporary metaphysical poet whose work fits this description. Its Catholic roots and its attention to the real daily presence of good and evil are its pragmatic dimension; its search for belief in beauty through and in form is its transcendence. Two elements in Gioia's poetry define its Christian spirit—an ethical stance and a sacramental vision. His work is a significant presence in current Christian literature.

Gioia was recognized during his term as chairman of the National Endowment for the Arts for his focus on reawakening interest in classic forms and figures, for the wave of renewed interest in Shakespeare in the schools his programs have brought about, for his workshops for war participants, and for many other programs that seek to revitalize interest in serious literature on a broad-based level. A spokesman for the New Formalist movement, Gioia is noted for reviving interest in Longfellow and other semi-neglected formalists. In his essay "Can Poetry Matter?" he argues for a number of techniques and devices that could help bring poetry back to the reading public, including a shift away from the professorial type of reading toward mixed evenings of poetry and music, poetry and art, poets reading others' work as well as their own, and a general opening wide of the narrow room he believed the art had stuffed itself into by the mid-1980s. His public presence provides a surge of confidence and enthusiasm among many who think poetry should be an important part of the wider culture and disconcerts some experimental poets who believe that poetry's most important responsibility has always been to challenge. Gioia places the primary responsibility of poetry elsewhere, in instruction and experience.

From his public role, a reader might expect Gioia to write traditional poetry, metrically exact and freely accessible, on social topics and on the role of poetry today. We might expect a classicism in form and content. And if one reads a few of his best-known poems, such as "Words" and "Veterans' Cemetery," these expectations appear to be met. Some of his poems are graceful reflections noted for their wit and precision. Their subjects are timeless; they may remind the reader of Martial and lapidary verse. This kind of crafted poetry is not usually thought of as metaphysical, though it can be. Certainly, it is closer to George Herbert's or even Ben Jonson's work than it is to John Donne's. This is in fact the kind of poetry one memorizes almost accidentally in rereading it, like certain poems of Robert Frost's. "Unsaid," which concludes the 2001 collection *Interrogation at Noon*, is one such poem:

> So much of what we live goes on inside —
> The diaries of grief, the tongue-tied aches
> Of unacknowledged love are no less real
> For having passed unsaid. What we conceal
> Is always more than what we dare confide.
> Think of the letters that we write our dead. (*IN* 69)

The frequently quoted "Words" opens the book and "Unsaid" closes it; in between are the words said. This kind of careful parenthesis is typical of the poet. These poems express and practice an ethic. They underscore the theme that love in its various dimensions and definitions is the key to right living, and their finely crafted expression may suggest that poems themselves have a duty—are accountable—to the society they serve.

Certainly, Gioia has some light and humorous poems, and a lot of wordplay and allusions that show the funny side of writers and writing, artists and art. These are entertaining and enlightening; they show how an agile sensibility unencumbered by any critical bias or apparatus delves into literary culture to find a singular perspective. An example is "Elegy with Surrealist Proverbs as Refrain," which gives startling, gossipy portraits of poets, writers, and artists linked by famous Surrealist statements, which appear as refrain lines: "There is always a skeleton on the buffet. / I came. I sat down. I went away" (*IN* 9).

Gioia's poetry is not generally optimistic and upbeat. Its universe is filled with forces that are inhospitable to humans and cannot be fully dealt with by any of the traditional means: education, art, religion. And yet, they sometimes emphasize the need for these very institutions that are shown as vulnerable and even failing. So the poetry presents conundrums, not solutions, and conflicts, not resolutions. Its world is a field of struggle which has no positive outcome promised or even suggested. Human beings and their art are in a situation that is threatening and is likely to prove overwhelming. Some of these poems have the somber mood of *Beowulf* or Norse myth, rather than of belief in progress; they are inhabited by the sense of an age that is passing away, leaving only uncertainty. Behind the shifting surfaces of contemporary life remains a belief or faith, but this faith motivates rather than consoles; it is linked to a sense of responsibility.

Perhaps because of his range in tone and content, Gioia's work is satisfying in a way that the poetry of many past and present formalists is not. Its layers of meaning and its refusal to accept closure sometimes have more in common with the postmodernists or at least the modernists than with the nineteenth-century traditional poets whose work Gioia admires. These are not cozy poems like many past formalists' poems, nor do they directly instruct. They are stages of quest, which makes of Gioia, a romantic poet, not what we consider recent romanticism (Allen Ginsberg et al.), but the original Romantic impulse with its attention to craft, its involvement with myth, its desire to find a more vital source of power than ordinary life provides. They seek transcendence, and sometimes they find it. And there is often a veil of romantic irony over the search itself, as can be seen in the closing lines of "A Curse on Geographers":

> Let oceans spill their green from off
> The edges of the earth, and let
> The curving plain unbend itself
> Behind the mountains. Put wind back
> Into the cheeks of demons. Voice,
> Pronounce your reasonable desire
> And sing the round earth flat again! (*DH* 39)

Like Wallace Stevens, one of his most significant influences, Gioia finds writing a realm of spiritual exploration. Like Stevens throughout most of his life, Gioia does not seem to find "a point of central arrival." There is always something beyond. But his work like Stevens's compresses emotion into form, devising forms of his own that fit the theme and direction of the work. One can think of Gioia's poems as having specific gravity; their nature is identifiable by the proportion of weight to mass. Conventionally this might be called decorum, but it is more subtle and varied than traditional notions of decorum. The forms fit their subject in such a way as to provide pleasure, emphasize lightness or depth, and underscore elements of theme, but frequently the forms have been invented for the poems, and seem like the essential music of the theme. Without this specific gravity, poetry loses a significant element of tone. The poems seem more undetachable from the poet, his or her voice easily recognizable but the range limited. Gioia works with or against a traditional form, or adapts one, or creates a new one, or writes in a modified free verse that nevertheless feels controlled by its thought. The work represents a range of organic poems from light to dark, with most of the notes in the deeper registers. His poems are richly allusive, peopled by figures from history, myth, literature—often humanity's more frightening real and imagined representatives. In form and content, the poems are various and unpredictable.

Therefore, although Gioia has been a spokesman for the New Formalist movement, he is not always an adherent to its principles or its subject, particularly as embodied in the *Formalist* journal. There are no prescriptions and he stays nowhere too long. In her essay "Against Ornamentation" in the 1998 collection *Viper Rum*, Mary Karr accuses the New Formalists of exalting trivial subject matter through rhyme and the postmodernists of obscurantism; there is some truth to both charges. But although Gioia may be a spokesman, even a defining one, for the New Formalists, he is limited by no one's rules, and his subjects range from pornography to jazz to mythology to the California countryside, while his forms include everything from sonnets to patterned free-verse tercets.

Gioia is a poet who from the beginning has shown this range of tones and moods, but it is still possible to trace directions in his work. His earliest pieces seem more separate, each poem more completely itself, than some of his later poems, which tend to be more complex and to overflow from one into the next, drawing them together in streams of thought and image. Wallace Stevens commented, "Thought tends to collect in pools," and this is more true of Gioia's later work. From the beginning, however, there is a sense of fatality, of the thin line between fortunate and ominous. In the later work the role of free will is explored and the questions involved in this issue tie the poems together. And then the romantic's heights and depths come into play—the possibility of good versus the knowledge of evil and the question of existential freedom.

Looking at his books in the order of their publication, one can trace the developing direction. The first book, *Daily Horoscope*, has heights and depths sometimes enclosed in rhyme, sometimes not. The title itself suggests one of its themes—the world is a jumble of meaning and meaninglessness. We find meanings and make them up, try to discover synchronicities, read the stars. The poems suggest that life holds obligations to do more than simply get through it making the best of things for oneself given the circumstances. There's a balance in these poems between the ordinary and the extreme. Everyday life, with its minor rewards and punishments, exists alongside another more fateful realm which bears an indecipherable relation to this one. Many of the scenes are ordinary at first and the actions apparently routine, but there is always another perspective, a glimpse at a wholeness of which these things are part. This makes the work comforting and ominous at once.

There is also the tension between daily and seasonal renewal and linear time, and between the day-world and the night-world, which seem reminiscent of Stevens's reality and imagination—and for Gioia like Stevens imagination derives its value from the way it cleaves to reality, not the way it departs from it. "In Cheever County" comments on the late novelist John Cheever's middle-class world and its values as it takes the reader on an uneventful and yet rich train trip home at dusk. It concludes:

> Here in the odd light of a rainy afternoon
> a ledger is balanced and put away,
> a houseguest knots his tie beside a bed,
> and a hermit thrush sings in the unsold lot
> next to the tracks the train comes hurtling down.
>
> Finally it's dark outside. Through the freight houses
> and oil tanks the train begins to slow
> approaching the station where rows of travel posters
> and empty benches wait along the platform.
> Outside a few cars idle in the sudden shower.
>
> And this at last is home, this ordinary town
> where the lights on the hill gleaming in the rain
> are the lights that children bathe by, and it is time
> to go home now—to drinks, to love, to supper,
> to the modest places which contain our lives. (*DH* 21)

Daily Horoscope is also full of shadows on the soul and on society. The poems play music in the dark—the music of their language and actual reverberations of musicians and their works. The music of the musicians infiltrates the music of words. It is as if Gioia is (again like Stevens) searching for a plastic art of words and music, to model or sculpt a work that immediately involves all the senses. No one accuses Gioia of postmodernism, exactly, yet he does share the postmodernist's desire to break down boundaries between disciplines and he like them is ready to apply the vocabulary of one art or system to another.

A powerful poem on an offbeat topic, "My Secret Life" is a response to what Gioia describes in a note as "an eleven-volume sexual autobiography published privately in 1888" by "a Victorian gentleman of private means" who "has never been identified" (*DH* [89]). It's about sex and sexuality, about the roles people play, about the unbridgeable otherness of the self. The dark side, the power we don't know how to control, but think we do, later becomes the vampire of Gioia's libretto *Nosferatu*. "My Secret Life" is a quiet poem beginning with an epigram. The obsessive sexual experience and recording of it by the autobiographer becomes a meditation on human compulsion and how the basest compulsions can be given mythic stature by those compelled by them—how the author or the book tries to convert the self-indulgent baseness of his experience, without success, to the gold of art. The poem speculates about the distorted, ingrown character of the wealthy experimenter who collected his sexual experiences into eleven volumes. "These memoirs are entirely pornographic, / an endless travelogue through a country / where no one wants to linger, where every church / and palace sounds identical" (*DH* 48). The reduction of a life to a series of sexual encounters is examined from all angles, the "scholar of seduction" finally summed up as "more antiquarian than lover," who wanted to keep his experiences in albums like stamps. The conversational poem opens up questions of value and meaning, of self-assessment and history's judgment, and suggests how love misdirected can poison the soul.

The first book is more stately, reflective, epigrammatic. The second book, *The Gods of Winter*, has some of Gioia's most chilling and yet cathartic work. Written mostly after the death of his baby son from sudden infant death syndrome, the poems present an effort to factor the unthinkable into a normal life. It works. What emerges from the reading is not rage at the unfairness of life, but a resigned acceptance of the world scheme with its loss and grief as counterbalance to its discovery and joy. The position is not comforting but it is honest. Attempts to explain away the horror of life do not work, and this is a major strength of these poems—their refusal to compromise, to settle for facile consolations.

"Planting a Sequoia" assumes personal grief into family and cultural myth as the father plants the sapling in commemoration of the dead son. The poem takes the Italian tradition of planting a tree for each child, and describes what it means to plant the tree in the case where the child did not live—a poem both desperately sad and yet healing, as it reaffirms the meaning of the family and its continuity.

> We will give you what we can—our labor and our soil,
> Water drawn from the earth when the skies fail,
> Nights scented with the ocean fog, days softened by the circuit
> of bees.
> We plant you in the corner of the grove, bathed in western light,
> A slender shoot against the sunset. (*GW* 10)

The sequoia will be there to witness the love that produced the child, even when "our family is no more, all of his unborn brothers dead" (*GW* 10). Thus the ritual is a step toward healing by placing the birth and death within the family history, never to be erased, the tree marking the membership of the child in that family, despite death and time. What we do means something, Gioia's work says, here and elsewhere. Losses are recorded twice, in their happening and in our memorializing of them. The record or memorial places the event within the context of our lives and underscores the meaning of those lives. This poem illustrates the sacramental vision in and through the images of the family ritual and the broader implication that our acts have meaning, now and throughout time.

"Counting the Children" is a terrifying poem about the fragility and vulnerability of children; it has been choreographed and performed. The Easternization of Gioia's name into the "Mr. Choi" of the poem is playful, but the poem is not. Mr. Choi is an accountant sent to audit the estate of an old woman who died intestate, leaving hundreds of battered, broken dolls. The dolls come to haunt Mr. Choi who identifies himself in a dream as their inept protector, and who is tortured by anxiety over his own daughter. Choi goes through a sequence of metaphysical speculations which bring him only more anxiety—but the poem is intensely gripping and anxiety-producing itself, for these are everyone's speculations, and everyone's fears for their children. Mr. Choi's feelings of loss, failure, and accountability are the price paid for being a parent.

Nothing I did would ever fit together.
In my hands even 2 + 2 + 2
No longer equaled anything at all.

And then I saw my father there beside me.
He asked me why I couldn't find the sum.
He held my daughter crying in his arms.

My family stood behind him in a row,
Uncles and aunts, cousins I'd never seen.
My grandparents from China and their parents,

All of my family, living and dead,
A line that stretched as far as I could see.
Even the strangers called to me by name.

And now I saw I wasn't at my desk
But working on the coffin of my daughter,
And she would die unless I found the sum.

But I had lost too many of the numbers.
They tumbled to the floor and blazed on fire.
I saw the dolls then—screaming in the flames. (*GW* 15–16)

The poem reflects the reality that there is no solution for parental anxiety, but that there is immense tenderness in it—it is a humanizing force. Mr. Choi does not lose his daughter and she begins to grow up (and away). The poem is nevertheless frightening, because the vulnerability, the possibility of suddenly losing what we love most, is an inseparable part of the risk of loving—a risk we have to take if we are to be fully human.

Nosferatu, the libretto written by Gioia in response to the film by F. W. Murnau, is a work that cannot be sampled, but must be experienced as a whole, including the music. But it is an example of many of Gioia's concerns—the shadow, the power of the psyche, and the need to fuse words and music. The traditional narrative of the vampire is a fine vehicle to represent the darkness of the human soul and also to show that choice has consequences. Moreover, the vampire myth is a way of dealing with the uncontrollability of death and the fading power of other consoling myths. And the vampire story is a way of dealing with death, too—in it, death must be positive as compared with the in-between state between it and life—the condition of the vampire, who is forced by his uncontrollable appetites to destroy life and add to the legions of the undead. The vampire is the image of the tormented destroyer, and the implications about the uneasy balance between good and evil in human nature, and the relationship between destiny and free choice, are many. In the libretto Gioia moves far from the closed epigrammatic meditations and the wit and wordplay of *Daily Horoscope*—the words mingle with the music, and language and passion flow over the barriers of genre.

The next book, *Interrogation at Noon*, is a sampling of all Gioia's styles and directions. While the title suggests a self-assessment at middle life, the thing that seems to hold the poems together most strongly is the question: what does it mean to devote your life to being a poet, to writing and celebrating poetry? Gioia is a charismatic person with the ability to effect changes in whatever field. What did it mean to put this soul, this self into the service of an art that many believe to be dying or dead? And what does it mean to the rest of us to do the same? What is poetry, that we should so value it? "Words" and "Unsaid" begin to answer, but so does a perhaps less noticeable poem, "The Voyeur":

> She is the moonlight, sovereign and detached.
> He is a shadow flattened on the pavement,
> the one whom locks and windows keep away.
>
> But what he watches here is his own life.
> He is the missing man, the loyal husband,
> sitting in the room he craves to enter,
> surrounded by the flesh and furniture of home. (*IN* 4)

This is the poet, looking in at the secret side of life—his own life, trying to see it, craving to see it, to cross the frontier between self and other. The book provides other views of the poet, public and private, as it wrestles with the question that forms the title of Gioia's most well-known essay, "Can Poetry Matter?" And it engages the questions that lie beneath this one: Can there be poetry after Auschwitz? In such a troubled time, how can we justify spending our brief allotment of days writing or reading at all? If poetry is indeed to have weight and occupy space in these times, what should it be doing?

Gioia's work has a compelling dark side. But what makes literature "dark"—and what does darkness run counter to—light? Nihilism is dark, but this poetry isn't nihilistic, nor is it unforgiving. Some of the poems are shadowy, containing ominous figures. Some are peopled by Gothic horrors. Some are not optimistic about human nature or about the immediate outcome of situations or events. They may be sardonic or may reach through surface brightness to an unyielding darkness that seems to lie at the heart of things, as in Joseph Conrad's story. They are often uneasy and resistant to conclusion or solution. The admixture of religious elements or considerations does not lighten the experience of the poetry or of the world. It does, though, suggest other perspectives which make the experience of darkness meaningful.

Reared a Catholic, Gioia has the sacramental imagination that distinguishes Catholic writing not only from secular but from other Christian poetry; he is steeped in the work of Flannery O'Connor and Graham Greene, neither of whom makes for comfortable reading. Perhaps Greene is more upbeat than O'Connor because he focuses on the strangeness and unpredictability of grace and the notion that salvation is not doled out by that human and fallible institution, the Church, but according to the impenetrable will of God. O'Connor's version is more frightening. Her morality tales suggest that human nature is irremediable and suggest that the path to damnation is almost inevitable. In Greene's work we are struck with wonder that someone with sins and weakness might achieve salvation; in O'Connor's we are struck with horror that someone with some moral good in them might be damned. Gioia's vision to the extent that it too is Catholic seems to have elements of both but is perhaps closer to that of Greene. And as in Greene, the hells and heavens are closely bound to this world. Metaphysical considerations are underneath; the meaning of individual choices, the importance of the seemingly unimportant, are in the forefront. The sacramental vision focuses on physical signs of spiritual presence—traditional ones sometimes, such as suggestions of baptism, marriage, burial of the dead, and so forth. But more deeply, this way of seeing contemplates the particulars of the world as possible signs of God's presence. There are connections between time and timeless in places, actions, people. Gioia's work often takes this perspective, implicitly and explicitly, and chooses to translate poets with whom he shares these conclusions, such as Rainer Maria Rilke and the Italian poet Valerio Magrelli. In the fourth segment of "Homage to Valerio Magrelli," a free translation of Magrelli's work, the poet refers to the soul-making quality of tears:

> Especially in weeping
> the soul reveals
> its presence
> and through secret pressure
> changes sorrow into water.
> The first budding of the spirit
> is in the tear,
> a slow and transparent word.
> Then following this elemental alchemy
> thought turns itself into substance
> as real as a stone or an arm.
> And there is nothing uneasy in the liquid
> except the mineral
> anguish of matter. (*IN* 57)

Gioia's faith as glimpsed in these poems is a questioning Catholicism, querying both itself and the world. But the poems clearly communicate the sense that there are interconnections between this present world and another—crossing points, transactions. These may be physical places and things, and subject to some extent to the will of the seeker. He reads the rocks and trees, but with the sense that every action has consequences and even to look at something is an action. For Gioia as for Greene the sacraments are real, true connections between the transitory and the eternal, but their meanings are not always predictable or apparent. Both the mystery and the portent are expressed in his pantoum "Divination," which concludes:

> Is it an old friend you do not recognize?
> Notice the cool appraisal of his eyes.
> Who is the stranger standing at the door?
> You sometimes wonder what you're waiting for.
>
> Notice the cool appraisal of his eyes.
> Better clean house to make the right impression.
> You sometimes wonder what you're waiting for.
> Always be ready for the unexpected. (*IN* 7)

Gioia is a poet of romance, mystery, and metaphysical homes. Americanist critic Albert Gelpi presents an insightful analysis of the relationship between Romanticism and modernism, showing how modernism was a reaction to romanticism and how subsequently post-modernism branched off into the works of the language poets and other postmodern trends.[1] As a reaction to postmodernism, Gelpi described another direction developing:

> Romantic epistemology, psychology, and aesthetics proposed an intrinsic, organic triad of correspondence or continuity between the perceiving subject, the perceived world, and the medium of expression in the subtending activity of Spirit. The most influential theoretician of the Romantic Imagination in England was of course Coleridge, and in America Emerson; its most influential exemplars were Wordsworth and Whitman. But visionary insight is difficult to attain, much less to maintain, and Romanticism put such stress on the individual's momentary experience that the Romantic synthesis of subject and object through the agency of the Imagination began to deconstruct almost as soon as it was ventured.[2]

---

[1] Albert Gelpi, "The Genealogy of Postmodernism: Contemporary American Poetry," *Southern Review* (Summer 1990): 517–41.

[2] Ibid.

This kind of deconstruction is present in contemporary literature as well; the Romantic is still a vital force in literature, and its visions remain hard to achieve and harder still to maintain: "The literature of the nineteenth century records the interplay between Romantic ecstasy and, increasingly, Romantic irony, from Blake's visions and Wordsworth's early nature mysticism to the decadence of the Romantic ideology at the *fin de siècle* in art for art's sake."[3]

Gelpi appears to value what many postmodernists would screen out of their work—passion, emotion, connection. The hunger for the transcendent. He continues:

> I recognize these issues as central to our poetry and culture since World War II. At the same time, in pondering recent answers to Frost's query to twentieth century poets—"what to make of a diminished thing"—I also find a countertendency that I would call Neoromantic in the work of poets like Roethke, Lowell, Berryman, Olson, Duncan, Everson, Levertov, Rich, Berry, Snyder. And, from the generation of the language poets, Fanny Howe and Susan Howe. Neoromanticism has to be a roomy rubric to admit the mystical Roethke and the skeptical Lowell, Rich the radical feminist and Everson the Dionysian Catholic, Duncan the occultist and Berry the agrarian. However, through their differences all these poets express a passionate desire to press limits and extend possibilities, an insistence that language penetrate rather than maintain surfaces, a compulsion to fathom the mystery linking subject and object, person and person, word and thing in a constructive act of signification.... The poets I am designating Neoromantic all believe, even in the face of the violence of contemporary history, that the word can effect personal and social change, that poetry can, almost against the odds, make things happen—psychologically, morally, politically, religiously.[4]

[3] Ibid.
[4] Ibid.

I believe that Gioia would echo the last line of Gelpi's insightful analysis. Dana Gioia's poetry is Neoromantic and Christian. It is a melding of music and meaning that provides a whole range of effects, from the playfully comic to the epigrammatic to the sardonic and the elegiac; Gioia uses music as the Romantics did, to complement theme and image. Gioia's work is, moreover, a poetry of story, exploring the big stories as well as stories by marginal people, real or invented onlookers of history.

Poetry traditionally dealt with the big myth, and modernist poets undertook the search and redefinition of the big myth. Postmodernist poems tend to be anti-mythological or to be based on pagan myth which is then itself demystified. Gioia's work is more modernist in the sense that it too is in search of the story of stories, but is very cognizant of the difficulty in this quest—in a flat surface, where everything is only itself, it asks: where can we find the power that went with the old mythologies when they were believed in? Anything too simple cannot fit the complexities of the world, and anything that can be stated is too simple. It may be this conundrum that creates the sense of ominousness in some of Gioia's work. There are myths—but they are dark myths. We believe in 9/11, but hope often seems vague and indefinable. And the romantic believes in the dark myths, there at the edge of his mind where the realization of infinite possibility meets the possibility of total despair. Gioia has the romantic attribute of attempting to discover the big story, the one that is under or the source of all the grand narratives which must hold for a while, then change or expire.

Wit and irony, self-assessment, dark expansive explorations, idealism that is based on the practical, cultural criticism, probing the walls for solidity, searching for what is possible—these are the activities of Dana Gioia's poems. The bedrock of Catholicism is glimpsed sometimes within, sometimes just beyond their margins. Their sacramental vision and their insistence on the accountability of art are rooted in their religious faith. They ask what the role of art is and could be in such an uneasy and unreliable world. Their answers are further questions, but questions redefined by meditation, prayer, and hope.

10

ON DANA GIOIA (2001)

William Oxley

I

Dana Gioia is probably the most interesting poet to have emerged in the United States since the 1980s. He clearly thinks about the craft and role of the poet, and because he thinks critically, he has become a highly controversial figure. He writes about poetry and his fellow poets with both sympathy and clarity. Nonetheless, American letters—especially poetry—is heavily academic, wedded to the theory of free verse, and populated largely by professionals in higher education, and Gioia—who comes from the world of commerce and who, like Poe, believes strongly in formal metrics—has been forced into the role of outsider.

In his poetry Gioia often reminds me of the Italian painter Giorgio de Chirico—the melancholia of frozen seasons, the chiaroscuro framed, and the metaphysicality:

> The architecture of each station still preserves
> its fantasy beside the sordid tracks—
> defiant pergolas, a shuttered summer lodge,
> a shadowy pavilion framed by high-arched windows
> in this land of northern sun and lingering winter. (*DH* 19)

Is it deep-seated memory of Gioia's distant Italian background coming through—a touch of baroque on modern American functionalism? I don't know. But "In Cheever Country," which begins "Half an hour north of Grand Central" and from which these lines are taken, is a marvelous poem that exactly captures that feel the city worker experiences commuting home by train "to the modest places which contain our lives."

Donald Justice describes Gioia's poetry as being "work—in which dream and reality keep intersecting most beautifully," and, as Eliot would have said, "that's a way of putting it." But there is more to be said than that, for Gioia is no mere dreamy fantasy but rather a true poet of the imagination. He is one who operates not through strained metaphors of the fancy but by focusing on real particulars, and he knows it:

> Look for smaller signs instead, the fine
> disturbances of ordered things when suddenly
> the rhythms of your expectation break
> and in a moment's pause another world
> reveals itself behind the ordinary. (*DH* 29)

That is the heart of his art; its program is to make accessible transcendent reality through the commonplace. His poetry is calmly and unobtrusively measured, and where Pound endeavored to make poetry concrete, Gioia keeps it simple—hence his accessibility. If I may be forgiven a pun, he makes the subtle and the complex simply accessible, and this is because, in part, like Donne, thought is its own experience—*is* experience.

In Gioia's volume *Daily Horoscope* there are many poems whose ostensible settings are old ruins, museums, neglected mansions, chapels, and so forth, and at first one thinks, "Ah, another poet playing with the past… a poet with a strong historical sense!" But very quickly one perceives not merely the historical sense but also the religious or, more properly, the metaphysical sense at work and preponderant. True, "The bankrupt palace still remains / beyond the wall that summer builds, / doors bolted shut, the roof caved in" (*DH* 59), yet it is not merely a poetry to evoke spent or derelict feeling but rather one to question and, as it were, re-envision such dead places:

> wasn't this the purpose of our listening:
> to sit in the same place with our eyes open
> and know that we have moved? That finally
> we've woken up into the place from which
> we've always woken out of, that strange place

that's always changing, constantly drifting
between the visible and invisible,
that place that we must stumble onto, now
as an unkempt garden. (*DH* 61)

How marvelously he has grafted Rilke onto the tree of contemporary American poetry and regrafted the Eliot of "Little Gidding" back onto his American roots.

I would not wish to mislead and to misrepresent Gioia and his style as that of only a new metaphysical poet. There are a number of highly contemporary, self-expressive, even "social" poems scattered throughout his books as well. I am thinking of poems like "Cruising with the Beach Boys" or "Bix Beiderbecke." In the former the poet, "Travelling on business in a rented car," listens nostalgically to a pop record of the 1960s; in the latter the poet works through the persona of the jazz musician who died in 1931, creating a miniature life story in twenty-five lines and concluding with

He lit a cigarette and closed his eyes.
The best years of his life! The Boring 'Twenties.
He watched the morning break across the snow.
Would heaven be as white as Iowa? (*DH* 42)

Thus, Gioia also is a very contemporary poet, down to his marvelous particularity of detail: "Another sleepless night, / when every wrinkle in the bedsheet scratches / like a dry razor on a sunburned cheek" (*DH* 7). But it is contemporaneity not for its own sake but only as the grist of fact awaiting his unique poetic interpretation. Gioia knows, and in his poetry shows, as Robert Graves said, that "fact and truth are not the same thing"; truth is the conclusion drawn from fact. Gioia has a great eye for fact and a mind set on telling truth, which is to say that he has vision.

Gioia's poems, as I have suggested, are a consequence of thought—even thought about thought—not "the spontaneous overflow of powerful feelings" but rather "emotion recollected in tranquility." This is possibly why there is here and there a movement into narrative, for example, as in "The Journey, the Arrival and the Dream," from *Daily Horoscope*, or in the desperately sad and faintly unpleasant "Homecoming," from *The Gods of Winter*. Both poems are characteristic of the soliloquy, that is, imbued with memory. The reflective disposition, as with Philip Larkin, shows up in the perusing of old mementos, such as photographs that evoke the poet's past. I am thinking especially of "Photograph of My Mother as a Young Girl" and "The Sunday News," both of which reveal an obsession with the past, a subliminal wish to stop the passage of time and its consequences—"and watched, as I do / years later, / too distantly to interfere"—and, similarly, the desire to find a way of resisting loss through time—"A scrap I knew I wouldn't read again / But couldn't bear to lose" (*DH* 71, 77). In his own words it is the being of "an eternal witness trapped in time" (*DH* 79).

A personal tragedy, the death of an infant son, brought about a shift in Gioia's poetic impulse in his second volume, *The Gods of Winter*. In this collection there is a touch of anguish, a darkening of tone, an intensification of feeling, bringing his poetry closer to lyrical spontaneity as in the opening of the title poem:

> Storm on storm, snow on drifting snowfall,
> shifting its shape, flurrying in moonlight,
> bright and ubiquitous,
> profligate March squanders its wealth. (*GW* 9)

Gradually, however, after writing the strange, perhaps therapeutic poem "Counting the Children"—a poem motivated at bottom by the fear of sudden infant death syndrome, I would guess, but which also incorporates examination of questions of mortality and immortality—Gioia gets back into his more normal urbane stride. Measured reflection takes over again, leading from time to time to poems like "My Confessional Sestina," "Money," or "News from Nineteen Eighty-Four," all of which have something of the odor of the occasional poem about them. He has also moved into the field of translation, often a worrying sign in all but the most prolific of poets, for it can indicate a diminishing of original impulse and a conscious searching for themes.

Between Gioia's two principal volumes of poetry, however, there are a fair number of different themes, two more of which deserve mention. One that appears early in *Daily Horoscope* is that of the suppressed nature poet, which every poet is at heart: "suddenly I realize the obvious: / that even this parking lot / was once a field" (*DH* 11). It is a conflict that shades off into another theme—or variant thereof—in his later poem "Rough Country," a quiet paean to the wide-open spaces where the poet seeks "a sign that there is still / one piece of property that won't be owned" (*GW* 23). It is an interesting thought coming from a poet with a background in business and from a poet who has written one of the few respectable poems—albeit ironically toned—to money, beginning with an approving epigraph from Wallace Stevens—"Money is a kind of poetry" (*GW* 33).

Gioia is often panned for being in the vanguard of the so-called New Formalist movement. It is more true, however, to observe of his work, as Charles Causley wrote in a glowing blurb for the UK edition of *The Gods of Winter*: "These lucid, varied and beautifully-crafted poems are the work of one of the most accomplished and compelling poets to have emerged on either side of the Atlantic over the past decade."

II

In Dana Gioia's work spiritual generosity exists side by side with a melancholia (perhaps the melancholia of doubt, such as the Elizabethan poets began to suffer from with the retreat of the faith of the Middle Ages?). But it is an exquisite combination that makes him probably the most exquisite poet writing today in English. Couple this with an unerring sense of form covering the full spectrum from the most formal to freer verse, and one has elegance of writing too. When I use terms like "exquisite" and "elegance" of this poet I mean the very opposite of precious; rather I intend something much closer to the quality of Pater's "hard, gemlike flame," but without any euphuistic properties. There is nothing vulgar in this poet either, and there is no other poet today of whom I can so emphatically say that. It gives Gioia that rarest of all qualities—both in his prose and in his poetry—namely, *authority*.

If I had one wish today for poetry it would be that, in terms of language (not subject matter) it would escape the contemporary. By this

I mean that more poets would employ not just the present conversational or the high academic in their work, but all of that poetic language built up from Chaucer to Whitman, Milton to Auden—picking and choosing the best syntactical and verbal felicities—and employ it in their own ways. Dana Gioia does.

Gioia's authority derives from humility, perhaps a troubled humility, but humility all the same. And the real subtle truths, nay truth itself, will only reveal themselves/itself, as Hugh MacDiarmid—a far from humble man—once said, "through a proper attitude of humility." The opening poem of *Interrogations at Noon* sets the tone of humility by beginning in arrogance with the assertion, "The world does not need words"—a richly ironic statement coming from a poet! But look more closely at this poem, called simply "Words," and see how words do come gradually to matter:

> The world does not need words. It articulates itself
> in sunlight, leaves, and shadows. The stones on the path
> are no less real for lying uncatalogued and uncounted.
> The fluent leaves speak only the dialect of pure being.
> The kiss is still fully itself though no words were spoken.
>
> And one word transforms it into something less or other—

By subtlety of poetic argument and insight, words do count:

> Yet the stones seem less real to those who cannot
> name them, or read the mute syllables graven in silica.
> . . .
> To name is to know and remember.
>
> The sunlight needs no praise piercing the rainclouds,
> . . .
> The daylight needs no praise, and so we praise it always—
> greater than ourselves and all the airy words we summon. (*IN* 3)

I have quoted a good deal of this poem to illustrate the decline from the high but negative arrogance of the first line to the low but positive humility and truth of the final two lines. A truly marvelous poem.

It is the same with the title poem "Interrogations at Noon," with its almost savage self-deprecation of the "cool and insistent" voice "in my head," telling the poet, "It is the better man I might have been, / Who chronicles the life I've never led" (*IN* 5). This is poetry expressing not so much the sense of failure, as one leading to humility, which, in turn, leads to the wisdom of the fourth poem in this fine first section of the book: "Failure doesn't happen by itself. It takes time, / effort, and a certain undeniable gift. / Satisfaction comes from recognizing what you do best" (*IN* 6).

Finally, in the fifth poem of the first section, we have the reminder of why we need this proper attitude on the part of the poet, which MacDiarmid called "humility" and Keats "negative capability": "You sometimes wonder what you're waiting for. / Always be ready for the unexpected" (*IN* 7). Significantly, the poem is called "Divination."

Later in the book, in a wonderful poem of refined irony and humor called "The Archbishop," which is dedicated to "a famous critic" (one wonders whom?) the same point about the miraculous understanding, the poetry, which alone can flow from humility, is returned to yet again:

His Reverence is tired from preaching
To the halt, and the lame, and the blind.
Their spiritual needs are unsubtle,
Their notions of God unrefined.

The Lord washed the feet of His servants.
"The first shall be last," He advised.
The Archbishop's edition of Matthew
Has that troublesome passage revised. (*IN* 30)

Interrogations at Noon is a more varied volume than my remarks may have so far suggested. There is, for example, a longish poem called "Juno Plots Her Revenge," based on the opening speech of Seneca's

Hercules Furens which is excellently modernized, but without being clever-clever or mannered, as Christopher Logue's *Kings* tends to be at times.

Then there are more personal poems like "Corner Table" or "My Dead Lover," where understatement combines with elegance to give even the anecdotal that exquisite sense I referred to earlier. Sometimes Gioia's penchant for nostalgia cannot be properly overcome; sometimes it can be brilliantly "turned," for example, with the single word "concertize" in these lines from "The Lost Garden":

> If ever we see those gardens again,
> The summer will be gone—at least our summer.
> Some other mockingbird will concertize
> Among the mulberries, and other vines (*IN* 68)

Gioia is never costive for a poet who "is meticulously painstaking and self-critical about his own poems." Just occasionally, as in "Borrowed Tunes," his ear lets him down, and there are signs of overworking in some of the pieces. But it is rare in this otherwise fine book of poems which, as I say, is something of a relief to encounter in a world where the rough, the vulgar and, very often, the pointless, predominate. A world which has quite forgotten Ronald Tamplin's words, "Poetry is a type of alternative speech, not an imitation of everyday speech," or Thomas Gray's, "The language of the age is never the language of poetry."

I can take any amount of realism (or romanticism) or whatever in poetry; but I resist anything once it becomes a convention. But nothing is a convention in these poems, despite all the fuss and false-prejudice and mis-expectations which have been created by associating Dana Gioia's work with "New Formalism." His is simply good, beautifully crafted poetry, written from within the timeless tradition set up by the best English language poets of the past.

11

THE ACHIEVEMENT OF DANA GIOIA (2008)

Jack Foley

The title of "The Achievement of Dana Gioia" sounds a little as though Dana Gioia's "achievement" were over, finished. We usually deal with the "achievement" of dead writers such as Robert Frost or T. S. Eliot. Perhaps we should say instead, "The *Continuing* Achievement of Dana Gioia"; perhaps even—since he is still a young man—the possible *future* achievement of Dana Gioia.

Since childhood, Dana Gioia has been an achiever. "In my childhood milieu," he writes in his essay "Lonely Impulse of Delight"—the title is from Yeats's "An Irish Airman Foresees His Death"—

> reading was associated with self-improvement. I suppose this uplifting motive played some role in my intellectual pursuits, but my insatiable appetite for books came mostly from curiosity and pleasure. I liked to read. I liked to study and investigate subjects that interested me.... My interests changed and developed year by year.[1]

He describes himself lying in bed and reading while his brother slept:

> Once we were in bed, [my parents] never forced us to turn off the lights—one of their countless kindnesses. Consequently, every night I read in bed, often for hours. When I remember my childhood reading, I see myself in Sears and Roebuck pajamas propped up under the covers devouring *The Circus of Dr. Lao*, *The Time Machine* or *The Lost World* while my younger brother Ted sleeps in the twin bed beside me. I usually kept the next book I planned to read on my nightstand—not so

---

[1] Dana Gioia, "Lonely Impulse of Delight: One Reader's Childhood," *Southern Review* 41/1 (Winter 2005): 49.

> much as an incentive to finish my current selection but simply to provide anticipatory pleasure.[2]

One thinks of him, not only as a child but as an adult, as continually *awake*, at the service of a consciousness (embodied initially in books) which is always prodding him to one more thought, one more new idea. "Even as a young boy," he writes, "I had trouble falling asleep."

Dana Gioia is the only member of the Bush administration consistently to receive good press—even ecstatic press—and that in itself is no mean achievement. His enormous energy and his boundless sense of creative possibility—his sense of *play*—matched with his good sense, his practicality, have made him a magnificent chair of the National Endowment for the Arts. We all know this and are grateful. That too is an achievement. It is also of some importance that, though he is no priest, a public intellectual of Gioia's stature is speaking to a predominantly Protestant country from the point of view of Catholicism—nor from the ordinary sense of Catholicism, perhaps, but from the point of view of Catholicism nonetheless. Hispanics, Italians, the Irish—all are predominantly Catholic people, and it is their voices that we can find echoed in his. Even further, he is a Westerner speaking to a country in which the principal sources of power—both cultural and political—tend to reside in the East: "I am a Latin," he writes in "On Being a California Poet,"

> without a drop of British blood in my veins, but English is my tongue. It belongs to me as much as to any member of the House of Lords. The classics of English—Shakespeare, Milton, Pope, and Keats—are my classics. The myths and images of its literature are native to my imagination. And yet this rich literary past often stands at one remove from the experiential reality of the West. Our seasons, climate, landscape, natural life, and history are alien to the world-views of both England and New England.... Spanish—not French—colors our regional accent. The world looks and feels different in California from the way it does in Massachusetts or Manchester—not

[2] Gioia, "Lonely Impulse of Delight," 48–49.

> only the natural landscape but also the urban one.... There is no use listening for a nightingale among the scrub oaks and chaparral....
>
> Our challenge is not only to find the right words to describe our experience but also to discover the right images, myths, and characters. We describe a reality that has never been fully captured in English. (*DI* 157, 158)

Gioia is also famous for his criticism, which is always articulate, provocative, intelligent, and passionately conceived. His essay—and then later the book—*Can Poetry Matter?* was a kind of trumpet blast of a new sensibility which had many important things to say and which—amazingly—was defending rhyme and meter in an intelligent, even compelling way. When recently I was putting together a collection of my essays, I discovered that almost all my best pieces referred to Gioia in some way. I didn't always agree with him, of course, but the effect he had on my thought was clearly far-reaching and profound. One could write a long essay on Gioia the critic. But, as is often the case with poet/critics, Gioia's criticism arises out of issues which inform his poetry. It is Dana Gioia the poet—the man of ideas who is also the man of emotions—that I wish to speak of today. Gioia's criticism is of considerable cultural importance—and it is beautifully written—but it is in poetry that his deepest achievement lies. In talking about his poetry, I will move perhaps overly freely in and around various of Dana Gioia's books.

I once remarked upon the number of times the word "dark" appears in Dana Gioia's poetry; it is almost omnipresent. One finds it for example in the concluding lines of "Insomnia": "The terrible clarity this moment brings, / the useless insight, the unbroken dark" (*DH* 18).

Elegy and loss are important themes in this poet's work, but have you noticed how often violence enters Gioia's poetry? His most recent book of poetry, *Interrogations at Noon*, has these lines via Seneca:

> Now, servants of the underworld, begin!
> Let my voice shake the deepest pit of hell
> And wake the Furies, daughters of the Night.

> Come to me, sisters, with your hair aflame,
> With savage claws. Inflict your punishments. (*IN* 47)

The concluding two stanzas of his brilliant poem, "Homecoming" from *The Gods of Winter*, are first, an ecstatic affirmation of violence—a giving in to it—and second, a disillusioned movement away from it. The word "dark" appears in the first stanza; the word "darkness" appears in the second. Interestingly, the first phrase of the first stanza, "I felt a sudden tremor of delight," comes close to Gioia's description of his childhood reading as "a lonely impulse of delight." (The books read by the protagonist of "Homecoming" as a young man are essentially the same books Gioia read as a young man.)

"Homecoming" is a dramatic monologue spoken by a man who has just escaped from prison; at the conclusion of the poem, the man murders his foster mother. His reaction to the murder is,

> I felt a sudden tremor of delight,
> a happiness that went beyond my body
> as if the walls around me had collapsed,
> and a small dark room where I had been confined
> had been amazingly transformed by light.
> Radiant and invincible, I knew
> I was the source of energy, and all
> the jails and sheriffs could not hold me back.
> I had been strong enough. And I was free.
>
> But as I stood there gloating, gradually
> the darkness and the walls closed in again.
> Sensing the power melting from my arms,
> I realized the energy I felt
> was just adrenaline—the phoney high
> that violence unleashes in your blood.
> I saw her body lying on the floor
> and knew that we would always be together.
> All I could do was wait for the police.
> I had come home, and there was no escape. (*GW* 51–52)

The second stanza, beginning "But as I stood there gloating," is a point-by-point refutation of the first stanza. If "I was free" in the first stanza, in the second "there was no escape." If "I was the source of energy"' in the first stanza, in the second stanza "the energy I felt / was just adrenaline—the phoney high / that violence unleashes in your blood."

Gioia clearly wishes us to feel that the protagonist's experience of "radiance" and "invincibility" is a false form of true mystical experience: that it "was just adrenaline." Yet, don't the lines as we initially experience them feel like a genuine evocation of a mystical state? True, it is violence which causes this feeling of radiance and invincibility, but isn't there something about that passage which is utterly convincing? Aren't all mystical states temporary? Doesn't even the highest of mystical states involve a rush of "adrenaline"? Gioia writes in "Lonely Impulse of Delight" that he "found spiritual sustenance ... in *The Lives of the Saints*, especially in its vivid accounts of legendary hermits and martyrs."[3]

What is the theme of violence doing in the consciousness of this most gentle of men, whom I have never once heard raise his voice in anger? Freudian notions of "repression" and the violence with which repressed contents sometimes announce themselves are of course relevant here. Like Freud, Gioia understands the mind to be a deeply divided entity. "I like writing poems that have a surface which executes one shape and a sub-text which executes another," he writes in the *Irish Review*.[4] From this point of view, the "I" who says "I was free" represents deep-seated desires which the protagonist has suppressed and which are "let out"—freed—in a cathartic moment; this "I" is "Mister Hyde." But there is more to it than that. That we live in a violent nation and in an extremely violent historical period will come as no surprise to anyone in this audience, and in part the violence of Gioia's poems is an expression of this greater societal violence. (As a child, Gioia says, he lived in a "violent" neighborhood.)

I would suggest that the violence we encounter in Gioia's poetry

---

[3] Ibid., 46.

[4] Isabelle Cartwright, "Dana Gioia Interviewed: Killybegs, County Donegal, 3rd May 1994." *Irish Review* 16 (Autumn/Winter 1994): 113.

goes beyond Freudian or sociological categories. *It is the violence of thought itself.* Imagination, feelings of radiance and invincibility, announce themselves to Gioia in a profoundly disturbing, alienating way. They thrust him *out*, away from community, into what he calls in "Lonely Impulse of Delight" "odd behavior," "secrecy," "the pattern of a double life," into behavior which is—as he writes—"clearly excessive, indeed almost shameful": "Not able to control this passion," he says, "I needed to hide it."[5] This is his poem, "The Country Wife"—the title perhaps echoes Frost's "The Hill Wife"—from *Daily Horoscope*. Each stanza of the poem is a triolet:

> She makes her way through the dark trees
> Down to the lake to be alone.
> Following their voices on the breeze,
> She makes her way. Through the dark trees
> The distant stars are all she sees.
> They cannot light the way she's gone.
> She makes her way through the dark trees
> Down to the lake to be alone.
>
> The night reflected on the lake,
> The fire of stars changed into water.
> She cannot see the winds that break
> The night reflected on the lake
> But knows they motion for her sake.
> These are the choices they have brought her:
> The night reflected on the lake,
> The fire of stars changed into water. (*DH* 78)

In the famous crossing-the-Alps passage of Wordsworth's *Prelude* (Book VI), imagination is first seen as a negative force:

> Imagination—here the Power so called
> Through sad incompetence of human speech,

---

[5] Gioia, "Lonely Impulse of Delight," 49.

> That awful Power rose from the mind's abyss
> Like an unfathered vapour that enwraps,
> At once, some lonely traveler. I was lost

But the force's "strength / Of usurpation" transforms itself into sheer vision:

> the light of sense
> Goes out, but with a flash that has revealed
> The invisible world ...
> ...
> Our destiny, our being's heart and home,
> Is with infinitude, and only there

The great "achievement" of Dana Gioia's early life must have been the tempering of this impulse, the discovery of ways in which this ambiguous, violent, sleep-preventing wildness of consciousness could be used to good purpose, "the fire of stars changed into water." As "Homecoming" demonstrates, "energy" is a violence which may result in the most appalling events. Yet, as Blake says—and as Gioia's poetry often demonstrates—energy is also eternal delight. Words are a place in which this violence—this power of imagination—can find a home, yet, as Gioia writes in *Interrogations at Noon*, "So much of what we live goes on inside," "The world does not need words" (*IN* 69; 3). Form is a tempering device, and if Gioia is a formalist, he is a formalist whose stanzas burst with a Romantic understanding of consciousness and the poet's role. He opens *Interrogations at Noon* with a quotation from Flaubert: "Human speech is like a cracked kettle on which we beat crude rhythms for bears to dance to, while we long to make music that will melt the stars."

One of the great tenets of American Puritanism is the notion that choosing is an unqualified good: it is what affirms us as human. (The great poem of Puritanism, Milton's *Paradise Lost*, is all about a *wrong choice*.) Dana Gioia's work is alive with choices which are not quite made—or, if made, made in the context of elegy rather than triumph, so that the thing chosen against retains some power. His work is a way of giving "local habitation and a name" to forces which exist in pure darkness and which simultaneously energize and threaten; indeed, the poet's task is precisely to retain the energy and to diminish the threat.

In Gioia's work there is always a secret world which intrudes itself upon the daylight world of ordinary consciousness. In "Lonely Impulse of Delight" he asserts that "every true reader has a secret life, which is… intense, complex, and important…. Our inner lives are as rich and real as our outer lives, even if they remain mostly unknowable to others."[6] And he writes in "Unsaid," the beautiful concluding poem of *Interrogations at Noon*, "What we conceal / Is always more than what we dare confide. / Think of the letters that we write our dead" (*IN* 69).

Dana Gioia's energies extend in an extraordinary number of directions, and his poetry often circles around the notion of rediscovery—even, at times, of resurrection. Yet the elegiac is always at work as well. One sometimes wonders why a man named Joy writes poems of such sadness. At the core of his work are not only themes of the Romantic Imagination or violence or "the contradictory impulses at the center of the human heart"; at the core of his work are what Virgil called "*lacrimae rerum*" ("the tears of things"). Gioia's Nosferatu is a villain, yes, but he is also the secret hero of the play. And like everything else—like us—he vanishes. It is Dana Gioia's achievement to tell us these things in a way which is profound, funny, compelling, and always—like violence—provocative. He gives us the "fire" not as it is in itself but as it is reflected in the deep water of a poet's consciousness.

[6] Ibid., 44.

12

DANA GIOIA'S DRAMATIC MONOLOGUES (2002; 2024)

Samuel Maio

Dana Gioia's poetry—collected in six volumes to date, representing four decades of sustained excellence from *Daily Horoscope* (1986) to *Meet Me at the Lighthouse* (2023)—is distinguished by its lyric grace and exceptional technical accomplishment. This is as it should be for the poet at the center of the formalist revival and the most famous spokesman for the New Formalism, which advocates for metrical forms and a return to populist poetic narratives such as the epic, the ballad, and the idyll. Gioia's well-known polemics and his singular achievements as a critic, translator, librettist, chairman of the National Endowment for the Arts and distinguished professor of poetry and public culture at the University of Southern California have made the literary arts, especially poetry, matter in our prosaic age. While Gioia has led his professional life as the rare man of letters, it is his own verse that centers all his work and will prove to be his considerable and lasting legacy. This is particularly true of his narrative poetry, expressly his memorable dramatic monologues, which must be regarded among his best and most important poems, and which move forward, in new and influential ways, one of the great poetic traditions.

In *Daily Horoscope*, Gioia began to explore the range of narrative methods and techniques that he would later broaden and amplify. Poems such as "The Man in the Open Doorway," "Speech from a Novella," "My Secret Life," and "The Room Upstairs" from that collection are all essentially lyric poems that move *halfway* into narrative. Each contains a "secret" narrative that is presented through a series of seamlessly interwoven lyric episodes. Gioia skillfully manages these episodes without losing the narrative thread of the poem. This is best exemplified by the poem "In Chandler Country," where the story line is not immediately discernible. Rather, it must be gleaned from the speaker's lyrical evocation of place and circumstance. The speaker of this dramatic monologue is Philip Marlowe, Raymond Chandler's famous private detective, who opens the poem with a number of general and seemingly directionless observations, however gracefully stated:

> California night. The Devil's wind,
> the Santa Ana, blows in from the east,
> raging through the canyon like a drunk
> screaming in a bar.
>   The air tastes like
> a stubbed-out cigarette. But why complain?
> The weather's fine as long as you don't breathe.
> Just lean back on the sweat-stained furniture,
> lights turned out, windows shut against the storm,
> and count your blessings.
>   Another sleepless night,
> when every wrinkle in the bedsheet scratches
> like a dry razor on a sunburned cheek,
> when even ten-year whiskey tastes like sand,
> and quiet women in the kitchen run
> their fingers on the edges of a knife
> and eye their husbands' necks. I wish them luck. (*DH* 7)

We learn from these lines a number of things about the speaker Marlowe, if not exactly where the narrative might be going. First, and most memorably, we are given highly effective and exact similes that portray Marlowe's state of mind. "The air tastes like / a stubbed-out cigarette," he remarks, and tells us that the bedsheet on this hellishly hot night "scratches / like a dry razor on a sunburned cheek." Given the poem's title—"In Chandler Country"—we are, of course, expecting the Los Angeles setting and perhaps even Marlowe's distinctive voice. After all, Chandler wrote his novels in the first person with Marlowe as the narrator. While we are not disappointed in these expectations, we are also delighted to encounter the poet's deft and lyric use of

Marlowe's idiom. Notice the clipped cadence of Marlowe's speech rhythms and his penchant for coarse similes, accurately descriptive. These are Marlowe's unique speech patterns and voice, dictional traits created by Chandler which have since become commonplace requisites—if rarely done well—of all fictional private detectives of the hard-boiled school. Gioia's tonal control and use of diction, syntax, and rhythm recreate the sound of Marlowe's voice exactly—yet Gioia goes beyond mere expert imitation. He puts in the mouth of Marlowe perfectly apposite similes and metaphors, something that the Marlowe of the Chandler novels had never shown himself capable of doing. In Gioia's poem, Marlowe chooses for his memorable similes such generic staples as "a drunk," a "razor," and "whiskey," but they are each used in fresh and insightful ways. In short, Gioia has crafted signal and salient similes out of the premises of cliché and used Marlowe—and, incongruously, his edgy, gruff manner of speaking—to give them voice.

Further, we learn from Marlowe's word choices something about why, other than the very hot Santa Ana winds, his night is restless—that his mood is gloomy, that he is troubled, and that he sees the aggravating night only through violent images. It is not until the penultimate stanza, however, that we can place Marlowe's mood and dark vision into a larger, narrative context:

> I remember
> the headlights of the cars parked on the beach,
> the narrow beams dissolving on the dark
> surface of the lake, voices arguing
> about the forms, the crackling radio,
> the sheeted body lying on the sand,
> the trawling net still damp beside it. No,
> she wasn't beautiful—but at that age
> when youth itself becomes a kind of beauty—
> "Taking good care of your clients, Marlowe?" (*DH* 7–8)

Here the dramatic situation, which has occasioned Marlowe's sleepless and haunted night, is abruptly brought into immediate, chilling focus. Earlier in the evening, the corpse of a young woman was dragged from the lake by the police. Marlowe assumes responsibility for her death, her care having been entrusted to him. The mordant gibe by an unknown speaker (probably a police officer, perhaps also of Chandler's invention) that replays in his mind—"Taking good care of your clients, Marlowe?"—bitingly reinforces Marlowe's guilt over his abject failure to take "good care" of the young victim, his now deceased client.

Yet the narrative line of "In Chandler Country" is only implicit and incomplete. The central drama of the piece—the young woman pulled from the lake—engenders more questions about the situation than the poem answers. Was the young woman murdered? If so, does Marlowe resolve the case, finding out why and bringing her killer(s) to justice? We cannot reasonably speculate, for the poem does not provide the necessary clues, unlike a Chandler mystery. The final stanza, rather than bringing closure to the implied narrative thread, ends the poem as it began—with a lyrical flourish depicting the dry and torrid Southern California night of ceaseless Santa Ana winds, the night so hot that it is like hell to Marlowe, made even more so by his deeply troubled conscience, and the nearby dogs "catching a scent":

> Relentlessly the wind blows on. Next door
> catching a scent, the dogs begin to howl.
> Lean, furious, raw-eyed from the storm,
> packs of coyotes come down from the hills
> where there is nothing left to hunt. (*DH* 8)

Even though the story line of "In Chandler Country" remains mysteriously oblique, one significant aesthetic trait of Gioia's narrative practice emerges in this early poem. He typically tells stories by portraying the psychology and personality of a single character in a specific setting. This central character is also the speaker of the poem, following in general the tenets of the dramatic monologue form. In relating personal experiences as well as his emotional and intellectual reactions to them, the speaker reveals through monologue his true nature and most intimate self. Any narrative arising from such portraiture seems a subtext to the principal context of the poem, which is a self-revealing character study of the speaker. As is true of any successful dramatic monologue, the speaker may be unaware of revealing his true self to us. By the end of the poem, we may know the speaker better than he knows himself—or better than he wants us to know him.

Yet as accomplished as "In Chandler Country" is, Gioia grew dissatisfied with this type of "secret" or hidden narrative poem, however lyrical and evocative he might make it. That kind of poem, with its lyricism elevated above its story line, proved to be a testing ground for the longer poems to come in his second collection. In *The Gods of Winter*, Gioia features two long narrative poems, each a prolonged and meditative character study: "Counting the Children" and "Homecoming." Each poem comprises one of the five sections of the book, thereby emphasizing the predominant emotional tones of melancholy, darkness, and grief which preside over the collection. The lyric sensibility seen in "In Chandler Country" is still very much evident in these two long poems, and the lyricism is integral to our understanding of the poems' speakers and, therefore, of the narratives they tell. But it is character development, as suggested by the speakers' reactions to key circumstances and predicaments, that is the prevailing structural method Gioia uses to organize and bind the poems. Unlike "In Chandler Country" where character development gives way to lyrical episodes—Marlowe, being a mythopoeic extension of a character already existing in literature, perhaps not in need of further development—both "Counting the Children" and "Homecoming" present speakers wholly of Gioia's imagining, so their distinctive mental and moral qualities must be explored in order for them to be engaging and the stories they tell convincing.

The 166-line "Counting the Children" is principally a character study of one Mr. Choi, presented to us through Choi's own eyes and mental processes as the speaker of the dramatic monologue. The poem recounts the psychological effects that Choi's professional duties have on himself and his family, specifically his personal challenges in trying to be a responsible and loving father. He is an accountant who has been "sent out by the State / To take an inventory of the house," as he explains in the opening of the poem: "When someone wealthy dies without a will, / The court sends me to audit the estate. / They know that strangers trust a man who listens" (*GW* 13).

Choi is a quiet man, and it is true that he is a good listener. He not only listens to the neighbor guiding him through the house of a wealthy woman who has just died, he also hears the various nuances emanating from the items to be inventoried. He is struck by one room in particular, a ghosted atmosphere, described by his guide as "hell":

> I walked into a room of wooden shelves
> Stretching from floor to ceiling, wall to wall,
> With smaller shelves arranged along the center.
>
> A crowd of faces looked up silently.
> Shoulder to shoulder, standing all in rows,
> Hundreds of dolls were lining every wall.
>
> Not a collection anyone would want—
> Just ordinary dolls salvaged from the trash
> With dozens of each kind all set together.
>
> Some battered, others missing arms and legs,
> Shelf after shelf of the same dusty stare
> As if despair could be assuaged by order.
>
> They looked like sisters huddling in the dark,
> Forgotten brides abandoned at the altar,
> Their veils turned yellow, dresses stiff and soiled.
>
> Rows of discarded little girls and babies—
> Some naked, others dressed for play—they wore
> Whatever lives their owners left them in. (*GW* 13–14)

Detailed, descriptive, reflective, and rhythmic, these stanzas represent a heightened lyricism, one made even more sonically pleasing by the lines' pentameter measure and iambic beat, the blank verse cadence matching Choi's natural and flowing rhythm of speech. With slight variances from a rigid, exacting meter at well-timed intervals in the monologue, Gioia carefully avoids Choi sounding like a metronome and, more pleasingly, renders his delivery more conversational and seemingly spontaneous than stilted and practiced. The lines and their resulting cadence are well controlled, each tercet stanza replete with internal assonance—"wall to wall" and "smaller," "dolls" and "wall," "want" and "dolls," "stare" and "despair" to mention just a few occurrences of such subtle rhyme. Here, then, we find an extension of Gioia's previous use of the lyric mode, "Counting the Children" being lyrical while structured along clear and compelling narrative lines. The tercet stanzaic pattern evokes Dante, as do the poem's general narrative frame and its atmospheric presentation of the story which opens in "hell." The narrative thread progresses as we are given privilege to Choi's rumination and visceral reactions to the shelves of dolls he encounters for the first time, and to which he ascribes animistic qualities, reactions that are both spiritually imaginative and self-revealing as is customary of a dramatic monologue.

Choi, like Gioia's Marlowe, draws interesting and illustrative similes, such as: "They looked like sisters huddling in the dark, / Forgotten brides abandoned at the altar," images of fright, betrayal, and forsakenness (*GW* 14). The overwhelming vision of the "hellish" room filled with dolls—each with "the same dusty stare / As if despair could be assuaged"—invites Choi to speculate:

> Where were the children who promised them love?
> The small, caressing hands, the lips which whispered
> Secrets in the dark? Once they were woken,
>
> Each by name. Now they have become each other—
> Anonymous except for injury,
> The beautiful and headless side by side.
>
> Was this where all lost childhoods go? These dim
> Abandoned rooms, these crude arrangements staged
> For settled dust and shadow, left to prove
>
> That all affection is outgrown, or show
> The uniformity of our desire?
> How dismal someone else's joy can be. (*GW* 14)

His reflections focus on parental and familial concerns. The dolls act as a collective specter of a once loving and joyous past, now a ghosted, broken, and dismal present, somehow casting a knowing and accusatory light on Choi. A father himself, he wonders if his love for his daughter will be similarly abandoned in time.

That night—the inventory of the estate acting as catalyst—Choi's dreams fuse his two preoccupations: his professional life as an accountant, and his personal life as a son, husband, and father. Upon waking, he admits to having had an obsessive fear of "crib death" befalling his only daughter:

> And I remembered when she was a baby,
> How often I would get up in the night
> And creep into that room to watch her sleep.
>
> I never told my wife how many times
> I came to check each night—or that I was
> Always afraid of what I might discover.
>
> I felt so helpless standing by her crib,
> Watching the quiet motions of her breath
> In the half-darkness of the faint night-light.
>
> How delicate this vessel in our care,
> This gentle soul we summoned to the world,
> A life we treasured but could not protect. (*GW* 16–17)

This last-quoted stanza correlates Choi's instinctual response to the dolls with his besetting doubts about his capacity as a father-protector. Through his own daughter, Choi sees all children, and beyond them, the dolls, reminding him once more of the desperation—whether in the form of debilitating self-doubt or of a living condemnation in the fragile world of dreams and broken children's toys—which prevails in his thoughts. The poem ends with Choi standing beside his daughter's bed glancing at her dolls, a few of which are poised exactly as the broken and abandoned ones were at the estate house:

I felt like holding them tight in my arms,
Promising I would never let them go,
But they would trust no promises of mine.

I feared that if I touched one, it would scream. (*GW* 19).

His desire to cling to his daughter, to her innocence and young life, offering her a lasting promise of comfort and trustworthy care, can be expressed only through his emotional reactions to the inanimate dolls—dolls made "real" simply in the minds of young girls. What Choi really wants—but sadly realizes he cannot have—is to retain forever his daughter's childhood purity and his own perfect love for her. Yet he fearfully knows that his daughter will grow independent of him and, correspondingly, his present, consummate love for her will alter with time.

A brilliant dissection of the most basic of all human feelings—parental love and its ensuing responsibilities—as well as a vivid evocation of both the emotional and psychological constitution of Choi's character, "Counting the Children" artfully blends sonically pleasing lyricism with narrative exposition in order to demonstrate many of Gioia's principal themes. *The Gods of Winter* opens darkly with graceful meditations on the loss by crib death of Gioia's first son. These elegiac poems, such as "Planting a Sequoia," are appropriately replete with images and thoughts of loss, grief, mourning, and remembrance. But in "Counting the Children," Gioia distances himself from this personally painful subject matter by having his created character—whose name is cleverly similar to the poet's own—reflect on the full emotional range of a father's love for his child, and to fear obsessively a crib death rather than tragically experience it. The poem, therefore, becomes more universal, probing the general fears, doubts, and guilt that accompany responsible and loving parenthood. "Counting the Children" stands as a complete projection, through the interior meditation of a single character, of a vision that recognizes the inseparability of human weaknesses and strengths, of love and its ephemeral nature, of innate goodness and darkness—what William Faulkner famously phrased "the problems of the human heart in conflict with itself," as revealed to us by Choi's introspection.

Nearly three times the length of "Counting the Children," the dramatic monologue "Homecoming" embodies the entire range of narrative techniques so far discussed. This 408-line poem is Gioia's longest original poem, and it also draws on the lyric form to frame its story line. The poem's aesthetic allows the speaker to reveal—in his own words and through his choice of images, metaphors, and the experiences he relates to us—his personal psychological profile. Further, the speaker recounts his private history, which neither Marlowe nor Choi do. Fundamentally, "Homecoming" is a character study of someone who chooses evil, an evil that manifests in certain environmental and social circumstances. The speaker, however, feels that he had no "choice" to make, that he was born with an inherently evil nature, a psychopathology that cannot be changed. The unnamed speaker chronicles in summary manner his life's path that led to murdering his foster mother for no apparent reason other than her having imposed moral boundaries on him. No one wanted him, his father having disappeared when he was three, his mother leaving a year later. He detested his foster mother's Christian teachings, believing that he was already foreordained to damnation. He tried to run away. He picked fights at school even though he was naturally bright and liked to read:

> My teachers always wondered why a kid
> as smart as me would lie so shamelessly
> or pick a fight for no apparent reason.
> She wondered, too,—as if intelligence
> was ever any guarantee of goodness. (*GW* 43)

He realized that "power was the only thing that mattered," and he repudiated any communal morality, becoming "born again," reinventing himself with those tenets of his personal code of conduct in mind, "not out of death, but into it" (*GW* 46). He was, in essence, "dead" to any acceptable and expected moral behavior, killing a neighbor's dog, then later a cat and other neighborhood pets. His new life began with these merciless killings. He was eventually imprisoned for robbery, escaping by murdering a guard. While in prison, his obsessive thoughts focused on his foster mother. She became the sole object of his anger and hatred, the representative of all societal rules to which he never could adhere. Once escaped, he made his way back to her—and killed her in the kitchen where she was preparing his supper, thereby destroying the only home he ever really knew.

This story, so fully narrated by the baleful speaker, is much more straight forwardly presented than are the narrative lines of either "In Chandler Country" or "Counting the Children." Gioia allows the speaker of "Homecoming" to tell the story of his life directly, unmediated by the lyrical episodes found in Marlowe's dramatic monologue or the introspective meditations found in Choi's, yet his measured language still rises far above the prosaic. The passage of time in "Homecoming" is condensed as well, covering a lifetime, whereas "In Chandler Country" spans but an evening and "Counting the Children," a single day (including night).

In his introduction to Robert McDowell's book-length narrative poem *The Diviners*, Gioia states that "the new narrative must tell a memorable story in language that constantly delivers a lyric *frisson*."[1] Gioia has made prominent the use of narrative poetry in our time in large part because of his special gift for telling original and compelling stories in verse that elevate to a unique *frisson*, or emotional resonance, we expect from the language of lyric poetry. Both "Counting the Children"—which is so inherently musical that it has been staged as a ballet—and "Homecoming," Gioia's consummate narrative piece, deliver such pleasures of memorability and sound in extremely effective ways. Such a masterful and inventive blending of the lyric and narrative modes led Gioia to extend further his artistry of narration. He has translated Seneca's verse tragedy *Hercules Furens*, and he has written an opera libretto for *Nosferatu*, which has been both published and produced on stage. Selections from those works appear in Gioia's third collection, *Interrogations at Noon*, as does the 165-line dramatic monologue "Juno Plots Her Revenge," adapted from Seneca.

---

[1] Dana Gioia, "Introduction," in *The Diviners,* by Robert McDowell (Calstock: Peterloo Poets, 1995), ix.

Having demonstrated in his first two poetry collections a mastery of dramatic monologues with clearly identifiable speakers such as Chandler's Philip Marlowe and his own fictional character Mr. Choi, Gioia in mid-career continued to use the framework of a speaker's interior monologue as the means of self-reflection and introspection with no implied interlocutor, but now the speaker is unnamed, personal identity being less important than the emphasized interiority. This type of poem on its surface may seem to be a lyric, a "personal" poem in the manner of a W. D. Snodgrass or Robert Lowell "confessional." Yet Gioia transcends the merely personal by centering the poem on the speaker's self-confrontation of his internal conflict or drama, thereby subtly extending the lyric mode into the dramatic monologue—or interior monologue—form.

The poem "Summer Storm" from *Interrogations at Noon* is one of Gioia's most memorable examples of such an interior monologue. Occasioned by a summer rainstorm, the middle-aged speaker suddenly remembers a long-ago chance encounter with a charming and beautiful woman, his rumination concluding with a mature and profound realization. This artfully deceptive poem comprised of rhyming ballad stanzas conceals until the midpoint that it recounts a memory of some years past, the reader assuming at the outset that the situation depicted—a brief conversation at a wedding reception—is set in the present and that the speaker is implicitly addressing his companion. Not all of the guests at the reception knew each other, as the opening stanza suggests:

We stood on the rented patio
While the party went on inside.
You knew the groom from college.
I was a friend of the bride. (*IN* 66)

The speaker and his alluring new acquaintance stand outside apart from the crowd, and, momentarily isolated together, they watch the sudden storm, the rain "like a waterfall / Of brilliant beaded light." Their shared witness to this refreshing natural splendor initiates an unspoken intimacy:

To my surprise, you took my arm—
A gesture you didn't explain—
And we spoke in whispers, as if we two
Might imitate the rain. (*IN* 66)

Then, just as quickly as the storm began, it receded and the incipient romantic bond between them was cut short. She returned inside, "Aloof and yet polite," the interlude now over as abruptly as the storm, their not speaking "another word / Except to say good-night."

Here, halfway through the poem, the speaker reveals that there is no interlocutor present, that the described episode was a fleeting encounter from decades past, the memory of which having been engendered by a sudden summer storm in the present, the rainy night putting him in a reflective mood:

Why does that evening's memory
Return with this night's storm—
A party twenty years ago,
Its disappointments warm? (*IN* 66-67)

The "Summer Storm" of the title refers to the actual rainstorms alluded to in the speaker's past and present, of course, as well as to the sudden "storm" of passion, the emotions he is now unexpectantly feeling. His self-interrogation, reflection in middle age, leads to his regarding "that evening's memory" less romantically and to articulating the wisdom learned from life experience rather than an idealized memory of it:

There are so many *might-have-beens*,
What-ifs that won't stay buried,
Other cities, other jobs,
Strangers we might have married.

And memory insists on pining
For places it never went,
As if life would be happier
Just by being different. (*IN* 67)

The speaker's self-inquiry leads to a tenuous resolution, an acceptance of *what is* rather than a yearning for an uncertain *what might-have-been*, a well-earned epiphany—such conclusionary understanding a prominent characteristic of an interior monologue—and lyrically expressed in more declaratory terms in the final stanza of "The Lost Garden," somewhat a companion piece to "Summer Storm" and the poem immediately following it in *Interrogations at Noon*:

> The trick is making memory a blessing,
> To learn by loss the cool subtraction of desire,
> Of wanting nothing more than what has been,
> To know the past forever lost, yet seeing
> Behind the wall a garden still in blossom. (*IN* 68)

Yet knowing "the past forever lost" can also make it present, evoking the spirits of the dead to return and comfort the living through memory. The poem "Tinsel, Frankincense, and Fir," a short interior monologue from *Meet Me at the Lighthouse*, Gioia's most recent collection, concludes with an astonishing epiphany both deeply private and universal, a truth revealed to the poem's elderly speaker on Christmas Eve (presumably) as he trims the family tree with his long-deceased mother's old and worn decorations. The tree trimming is seemingly not just a holiday tradition but a spiritual meditation, the "frankincense" in the title suggestive of a rite as it was used in religious ceremonies in ancient times. "Hanging old ornaments on a fresh cut tree"—the poem's opening line—is the speaker's way of including the ghost of his mother in the annual ritual:

> How carefully she hung each thread of tinsel,
> Or touched each dime-store bauble with delight.
> Blessed by the frankincense of fragrant fir,
> Nothing was too little to be loved. (*MML* 12)

When alive, his mother "had so little joy to share" aside from the box of ornaments she kept hidden away until "on the darkest winter nights—*voilá*— / She opened it resplendently to shine." Now, these "scratched and shabby" decorations, "each red glass bulb and tinfoil seraph," elicit the speaker's remembered shining joy of Christmases in his youth shared with his beloved mother, whose ghostly visitation on this Christmas blesses him with peace and a loving appreciation of the hardships and selfless sacrifices of his ancestors made in his behalf that he never can repay:

> Why do the dead insist on bringing gifts
> We can't reciprocate? We wrap her hopes
> Around the tree crowned with a fragile star.
> No holiday is holy without ghosts. (*MML* 12)

Another ghost, much less comforting but proving to be a savior, makes a frightening appearance in the 213-line dramatic monologue "Haunted," the central poem of *Pity the Beautiful*, Gioia's collection following *Interrogations at Noon*. The principal speaker of "Haunted" is an older man, a monk who is addressing a silent bartender to whom he is "delivering brandy from the monastery," declaring that he has little faith and does not believe in ghosts even though decades before he actually saw one. That encounter with a spirit is the essence of his narrative related:

> It happened almost forty years ago.
>
> *
>
> I was in love with Mara then, if love
> is the right word for that particular
> delusion.
>
> *
>
> Mara was brilliant, beautiful, refined.
> She'd walk into a room dressed for the evening,
> and I would lose a breath. She seemed to shine
> as movie stars shine, made only of light.
> And did I mention she was rich? And cruel?

> Do you know what it's like to be in love
> with someone bad? Not simply bad for you,
> but slightly evil? (*PB* 35)

Upon mature reflection, he states that he does not despise Mara for being the object of his obsessive desire, but rather he despises himself for having been delusional about her. One late autumn, they traveled to her uncle's vacated country manor in the Berkshires. Their first evening in the Gothic-style house, they enjoyed fine wine:

> That night we drank in the high paneled library,
> a great inferno blazing in the fireplace.
> Naked Diana stood in tapestry
> above us on the wall. Below her, Mara,
> stylishly overdressed, refilled our glasses. (*PB* 37)

A "connoisseur of *Schadenfreude*," she delights in emotionally manipulating him, sitting "half illumined by the fire / and half in shadow, spinning out long stories" of "her former lovers—imitating them, / cataloguing their signature stupidities, / and relishing their subsequent misfortunes. / (I'm surely in her repertory now.)" He is "embarrassed by her candor" and jealous, feeling "more like a confidant than lover" (*PB* 38).

They drunkenly quarrel, Mara "slamming doors theatrically" while he "went to the other wing to sleep." He resolves not to submit to her will and be first to make amends:

> Let her find me, I thought. Let her apologize.
> She won't like sleeping in this house alone.

Brooding in the cold room, "too annoyed / to fall asleep," he reads Shakespeare's sonnets, "each poem," he feels, "seemed written just for me," particularly lines that foreshadow the ghost's appearance: "*What is your substance, whereof are you made, / That millions of strange shadows on you tend?*" Then he sees the apparition, "a handsome woman in her early forties" who "seemed at once herself and her own reflection /

shimmering on the surface of clear water / where fleeting shadows twisted in the depths" (*PB* 39).

The salient drama of the poem is the speaker's internal conflict between what he is witnessing and what he intellectually accepts:

> I found it hard admitting what I saw.
> She seemed to be a ghost, though that sounds crazy.
> Oddly, I wasn't scared—just full of wonder,
> watching this thing I knew could not exist,
> this woman standing by her dressing table,
> translucent, insubstantial, but still there,
> and utterly oblivious of me.
> First to be haunted, then to be ignored! (*PB* 39-40)

His vanity wounded for the second time that evening, he fails to seize the opportunity to resolve his spiritual skepticism:

> Here I was face to face with a dead soul,
> some entity regathered from the dust,
> returned like Lazarus from the silent tomb,
> whose mere existence, right before my eyes,
> confounded my belief there could not be
> an afterlife. Think what this meeting represented—
> a skeptic witnessing the unexplained.
>
> I could have learned the secrets of the dead
> if there are any secrets, which I doubt. (*PB* 40)

Yet he says "nothing at all," asks no questions and learns no secrets of the afterlife but rather receives a chilling message instead, "almost in a hiss." The ghost says: "You don't belong here. No, you don't belong here." He thought she meant that he did not belong in her ghostly realm so, frightened, he ran—straight to Mara's room, where she was waiting for him, "naked under satin sheets," smirking.

> That night I held her, feeling our hearts beat—

> first hers, then mine—always out of sync,
> and in the dark I thought, *I don't belong here,*
> *I don't belong here.* (*PB* 41)

Now understanding the ghost's words as a whispered warning to free himself from Mara and her evil pleasure she takes in causing him emotional pain and psychological suffering, he leaves quickly, leaving behind "the clothes, the books, the camera," all things he believed he wanted from a wealthy life with her. "What a surprise to first feel / the liberations of divestiture," he thinks as he leaves the haunted manor with "new lightness down the stairs" and out the door, closing it quietly: "The lock clicked shut. Good-bye to both my ghosts" (*PB* 41). Both ghosts, the well-intended one haunting the Berkshires manor and the desired illusion of Mara, not the person in reality.

While the speaker confesses to the bartender that he still has doubt about the afterlife, he is nevertheless forever haunted by his experience with the ghost and the belief that her visitation ultimately led to his becoming a monk, "the life I didn't want to waste," for fifteen years now, freed from the bondage of Mara and earthly delights, a life of "Poverty, Chastity, and Growing Grapes," seeking answers to the spiritual questions he could not ask the ghost. However, the speaker does not realize that through his dramatic monologue he has tacitly admitted to having resolved his doubt. His believing that he was called to be a monk, and to the life he would have otherwise "wasted" but for spiritual intervention, is an acceptance of a metaphysical existence, an afterlife. As seen in the great dramatic monologues of the Old Testament, the speaker's self-conflict, his doubt and imperfect faith, compels his choosing between worldly goods—which Mara represents—and the promptings of the Holy Ghost, whose agent is the Berkshires manor ghost, toward the life he "didn't want to waste" by being of the world and not of the spirit. "Haunted" stands as Gioia's most visually arresting dramatic monologue—it has been stunningly staged as a dance opera—as well as his most memorable poem in that it suggests an affecting spiritual presence in our faithless age.

Gioia's poems, so startling original that they seem familiar on first reading, are as haunting as the ghosts and spirits he has composed, an image or theme returning to us like a sudden memory made new with striking insight into the complexities of experience. He has spent his lifetime in poetry carefully cultivating his prodigious talent and fine musical sensibility for language to achieve what so few before him have done: gift us with timeless poems, selective in subject matter, that resonate personally, emotionally, and comprehensively.

III

Later Career

Pity the Beautiful, *99 Poems*, and
Meet Me at the Lighthouse

13

NAMING AND TAMING THE TRUTH: DANA GIOIA'S TRANSFORMATIVE POETRY (2021)

Roxana Elena Doncu

Introduction: Not Form but Transformation

Our private and public lives are shaped by the truths we fight for, and we are constantly at war with those who misunderstand us. Knowledge is power, yet true knowledge is scarce and not easily discernible among the heaps of disposable errors. Science has developed procedures and protocols to ascertain the truth of facts, and logic has its own methods to check the truth of statements. Yet while scientific, logical truth is always predicated of a specific object, there is another kind of truth (sometimes capitalized as the Truth), which we find in religion, metaphysics, or esoteric knowledge—modes that emphasize the meaning of life—and we identify with. These two forms of truth—the universal truth of propositions, sentences, axioms, facts—and the fuzzier, individual Truth share a certain kind of efficiency: they are foundational values which enable us to proceed further.

For John Keats, the visionary moment that crowned his contemplation of the Grecian urn revealed that "Beauty is Truth, Truth Beauty," a conclusion that a modernist like T. S. Eliot found meaningless—and a "serious blemish on a beautiful poem"—strange perhaps, if we think of the modernist *topos* of epiphany, of those myriad aesthetic revelations experience afforded writers like James Joyce, W. B. Yeats, Katherine Mansfield, and Eliot himself. Yet Eliot's criticism of the final lines of Keats's poem is not ungrounded: beauty is often in the eye of the beholder, while truth and subjectivity are sworn enemies. Eliot remarked that either he had failed to understand Keats's meaning or the statement that "beauty is truth, truth beauty" was simply "untrue."[1] His observation was not, as we might be tempted to understand, some kind of gentle irony directed both at himself and Keats. This modern—and modernist—failure to understand sprang from the gap that separates the Romantic aspiration toward a unity of the metaphysical and the natural from the subject/object divide that plagues the modern soul. Keats's beauty was a sort of "true beauty," an ideal that served to erase distinctions between higher values; for Eliot, any idea of beauty was inherently subjective and particular, whereas truth remained an aspiration toward the universal.

My analysis of Dana Gioia's "poetic revelations" starts with this comparison between the Romantic and modernist artistic credo because Gioia's aesthetic positioning is the result of a dialectical movement from Romanticism to modernism and then to the new direction in American poetry (variously called New Formalism or Expansive Poetry) that he helped to define. Matthew Brennan contends that the key to understanding Gioia's aesthetics lies in his allegiance to New Formalism, which he goes on to define as "less an organized movement than a generational change in poetic sensibility," drawing together "poets dissatisfied with the entrenched tradition of the first-person lyric in free verse."[2] Gioia's article "Notes on the New Formalism" was instrumental in helping the new movement coalesce and gave it a definite orientation toward experimenting with traditional forms. To see how this apparently paradoxical injunction worked for Gioia, it is necessary to go back to the idea of Romantic and modernist poetry.

For most Romantics poetry, the highest exercise of the imagination, rested on the unity of the material and the spiritual, the subject and the object, beauty and truth inseparable from each other. For modernists like Eliot and Yeats, however, "the center cannot hold" (see "The Second Coming"): subjected to the centrifugal forces of modernity, poetry becomes as fragmentary and unstable as modern life. For those who still retain a religious feeling like Eliot, truth is hidden or

---

[1] T. S. Eliot, "Dante," *Selected Essays* (London: Faber, 1999), 270.

[2] Matthew Brennan, *The Colosseum Critical Introduction to Dana Gioia* (Steubenville, OH: Franciscan University Press, 2020), 15.

unspeakable, not a direct object of poetry, but that "absent" God that so terrifies Prufrock (the rock of scientific proof, not the rock of faith upon which Jesus had built his church), an impossible desire. The search for truth is replaced by the search for new gods, new modes of expression, new "objective correlatives" which can truthfully render the process of a dying order, of a world on the brink of extinction.

This desperate need for creation, for new and original modes of expression was perhaps unparalleled in the history of poetry, and it led to formal innovation as well as formal dissolution. Traditional poetic technique, meter, and rhyme were discarded in favor of free verse. Since this choice rested on more than a desire for artistic reform, being predicated on a revolutionary poetic spirit, it gave rise to what Octavio Paz called the "tradition of rupture."[3] The followers of modernism turned formal experimentation and innovation into a mandatory requirement of poetry—which arguably led to a fossilization of free verse. Thus, while the formal discontinuities of modernist poetry mirrored an age of rupture, turmoil, and dissolution, the requirement of constant innovation appeared ridiculous and unproductive to a number of contemporary American poets. Among them, Gioia is an outspoken critic of the negative consequences that such a demand spelled for poetry, in particular its imprisonment in academic circles and creative workshops and its marginalization in the wider framework of contemporary culture.

The legacy of modernism—"the free verse orthodoxy of an older generation of modernists like Ezra Pound and Williams Carlos Williams," as Robert McPhillips calls it—came under harsh scrutiny in Gioia's influential essay "Can Poetry Matter?," and was criticized for having transformed poetry from a popular oral art into an elitist written form, responsible for the current marginal status of poetry.[4] The focus on formal innovation, which had done away with rhyme and meter, structures that attested to the orality of poetry and made it a kind of concise art for the relaying of experience, had also turned poetry into

---

[3] Octavio Paz, "Poetry and Modernity. The Tanner Lectures on Human Values," Tanner Humanities Center, University of Utah, 18 October 1989, tannerlectures.utah.edu, 73.

[4] Robert McPhillips, *New Formalism: A Critical Introduction* (Cincinnati, OH: WordTech / Textos Books, 2005), 33.

an exercise reserved only to the few. Gioia, together with a generation of poets who later came to be subsumed under New Formalism, sought to change this by a counter-revolution which was mistakenly perceived, by some American critics and poets, as a restoration, a conservative return to traditional poetic techniques. After the initial enthusiastic reception of poetry books written by New Formalist poets, there was, according to McPhillips, "a critical backlash among many free-verse advocates."[5] The outrage at this revival of poetic form was stronger as the free verse had been perceived as the hallmark of American democracy. One reason why New Formalist poetry met with such—disproportionately—sharp criticism in an age when everybody can write what and how they desire may be the fact, duly noted by Gioia, that "The New Formalists put free verse poets in the ironic and unprepared position of being the status quo" (*CPM10* 29).

Political considerations apart, if one were to judge objectively, there was as much conservatism in the modernist poetic revolution as there is a revolutionary spirit in the New Formalist/Expansivist return to traditional forms. Modernist literature mirrored its age of technical inventions quite faithfully in its preoccupation with doing away with old forms and inventing new ones.[6] It was less inventive, however, in the mode and modality through which it related to reality, as its technical innovations were still tied to a mimetic conception of art, where the fragmentariness of form was supposed to be an "objective correlative" for the gaps and discontinuities of a worldview shaped by secularization, technologization, and two world wars. On the contrary, the revitalization of contemporary poetry that McPhillips identified as the main objective of New Formalism is envisaged not only as a return to traditional forms but also as a means of its achieving transformative power.

The impulse that lies at the heart of Gioia's poetry, in spite of its exquisite imagery (or artfully disguised underneath it), is not

---

[5] Ibid., 3.

[6] Trying to explain the emergence of non-metrical verse, Timothy Steele emphasizes the influence that scientific progress exerted on modern culture. See Timothy Steele, "Tradition and Revolution: The Modern Movement and Free Verse," *New Expansive Poetry*, ed. by R. S. Gwynn (Pasadena: Story Line Press, 1999), 47.

representational and mimetic, but imaginative and transformative. Poetry goes beyond expression and representation, acquiring a sort of power which acts on the individual psyche and transforms it. Rhyme, meter, and orality become essential for this type of poetry, because these are the features that enable it to have an effect, to move the audience. Since it is transformation and not representation that constitutes poetic desire, truth as the liminal space that creates the conditions for transformation becomes part of its aesthetic: here we can speak, once again, of a beauty that partakes of truth and of a truth that shines forth through beauty. Gioia's truth and beauty are far from the Romantic imagination; yet the fact that they work together shows how strange the ways of poetry are. In what follows I will show what kind of truth becomes necessary for poetry to achieve transformative power and how, in Gioia's poetry, beauty becomes the only way of accessing a higher truth.

The Necessary Truth

Gioia's first poem in his first published collection, *Daily Horoscope* (1986), is titled "The Burning Ladder." It is a modern parable that draws on the dialectic of gravity (*gravitas*, the earthly, embodied quality) and desire to show the insurmountable difficulties of surpassing our own frail human nature to reach for God. In the poem "Jacob / never climbed the ladder / burning in his dream," while "Sleep / pressed him like a stone / in the dust," preventing him from seeing the angels descending and ascending toward God (*DH* 3). Sleep and dust, two metaphors of death, point to the human limitations that endanger our path to perfection, conceived, in the biblical story of Jacob's ladder, as a gradual ascension. Sleeping through it all, "a stone / upon a stone pillar," Jacob is denied the vision of the angels "slowly disappearing / into the scattered light / between the stars," but not the capacity for sensing the sacred, as he is shivering in his dream—an allusion perhaps to one of Gioia's favorite figures of Christianity, the Danish philosopher Søren Kierkegaard (*DH* 3). Although the overt message of the poem is pessimistic—our human limitations prevent us from reaching God, the visual form of the poem (written in the shape of a five-rung ladder), as well as the enjambment of most lines, which gives an impression of continuity and coherence, resist this first interpretation: the ladder-shaped poem stays there, as a reminder that perfectibility takes time and requires second chances.

In "Sunday Night in Santa Rosa," the last poem in the collection, the post-carnival scenery contrasts both with the upside-down world of the carnival and with the ordinary life which is being resumed. Although Gioia's imagery is profoundly resonant with the carnivalesque, we are as far here from Mikhail Bakhtin as possible.[7] The carnival is revealed to be a world of props, appearances and false promises, a pageant of shining illusions, which collapses as soon as the spectacle is finished. Nature (the wind and the mice) takes over, revealing the misery beneath this made-up world. Gioia's carnival is devoid of any subversive artistic potential; it is the final gesture of the clown who "peels away his face" in front of a mirror which restores dignity to the human species, and not the freedom that the carnival is supposed to foster by the temporary suspension of all social hierarchies and rules, according to Bakhtin (*DH* 87). The "peeling away" of the clown's face, the removal of the mask, carries a double symbolic load and works on two levels: first, as this is the staple gesture of the actors at the end of the play, it signals that the spectacle is over and refers back, like in a circle, to the first line of the poem: "The carnival is over"; secondly, as this unmasking takes place in front of a mirror, the contrast between illusion and reality becomes reflected in one's self. Truth and illusion are thus internalized at the very core of identity. While other characters in the poem are defined by their masks (the Dog-Faced Boy who sneaks off to join the Serpent Lady for the night, the Dead Man who loads his coffin on a truck) and thus become inseparable from the roles they perform, the anonymous clown who stares in his dressing mirror and peels away his face stands for the emergence of self-reflection, awareness, and consciousness. The gesture of unmasking marks the moment of truth, and, for Gioia, truth is the precondition for developing self-reflection and consciousness.

The ladder and the mirror point to different ways of accessing the truth. As a symbol of ascension, the ladder shows the way to a higher

---

[7] Mikhail Bakhtin, *Problems of Dostoevsky's Poetics*, trans. Caryl Emerson (Minneapolis: University of Minnesota Press, 1963), 61–63.

Truth, a metaphysical or transcendent one, which tired Jacob misses in his dream. The burning ladder in the dream, the impossibility of desire, the gravity that pulls him down toward the earth work as signs for the limitations of human nature, which proves incapable of reaching a higher truth. Yet the tone of the poem is not despairing—as Robert Frost managed to define and settle the conflict between the two opposed pulls in the human being, one toward nature and its freedom and the other toward society with its burden of responsibility in the famous "Stopping by Woods on a Snowy Evening," in a similar way Gioia contrasts man's pull toward the duties and responsibilities of ordinary life with the metaphysical impulse.[8] One might even imagine Gioia's fictional Jacob as the fictional "I" of Frost's poem: the promises he had to keep and the miles he had to travel had exhausted and dulled his consciousness to such an extent that he did not manage to keep even that small grain of awareness which would have enabled him to climb the burning ladder in his dream.

The mirror, on the other hand, points to a different kind of truth, an insight that cannot be reached by degrees, like in ascension, but at once, by a gesture of unmasking. The mirror in itself is a neutral medium: it can show us either the mask we wear, or the true face we hide from the world. The act of unmasking before the mirror points to a desire for self-reflection in a human being, a desire that shapes consciousness. This is a truth that we are all capable of reaching, but only few have the courage to pursue it. Perhaps Gioia's attraction to Kierkegaard stems from this conviction, whose root is religious and Christian, that one's identity can be established only in the light of truth. In "Homage to Kierkegaard," by mixing quotes and facts from the life of the Danish philosopher, Gioia describes an exemplary life lived in the light of truth: it is a story of suffering and alienation, of an outcast who stands "*alone before God in fear and trembling*" (*99P* 24). In a sense, God is the mirror that the clown-philosopher looks into, and the trembling (Jacob's shivering in "The Burning Ladder") is the sign of the painful awareness of one's limitations. A life lived in this awareness contains

[8] Robert Frost, "Stopping by Woods on a Snowy Evening," *Selected Poems* (New York: Penguin, 1973), 130.

within it the promise of salvation, of perfection granted: "*Now with God's help I shall at last become myself*" (*99P* 24). The transformation of the human being which was refused to Jacob and only alluded to in the "peeling away" of the mask is fully granted to Kierkegaard, even if it happens post-mortem: the crippled Søren, whose hair "rose in waves six inches above his head," looks radiant in death, his skin becoming "almost transparent," almost revealing his soul (*99P* 23, 24).

The courage one needs in order to achieve this transformation is the courage it takes to see the world for what it is: "an uninhabitable place, temporary at best" ("The End," *DH* 51). Every day of our life feels like an apocalypse, to which, like the speaker in the poem "The End," we are dumb witnesses: "like a sleeper shaken from a dream / I witnessed what I could not understand" (*DH* 52). No wonder modern man looks for escape from such a harsh reality. In the six poems that make up the "Daily Horoscope" in the eponymous collection, Gioia plays both with the early Christian theme of reading the Book of Nature and the modern search for the miraculous, in a disenchanted world, in various divination practices. The titles of the poems ("Today Will Be," "Nothing Is Lost," "Do Not Expect," "Beware of Things in Duplicate," "The Stars Now Rearrange Themselves," "News Will Arrive from Far Away") build up an expectation of mystery, of wonderful things that will come true. Without exception, these expectations will be thwarted: the wonderful rhetoric of the title announces just another ordinary day, or a phone call from a distance that melts space and time into a nostalgic whole.

In "Nothing Is Lost," the principle of material accumulation is ironically converted into the law of spiritual loss, as a coin that circulates and returns to its owner is made to stand for the gradual dwindling of possibilities. "Beware of Things in Duplicate" plays with the idea of the evil double, which turns out to lie in a host of ordinary household stuff, harmless at first sight. Yet the listing at the beginning and at the end of the poem starts with ordinary objects like knives, cufflinks, keys, only to end, disturbingly, with "the eyes / of someone sitting next to you" and "your own reflection in the glass" (*DH* 28). It is in these ordinary things that the mystery lies, but we refuse to see it, just as we refuse to see ourselves as we truly are. Instead of looking at the stars, which "rearrange themselves above you / but to no effect," we should look "for smaller signs instead, the fine / disturbances of ordered things": they will reveal to us "another world ... behind the ordinary," if only we can accept and live with our broken expectations (*DH* 29). This is a difficult truth that each of us has to come to terms with, and Gioia teaches us this lesson with so much style and elegance that it is difficult to ignore it. Paradoxically, the experience of mystery does not come from reading and interpreting the Book of Nature—we misuse it by using it as a form of divination—but by confronting it as otherness. Since "nothing is hidden in the obvious / changes of the world," "the dim / reflection of the sun on tall, dry grass / is more than you will ever understand" (*DH* 27). Only by pressing "against / the surface of impenetrable things" can one partake of the true mystery of the world (*DH* 27). Gioia prefers this negative theology of Nature, since any attempt to understand it is doomed to fail. It is this awareness of the mysterious otherness of Nature that can shield us from the devastating effects of disenchantment, by preserving and revering the mystery inherent in the natural world.

Gioia's Poetry between Reality (Truth) and Imagination (Form)

The poetic worlds of the modernists are born of despair. The cultural reconstructions of Ezra Pound, the ghostly visitations in T. S. Eliot, the esoteric visions of Yeats relate and are responses to the sickness of a dying order. Their poetic worlds are havens, more or less safe, more or less comfortable, from the catastrophes of the real world. This large-scale orchestrated escape from the real world, together with the growing power of technology and the new media, gave rise to the postmodernist concept of simulacra, which had supposedly supplanted reality. Human beings no longer had to confront a rapidly shifting reality, as there was no reality to confront: we live in a world of simulacra that do not refer to any originals; they are not even bad copies of a worthy original, so that, like in Plato, we only have to become aware of the cave we live in.

Opposing the centrifugal forces of modernity, driven by a centripetal impulse, Gioia's poetry provides a refreshing sense of reality and groundedness, even if this reality is a difficult thing to grapple with, burdensome and oppressive. In a world of simulacra, truth makes no sense; in Gioia's world, it becomes a necessity. It is the counterpart of Wallace Stevens's necessary angel of the earth, the angel of reality, who announces "in my sight you see the earth again."[9] For Stevens, the pressure of the contemporary reality worked so intensely that the spirit needed imagination to counter it. However, he noted that "the imagination loses vitality as it ceases to adhere to what is real."[10] Though painfully conscious, like most modernists, of the disorientation that characterized his times, Stevens managed to overcome the modernist despair by placing his trust in the imagination, the Romantic concept that he reshaped to fit contemporary reality. Stevens's imagination has nothing of the prophetic quality or the transcendental impetus of the Romantic imagination; it exists only in relation with reality (in a "precise equilibrium"), which it ennobles. One might even say that imagination is the angel of reality, in so far as it abstracts from reality what is necessary for the psychic survival of the individual. However, it does so not in a mechanistic fashion, by selecting and arranging elements with a fixed purpose in mind. Following I. A. Richards's discussion of the difference between imagination and fancy outlined by Samuel Taylor Coleridge, Stevens remarks that the purpose imagination is working for when abstracting from reality is being created at the same time as the work itself. The work and its purpose are simultaneously created by imagination, whereas fancy does its work with an already fixed objective. It is interesting to note that Gioia shares with Stevens this view of the work and its purpose being simultaneously shaped: clearly stated in his *ars poetica* "The Next Poem," extended to comprise the creation of our own lives in "Curriculum Vitae": "We shape our lives / Although their forms / Are never what we meant" (*IN* 39). Creation as contingency shaped by the work of poetic imagination is also rendered in one of Gioia's translations of Valerio Magrelli as "a tailor / who is his own

[9] Wallace Stevens, "Angel Surrounded by Paysans," *The Collected Poems of Wallace Stevens* (New York: Knopf, 1971), 496.

[10] Wallace Stevens, *The Necessary Angel: Essays on Reality and the Imagination* (New York: Knopf, 1951), 6.

fabric" ("Homage to Valerio Magrelli," *IN* 60).

This may be the reason why, for Stevens, imagination and reality are so intimately bound together that a new era always gives rise to a new imagination: "It is one of the peculiarities of the imagination that it is always at the end of an era. What happens is that it is always attaching itself to a new reality and adhering to it. It is not that there is a new imagination, but that there is a new reality."[11] With its ability to make the remote near and the dead live with "an intensity beyond any experience of life," imagination is the domain of the poet, and the "measure of his power to abstract himself, and to withdraw with him into his abstraction the reality on which the lovers of truth insist."[12] A possible poet "must be able to abstract himself, and also to abstract reality, which he does by placing it in his imagination."[13] Stevens's definition of the poet and poetry is not far from esotericism: imagination appears as a kind of alchemical alembic which distills reality, the crucible of transmutation. It is far from Platonism and Neoplatonism, though, which he criticizes for adhering to the unreal: he uses the word *possible* and not *ideal* to define the poet, while the title of one of his poems alludes critically to Plato, echoing William Carlos Williams's poetic manifesto: "Not Ideas about the Thing but the Thing Itself."[14] Thus, although more attuned to reality than the majority of his fellow modernists, Stevens remains captive inside its atomistic, purely individual world; neither imagination nor reality partake of the substance of universals.

With Gioia, American poetry witnessed not only a return to form, but also a return to the universal, or at least to a passionate search for it. Stevens's necessary angel, which is quoted in the dedication of the

---

[11] Ibid., 22.

[12] Ibid., 23.

[13] Ibid.

[14] William Carlos Williams's poetic credo "no ideas but in things" as well as Stevens's anti-Platonic and anti-Kantian "Not Ideas about the Thing but the Thing Itself" are typical manifestations of the literary nominalism of modernists, which sought to abolish the Kantian distinction between *noumena* and *phenomena*. See William Carlos Williams, "The Delineaments of the Giants," *Paterson*, rev. ed. (New York: New Directions, 1995), 21.

volume *Pity the Beautiful*, becomes "The Angel with the Broken Wing," a wooden statue imprisoned in the "air-conditioned tomb" of a museum, whose incapacity to rise to its mission as a mediator between human suffering and divine mercy oscillates between the tragic and the merely pathetic:

> There are so many things I must tell God!
> The howling of the damned can't reach so high.
> But I stand like a dead thing nailed to a perch,
> A crippled saint against a painted sky. (*PB* 5)

It is obvious that for Gioia the necessary angel is no longer an imagination that abstracts from reality without in some way lifting it to God and transforming it. "The thing itself," untouched by emotion or dissociated from human life is meaningless and even threatening, yielding only a "useless insight"; in "Insomnia," the punishment for a life devoid of love and meaning is ending up subjected to the power of the naked things:

> Now you hear what the house has to say.
> Pipes clanking, water running in the dark,
> the mortgaged walls shifting in discomfort,
> and voices mounting in an endless drone
> of small complaints like the sounds of a family
> that year by year you've learned how to ignore.
>
> But now you must listen to the things you own,
> all that you've worked for these past years,
> the murmur of property, of things in disrepair,
> the moving parts about to come undone,
> and twisting in the sheets remember all
> the faces you could not bring yourself to love.
>
> How many voices have escaped you until now,
> the venting furnace, the floorboards underfoot,
> the steady accusations of the clock

> numbering the minutes no one will mark.
> The terrible clarity this moment brings,
> the useless insight, the unbroken dark. (*DH* 18)

By contrast, the unnamed character in "The Journey, the Arrival and the Dream," who finds herself re-living the last moments of an unnamed ghost, departs from a reality "more sinister than any clerk's revenge" to find herself in a strange house, surrounded by things so tinted and saturated by another life that they manage to trigger the dream, or the vision of herself as the other, dying woman:

> Emptying your pockets on the dresser, notice
> how carefully you put down all the useless keys
> and currency you've brought from home, so terrified
> of scratching the patina of the varnished wood
> that innocently reflects the lamp, your hand, the curtains,
> and the badly painted cherubs on the ceiling,
> who ignore you. Light a cigarette and watch
> the lazy smoke creep up and tickle them
> to no effect and realize you don't
> belong here in their world where everything
> is much too good for you, and though the angels
> will say nothing, they watch everything you do.
>
> III.
>
> But you are also in another room
> finishing a letter in a language
> you don't understand, your dark hair pulled
> back loosely in a bun, and the crucifix
> you bring everywhere set upon the desk
> like a photograph from home. (*DH* 64)

The things that had belonged to the dying woman, humanized by her touch and transfigured by her feelings and thoughts now make up a world of their own, whose presence is so strong that the young woman feels she does not belong among them. They are no longer simply "things themselves," but things that have acquired a history, and, having been so impregnated by human life, they manage to evoke it to foreigners in a kind of ghostly fashion. Thus, "the thing itself" has managed to transcend its "thingishness" and cross the boundary into human life.

Even more repulsive than "the thing itself" is for the poet the world of simulacra, of appearances that pander to consumerist desire. In "Shopping," an upscale shopping mall, one of the landmarks of consumer capitalism, is ironically compared to a temple. The speaker walks around the aisles like a modern prophet taking in the illusory attractions of the department store and invoking the gods of capitalism in a mock-religious tone:

> Redeem me, gods of the mall and marketplace.
> Mercury, protector of cell phones and fax machines,
> Venus, patroness of bath and bedroom chains,
> Tantalus, guardian of the food court.
> ...
> Because I would buy happiness if I could find it,
> Spend all that I possessed or could borrow.
> But what can I bring you from these sad emporia?
> Where in this splendid clutter
> Shall I discover the one true thing?
> ...
> There is no angel among the vending stalls and signage.
> (*PB* 10–11)

There is no necessary angel, not even an angel with a broken wing, in the world of simulacra, a world of superficial beauty ("splendid clutter"), but devoid of truth. As such, this world is irredeemable and its "Divinities of leather, gold, and porcelain" are powerless (*PB* 10). But where does Gioia find what he misses in the department store? We can find a clue in the word *clutter*: true beauty, that Platonic splendor of truth, can be apprehended only in the meaningful order of form. This aesthetic adherence to a notion of truth makes it impossible to call Gioia's poetry truly postmodern.

In his critical introduction to *The New Formalism*, McPhillips defines Gioia's poetry as "visionary realism": on the one hand, he argues, there is "a tantalizing sense of the imminence—yet frustratingly elusive sense of transcendence—of the quotidian," while on the other the poet, "like Stevens, is in quest of 'another world... / behind the ordinary.'"[15] The tension between the quotidian and the transcendental is at the heart of Gioia's poetry; and so is the paradox, as McPhillips calls it, stated in "Words," the opening poem of *Interrogations at Noon*, that "The world does not need words," "Yet the stones remain less real to those who cannot / name them, or read the mute syllables graven in silica" (*IN* 3). The world and the word are of different orders, but if the poet acknowledges the gap between the *noumena* and the *phenomena*, he does not do it with a sense of fatalist resignation in the face of reality. Gioia sees the paradox inherent in reality: devoid of the transcendental creative power of the word, the world makes no sense. He also sees the creative, redemptive potential of this paradox. While for Stevens the word belongs to the order of imagination or abstraction, for Gioia it comes from an order which lies outside experience. The word is the other of the world, a power that comes from the outside and endows it with meaning. This is why ordinary reality is so tantalizing in its immanence, so full of *gravitas*. Outside language, outside poetry, the world has no meaning ("is less real") for the human being. It is the thing itself which turns into an abstraction—and a menace.

The function of language and poetry (in short, of the word), which belong to a transcendental, magical order outside the realm of experience, is to transfigure reality or daily experience. Gioia is a magician of the quotidian as well as a sorcerer of words, in the tradition of Vladimir Nabokov: his fusion of the "heaviness" of reality and the "lightness" of the "airy words we summon" produces "poetry as enchantment." The tougher the reality, the more intense the enchantment: Gioia does not shrink from touching upon the most delicate or forbidden of subjects; he is, as McPhillips notes, a great poet of love, but also of death, of ghostly visitations and that eerie quality of in-betweenness, of liminal ontology that some of his characters experience while being visited by

[15] McPhillips, *New Formalism*, 43.

or becoming ghosts. The healing musical quality of his verse transfigures death, suffering, loss, imperfection, all the limitations of human nature. The dignity of man resides neither in ignoring them, nor in trying to overcome natural limits by artificial/technological means, but in accepting and transfiguring them.

One of Gioia's major themes is that of how we shape our identity and our lives. From a million possibilities, we choose one (often quite accidentally, without too much consideration, as it happens to the character in "The Road," who asks himself "Where was it he had meant to go, and with whom?"), and so all the others are forsaken. Oftentimes our choices are not free, but forced by circumstances, and then we ask ourselves "What would have been if ...?" In "Equations of the Light," the possibility of love is rendered through the extended metaphor of turning the corner into a "quiet, tree-lined street," prompted by "the strange / equations of the light" (*GW* 61). The magical quality of the light made the two unnamed characters believe that the "brief / conjunction of our separate lives was real," yet the moment which "lingered like a ghost, / a flicker in the air, smaller than a moth, / a curl of smoke flaring from a match," seems to be "haunting a world it could not touch or hear" (*GW* 61). The ghost, the moth, and the smoke suggest the impalpable quality of this possibility of love, which makes the speaker finally ask himself: "at the end what else could we have done / but turn the corner back into our life?" (*GW* 62).

The lure of the "what ifs" and "might-have-beens" is quite dangerous as it is an eternal temptation for human beings, whose "memory insists on pining / For places it never went, / As if life would be happier / Just by being different" ("Summer Storm," *IN* 67). This is Hegel's bad infinity, the endless proliferation of choices that can never be realized in one finite human life. The antidote to bad infinity is "making memory a blessing" and learning to be content with what one has ("wanting nothing more than what has been") ("The Lost Garden," *IN* 68). In "The Lost Garden," the nostalgic speaker, thinking of his lost youth and love, imagines what would have happened if "we had walked a different path one day" (*IN* 68). As the past cannot be changed, however, it is better "to learn by loss subtraction of desire," yet, at the same time, to be able to see "behind the wall a garden still in blossom" (*IN*

68). This delicate balancing of impossible desires, acceptance of loss and nostalgic indulgence (another thing that connects Gioia to Nabokov) is the best recipe for surviving and at the same time preserving our humanity.

The possibility of different choices implies the possibility of a different identity, as our choices determine who we are. Identity is not a given, but a process in which we all contribute our share, as the motto to the first part of *Pity the Beautiful*, from the *Proverbs and Songs* of Antonio Machado testifies: "*caminante, no hay camino / se hace camino al andar*," which Gioia translates as "traveler, there is no road, / the road is made by walking (*PB* 1). The worst mistake is not to make the wrong choice, but not to make any choice at all. The character in "The Road" misses out on his true identity, by not choosing to make a choice: "no one chose the way— / All seemed to drift by some collective will" (*PB* 9). In "Interrogations at Noon," the "I" of the speaker is reprimanded by his better self for failing to live up to his real potential:

> Just before noon I often hear a voice,
> Cool and insistent, whispering in my head.
> It is the better man I might have been,
> Who chronicles the life I've never led.
> ...
> "Who is the person you pretend to be?"
> He asks, "The failed saint, the simpering bore,
> The pale connoisseur of spent desire,
> The half-hearted hermit eyeing the door?
>
> "You cultivate confusion like a rose
> In watery lies too weak to be untrue,
> And play the minor figures in the pageant,
> Extravagant and empty, that is you." (*IN* 5)

The theme of the better self is a familiar one in Spanish literature, and Gioia's poem seems to resonate with Juan Ramón Jiménez's "*Yo no soy yo*," in which the Spanish author seemingly denies his identity in order to establish the existence of a shadow self.[16] Both Gioia's and Jiménez's poems deal not so much with a Freudian super-ego as with the possibility of difference within identity. The better self makes sense not as a self that is actually superior to the existing one, but as a possibility that leaves the question of identity open and by this "incompleteness," like in Jiménez: "*el que quedará en pie cuando yo muera*," denies the completeness/closure of life which is death.

The life-affirming quality of possibility is the subject of another hauntingly beautiful poem, "Majority," in which Gioia imagines the trajectory of his first son who had died in infancy. The poem is quoted in its entirety:

> Now you'd be three,
> I said to myself,
> seeing a child born
> the same summer as you.
>
> Now you'd be six,
> or seven, or ten.
> I watched you grow
> in foreign bodies.
>
> Leaping into a pool, all laughter,
> or frowning over a keyboard,
> but mostly just standing,
> taller each time.
>
> How splendid your most
> mundane action seemed
> in these joyful proxies.
> I often held back tears.

[16] Juan Ramón Jiménez, "Yo no soy yo," *Poemas del Alma*, www.poemas-del-alma.com/juan-ramon-jimenez-yo-no-soy-yo.htm.

Now you are twenty-one.
Finally, it makes sense
that you have moved away
into your own afterlife. (*PB* 68)

This interplay between memory and imagination, the power of memory to revive the past allied with the possibility-designing capacity of the imagination opens the door to art and freedom: the Nabokovian all-encompassing memory, triggered by nostalgia, acts as an archive to the ordering principle of the imagination, and the result is an art that sets free both its creator and itself.

Unlike Nabokov, who delighted in the creation of parallel worlds, Gioia only plays with the power of possibility in order to recreate lost chances and lost lives. His sense of the mystery being played out in human life is so great that the idea of embodiment or incarnation figures prominently in his poetry. While in religion incarnation refers to the mysterious and unbreakable unity of the human and the divine, for Gioia incarnation may refer either to the mysterious unity of poetic form and content, the embodiment of truth in beauty or the coming together of the universal and the particular within the boundaries of human life. Incarnation works as *perichoresis*, a theological concept that defines the mutual indwelling and the interpenetration of the human and the divine natures in Christ. The divine nature of Christ redeems human nature by assuming (taking onto itself) the evil and the imperfection in human nature. Form, on the other hand, works as a kind of divine order, which, by in-forming redeems the imperfections in human nature and the suffering these imperfections bring about.

Conclusion

However paradoxical it may sound, Gioia's poetry is simultaneously a return to form and a return to truth. Form is endowed with a creative agency of its own insofar as it serves as a means to a transformational end: it translates notions of truth (be it the truth of Nature, divine truth, our inner truth) into poetry, at the same time redeeming, by the order and harmony it brings about, the ordinary imperfect human life.

Gioia's use of form relates to, and simultaneously differs from

Romanticism, modernism, and postmodernism. His formalism takes up the notion of a connection between Truth and Beauty, without presuming to identify one with the other. On the other hand, it resists both the modernist obsession with dissolution and fragmentariness, and postmodernism's skepticism toward grand narratives: form is a coalescing agent, uniting different aspects and levels of reality; and narratives are instrumental in shaping both the individual and the social body. The power to name (point to and describe) and to tame (to translate dark or incomprehensible aspects of reality) which resides in language is the main means by which poetry contributes to the shaping of our social and cultural world. Without it, we would be doomed to be either eternal witnesses to what we do not understand or to speak a language that is purely our own, separate from the reality of the world, incomprehensible, immanent. An engagement with form is always an engagement with a transformative force which, by compressing experience into words, lends meaning to our lives.

14

IN CHRIST-HAUNTED CALIFORNIA: DANA GIOIA'S *99 POEMS* (2016)

James Matthew Wilson

At the heart of Dana Gioia's 2012 collection, *Pity the Beautiful*, lies a ghost story. "Haunted" tells the tale of a young man who has gone for a secluded and intimate weekend in an ancestral New England mansion with a woman of great beauty and even greater vanity. Mara, the narrator tells us, "loved having me as audience," as she described "her former lovers—imitating them, / cataloguing their signature stupidities" (*PB* 38). He, meanwhile, sits in awe. As the story unfolds, we sense the narrator is of humble origins but of a sensibility that has already warmed up to obscene wealth. He describes the mansion's art as "grand, authentic, second rate," and while Mara showers, he distracts himself from contemplating her body by exploring the wine cellar, where he recognizes and appreciates the collection of Bordeaux.

Invited into the world of affluence, a quick study in its ways, but held slightly in contempt by its prize beauty, the narrator argues with Mara and storms off to another wing of the mansion. There, disrupting his sulking over a volume of Shakespeare's sonnets, enters a woman, a housekeeper—no, a ghost: "She seemed at once herself and her own reflection / shimmering on the surface of clear water / where fleeting shadows twisted in the depths" (*PB* 39).

He tries to address her. She ignores him. But then, turning her face to him, she hisses, "You don't belong here. No, you don't belong here" (*PB* 41).

Other things happen in the story before its end, but we soon learn that this haunted man has fled the mansion in his socks, leaving his shoes behind, and hitchhiked until he, by chance perhaps, arrives at a monastery. The story begins with him insisting to us that he does not believe in ghosts. It ends with him confessing that he does not even believe in an afterlife. And yet, after this encounter with the "unexplained," he has become a monk. He relates all this while delivering brandy from the monastery to a local tavern. And he is content indeed, for monastic discipline somehow is the only means of ensuring that this life, this earthly life, will not be wasted.

With the publication of *99 Poems: New and Selected*, readers are brought to see with clarity how central the themes of this ghost story are to understanding the career of one of America's most admired, controversial, and accomplished poets and critics. We see that, for all the great variety of form, style, and subject, Gioia's poetry reminds us again and again that the world is a mystery where the things of God wait, hidden inside the heart of the world.

Half a century ago, Flannery O'Connor wrote that modern America had grown "hard of hearing" to the voice of grace. We live in a world disfigured by its unconcern for anything but a life spent in the pursuit of pleasant vanities. And yet, those few persons who sense that something has gone wrong without quite knowing what or why will be "Christ-haunted"; they may not believe in God, but they spend their lives running away from, driven to the edge by, his presence.

To encounter Gioia's poetry is to discover the superficial brilliancies that make up the lives of modern Californians and New Yorkers and to see how they shine on almost totally unperturbed. We pass through the landscapes of a country of power and splendor falling silently into decline. An early poem, "In Cheever Country," for instance, captures the landscape along the railway as one travels north from New York City into the wealthy counties just upstate along the Hudson River. What sounds from the title like a minor homage to a great midcentury American storywriter soon reveals itself as a perceptive and precisely imagined landscape poem that stands comparison with any in the long tradition of that form. Gioia writes,

> The architecture of each station still preserves
> its fantasy beside the sordid tracks—
> defiant pergolas, a shuttered summer lodge,
> a shadowy pavilion framed by high-arched windows
> in this land of northern sun and lingering winter.

Speaking of those "palaces the Robber Barons gave to God," he continues,

> And some are merely left to rot where now
> broken stone lions guard a roofless colonnade,
> a half-collapsed gazebo bursts with tires,
> and each detail warns it is not so difficult
> to make a fortune as to pass it on. (*99P* 32, 33)

Gioia worked in the Northeast for decades, but his home is Southern California, so he also depicts the people of a dry and sunny land of "bright stillness" so in thrall to the little gods of the shopping mall that the pleasures of this world blot out the thought of any other. "Shopping," another poem from *Pity the Beautiful* and included in *99 Poems*, begins, "I enter the temple of my people but do not pray. / I pass the altars of the gods but do not kneel / Or offer sacrifices proper to the season" (*99P* 46).

In a similar vein, "A California Requiem," from *Interrogations at Noon* (2001), resurrects the scathing social critique of Jessica Mitford's *The American Way of Death* (1963). Californians, Gioia suggests, so jealously clutch those gods of the shopping mall that they make every effort, in their cemeteries, to pretend that death does not exist. He describes one thus:

> There were no outward signs of human loss.
> No granite angel wept beside the lane.
> No bending willow broke the once-rough ground
> Now graded to a geometric plane.
>
> My blessed California, you are so wise.
> You render death abstract, efficient, clean. (*99 P* 43)

If we reduce the monuments of death to the pleasant and gentle grades of a public park, perhaps death itself will disappear. Perhaps. As "Shopping" hints, perhaps not: Gioia's speaker relishes the gods of the mall, from "Mercury, protector of cell phones and fax machines," to

"Venus, patroness of bath and bedroom chains," but finally confesses, "I would buy happiness if I could find it" (*99P* 46). We all would, but each of these little gods, after a time, turns upon us like the ghostly presence in "Haunted," to warn, "You do not belong here."

The difficulty for us modern persons, so anxious to discover for ourselves just how much happiness money can buy, is that, as O'Connor wrote, we are hard of hearing. If the thought of living another kind of life whispers through our minds—one that will not be squandered or that will be found worthy as we enter by way of divine judgment into another—we will finally notice the sound only belatedly, suddenly, and with fear. The divine comes only as a ghost comes, passing through a shut door into our lives.

99 Poems appropriately begins with poems on the theme of "mystery," for from his first book, *Daily Horoscope* (1986), onward, Gioia's work has sought to remind us that our secular age, our world too enlightened and uniform for any depths of darkness to remain, is not the place we think it is. Around every corner, haunting us, some strange revelation awaits. You awake in the middle of the night and hear "what the house has to say," "How many voices have escaped you until now" (*99P* 4). We look up at the stars, not as astrologists who seek to discern and master the astral powers, but as complacent worldlings who discover that everywhere we look is a sacramental sign, however subtle:

> Look for smaller signs instead, the fine
> disturbances of ordered things when suddenly
> the rhythms of your expectation break
> and in a moment's pause another world
> reveals itself behind the ordinary. (*99P* 5)

Many of the poems in Gioia's second book, *The Gods of Winter* (1991), consider such disturbances with alternately imaginative and spiritual brilliance. "All Souls'" begins with a curious conceit,

Suppose there is no heaven and no hell,
And that the dead can never leave the earth,
That, as the body rots, the soul breaks free,
Weak and disabled in its second birth. (*99P* 9)

The poet proceeds to depict just such a world, as if to show us that even for those who envision the world as smaller, narrower, and less spectacular than does, say, Dante in *The Divine Comedy*—with its sublime architecture of Earth, Hell, Purgatory, and Paradise—the reality of the soul refuses to disappear. It just becomes harder to understand and so our present lives become harder to live well, so much of what makes them worth the living having been consigned to the spectral margins of superstition.

It is in *The Gods of Winter* that Gioia's reflection on the mystery of things finds mature and most poignant articulation. Dedicated to Michael Jasper Gioia, the poet's first-born son who died in infancy and whose loss left him, for years, mute with grief, *The Gods of Winter* is a book whose perfect stanzas express a wisdom dearly bought. The haunting grief that hangs over the volume attests that sorrow has much to teach us about the same mystery of the quotidian that Gioia's first book strained to show us. One of its lessons is that the decision we must make about the nature of the world is not between secular materialism and "superstitious supernaturalism." We choose, rather, between a world, as Thales once wrote, full of gods, and one made and ordered by the love of God and guarded by his angels.

It was a wise choice to gather together in this new volume all of Gioia's poems about his lost son alongside others on the theme of "Remembrance," for there we see not only some of his most finely wrought lines but also his most compelling accounts of life and death. "Planting a Sequoia" stands out as one of the great poetic elegies of a century that produced many fine ones, but "Prayer" testifies most richly and suggestively to the depth of insight the tragedies of our lives can bring. The first four stanzas address the "object" of prayer in a series of epithets. Some of them could conceivably apply to the spectral presence of some pagan earth god, or simply to Fate, while others clearly could only speak of the one God. We hear this presence first named as "Echo of the clocktower, footstep / in the alleyway, sweep / of the wind sifting the leaves" (*99P* 55).

As Gioia's early poems had suggested, the "rearrangement" of the stars or the mundane order of our lives to reveal divinity, spirit, and mystery at their depths generally feels like a haunting: an echo that troubles the otherwise insensitive ear, the sound of an approaching footstep just out of sight, the wind among the leaves. But, he continues the address,

> Jeweller of the spiderweb, connoisseur
> of autumn's opulence, blade of lightning
> harvesting the sky.
>
> Keeper of the small gate, choreographer
> of entrances and exits, midnight
> whisper traveling the wires. (*99P* 55)

Beginning with an image of minute yet precise beauty that Gioia will echo many years later in "Prophecy," these lines suggest not a god stalking through nature, haunting us, but the God of nature giving measured form to his creation, crafting each blessed thing as a revelation, as a sign of his work—including, at last, the form of our lives, whose shape is delimited by our birth and death. The epithets continue, and then at last a complete sentence follows:

> Seducer, healer, deity or thief,
> I will see you soon enough—
> in the shadow of the rainfall,
>
> in the brief violet darkening of sunset—

This God will be seen in nature, but of course he will also be the thief who steals our lives away, thus every sunset is a brief intimation of a "violet darkening" that will come later but "soon enough." The poem has been a prayer of awful praise, thus far, but now it becomes one of petition: "but until then I pray watch over him / as a mountain guards its covert ore // and the harsh falcon its flightless young" (*99P* 55).

We hear in such lines the supplication of every father who has ever buried a son. It is a prayer to the gods of winter, those deities who would pull us under the earth, even as it is finally a prayer to the true God. Death and grief have a way of reminding us there is always someone to whom we owe our existence and the shaping of our lives. Grace feels like a weight when marred by loss.

In 2013, Gioia published his important essay "The Catholic Writer Today," initially in *First Things* magazine and subsequently in a popular pamphlet from Wiseblood Books. Its argument and insights help us to see his poems as joining a great tradition of Catholic writing in America, where a sacramental vision of the things of this world as signs of the divine disrupts, transforms, and instructs our otherwise unobservant and complacent engagement in the business of daily life. We could name many other important poems that are so disruptive, including such magnificent lyrics as "Words," "Interrogations at Noon," "Night Watch," and "Veterans' Cemetery." These and other later poems move beyond the mere suggestion that the secular world remains haunted by a spiritual one in order to give us a truer vision of reality as a whole.

It would, however, mischaracterize Gioia's achievement to describe him only as one of the great Catholic poets of the last century. When *Daily Horoscope* was published, critics recognized it as a seminal volume in what had just been dubbed the "New Formalism," the revival of meter and rhyme as central techniques of poetic craft. Gioia's critical essays from this period helped give this poetic movement its bearings. The poems in *Daily Horoscope* were also recognized for reconnecting the fine arts with the landscapes, the popular culture, and even the business world as these things filled out 1980s American life (as in the award-winning poem, "Cruising with the Beach Boys").

By the time he published *The Gods of Winter* five years later, Gioia had become the most prominent single advocate of poetry as a central and public art form for American culture. In his hands, poetry once more became a medium of rhythmically brilliant songs but also of great storytelling. "Counting the Children" and "Homecoming," both collected with Gioia's other tales in verse in *99 Poems*, are stories of great power, deepened by their respective main characters' sense of being haunted, even hunted, by the destiny of the soul. That same year, he published his best-known essay, "Can Poetry Matter?" The answer, his book showed, was, yes, if poets would only let their art rejoin the central concerns of human life. The elegies in the volume are of such hard-won power that they remain his best-known poems.

In 2001, *Interrogations at Noon* showed Gioia reasserting poetry's role as words for music, words for the stage, and words for interior meditation. The movements between dramatic monologue, song, and lyric seemed to invite readers to join in a shared public culture that valued the way words can deepen our engagement with the world. From 2003 to 2009, Gioia served in a role suited to one concerned with the place of art in public life, as chairman of the National Endowment for the Arts. He revitalized that organization, bringing its programs into schools, military bases, and towns across the country.

After a hiatus from publishing on account of his public position, his most recent collection of new poems, *Pity the Beautiful*, continued to offer poetry as an art form of public reflection for the members of a shared, national culture. The occasional poem "Autumn Inaugural" is one of the finest works in its genre written by an American. It reminds us of how essential ceremony is to the life of a people if it really is to have a common life.

That is not all. Like many poems in *Pity the Beautiful*, "Autumn Inaugural" manifests Gioia's Catholic sense that culture matters, poetry matters, because it is a temporal sign of something deeper, eternal, and more mysterious: the way divine truths come to appear, if only by "indirection and ellipses," in the things of this world. "Symbols betray us," he writes, because they "are always more or less than what / Is really meant" (*99P* 94). The poem resolves, "Praise to the rituals that celebrate change, / Old robes worn for new beginnings" (*99P* 95).

Human beings are not only haunted by the divine. For the common blessed multitudes, the sacred weaves its way through our everyday lives and gives to the mundane a significance that transcends the horizon of this world. Down to the socks we wear, and the shoes we sometimes forget, our lives are cluttered with symbols, material things waiting to show us the spirit. The divine only rebukes our consciences when we grow deaf and forgetful or treat created things as subject to our dominion (as another great poem, "The Angel with the Broken Wing," suggests). The rest of the time, it guides us down the path to living lives informed by a consciousness of good and evil, salvation and sin, evanescence and permanence.

Fifteen new poems are included among the ninety-nine, including a bizarre and important blank verse story called "Style." But, given how various and full of surprises Gioia's poetic career has been so far, it would be idle to speculate where his work will take us next.

15

"FAITH'S ARDOR IN AN AIR-CONDITIONED TOMB": SIGHTS OF THE UNSEEN IN A SECULAR AGE (2023)

Joshua Hren

"Foght. On the site of the Angel's."
—James Joyce, *Finnegans Wake*

In its earliest usage (c. 1300) the adjective *secular* meant not godlessness but "living in the world but not belonging to a religious order." From the 1850s, however, *secular* has been used "in reference to humanism and the exclusion of belief in God from matters of ethics and morality."[1] That is to say, secularization is bound up with the religious against which it defines itself. In turn, the religious is increasingly bound up with the secular which it defines itself against.

The lines dividing secular and sacred are increasingly written with chalk, and for decades our supposedly secular age has been haunted by sights of the unseen. In *Partial Faiths*, John McClure strives to define a growing body of literature which he gives the ugly, if useful, name "post-secular." Such a literature merits this appellation because it contains stories that "trace the turn of secular-minded characters back toward the religious; because its ontological signature is a religiously inflected disruption of secular constructions of the real; and because its ideological signature is the rearticulation of a dramatically 'weakened' religiosity with secular, progressive values and projects."[2] Dana Gioia's poetics of faith in a secular age has given us a number of poems that embody

---

[1] "Secular," *Etymology Online*, www.etymonline.com/word/secular.

[2] John A. McClure, *Partial Faiths: Postsecular Fiction in the Age of Pynchon and Morrison* (Athens: University of Georgia Press, 2007), 3.

the first two of these characteristics, even as it departs from the third. Instead of dramatizing a weakened religiosity that fits cozily into the humanist project, Gioia presents "secular-minded" persons who are "drawn back toward the sacred by promptings [they do] not invite but cannot ignore."[3] In these poems the sacral haunts and interrupts lives spent inhabiting the mundane and materialistic, abstracted and disenchanted spaces of a secular age, unveiling the metaphysical and reorienting the soul.

"I Enter the Temple of My People but Do Not Pray"

As Charles Taylor relates, disenchantment "designat[es] one of the main features of the phenomenon we know as secularization."[4] The German word for "disenchantment" is "*Entzauberung*," which contains the word "*zauber*," or *magic*: it literally translates as "de-magicification." Taylor traces two main features of the enchanted world that "disenchantment did away with."[5] The first is that the world "was once filled with spirits [God, angels, Satan, demons, spirits of the wood]" that were "almost indistinguishable from the *loci* they inhabit, and moral forces [that] impinged on human beings."[6] The boundary between these super-natures and humans were profoundly porous.

Although secularization has advanced a rosy understanding of disenchantment, any reduction of reality to materiality and mundanity ignores the magic that persists in a purportedly demystified world. If Karl Marx's corpus is ridden with foundational errors, even the materialist is privy to this phenomenon: "A commodity appears at first sight an extremely obvious, trivial thing. But its analysis brings out that it is a very strange thing, abounding in metaphysical subtleties and theological niceties."[7] When a person transforms a tree into a table, although the object has changed, it remains a common, everyday thing: wood.

---

[3] Ibid., 9–10.

[4] Charles Taylor, *A Secular Age* (London: Belknap Press, 2018), 287.

[5] Ibid.

[6] Ibid., 287, 290.

[7] Karl Marx, *Capital: A Critique of Political Economy,* vol. 1., trans. Ben Fowkes (New York: Penguin, 1990), 163.

However, as soon as this table is changed into a commodity, it becomes "transcendent," assumes a "mystical character."[8] Marx names this transformation "commodity fetishism," borrowing from anthropology the word "fetish," which denotes the belief that divinities and gods inhere in material things.[9]

If Gioia the former businessman departs from the Marxian labor theory of value, he captures the same "enchantment" Marx spies in materialist obsession. In his poem "Shopping," the narrator proclaims, "Blessed are the acquisitive, / For theirs is the kingdom of commerce." Entering a shopping mall, the speaker describes it in sacred terms:

> I enter the temple of my people but do not pray.
> I pass the altars of the gods but do not kneel
> Or offer sacrifices proper to the season.
> ...
> But I wander the arcades of abundance,
> Empty of desire, no credit to my people,
> Envying the acolytes their passionate faith. (*99P* 46)

In her essay "Dana Gioia: A Contemporary Metaphysics," Janet McCann contends that Gioia's work "cognizant of the difficulty [of a deeper] quest [in modernity]—in a flat surface, where everything is only itself, it asks: where can we find the power that went with the old mythologies when they were believed in?"[10] In "Shopping" at least one answer to McCann's question is "the mall." Instead of satirizing or ironizing the mall in a mode that enunciates its secular vapidity, Gioia dramatizes a mystical and religious register that give a compelling account of why devotees of secularity find such satisfaction in a purportedly materialistic place. The mall, with its "hymns of no cash down and the installment plan, / Of custom fit, remote control, and priced to move," with its pseudo-incense of "coffee, musk, and cinnamon" celebrates the supernatural nature of commerce:

---

[8] Ibid.

[9] Ibid.

[10] Janet McCann, "Dana Gioia: A Contemporary Metaphysics," *Renascence* 61/3 (2009): 204.

Redeem me, gods of the mall and marketplace.
Mercury, protector of cell phones and fax machines,
Venus, patroness of bath and bedroom chains,
Tantalus, guardian of the food court. (*99P* 46)

Why? Because the arts of commerce have seemingly surpassed nature itself; piles of crêpe de chine, silk, and satin heap "like cumuli in the morning sky" (*99P* 46). Because all of this seems to have been brought not by mechanistic semi-trucks and overnight airplane deliveries, but by "caravans and argosies"—emblems of the exotic east (*99P* 46). Yet, if at first this mall-pilgrim experiences a *mysterium termendum* before the "crowded countertops and eager cashiers," he eventually exclaims in frustration:

But what can I bring you from these sad emporia?
Where in this splendid clutter
Shall I discover the one true thing?

Nothing to carry, I should stroll easily
Among the crowded countertops and eager cashiers,
Bypassing the sullen lines and footsore customers,
Spending only my time, discounting all I see. (*99P* 47)

"There is no angel among the vending stalls and signage," he concludes. The absence of the sacramental stokes a visceral search for the "errant soul and innermost companion" (*99P* 47). That this pilgrim would fail in such a place was evident from the poem's beginning, for, wandering the "arcades of abundance," he is "empty of desire" (*99P* 46). That is to say, although he envies the faithful their passionate faith in the fetishes that fill the mall, although he "spends his time" trying to acquire it, he receives no answer to his demand that someone "Tell [him] in what department [his] desire shall be found" (*99P* 47). What he desires, and what, he confesses, he would buy if he could, is "happiness," and here we encounter that enduring problem, noted by Aristotle in the *Nicomachean Ethics* and which St. Augustine addresses with characteristic jocularity in *City of God*: "That all men wish for happiness is a certitude for anyone who can think. But so long as human intelligence remains incapable of deciding which men are happy [and, he elaborates elsewhere, why], endless controversies arise in which philosophers waste their toil."[11] The narrator of "Shopping" pronounces the equally wasted toil of the "footsore customers" standing and waiting in their "sullen lines" (*99P* 47).

That this pilgrim departs from his peers is no guarantee that his new direction will be guided by a more profound beatitude. However, because he experienced the mall as an enchanted realm rather than a merely materialistic, secular space, this spiritually charged vision permits a turn toward the soul, whom he looks for "among the pressing crowds" (*99P* 47). If his experience of this commercial temple could be explained as mere configurations of chemicals, with dopamine falling while one waits in line and peaking from the time he sees that satin and silk until he makes a purchase, his disappointment would need to be resolved materially, through some sort of mundane divertissement. But, seeing the spiritual and mystical dimensions of the mall, knowing that the goddess of love herself protects and assists the lingerie stores, he also has eyes for his mysterious soul, whom he addresses in ardent apostrophe: "Where are you, my fugitive?" (*99P* 47). His epiphany, coming after he has exhausted time spent "stalk[ing] the leased arcades," elicits a series of questions, whose rhetorical expression and effect carries echoes of the beginning of St. Augustine's *Confessions*:

> How shall I call upon my God, my God and Lord? Surely when I call on him, I am calling on him to come into me. But what place is there in me where my God can enter into me? "God made heaven and earth" (Genesis 1:1). Where may he come to me? Lord my God, is there any room in me which does not contain you? Can heaven and earth, which you have made and in which you have made me, contain you? Without

---

[11]Augustine, *The City of God*, Books I–VII, ed. Demetrius B. Zema, Gerald G. Walsh, and Etienne Gilson (Washington, DC: Catholic University of America Press, 2008), 186. Note: In an *Image: Art, Faith, Mystery* interview, Gioia says that St. Augustine's *City of God* "probably shaped my adult life more than any other book except the Gospels."

> you, whatever exists would not exist. Then can what exists contain you? I also have being. So why do I request you to come into me when, unless you were within me, I would have no being at all. I am not now possessed by Hades; yet even there are you (Psalms 138:8).[12]

After asking where his soul is, he questions, in confessional form, "Why else have I stalked the leased arcades / Searching the kiosks and the cash machines?" (*99P* 47). And then the Augustinian inquiry crescendos:

> Where are you, my errant soul and innermost companion?
> Are you outside amid the potted palm trees,
> Bumming a cigarette or joking with the guards,
> Or are you wandering the parking lot
> Lost among the rows of Subarus and Audis?
>
> Or is that you I catch a sudden glimpse of
> Smiling behind the greasy window of the bus
> As it disappears into the evening rush? (*99P* 47–48)

The poem ends here, without answers. Still, the barrage of inquiries provokes the reader to also seek after the nature of the soul. Further, the questions contain clues as to the nature of the narrator's crisis. One thing cannot, on a literal level, be simultaneously errant and innermost, and so we are cued into the symbolic key of these final inquiries. His soul cannot literally be outside amidst the potted palm trees, but the key word here is "outside." The soul either refused to enter the mall, or the man left the soul there—again, not literally, but metaphorically. Left outside, the soul might be joking with the guards, a gesture suggestive of joy. But perhaps the outside of the mall is also foreign territory for the soul, and it is misplaced, drifting without a clear destination through the sea of cars. Or, finally, is the soul "smiling"—again here suggestive of that joy that the narrator had sought without knowing

---

[12] Augustine, *Confessions*, ed. Henry Chadwick (Oxford: Oxford University Press, 1991), 4–5.

it—behind a window so different than those that line the leased arcades? Perhaps, and here the chill of the ending emerges, the soul simply departed. The pilgrim sought too long in the mall, did not accept or act upon the soul's jealous insistence upon a joy that can only come with beatitude, so that epiphany the man may have had, but this epiphany does not preclude the possibility of irreversible tragedy, of a case wherein the soul has been veritably excluded and at last excised from his existence.

"Faith's Ardor in an Air-Conditioned Tomb"

We move from the mall to the museum as we leave "Shopping" and consider "The Angel with the Broken Wing." Both of these spaces can be read as temples. As Giorgio Agamben argues, "The Museum occupies the space and function once reserved for the Temple as the place of sacrifice. The faithful in the Temple—the pilgrims who would travel across the earth from temple to temple, from sanctuary to sanctuary—correspond today to the tourists who restlessly travel in a world that has been abstracted into a Museum."[13] It would be absurd to declare Agamben's contention absolutely true, but he rightly reads the phenomenon of a secular space replacing a sacred one, a pattern evident in "Shopping" and repeated in "The Angel with the Broken Wing." In the latter, the beautiful is replaced by the aesthetic, which is to say that when sacred art has been "abstracted into a Museum," it is cut off from its relation to the sacred order: art's metaphysical meaning is "mercifully" mummified and put to sleep.

McCann is right to note that in Gioia's poems, "The bedrock of Catholicism is glimpsed sometimes within, sometimes just beyond their margins. Their sacramental vision and their insistence on the accountability of art are rooted in their religious faith."[14] This is perhaps clearest in "The Angel with the Broken Wing," where the poem's protagonist and narrator is a statue exiled to solitary confinement in a museum:

---

[13] Giorgio Agamben, *Profanations* (New York: Zone Books, 2007), 84–85.
[14] McCann, "Dana Gioia," 204–205.

I am the Angel with the Broken Wing,
The one large statue in this quiet room.
The staff finds me too fierce, and so they shut
Faith's ardor in this air-conditioned tomb. (*99P* 16)

The angel alleges that his fate grows out of the fact that "the staff finds [him] too fierce." Here the poem registers the terrible irony: the angel's purported advancement from "a country church" to a museum complete with air-conditioning and quiet is actually a death. This death comes in large part because the rarefied docents, and presumably the "chatter[ing]" museumgoers, relegate their praise to the angel's "elegant design." Such a reductive reading of the angel elicits his sardonic, melancholic conclusion that if he is a "masterpiece of sorts," it is only in the sense that he is "the perfect emblem of futility" (*99P* 16).

Describing the convergence of atheism and aestheticism, Philip Rieff writes, "having abandoned their belief in God, poetry—art generally—can take its place as the style of redemption."[15] One of the consequences of this replacement is that art comes to be judged only according to the categories of aesthetics. For Thomas Aquinas, the beautiful cannot be compartmentalized: where there is beauty there is also goodness and truth. Further, we cannot draw from an object all its beauty. This implies that when we behold a beautiful object, we are captivated by it in part because some of its beauty fastens us to itself in that, so to speak, it does not quite arrive. "To experience the beautiful is not only to be satisfied," John Milbank writes, "but also to be frustrated satisfyingly; a desire to see more of what arrives ... is always involved."[16] For Milbank, this desire to see more is actually a desire to see the unseen; to truly see the beautiful is to see the invisible in the visible. He notes that Hans Urs Von Balthasar aptly articulated "Glory," as it occurs in the Bible, as the experience of a "hidden, divine force irradiating the

---

[15] Philip Rieff, *My Life among the Deathworks: Illustrations of the Aesthetics of Authority*, ed. Kenneth S. Piver (Charlottesville: University of Virginia Press, 2006), 17.

[16] John Milbank, Graham Ward, and Edith Wyschogrod, *Theological Perspectives on God and Beauty* (Harrisburg: Trinity Press International, 2003), 2.

finite surface."[17] Wherever this possibility of knowing both the true through the beautiful and the invisible through the visible remains, aestheticism has not conquered. There was, in the Medieval period, no branch of philosophy called "aesthetics." Kant, the supreme theorist of modernity's aesthetic maintains that the beautiful is ineffable, but he locates this ineffability "on the side of subjective feeling alone."[18] He refuses the possibility of glory, or the *presence* of the invisible in the visible. Superficially, the museum docents do the same, limiting their critiques to the "elegant design," but we cannot forget that, though they may not admit this to be the case, they have confined the angel to solitude in part because they "find [him] too fierce" (*99P* 16). That is to say, they cannot mute the way in which the invisible irradiates the visible: their aesthetic categories cannot clip the wings of the transcendentals: the beautiful angel bespeaks truth to them, a truth that feels fierce to those who have inherited and who proselytize a horizontal world.

For Rieff, a world ordered around the horizontal leaves us with an understanding and experience of culture that is all-too-human: in such a social order, the truths do not intersect with and so do not inflect our culture. However, "Our own motions in sacred order are locatable once each of us has restored to himself the notion of sacred order. The basic restorative is to understand the purity and inviolate nature of the vertical in authority ...That we do not now find safety... reflects our loss of the radically contemporaneous memory of sacred order and our present time and place in it."[19] According to the angel, though, the docents have not been able to forget this memory of the sacred order: taxonomize him according to the categories of a museum's secularized aesthetics they may, but encountering him they cannot help but know terror when they glimpse their existences as transcending that which can be empirically mapped. As Rieff continues to explain,

> Cultures give readings of sacred order and ourselves somewhere in it. Culture and sacred order are inseparable, the former the registration of the latter as a systemic expression of

---

[17] Ibid., 2.
[18] Ibid., 4.
[19] Rieff, *My Life among the Deathworks*, 13.

> the practical relation between humans and the shadow aspect of reality as it is lived. No culture has ever preserved itself where it is not a registration of sacred order. The [secularist] notion of a culture that persists independent of all sacred orders is unprecedented in human history.[20]

The poem, Gioia notes, "is spoken by a *santo*, a devotional wooden statue carved by a Mexican folk artist" (*PB* 71). As the angel narrates the story of his life, we see that the docents' recognition of that which transcends his design was shared by the Mexican revolutionaries who despoiled his "country church" of origin. Sent to vandalize the chapel, the troops break only his left wing ("Even a saint can savor irony" [*99P* 16]). The revolutionaries cannot complete their mandate of desecration:

> They hit me once—almost apologetically.
>
> For even the godless feel something in a church,
> A twinge of hope, fear? Who knows what it is?
> A trembling unaccounted by their laws,
> An ancient memory they can't dismiss. (*99P* 16)

Their violence to the statue reinvigorates its—and faith's—ardor, to introduce a sacredness whose beauty is tied to numinous laws that announce truths that reveal the revolutionary's commandments to be radically incomplete and even inimical to the persistent divine.

At the poem's end, the angel with the broken wing with "so many things [he] must tell God!" finds himself "like a dead thing nailed to a perch, / A crippled saint against a painted sky" (*99P* 17). In Gioia's poems, then, sacramental realities are revealed through their failings: the prospective failure of the mallgoer to retrieve his soul in time; the failure of the revolutionaries or the docents to duly order their cultures around the angel's revelations; the pitiable, beautiful angel's failure to tell "so many things" to God, even though he knows he "must." He cannot, for it was not he alone who can tongue things to God. When he inhabited that "country church" for which he was carved, the angel served a

[20] Ibid., 15.

community of believers:

> I stood beside a gilded altar where
> The hopeless offered God their misery.
>
> I heard their women whispering at my feet—
> Prayers for the lost, the dying, and the dead.
> Their candles stretched my shadow up the wall,
> And I became the hunger that they fed. (*99P* 16)

The angel and his congregation transform each other. He becomes "the hunger that they fed"; that is to say, the faithful's "prayers for the lost, the dying, and the dead" were pulled forth upon seeing him. Without him their prayers would not achieve the verticality to which the poem gives literal articulation in the line, "Their candles stretched my shadow up the wall," and beyond the visible ceiling (*99P* 16). Once again, though, it is this poem's tragic ending, wherein the heights of the cosmos are reduced to the museum's "painted sky," that reveals the awful superiority of the sacred order. Secularity, ushered in by violent revolutionaries or elegant docents, makes us claustrophobic, crippling our souls, and even ("I stand like a dead thing") crippling us. But the poem's tragic end solicits our pity for those necessary angels of beauty who are ready to resurrect faith's ardor even from within the "air-conditioned tomb."

16

THE ART OF STORY-TELLING: DANA GIOIA'S "BALLAD OF JESÚS ORTIZ" (2018)

John Zheng

"The Ballad of Jesús Ortiz" celebrates the life story of Dana Gioia's Mexican great-grandfather, Jesús Ortiz.[1] In a note written when the poem was reprinted, Gioia says, "When I was ten, I had an astonishing conversation with my Mexican grandfather. He told me that he had quit school at my age to become a cowboy. When I asked him why, he replied, 'My dad got shot in a saloon. My brother and I had to support the family.' He then described his early life in frontier Wyoming. I never forgot his rough and violent story. I also never entirely trusted it."[2] This story had been intriguing to Gioia ever since. Forty years later, after Gioia mentioned the 1910 murder of his great-grandfather during a speech given in Casper, Wyoming, the state librarian, who was in the audience, sent him a large package that "contained copies of newspaper articles and official documents, concerning [his] great-grandfather's death and the search for his murderer."[3] These documents proved what Gioia's grandfather had told him and aroused him to shape the forgotten story of Jesús Ortiz into a ballad.

---

[1] Dana Gioia published the poem in three distinct editions and multiple journal reprintings between 2017 and 2023. Originally published without an accent mark in "Jesús," "The Ballad of Jesus Ortiz" first appeared in the *Los Angeles Review of Books*, September 30, 2017, https://lareviewofbooks.org/article/ballad-jesus-ortiz/. By popular demand, a limited edition of *The Ballad of Jesús Ortiz* was issued in 2018 by Providence Press of Ojai, California. We are citing "The Ballad of Jesús Ortiz" as reprinted in *Meet Me at the Lighthouse*.

[2] Dana Gioia, "Was the Story True?," a note accompanying the reprinting of "The Ballad of Jesus Ortiz," *Santa Clara Magazine*, March 27, 2018, magazine.scu.edu/magazines/spring-2018/the-ballad-of-jesus-ortiz/.

[3] Ibid.

Jesús, called "Jake" by Americans who felt uncomfortable with someone named Jesus, was born of a vaquero family. He learned to drive cattle with his father in Montana:

When Jake was twelve, his father
Brought him along to ride.
"Don't waste your youth in the pueblo.
Earn by your father's side." (*MML* 17)

A person's coming of age is like the flow of water. With the right guide, he flows to the right place. Jake's father planted in him a seed of earning a living by working hard as a cattle driver rather than by idling away his "youth in the pueblo" or by "sitting in a mission school with bare and dusty feet" (*MML* 17). However, learning to drive cattle at twelve also suggests the poverty of people like Jake's family in the Western frontier at the turn of the twentieth century.

Indeed, Jake's adventure started by herding cattle in "hot and toilsome" days and sleeping on the hard ground at night when coyotes roamed nearby. The images of coyote and weeping Jake set up a contrast between the dangerous wilderness and the comforting voice of his mother in order to intensify the harsh environment Jake had to face, as described in the following stanza:

At night when the coyotes called,
Jake would sometimes weep
Recalling how his mother
Sang her children to sleep. (*MML* 18)

The cattle drive changed little Jake into both a tough young man who was brave to overcome any hardships and a tender person who enjoyed himself in the sweet morning air of the desert. The hard and tender parts of Jake show especially in the following description:

Three thousand head of cattle
Grazing the prairie grass,
Three thousand head of cattle

Pushed through each mountain pass.

Three thousand head of cattle
Fording the muddy streams,
And then three thousand phantoms
Bellowing in your dreams. (*MML* 17)

These two stanzas present a spectacular view of early cattle drives in the Wild West: the three thousand head of cattle, the natural beauty through cattle grazing the prairie, the difficulty of driving the cattle through the mountain passes, and the breathtaking moments of cattle fording the streams. Each drive was made according to where the grass or water was, and yet each drive would also mean the slaughter of cattle driven to market. The bellowing phantoms haunting the vaquero's dreams reveal the mixed feelings of sadness and fear.

After returning to the pueblo as a man, Jake spent ten more years as a vaquero on the open range with "no children and no wife." Poverty forced him to move north to Wyoming to "find his winter keep / Among the Basques and Anglos / Who raised and slaughtered sheep." But the living and working conditions there were as harsh as where he had worked:

He came to cold Lost Cabin
Where the Rattlesnake Mountains rise
Over the empty foothills,
Under the rainless skies.

The herders lived in dugouts
Or shacks of pine and tar.
The town had seven buildings.
The biggest was the bar. (*MML* 18)

Jake was hired by John Okie, who owned Lost Cabin, to tend bar and allowed to sleep in the kitchen. According to Tom Rea, John Okie's flocks had grown to 12,000 head by 1891, so he was called the "Sheep King." Okie also owned stores. "Knowing his business depended on the good will of his customers, Okie cheerfully gave them credit. They could buy now and pay later when they had money—after shearing time or after lamb-shipping time."[4]

As a hardworking Mexican who never whined about life, Jake welcomed a new life in Lost Cabin, "married a sheepherder's daughter, / Half-Indian, half-white. / They had two sons" (*MML* 19). He began to feel that he lived a right life. But,

> One night he had an argument
> With a herder named Bill Howard,
> A deserter from the Border War,
> A drunkard, and a coward. (*MML* 19)

Jake had to ask Howard to pay the bill for his drinks because Okie no longer gave him any credit. Feeling humiliated by Jake, Howard returned to the bar at midnight and shot Jake to death. Gioia restores the murder scene:

> Three times he shot his rifle,
> And Jake fell to the floor.
>
> Then Bill beheld his triumph
> As the smoke cleared from the air—
> A mirror blown into splinters,
> And blood splattered everywhere. (*MML* 20)

The tone through these lines is ironic and painful. A reader would ask how Howard, a deserter, could see his triumph in the bloody killing of a civilian or a person as poor as he was and how this coward could be so brutal and wild. The answer can be found in Howard's question—"Is this some goddaman joke, / A piss-poor Mexican peon / Telling me I'm broke?"—which indicates that even though both men were poor,

---

[4] Tom Rea, "J. B. Okie, Sheep King of Central Wyoming," November 8, 2014, *Wyohistory.org*, www.wyohistory.org/encyclopedia/j-b-okie-sheep-king-central-wyoming.

Howard, who judged from his narrow mind about race, would think he was different from Jake (*MML* 20). To use a contemporary term, Howard committed a hate crime.

The tragic scene, intensified graphically through the use of alliteration in "splinter" and "splatter," is thought-provoking to readers one hundred years later:

> A sudden brutal outburst
> No motive could explain:
> One poor man killing another
> Without glory, without gain.
>
> The tales of Western heroes
> Show duels in the noonday sun,
> But darkness and deception
> Is how most killing is done. (*MML* 20)

The poet challenges us to question about the killing done in darkness that showed no glory or heroic tales. Jake, whose life was in conflict with the natural world and who never complained about society, was forced to be in conflict with his antagonist and died a tragic death. On the other hand, Howard, the murderer who did the killing in the dark, became a runaway, again proving he was nothing but a coward. On April 21, 1911, the *Lander Eagle*, a local newspaper, reported Howard's murder charge and the funeral of Ortiz:

> William Howard, the man who shot John Ortiz at Lost Cabin on the night of April 8th, and who was later arrested in the Rattlesnake range of mountains by Sheriff Johnson and a posse, now faces a very grave charge—in all likelihood murder in the first degree.
>
> Ortiz, the man shot by Howard, died at noon on Monday. He was attended by Dr. Jewell of Shoshoni, who extracted the bullets soon after the shooting occurred, but the wounds were of such a nature, both bullets perforating the lungs, that he had but little chance for his life from the start. The cause of death was hemorrhage.

> When told of the death of Ortiz by Deputy Gaylord, Howard was greatly depressed. He had hoped the wounded man would recover and lighten the charge against him.
>
> Ortiz was a Mexican by birth. He was a married man and leaves a wife and three children to grieve over his tragic death. The funeral took place at Lost Cabin on Tuesday morning. Rev. Father Keller went from Lander to conduct the services, the Ortiz family being of the Catholic faith. Interment took place in the cemetery at Lost Cabin.[5]

Human life was not worth much when killing was not unusual in those early days, as Gioia describes in the penultimate stanza: "There were two more graves in Wyoming / When the clover bloomed in spring. / Two strangers drifted into town / And filled the openings" (*MML* 21). The word "opening" is a verbal play, not just for the purpose of rhyme but also for the double meaning it suggests. Gioia says, the word "refers to the jobs opened by the deaths as well as suggests the open graves."[6] As the ballad concludes with two tall boys departing their mother and riding away for cattle drives, the poet's doubt about the Ortiz story his grandfather told him is removed as well.

"The Ballad of Jesús Ortiz" is a narrative poem of 116 lines in 29 quatrains. It was originally published in the *Los Angeles Review of Books* and broadcast on the BBC Radio 3 series *In the Studio*. The third-person narrator tells a reliable and objective story. Each stanza ends with a punctuation mark of period to indicate an end of an episode in Jake's life. Thus, reading each stanza is like following Jake's footprints and moving from place to place so as to learn bit by bit about his place, name, education, cattle drive, life, job, family, and tragic death.

The poet employs the form of ballad to tell a vivid story. He writes in the author's note, "The ballad has traditionally been the form to document the stories of the poor, particularly in the Old West. The

---

[5] "John Ortiz' Life Passes," *The Lander Eagle* 1/14 (April 21, 1911), [1]. pluto.wyo.gov/awweb/main.jsp?flag=browse&smd=2&awdid=1. See also: https://www.findagrave.com/memorial/75712766/john-j.-ortiz.

[6] Dana Gioia, "Re: Questions about *The Ballad of Jesús Ortiz,*" email to John Zheng, September 27, 2018.

people remembered in the poem sang and recited ballads. The form seemed the right way to tell their story." A traditional ballad maintains a form of rhymed quatrain (*abcb*) with four metrical feet in the first and third lines and three feet in the second and fourth. "The Ballad of Jesús Ortiz" is written in tradition with the *abcb* rhyme pattern, but it is also untraditional. Though it keeps the rhyme, it is not bound by the strict metrical pattern. Every now and then, the poet breaks through the metrical fetters in order to keep a smooth flow of the narrative voice.

One characteristic of the narrative voice in "The Ballad of Jesús Ortiz" is that the poet chooses the simple common words suitable for the story-telling and metrical beats. Thus, the voice becomes distinctively the poet's own. Gioia writes for the ear. Read these lines—"He came to cold Lost Cabin / Where the Rattlesnake Mountains rise / Over the empty foothills, / Under the rainless skies"—and you will feel the effective cadence through the working of rhythm, alliteration, and rhyme, which echoes what Robert Frost expected for the sound of sense, "the abstract vitality of our speech" (*MML* 18).[7] In other words, Gioia tells the story not just through the chosen words and their meanings in each stanza but through the tone of his voice as well.

"The Ballad of Jesús Ortiz" tells a painful story of a poor vaquero's life, his struggle for survival in frontier Wyoming, and his hardworking effort to raise a family. It is a tribute to Jake and millions like him. As a cowboy ballad written with vital voice and artistic mastery, it speaks well to both literary and general audiences. And for this purpose, this telling and retelling, this remembering and singing, we celebrate.

---

[7] Robert Frost to John Bartlett, 4 July 1913, qtd. in "Robert Frost on the 'Sound of Sense' and on 'Sentence Sounds,'" udallasclassics.org/maurer_files/Frost.pdf.

17

BELOVED COMMUNITIES: ON *MEET ME AT THE LIGHTHOUSE* (2023)

Ned Balbo

When it appeared in 2017, poet and critic Dana Gioia's *99 Poems: New & Selected* served as capstone to what was already a distinguished body of work. With *Meet Me at the Lighthouse*, he shows he still has much to say, and we as readers are the richer for it. The son of a Sicilian immigrant father and a mother whose heritage was Mexican, Gioia grew up in the Los Angeles metropolitan area, in a blue-collar, Catholic home surrounded by the cultural artifacts—books, art books, records, and musical scores—inherited from an autodidact uncle. These roots—and this community—form the backdrop of the new book, a wistful yet probing immersion into the necessary bonds of neighborhood and family, as well as a restless interrogation of history, social class, art, and faith.

That interrogation requires more than one thoughtful look back at the past. Theodore Ortiz, the uncle whose legacy helped fuel Gioia's intellectual and aesthetic interests, is remembered in "Seaward," its alternately rhymed, two-beat lines directed both to the young US Merchant Marine who died in a plane crash, and to the poet himself: "Stand on the dock / as the ocean swells. / Death is what happens / to somebody else" (*MML* 11). ("Night Watch," published in Gioia's 1991 masterpiece, *The Gods of Winter*, tells more about Ortiz's fate: "burned beyond recognition, / left as a headstone in the unfamiliar earth / … // and not scattered on the shifting gray Pacific" [*GW* 6].) Together, these poems underline the importance of his uncle's gift to Gioia, which was not just books to read or records to play but the idea that books, music, literature, and art matter—and, for some, could be a calling. (Gioia's mother, a telephone operator, influenced him, too, reciting poems by Poe, Tennyson, and more to her son's delight.) His uncle's death, therefore, is both a fateful crossroads and deeply formative: a loss without which Gioia's life in the arts, as embodied in the very books he held, might have seemed less real, less possible.

That community of the arts is also the subject of the new book's title poem. The Lighthouse, still in operation today with "Café" added to its name, began featuring jazz in 1949; there, some of the genre's biggest names performed and recorded, including Hampton Hawes, Gerry Mulligan, and Chet Baker, who also appear, with others, at Gioia's invitation:

> Meet me at the Lighthouse in Hermosa Beach,
> That shabby nightclub on its foggy pier.
> Let's aim for the summer of '71,
> When all our friends were young and immortal. (*MML* 3)

The meeting won't be at the real club, however, but at a timeless afterlife version where "only ghosts [sit] at the bar" while "the best talent in Tartarus" "shine[s] from that jerry-built stage." (Under other circumstances, it's an invitation Gioia's brother, revered jazz critic Ted Gioia, might appreciate, but since "Death the collector is keeping the tab," maybe not.) There will be other Dantean turns throughout the book: after all, "Time and tide are counting the beats" (*MML* 3). In the poem "Meet Me at the Lighthouse," Gioia skillfully blends local L.A.-area history with an autumnal affection that both celebrates the arts and mourns the passing of communities.

That elegiac impulse is even more pronounced in the book's third section, a triptych tribute to the City of Angels. This trio of psalms blends echoes of Catholic prayer with flashes of nostalgia and uniquely L.A. references that merge easily with Gioia's historical interests and concern for social justice. In "Psalm and Lament for Los Angeles," the speaker wanders the suburb of his youth to "revisit the precincts of memory," only to find "the silent ruins of my city. / What was there to sing in a strange and empty land?" (*MML* 25). There's beauty, but beyond the "dances of the surfers and the dolphins," there's suffering, too: "But, O Los Angeles, you dash your children against the stones. / You devour your natives and your immigrants. // ... You sprawl in the carnage and count the spoils" (*MML* 26).

The next poem, "Psalm of the Heights," perfectly balances regret and longing. After praising the city's nighttime splendor ("boulevards unfold in brilliant lines" and "freeways flow like shining rivers"), unrhymed couplets look to the heavens, invoking celestially named mid-century cars ("speeding Comets or sleek Thunderbirds") as if they were sky-chariots piloted by youthful gods locked in "lust or laughter" (*MML* 27–28). Its caveats aside, "Psalm of the Heights" is a love poem to L.A. where "the soul sings like a car radio" and Hollywood dreams become stellar transfigurations: "'Where else can you become a star?'" (*MML* 29).

It is "Psalm for Our Lady Queen of the Angels" that praises and prays most poignantly. Here, Gioia recalls the "forgotten forty-four" settlers who founded and named a riverside pueblo in honor of the Virgin Mary. Lines gather force in unrhymed quatrains, taking in

> the marriages and matings that created us.
> Desire, swifter than democracy, merging the races—
> Spanish, Aztec, African, and Anglo—
> Forbidden matches made holy by children. (*MML* 30)

Many are those whom history often forgets: "the hungry, the stubborn, the scarred." In a nod to Whitman's "Song of Myself," Gioia praises himself ("the seed of exiles and violent men"), his ancestors ("the unkillable poor, / The few who escaped disease or despair—"), and, finally, *Nuestra Señora*, God's Mother, "who watches them still / From murals and medals, statues, tattoos. / She has not abandoned her divided pueblo." The poem ends with the poet's prayers "for the city that lost its name," for "the flesh that pays for profit," for all those "mixed and misbegotten, / Beside our dry river and tents of the outcast poor" (*MML* 30, 31). In this quietly magnificent sequence, a modest community transforms into a major metropolis. Accordingly, the question of what connects us becomes more complex, history's cycles calling on new generations to reinvent the boundaries of unity and division.

Gioia's new collection includes an impressive range of work: rhymed quatrains on a lovely luna moth ("baneful vagrant from the stormy skies"), a witty, Baudelairean sonnet on boredom's burdens ("flies intone their imbecilic whir"), literate lyrics (available in full musical setting on Helen Sung's album *Sung with Words*), "The Ballad of Jesús Ortiz" (a story-song in the *corridos* tradition that tells of Gioia's great-grandfather's Old West exploits), fine translations of Rilke, Neruda, and Machado, and much more. In all these, Gioia's command of craft, deep knowledge, and restless curiosity offer a broad scope of pleasures and effects.

In a darkly ironic final sequence whose tone recalls Weldon Kees, Gioia embarks on an unsettling railway journey in the poem "The Underworld" that ends in a section titled "Disappointments":

> No triple-headed dog to guard the gate,
> No gate at all as far as you can tell,
> No burning wheel, no stones to push uphill,
> No Titans bound in chains, no serpent king.
> No sun, no moon, no stars, no sky, no end. (*MML* 54)

Elsewhere, death is the reality we accept in poems alive with vanished loved ones—that community of memory that's always with us. In "Tinsel, Frankincense, and Fir," the hanging of "scratched and shabby" Christmas ornaments compels the speaker to remember the mother who once hung them herself in times long past: "How carefully she hung each thread of tinsel, / Or touched each dime-store bauble with delight" (*MML* 12). It is a brief, beautiful poem. As Gioia concludes, "No holiday is holy without ghosts," we feel how faith and memory preserve those we loved most deeply (*MML* 12). *Meet Me at the Lighthouse* is a wonderful new entry in a vital body of work.

18

THE TURN IN DANA GIOIA'S *MEET ME AT THE LIGHTHOUSE* (2023)

Shirley Geok-lin Lim

Hailed early as a key mover in the shaping of New Formalism, a rethinking of twentieth-century American modernist poetics established by Ezra Pound's manifesto to "Make it new," William Carlos Williams's free verse stylistics, T. S. Eliot's *The Waste Land*'s incoherent coherence, and a seeming return to English prosodic traditions, Gioia's first collection, *Daily Horoscope*, was received as a confirmation of his already established reputation as a poet-critic. Not many poets are notable before their first book of poems appear, but in 1986, *Daily Horoscope*'s blurbs by three of the most distinguished American poets, Donald Justice, X. J. Kennedy, and Frederick Turner, all struck similar praise for the beauty of his verse. "If there is a turn now toward more traditional poetry," Justice boldly stated, "then Gioia is in the vanguard." Calling him "a voice of quiet authority," Kennedy admired how Gioia moves with "masterly ease from strict form to flexible cadences." Turner affirmed "the intellectual perspicuity, the moral maturity, the formal richness, the emotional complexity" of the debut collection. He found in Gioia's poetry "the evocativeness—the addictiveness—of the most perfectly wrought classical lyric" (*DH* back cover). These dual subjects, poetic beauty and moral authority, sound in every reception of his following four collections. Matthew Brennan's *Colosseum Critical Introduction to Dana Gioia* (2020) includes Gioia's poetry, criticism, opera libretti, interviews, and anthologies, and hews to this view of the author's identity as a composition balanced between New Formalist poetics, critical authority, and Catholic faith. "[H]is upbringing was saturated in the religion."[1] Gioia had early asserted the central force of Catholicism in his life: "Catholicism was everything to me," noting that the Roman Catholic Church was socioculturally fused with his family's "Latin community of Sicilian and Mexicans."[2]

My critical account of Gioia's most recent collection, *Meet Me at the Lighthouse* (2023), is grounded on a rereading of his first poetry collection to argue that this sixth collection, published when he was seventy-two, after forty years of prominence as a poet and public intellectual with a highly visible influence on the American arts, is both a kind of summation of his poetry trajectory and also a refusal of this long road taken. It focalizes instead on a turn to another identity, to go down a road not visibly taken until the last few years.

The dedication in Gioia's first poetry collection, *Daily Horoscope*, immediately signaled for readers his ancestral identity, his father, Michael Gioia, a Sicilian Italian and his mother, Dorothy Ortez, a mestiza of Mexican Indian ancestry. The epitaph below the dedication, "*Al cor gentil ripara sempre Amore*" ("To the noble heart, Love always returns"), is from the thirteenth-century Italian poet Guido Guinizelli and underlines Gioia's non-Anglophone linguistic roots.

These ancestral roots, Sicilian and Mexican Indian, otherized in white America, are almost effaced in the critical reception to his first five poetry collections, from 1986 to 2016, and to his work as critic, essayist, polemicist, biographer, lauded man of letters, and literary personage. For decades, in numerous published radio and television interviews and conversations and in the studies of his poetry, Gioia's comments on his immigrant generational history were chiefly ignored and remained near invisible. For these interlocutors, Gioia's life and career merge in the identities of the New Formalist poet, the critic-theorist, and the Catholic—his poetics and theology interwoven in the range of literary forms, genres, and rhetoric he produced in over fifty years.

Gioia, however, had flagged in his acclaimed debut collection, packed with poems earlier published in top-ranked journals such as the

---

[1] Matthew Brennan, *The Colosseum Critical Introduction to Dana Gioia* (Steubenville, OH: Franciscan University Press, 2020), 7.

[2] Robert McPhillips, "Dana Gioia: An Interview," *Verse* 9/2 (1992): 9–27, qtd. in Brennan, *Colosseum Critical Introduction to Dana Gioia*, 7.

Hudson Review, the *New Yorker*, the *Paris Review*, and *Poetry*, signs that his poetry is not quite in the mainstream of white, mostly male elite poets, and rooted in the tribe of recognized American public figures, many of whom Gioia was even then on first-name terms. Naming his parents and hailing them in his father's tongue, a reader may wonder how these parents' ethnic identities may serve as a counterweight presence to the Anglo-Saxon contextual heft of the poems' allusions, forms, and embeddedness in discernable traditions and values as vetted by the journal editors.

The reader in 1986 may have wondered if Gioia was himself familiar with the history of his parents' "people," if he was ever conscious of the racism Sicilian and Mexican immigrants to the US encountered, racism resulting in violence, including lynching, and discrimination in employment, education, housing, and other public sectors that kept these ethnic communities segregated and poor. (See, for example, Brent Staples's 2019 *New York Times* article "How Italians Became White."[3]) If his imagination had received these histories, were his poems inscribed with their traces overwritten in the invisible ink of images so subtle as to suggest that the imagination of this public poet may have disavowed these genealogical stories?

The first poem in *Daily Horoscope* opens and closes on allegorical figures. "The Burning Ladder" reimagines the biblical story in Genesis 28:10-19 in which Jacob's dream shows him angels ascending to heaven and descending. Gioia's poem, unlike the Genesis narrative, foregrounds not the dream but Jacob's insensate consciousness: "Sleep / pressed him like a stone"; he "closed / his eyes …/ … unconscious /of the impossible distances," missed the angels mounting, "slept / through it all" (*DH* 3). In this opening poem, the poet figured behind the scriptural patriarch, Jacob, is not a dreamer but "a stone," offering not moral authority but moral lassitude. The speaker upturns the figure of the patriarch with a vision of active "Seraphim" to a man "sick of traveling." Instead of a "flame rising" with the angels, the speaker slept through it

[3] Brent Staples, "How Italians Became White," *New York Times*, October 12, 2019, www.nytimes.com/interactive/2019/10/12/opinion/columbus-day-italian-american-racism.html?auth=login-google1tap&login=google1tap.

all, "a stone upon a stone," "gravity [being] always greater than desire." The poet-speaker cannot rise to scriptural or poetic vision. "Gravity," a metaphysical play on the earthly pull of weight and a sensibility of gravity, suggests in the word-play pun with "grave" the death-foreboding un-angelic mortality of humans; hence, the poem's subject—the eternal ("always") failure to rise to spiritual sublimity.

The allegory that closes the collection is drawn from popular culture, the opposing polar domain to Christian theology. The poem's title, "Sunday Night in Santa Rosa," posits a response to the call of Wallace Stevens's iconic modernist 1915 poem "Sunday Morning." However, Gioia's poem offers a secular figuration of late twentieth-century existence in the extended tropes of carnival freaks settling into their private lives at night after their public performances conclude. The poem's vision of humanity as a collective of freaks picks up on tropes of "Life Is a Carnival," widely popularized in the 1970s in the lyrics of a top pop song written by Levon Helm and Robbie Roberston. In Gioia's poem, the Dog-Faced Boy, Serpent Lady, giant, juggler, and others get on with their private lives. However, the final image of the clown sitting by a mirror peeling off his comic face leaves open what that private face may be. In classic drama, the clown mask is the iconographic opposite to the tragic. The poem's (and the collection's) closing figure, suggesting the tragic face disguised behind the clown mask, acts as the objective correlative to Gioia's late twentieth-century dark subjectivity. To read his poetics in *Daily Horoscope* as tonally "wry" is to misread the darkness and alienation that ground the admixture of low and high cultural referents deployed in Gioia's 1986 stylistics.

Daily Horoscope's success set the terms for the reception of the next four collections. Robert McPhillips's chapter on Gioia's poetry in *The New Formalism: A Critical Introduction* (2005) promulgated his poetics in the twenty-first-century interregnum school of New Formalism. Linking by violence two unlike attributes, "visionary" and "realism," McPhillips's close readings of the three extant collections authoritatively quote Gioia's biographical journey from working-class Los Angeles to academic success in literature and fine arts at Stanford and Harvard before his shift to an MBA earned at Stanford and the fifteen-year executive climb to Vice President of Marketing at General Foods in Westchester County, New York. Gioia, McPhillips recounted, "walked away from the Harvard program in Comparative Literature" for a "peculiar degree" in business, which corporate position (and salary) freed the poet from university constraints and allowed him to compose "highly polished poems … in prestigious journals" and to emerge as "a discriminating critic of contemporary poetry."[4] This profile of an outsider poet-critic (formalist instead of free-verse, MBA instead of MFA) whose unlikely success raises him to the center of literary influence "in the last quarter century" (1980–2005) is the narrative told of Dana Gioia, a poet who moved from a Californian identity to East Coast "Cheever Country," and later from a vice president corporate position to a six-year term from 2003 to 2009 as chairman of the National Endowment for the Arts, nominated by President George W. Bush and twice unanimously confirmed by the US Senate (a radical career shift that McPhillips's chapter did not address).

In 2011 Gioia returned to California and served for eight years at the University of Southern California as the Judge Widney Professor of Poetry and Public Culture. While teaching, he published his new and selected collection, *99 Poems* (2016), with a revelatory thematic organization. In the years since he resigned from his USC position, he has flourished in multiple roles. He published a new critical book, *The Catholic Writer Today* (2019); a literary memoir, *Studying with Miss Bishop* (2021); a book of interviews, *Conversations with Dana Gioia* (2021); and *Meet Me at the Lighthouse*, which arguably presents a fully new identity position.

David Mason's 2015 essay is perhaps the first to note the anomalies in Gioia's poetic career. "To understand Dana Gioia's contribution to modern American poetry, one must first acknowledge his position as an outsider": an outsider whose strengths of "feisty independence and clarity of vision" is yoked together with "intensely private grief."[5] As Gioia's poems often claim, his narratives and lyrical poems are "haunted." Mason connects this haunted sensibility to a "theme of unbelonging" that

---

[4] McPhillips, *New Formalism*, 33.

[5] David Mason, "The State of Letters: The Inner Exile of Dana Gioia," *Sewanee Review* 123/1 (2015): 135–36.

he sees cognizant with "a cultural tradition … his Mexican and Italian roots."[6] Mason, however, ignores the very ethnic differences he identifies to place these differences in "one basket," the category of Rome and the identity of the Catholic writer. Here Mason is accepting the lead Gioia had himself made over the years, and that underlines what Mason views as Gioia's predilection for "the unrecognized, the unseen, and a poet who knows all about the unsaid."[7] This aporia, the oversight of Gioia's ethnic identity in a nation historically riven by race and ethnicity, identities that enrich and problematize its literature, has been partially caused by Gioia's often stated agenda of writing for a "general public," and his praise of poetry accessible to general readers rather than only to an academic elite. This position, famously expressed in his *Atlantic* essay "Can Poetry Matter?," served to place him as the nation's chief civil servant for the Arts and also to cast his poetry as secondary to his public role as a man of letters. Mason laconically recognizes this aporia: "Of course Dana Gioia is more famous as a critic and public servant than as a poet."[8]

"Unsaid," the poem that appears on the dust jacket of 99 *Poems: New & Selected* (2016) picks up on Mason's acute apprehension of Gioia's poetics, what had been missed by many critics before Mason, the poetics "all about the unsaid."

> So much of what we live goes on inside—
> The diaries of grief, the tongue-tied aches
> Of unacknowledged love are no less real
> For having passed unsaid. What we conceal
> Is always more than what we dare confide.
> Think of the letters that we write our dead. (*99P* 66)

The six lines of blank verse confess to a profound repression of utterance, in ironic opposition to the definition of poetry as emotionally expressive. Speaking in a plural voice, "Unsaid" views the intense

[6] Ibid., 137.
[7] Ibid., 139.
[8] Mason, "State of Letters," 142.

interiority of lived experience as beyond the reach of communication and intimacy, "tongue-tied," "unacknowledged," "passed unsaid," "conceal," "letters" written not to the living but to the dead (*99P* 66).

The paradox of poetry that expresses obliquely, revealing by what it conceals, results in poems whose lines turn on paradox, each paradox strung on ideational tensions that, like John Donne's metaphysical wit, are surface play and depths-profound. "God Only Knows" (published in *Daily Horoscope* and republished thirty years later in *99 Poems*) uses the quotidian idiomatic phrase to meditate on Bach's "greatest work." Bach's sublime music opens the ordinary worshippers to an awesome heaven, "a terrifying sky" filled nonetheless with "angels," but angels on Judgment Day "holding ledgers / for a roll call of the damned," a Judgment Day the congregation averts by singing "to save their souls" (*DH* 38). This twenty-line free verse poem with its visual topographical design has been scarcely discussed despite the turns in its Christian metaphysical wit (fittingly, John Harbison set it to music in 2007 for soprano and piano). Publicly inserting his Catholic personhood into US poetic discourse (as in *The Catholic Writer Today*), Gioia is widely welcomed as a "Christian" poet by readers of the faith, at the same time as his particular praxis of challenging form and thought, underlined in his editing of the poetry of John Donne and Gerald Manley Hopkins, two British poets famed for the original genius of their verse and religious/metaphysical profundities, may explain the paucity of general attention to his Christian-thematized poems.

In 2018, during his three-year term as California's poet laureate, a period when he read in all fifty-eight California counties, Gioia began publicly to claim his family's ethnic history, identities he had overtly inscribed in his dedication to his Sicilian father and Mexican mother in *Daily Horoscope*, but which remained submerged in the critical reception of his works. The special publication of *The Ballad of Jesús Ortiz* by Providence Press in Ojai, California (a rare change from Gioia's decades-long relationship with Graywolf Press in Minneapolis, Minnesota), composed in the form of the Mexican *corrido*, his first and only use of this ballad form, explicitly narrates his great-grandfather's life as a vaquero. (The poem is also included in *Meet Me at the Lighthouse*.)

The author's note to "The Ballad of Jesús Ortiz" testifies to the veracity of the family story and links his deployment of the *corrido* to its evolution as "traditionally . . . the form to document the stories of the poor, particularly in the Old West. The people remembered in the poem [i.e., his Mexican forebears and descendent Mexican Americans] would have sung ballads" (*MML* 57). The author's note also dates its composition to his time as the Poet Laureate of California. More importantly, the *corrido* contextualizes Gioia's family history as immigrant, bilingual, and transnational: "Jake's real name was Jesús, / Which the Anglos found hard to take, / So after a couple of days, / The cowboys called him Jake" (*MML* 17). The swift anglicization of Jesús, a cattle driver raised in a pueblo in Sonora, to Jake settling down as a bartender in the Wyoming town of Lost Cabin is covered in ten quatrains. The ballad then introduces another ethnic identity, the maternal great-grandmother, "Half Indian, half white," and succinctly dramatizes the character of the white supremacist, Bill Howard. Affronted—"Is this some goddamn joke, / A piss-poor Mexican peon / Telling me I'm broke?"—when denied service unless he settles his bill, Bill Howard returns and guns down Jesús Ortiz (*MML* 20). The *corrido* closes this Mexican American tale with resonant sentiments on the murder and its consequences:

> There were two more graves in Wyoming
> When the clover bloomed in spring.
> . . .
> And two tall boys departed
> For the cattle drive that May
> With hardly a word to their mother
> Who watched them ride away. (*MML* 21)

Arguably the poem's closing image pulls back from the storyline to a longer future perspective, the next generation riding away from this violent racialized past and from the Indian-white mother. That is, the poem enacts Gioia's literary identity trajectory up to the publication of "The Ballad of Jesús Ortiz."

Because the family story pitches no special pleading for a retrospective inscription of his Ortiz Mexican forebears in his imagination (other than the story recorded in the ballad), the reception to the poem had likewise been critically muted on the ballad's re-shifting of Gioia's genealogical and poetic identities until the 2019 interview with John Zheng, published in *Journal of Ethnic American Literature* (reprinted in 2021 in *Conversations with Dana Gioia*). In the interview, Gioia sketches moments from his Mexican American childhood, focusing on his great-grandfather's violent death: "The poem tells a story I first heard as a child, but I didn't write the poem until I was sixty-five."[9] Gioia's responses to Zheng's questions deserve some unpacking: "The story helped shape my sense of my family history ... But the episode never emerged in my imagination as a poem."[10] When he finally composed the ballad in 2018, the act of writing the core origin story of his Mexican ancestor in the ballad form of that ancestral culture arrived from a source outside of poetics and religious dogma: "Writing the poem released all sorts of emotions. It felt affirming to tell a story that had gone untold for over a hundred years. I was proud to remember my great-grandfather. The stories of poor Mexican immigrants have mostly been forgotten. They have remained unsung."[11]

In these brief sentences, Gioia is calling on the direct diction of poets for whom poetry is expressive, psychologically a release of emotions, proudly and openly claiming ethnic identities, and engaged in their imaginations with the retelling of stories "forgotten ... unsung"—erased and/or effaced in mainstream Anglo-Euro-America. As Gioia recounts the reception of the ballad, one may infer that the ballad has released as well a public affirmation of the poet Dana Gioia: "It created an immediate stir ... It was translated into Spanish and Vietnamese... Finally, the sculptor and *santero* Luis Tapa [created] "El Cantinero," a statue of Jesús Ortiz. He said that the poem had moved him so deeply that he had felt compelled to carve it."[12] Ironically, in writing of his ethnic identity, Gioia has emerged as more accessible to a general audience than in his earlier collections where his poems were viewed

[9] John Zheng, *Conversations with Dana Gioia* (Jackson: University Press of Mississippi), 234.

[10] Ibid., 235.

[11] Ibid., 236.

[12] Ibid., 238.

through formalist and moral lenses.

Surprisingly, many reviews of *Meet Me at the Lighthouse*, which includes "The Ballad of Jesús Ortiz," praise it as the cumulative achievement of his oeuvre while continuing to ignore the evolution of his autobiographical and poetic identity. In *World Literature Today*, Fred Dings notes the poems' recollection of a "working-class family of immigrants," including the poem on Gioia's uncle, a US Merchant Marine, and "The Ballad of Jesús Ortiz," the latter of which is described as about "his great-grandfather, a Mexican vaquero who was shot dead at a tavern in Wyoming during a dispute over a bar tab."[13] But Dings chiefly generalizes the collection as a life-writing sequence "holding the entirety of lived life and so preserving it."[14]

Seth Wieck marks the collection with Gioia's age, "72 this last Christmas Eve," to commemorate its publication as the poet understanding that "he has reached the last stage of his life and career."[15] Yet, factually the dedication to the three generations of his mother's Ortiz genealogy—his great-grandfather (Jesús), grandfather (Francisco), and uncle (Theodore)—in praise of "the dignity of their destitution," linking Mexican ethnicity with working-class position, opens the collection which in its entirety foreshadows a burst of stories, multilingual stylistics, and a new poetics in future works.

The opening and title poem set in the imperative present tense is addressed to a friend long dead, in The Lighthouse bar, to listen to swing-jazz musicians now in Tartarus, the Inferno of Greek mythology:

> The crowd will be quiet—only ghosts at the bar—
> So you, old friend, won't feel out of place.
> You need a night out from that dim subdivision.
> Tell Dr. Death you'll be back before dawn.
>
> The club has booked the best talent in Tartarus.

---

[13] Fred Dings, review of *Meet Me at the Lighthouse*, by Dana Gioia, *World Literature Today* 97/2 (March 2023): 68.

[14] Ibid.

[15] Seth Wieck, "Dana Gioia's Bright Twilight," *Front Porch Republic*, February 7, 2023, www.frontporchrepublic.com.

Gerry, Cannonball, Hampton, and Stan,
With Chet and Art, those gorgeous greenhorns—
The swinging-masters of our West Coast soul.

Let the All-Stars shine from that jerry-built stage.
Let their high notes shimmer above the cold waves.
Time and the tide are counting the beats.
Death the collector is keeping the tab. (*MML* 3)

The poem, establishing the collection's thematic nexus, fuses the coeval recurring subjects in Gioia's half-a-century poetics—ghosts and the underworld, haunting figures for loss, memory of loss, of grief and mourning, and the dread of the something after death, "The undiscover'd country, from whose bourn / No traveller returns" (Shakespeare, *Hamlet*).

These subjects are "universal" in that myths, sacred rituals, and stories circulate them in every society conscious of its exceptionalism. Yet they are also shape-shifting, specifically original to sources embedded in tribal, racialized, ethnic, national, and religious communities. The sensibility in *Meet Me at the Lighthouse* weaves a matrix composed of Western and Catholic civilizations, US and Americas regionalism, Anglophone and Euro-American literatures, Los Angeles and the Underworld of Dante's *Inferno*, where what had been left unsaid in earlier collections comes as close to being said as Gioia's obliquity will let shine through its cracks.

Using an ironic pun, "Tinsel, Frankincense, and Fir" memorializes Gioia's mother, who "had so little joy to share / She kept it in a box to hide away" (*MML* 12). In the narrative of re-using her treasured Christmas tree baubles, the final quatrain strikes a despairing query on the disjuncture between the narrator-first person character and parental generation: "Why do the dead insist on bringing gifts / We can't reciprocate?" to close with yet another pun that sacralizes the lost mother: "No holiday is holy without ghosts" (*MML* 12). Can this poem be read as "Catholic"? Yes. But it is also memoirist and confessional, Robert Lowell's "Skunk Hour" paralleled by the "frankincense" of the Christmas fir tree hour.

The collection, opening with the friend and musicians now resident in Tartarus, the ancient Greek underworld, ghosts from the era of 1950s Los Angeles, is chained-linked to the lost mother, "old ornaments," haunting the poet's present-tense Christmas "fresh-cut tree," and closes with Gioia's newest reiteration of the Underworld. Through the decades of his poetry, Gioia has thematized the human failure to transcend its fallen condition; his sensibility has been strung not on Seraphim ascending to heaven but on souls cast down into Dante's *Inferno*. In the collection's final segment, seventeen stanzas or chapters track a collective second-person addressee through the trip to the underworld, elaborating on the fare, passengers, and the destination, "dark city . . . in the distance," hell itself (*MML* 54). The last seven-line chapter-stanza blows through a series of sixteen negatives, the last line of the poem composed with five no's: "No sun, no moon, no stars, no sky, no end," ironically punning at its end, "no end" (*MML* 54).

"The Underworld" is an ingenious narrative poem, succinct, classically allusive, Virgil and Dante as its guides, formally seventeen seven-line stanzas, occasionally end rhymed, frequently sonically consonantal, imagistic ("a piece of bread, / A sip of wine, a single pumpkin seed— / And you invite the darkness into you. . . . / You wake a dry husk turning in the wind"), packed with concrete particulars ("Jewelry boxes, satchels stuffed with cash, / Briefcases, laptops, thermoses, and urns"), and statements freighted with abstractions ("There are some truths that only darkness knows. / Such knowledge never comes without a price"), crafted with rhetorical figures that endow persuasive authority: "There are some," "only," "never" (*MML* 50–51).

These ghosts, losses, the Imaginary of Tartarus/Underworld/Hell, articulate an existential nihilistic Eternity. The translations (poems by Machado, Rilke, and Neruda) also thematize life as negative transience; in Machado's poem, "only a track of foam upon the sea," "nothing more," "no road," "you cannot walk again," "no road," anticipating the collection's final stanza; in Rilke's "Aimlessly wandering the empty lanes / Restless" and Neruda's "No longer with you, I am nothing but your dream" (*MML* 35–37). *Meet Me at the Lighthouse* is a dark poetics, its Catholicism one of awful dread, its stories twisting on the failures of mortal souls, its belief in the power of language, wording, uplifted by and cast down by ambivalent hope:

It is the luck to fail at what we started,
of letting language use us as a vessel
swept on a course we never could have charted—
to hope that once
the angel came, possessed us, and departed. (*MML* 13)

Meet Me at the Lighthouse, however, is unequivocally Gioia returning to his working-class Hawthorne and mestizo Los Angeles roots, emerging with another entirety of identities. Gioia's poetics before 2018 are that of the "unsaid," "letters to the dead" evocative of Matthew Arnold's "Buried Life" and wandering "between two worlds, one dead and another powerless to be born."[16] But in Section III, the poems claim a birthright that had been earlier left unsaid. With nothing left to lose, they shine a light on birthmarks now vivid as in "Psalm for Our Lady Queen of the Angels":

Let us sing to our city a new song,
A song that remembers its name and its founders—
Los Pobladores
...
They named the river for the Queen of the Angels,
Nuestra Señora la Reina de los Ángeles.
Poor, they were forced to the margins of empire,
Dark, dispossessed, not one couple pure.
...
I praise myself, a mutt of mestizo and mezzogiorno,
The seed of exiles and violent men,
...
I praise my ancestors, the unkillable poor, (*MML* 30)

What luck lies in one rapturous reception, that "in this entertaining collection," the "delightful poems" are "simple, clear, and permanent—exactly what poetry should be" and "amuse ... with lyricism and

---

[16] Matthew Arnold, *Matthew Arnold*, ed. Miriam Allott and Robert H. Super (Oxford: Oxford University Press, 1986), 161.

whimsy."[17] If beauty is in the eye of the beholder, can poetry matter if words are immutably in the heads of the readers and not on the page, as in *Meet Me at the Lighthouse*, to tease us "out of thought"? The answer lies in Gioia's complicated, ever evolving poetics, for yes, Jarvis rightly found poems in *Meet Me at the Lighthouse* that are simple, amusing, whimsical, and entertaining (see "Hot Summer Night," "Too Bad," and "Epitaph"). Like Walt Whitman, whose "Song of Myself" is echoed throughout Section III, Gioia is singing "a new song," where the poet praises "myself." Unlike Whitman, however, Gioia's poetry does not "contain multitudes"; it is layered on named singularities, New Formalist poetics that are also inclusive of diverse forms, a Catholic transcendentalism seen as through a glass darkly, and allusive and elusive imagery testifying to his critical academic intelligence. Poetry matters here, in this latest collection, in the release of an activist identification with his birth city, Los Angeles, and his city's and forebears' *ethnos*, his Mexican identity.

---

[17] Andrew Jarvis, review of *Meet Me at the Lighthouse*, by Dana Gioia, *New York Journal of Books*, www.nyjournalofbooks.com/book-review/meet-me-lighthouse-poems.

19

THE POET AS CRITIC AND PUBLIC INTELLECTUAL (2003, REV. 2020)

Matthew Brennan

Dana Gioia is a poet who writes criticism seriously and who undertakes editing projects that serve poetry's greater cause. This role of public intellectual was filled in Auden and Eliot's time by the quaint "man of letters." Not all freelance writers qualify as public intellectuals, however. In evaluating the career of Alfred Kazin, Thomas Bender distinguishes the public intellectual not just by the writer's status as nonspecialist but also by the uses of literature. Kazin "used literature for larger purposes, to talk about subjects that mattered to contemporary society. His capacity to speak to more general and deeply felt worries, questions and aspirations, and to do so in a common idiom, made him a public intellectual."[1]

This characterization of Kazin goes far in describing what Gioia does and why. Gioia told John Cusatis that as a graduate student he loved to read essays by Wendell Berry, Donald Hall, and Cynthia Ozick, "public intellectuals writing for a broad but mixed audience. I knew early that they were my people."[2] After Gioia left his job as a vice president at General Foods, he turned to writing for his livelihood. Gioia eventually left New York at age forty-five for his native California, where he forged ahead as a professional "man of letters"—not a university specialist in creative writing. Though a decade lapsed between his second and third books of poems and another eleven years between the

---

[1] Qtd. in Marjorie Garber, *Academic Instincts* (Princeton: Princeton University Press, 2001), 20.

[2] John Cusatis, "An Interview with Dana Gioia," in *Dictionary of Literary Biography: Twenty-First Century American Poets. Third Series*, vol. 380, ed. John Cusatis (Farmington Hills, MI: Gale Cengage Learning, 2017), 332.

third and the fourth, Gioia has never swerved from his primary identity as poet. Everything Gioia does simultaneously serves the cause of his own poetry and his quest for poetry to reach a wider audience of educated but nonspecialized readers. As a result, he was a natural fit for the National Endowment for the Arts.

As a public intellectual, Gioia's most deeply felt worry is the divorce of poetry from the educated general reader and the resulting isolation of poets from a common audience. In 1991, in "Can Poetry Matter?" he amplified the problem like this:

> The most serious question for the future of American culture is whether the arts will continue to exist in isolation and decline into subsidized academic specialties or whether some possibility of rapprochement with the educated public remains.... Given the decline of literacy, the proliferation of other media, the crisis in humanities education, the collapse of critical standards, and the sheer weight of past failures, how can poets possibly succeed in being heard? (*CPM10* 18).

Here Gioia expresses his greatest wish: "that poetry could again become a part of American public culture" (*CPM10* 19). Poetry, he feels, must recruit its readership from the people who in general support the arts, the well-educated people who cut across occupational boundaries but who commonly attend performances of symphonies and operas and screenings of foreign films, who buy jazz and classical music, who read literary fiction and biography, who listen to National Public Radio (*CPM10* 16). Gioia wants our culture to meet Walt Whitman's challenge that "'To have great poets, there must be great audiences, too'" (*CPM10* 10).

Through his essays in the eighties, Gioia established the defense of New Formalism in much the same way that Wordsworth's preface to *Lyrical Ballads* paved the way for Romanticism in 1800. Wordsworth conditioned his audience to accept the turn in literary history that his works embody. In other words, he exploited the preface as a marketing tool; its earliest incarnation in the first edition of 1798 was labeled an "Advertisement." Similarly, in "Notes on the New Formalism" and "The Poet in an Age of Prose"—both reprinted in *Can Poetry Matter?*—

Gioia argues for a revival of form in poetry to parallel the return to tonality in music, representation in art, and ornamental detail in architecture (*CPM10* 36). These shifts resemble the New Formalists' reactions against free verse, which once aided an earlier poetic revolution but now serves the old-guard establishment. Poets reviving formal verse, like painters returning from abstraction to realism, represent the fresh "unexpected challenge," Gioia says, which gives them appeal to audiences, as do their means (*CPM10* 29). In "The Poet in an Age of Prose," Gioia establishes that from the beginning the New Formalists made reaching an audience primary to their mission:

> New Formalism represents the latest in this series of rebellions against poetry's cultural marginality. The generational change in literary sensibility, which would eventually be called New Formalism, began ... when a group of young writers created—admittedly, only in their own minds—a new audience for poetry. Alienated from the kind of verse being praised and promulgated in the university, these young poets—like every new generation of writers—sought to define their own emerging art in relation to an imaginary audience. (*CPM10* 224)

The purpose of reviving form and meter, he argues, is to widen the audience for poetry and to provide poets with long dormant possibilities for fresh expression.

Gioia revives this concern for audience in "Disappearing Ink: Poetry at the End of Print Culture," the lead essay of his third critical collection. It speculates on the directions of poetry within American culture in the twenty-first century. In an age when print competes with technology and mass media, Gioia observes that the major change in the world of poetry is the rise of popular poetry—rap, cowboy verse, spoken word, performance poetry, and poetry slams. Gioia, whose essay is analytical and not evaluative, nevertheless allows that "most of this verse is undistinguished or worse" (*DI* 7). But what matters is that all these types of poetry are oral and all draw audiences "hungry for what poetry provides" (*DI* 19). Despite the challenges to print poetry and to the literary dominance of universities, the changes in literary poetry toward rhyme and meter locate it within the cultural "shift in sensibility toward orality" more obviously seen in rap or cowboy verse (*DI* 29). As a result, Gioia concludes, "For the first time in a century there is the possibility of serious literary poetry reengaging a nonspecialized audience of artists and intellectuals, both in and out of the academy" (*DI* 31). Ironically, much of this reengagement occurs during oral readings at bookstores—though, like ink, they're disappearing, too.

A prime goal of Gioia's at the NEA was to reverse the decline in reading, a cultural problem fully explored in the agency's 2004 report *Reading at Risk: A Survey of Literary Reading in America.* As a partial remedy, Gioia launched The Big Read, which through grants, discussion guides, and compact discs has encouraged residents of cities and towns to read and talk about a single work within their community. Choices originally included F. Scott Fitzgerald's *The Great Gatsby*, Ray Bradbury's *Fahrenheit 451*, Harper Lee's *To Kill a Mockingbird*, and Zora Neale Hurston's *Their Eyes Were Watching God.* Gioia's mission to boost reading derives from his belief that literary works fulfill the human "need for stories" that deepen "the meaning of our own lives,"[3] as he explains in a preface to a coedited textbook. His stint teaching at the University of Southern California clearly supported this longtime effort to boost reading, in this case the reading of poetry among undergraduates. As he told Father Sean Salai, who interviewed him for *America*, his course enrolled up to two hundred students whom he challenged not only by assigning papers and exams but also by making them recite poems they have memorized, all to emphasize the experiential approach to poems that can enchant readers.[4] Naturally, his textbook of choice was the one he coedited with X. J. Kennedy, *An Introduction to Poetry.*

Another key way to meet the challenge of creating readers, especially audiences for poetry, is to produce better anthologies, for these volumes "are poetry's gateway to the general culture" (*CPM10* 20). Among Gioia's books are fifteen textbooks and anthologies, including

[3] X. J. Kennedy, Dana Gioia, and Nina Revoyr, *Literature for Life* (New York: Pearson, 2013), 15.

[4] Sean Salai, SJ, "Catholic Poet Dana Gioia: Is Poetry Still a Spiritual Vocation?" *America*, May 6, 2019, www.americamagazine.org/arts-culture/2019/05/06/catholic-poet-dana-gioia-poetry-still-spiritual-vocation.

the two just mentioned. All of these texts are the kinds of books that not only serve the demands of the classroom but also just might remain in the private libraries of money-strapped students. Gioia longs for the days when poetry anthologies by the likes of Oscar Williams and Louis Untermeyer sold in huge quantities to general readers and consistently updated the best of contemporary writing. In *An Introduction to Poetry*, he and poet X. J. Kennedy demonstrate how college textbooks can fill the same role. Gioia's chief criterion for anthologies is that they present "masterpieces, not mediocrity," and this collection meets the requirement consistently (*CPM10* 20). But among its hundreds of poems, Gioia and Kennedy include not just warhorses but also samples from many up-and-coming poets.

This last distinction of his anthology points to the role his criticism has played in bringing notice to unfairly neglected poets. The poet who spent years plying his craft at night and holding his poems from circulation repeatedly focuses on previously neglected writers. His own years of loneliness as a writer primed Gioia to understand, as he puts it elsewhere, that "the contemporary poet has reluctantly learned to expect obscurity and isolation—not only from readers but from other artists—as conditions inseparable from his craft."[5] For example, *Studying with Miss Bishop* devotes a chapter to Ronald Perry, an all-but-forgotten poet who resided in Nassau and died in middle age, and large parts of *Can Poetry Matter?* cast light on previously overshadowed poets such as Jared Carter, Tom Disch, Weldon Kees, and Ted Kooser. Gioia writes with convincing, sympathetic intelligence about all of them. Just as he has worked to broaden the audience for poetry in general, so here he works to gain an audience for neglected talent. Through his appraisals of the noncanonical, then, Gioia teaches "remedial reading," as David Mason puts it.[6]

The other three collections of essays similarly strive to bring notice to poets who deserve to be better known. *Barrier of a Common*

---

[5] Dana Gioia, "Afterword: Creative Collaboration," in *Dana Gioia and Fine Press Printing: A Bibliographical Checklist*, comp. Michael Peich (New York: Kelly/Winterton Press, 2000), 19.

[6] David Mason, "The State of Letters: The Inner Exile of Dana Gioia," *Sewanee Review* 123/1 (2015): 133–46.

Language: An American Looks at Contemporary British Poetry advocates for Ted Hughes and Philip Larkin, whose slots in the canon are secure, as well as for Charles Causley, Tony Connor, and Dick Davis, who are less likely to land on Americans' reading lists. *Disappearing Ink* promotes the poetry of Samuel Menashe, Kenneth Rexroth, and Kay Ryan, who subsequently became US Poet Laureate. Moreover, in "Longfellow in the Aftermath of Modernism," Gioia takes on the task of rehabilitating the reputation of Henry Wadsworth Longfellow, once the most famous American poet in the world but now nearly eradicated from anthologies and represented by only a handful of lyric poems and short excerpts from narratives. Gioia accounts for this seismic change and argues that Longfellow's work, including his accomplishments in narrative and in prosody, need to be reevaluated not by the values of modernism but by those of his own time, the nineteenth century. Gioia keeps his eyes open to Longfellow's deficiencies, including the lack of tragic vision, but considers his place in American literature safe: "You will have to go a long way round if you want to ignore him" (*DI* 86). Finally, in separate essays, *The Catholic Writer Today* promotes the almost forgotten poets Brother Antoninus, Elizabeth Jennings, and Dunstan Thompson. Thompson's "early work has been out of print for seventy years" (*CW* 77). The reputation of Brother Antoninus has fallen in the last quarter century since he died, and his "legacy" is "still too little known, even by Catholics" (*CW* 100, 107). And Jennings, whose poetic life "began splendidly," saw her luck run out and her career stall as her inclusion in The Movement led to "a dead end" (*CW* 108). In his essays on these three Catholic writers, Gioia recovers their lost reputations.

Besides promoting good poems and neglected talent in his anthologies, as editor of *The Best American Poetry: 2018*, Gioia has shined attention on poetry's contemporary variety as well as its quality, a sure way to widen its appeal. Poetry, it would seem, no longer is trapped in dire straits. Making his selections from more than five thousand poems, Gioia discovered that poetry still matters and in more ways than ever. But the old culture wars that pitted free verse against formal verse now seem quaint, if remembered at all. "Anything goes," Gioia found:

> A benevolent sanity prevails in which poets seem free to write in whatever way inspiration suggests. I was pleased to see individual writers publish work in widely different styles, sometimes even in the same issue of a journal. Free verse remains the dominant mode, but rhyme and meter are widely used again, often in ways that imitate hip-hop. Prose poems still make a strong showing ... It was a pleasure to turn the pages of a journal and not know what to expect next.[7]

So, there is no mainstream anymore, only a gamut of alternatives, which includes forms of performance he could not reproduce in the print anthology. Above all, Gioia's selections mirror "the social complexity" of America and "poetry's regional variety." He learned "there are fine writers everywhere."[8] No wonder the audience for poetry is "rapidly growing," he concluded.[9]

Gioia's poetic versatility and his cause for poetry in general—the need to entertain, to find a broader audience, to find ways to merge low and high culture as well as to combine poetry and the other arts—are vividly embodied not only by his anthologies and his essays written for the common reader but also by his four libretti. His first, *Nosferatu: An Opera Libretto*, was written for composer Alva Henderson and published in 2001 as a book. Gioia based it on F. W. Murnau's great silent film of 1922, an adaptation of Bram Stoker's gothic novel *Dracula*. In Murnau's film, Gioia found a Romantic myth natural to opera. In an informative essay that Gioia appends to the libretto, "*Sotto Voce*," he comments that with each scene he first wrote the lyrics to the central aria and then wrote the parts that preceded and followed it.[10] He generated ten arias that provide the plot's emotional peaks. Among the best are the three arias that also appear in *Interrogations at Noon*: "Ellen's Dream," "Eric's Mad Song," and "Nosferatu's Nocturne" ("Nosferatu's

---

[7] Dana Gioia, Introduction, *Best American Poetry 2018* (New York: Simon & Schuster, 2018), xxx–xxxi.

[8] Ibid., xxix–xxx.

[9] Ibid., xxiii.

[10] Dana Gioia, *Nosferatu: An Opera Libretto* (St. Paul: Graywolf Press, 2001), 83.

Serenade" in *Interrogations at Noon*). These lyrics vary their rhyme schemes and meters, but all the verse is clear, direct, and musical. The second libretto was written for composer Paul Salerni's *Tony Caruso's Final Broadcast* (published in 2005 in *Italian Americana*). Gioia creates ten short scenes centering on Caruso's last show, "Opera Lover," and probes Tony's failed dream to become the "second Caruso." *Pity the Beautiful* excerpts four of the songs, including "Maria Callas's Aria," which is sung by the ghost of Maria Callas, who pays Tony a visit. Gioia's other two libretti are *The Three Feathers* for Lori Laitman (premiered 2014) and *Haunted* for Salerni (premiered 2019). In a sense, Gioia's own orality includes performance and recordings of these operas. Other works have been set to music by such composers as Morten Lauridsen, Ned Rorem, and Dave Brubeck. As librettist, Gioia extends the literary diversity that distinguishes his work. Like Auden, who wrote libretti and critical essays as well as poetry, Gioia has also published libretti and essays as well as translations. As with Auden, however, with Gioia what matters most is his own poetry.

20

THE STATE OF LETTERS: THE INNER EXILE OF DANA GIOIA (2015)

David Mason

The Outsider

> "As Marx maintained and few economists have disputed, changes in a class's economic function eventually transform its values and behavior."
>
> —Dana Gioia, *Can Poetry Matter?*

To understand Dana Gioia's contribution to modern American poetry, one must first acknowledge his position as an outsider. This will seem strange to some, who consider Gioia the ultimate insider—a man with his fingers in many cultural pies, a man of privilege, educated in the Ivy League, prosperous, prolific, and political. Dana Gioia, the corporate poet, who had attained a vice presidency at General Foods when he resigned his position there to write full-time. Dana Gioia, the coauthor (with superb assistance from his wife, Mary) of popular textbooks used in many of the colleges and universities of the United States. Dana Gioia, the Bush appointee as chairman of the National Endowment for the Arts, the man who talked a hostile Congress out of more money and in effect saved the institution he ran for six years. An originator of programs devoted to reading, Shakespeare, jazz, the writing of returning veterans, and Poetry Out Loud, a marvelous program helping high-school students develop skills in thoughtful performance. A man much honored in the public realm, his shoulders bowed by eleven honorary degrees—he could joke with Robert Frost about being educated by degrees, but unlike Frost he had already earned several the old-fashioned way. Dana Gioia, the cofounder of a prominent poetry conference held each June in West Chester, Pennsylvania. A manager of people, hiring and firing and running the show like some Republican Wizard of Oz. Now we have Dana Gioia, professor at the University of Southern California, able to make a living by teaching one semester a year without having to attend faculty meetings. Surely no one has ever been so privileged.

These external trappings, however, are not the privilege they appear to be but the result of Gioia's feisty independence and clarity of vision, a clarity deriving precisely from his status as an outsider. To be an insider is to lose *privilege* in its root sense, "a bill or law affecting an individual." To be an insider means to behave as part of a group, a tribe, or social class, and this Gioia has never done. He has maintained his privileged status as a contrarian, a visionary, and he has made enemies in the process. "Give me a landscape full of obstacles," he writes in a poem called "Rough Country," and you know he means obstacles in multiple ways. One of his favorite Shakespearean lines comes from Duke Senior in *As You Like It:* "Sweet are the uses of adversity." Gioia is not a duke but has had to claw his way up from working-class roots, the son of a Mexican American mother and a Sicilian American father. He received a rigorous Catholic education that no doubt helped him succeed at Stanford University, where he took a BA and confirmed his desire to be a writer (he was also a serious musician and linguist). At Harvard he studied comparative literature, taking classes from both Robert Fitzgerald and Elizabeth Bishop along the way. Like other poets in a scholarly program, he was a double agent, unsure how to reconcile his creative ambitions with increasingly theoretical and arcane modes of study. He disliked what was happening to literature in the academy and also saw how few options he would have for making a living if he continued on this course. So, he did something outlandish. He went back to Stanford and got a master's in business administration. As the dutiful oldest son in a large family without wealth, he knew he would have to make money.

I know I've used the word *privilege* perversely in some respects—reversing the usual expectations that come with it, but I want to differentiate real individuality from group thinking. Despite our protective tenure, we academics very often enforce the assumptions of our tribe concerning money, class, politics, literature, and theory. Often, we write for one another, not for a presumed audience outside our walls and corridors. There is a strangely hidden pressure to fit in, to enter the fold, and the flock can behave cruelly toward an outsider. The corporate headquarters Dana Gioia entered also had its group behavior, its cruelties, but Gioia could put on its uniform, survive by its rules, hide his identity as a poet while he made a living, and look back on the academic world with the privilege of apartness. To do so, however, took prodigious, even obsessive and exhausting work—ten-hour days at the office, plus late nights writing at home.

It was about this time—the late seventies and early eighties—when Dana and I began the correspondence that would lead to our friendship. We bonded partly as outsiders who loved aspects of poetry that seemed disallowed by the academy at that time—a sweeping generalization, I know, but we felt acutely that to love Robert Frost or W. H. Auden or Emily Dickinson or Richard Wilbur was to be thought insufficiently barbaric and American in the classrooms of the day, where poets responding to the Vietnam War practiced their own violent righteousness, where race and gender politics were understandably coming to the fore after years of neglect. A generation of American poets born in the twenties and thirties had largely abandoned traditional techniques like narrative, rhyme, and meter to forge a poetry they considered more authentic; and we were simply young writers who still felt affection for diverse techniques and wished to keep them, along with all the other tools at a poet's disposal.

I won't belabor what used to be called "the poetry wars" or waste time elucidating the cultural debates of the era. Others have done that *ad nauseam*. My purpose here is to understand Gioia's outsider status. It's not just that he made his living as a businessman, working late into the night several days a week on his poetry, essays, and reviews, keeping his literary life a secret from the steel-and-glass office—I actually visited General Foods with him in the early eighties, saw the security measures for entry, the sterile rooms, the glass ceiling beyond which unseen demigods maneuvered. Sacrificing a more romantic image of the artist, Gioia maintained his privileged outsider status, feeling no pressure to conform to academic criteria. He could write whatever he wanted, not what might have been required for tenure.

Though strongly associated with a poetry movement called New Formalism—and here I should acknowledge Wyatt Prunty's seminal study, *Fallen from the Symboled World*, as well as books by many other writers—Gioia was steeped in the modernist poetries of Europe and always wrote free verse as well as metered poetry. He maintained a devotion to narrative verse when it was utterly unfashionable in the university, and as a reviewer he proved small-c catholic in his tastes. He had a knack for seeing the talents of others and promoting them when no one else would do so. He had, in short, something in short supply in the literary world—integrity. And he was beginning to shape his independent vision in some of the most trenchant essays by any poet of his generation.

Dana Gioia is an outsider. He always has been. And the adversity he faced by writing outside the academy allowed him original insights, just as exile liberates Shakespeare's Duke:

> Sweet are the uses of adversity,
> Which, like the toad, ugly and venomous,
> Wears yet a precious jewel in his head;
> And this our life, exempt from public haunt,
> Finds tongues in trees, books in the running brooks,
> Sermons in stones, and good in everything.
> (*As You Like It*, II.i.12–17)

In his poetry, Gioia's outsider status has more private meaning, dramatizing a profound schism between his public and private identities. His increasing visibility in the public sphere has paradoxically moved him to guard private experience and make it the true subject of his poems. He has always written as a Catholic—large C—in a secular age, has never allowed his subjects or forms to fit the expectations of others. And his major point of view is that of the outsider, the inner exile, the man who cannot completely reconcile public and private realms, and who never feels that he belongs anywhere. He is a poet of psychic separation, longing for the intimate touch from which we have fallen, and it is from this intensely private grief that he has forged his humane and human vision.

The First Three Books of Poetry

"Here feel we not the penalty of Adam."
—William Shakespeare, *As You Like It*, II.i.5

When I first visited Dana in New York in 1981—at last meeting the literary brother with whom I had corresponded for years—he kept me up half the night reading poems by someone I had never heard of. This was a poet of quiet lucidity, irony, and dramatic flair, a poet whose personae were death-obsessed and strangely thwarted Americans. The poet was Weldon Kees, whose reputation had evaporated after his apparent suicide in the 1950s. Donald Justice had with typical generosity edited a *Collected Poems*, and Dana would later edit Kees's fiction and drama. Poets desire fame, I suppose, but they adore obscurity, partly because it is so central to their own lives, their own fears of insignificance. The lives of people like Kees represent the dreams America fosters and destroys in equal measure. Kees would also influence Gioia's technique, most obviously in the verbal fugue, "Lives of the Great Composers," which made such an impression that it was imitated by Howard Moss in a poem dedicated to Dana. "Lives of the Great Composers" is Keesian in its irony, observing how even artists who might tremble at the sublime come, like all chimneysweepers, to dust. "Liszt wept to hear young Paganini play. / Haydn's wife used music to line pastry pans" (*DH* 37). The poem arises from Gioia's own vision of a fallen world where, as he says elsewhere, "Gravity" is "always greater than desire" (*DH* 3).

Those words are quoted from "The Burning Ladder," the poem that opens *Daily Horoscope*, Gioia's remarkably assured first book, published in 1986. Though its poems vary greatly in form and subject, they are clearly the work of a refined sensibility—witty knowing, haunted. Half a dozen of the poems are explicitly about the business world, and a handful evoke the poet's native California. There are dramatic monologues and narratives as well as lyrics—something we find in all of Gioia's collections. The verse is formal but never rigidly so, lucid and even plain in a manner we sometimes associate with other Stanford poets from Yvor Winters to Timothy Steele. Yet Gioia's technique feels less obviously like technique, and I imagine the influence of Elizabeth

Bishop, as well as poets writing in other languages, might have contributed to this flexibility.

Whatever landscape Gioia writes about—New York, California, Italy—and whether his poems are set in airports or offices, bedrooms or the out-of-doors, he never evades the central problem of his work—this schism between public and private, dream and reality, the workaday world and the imaginal. "The Journey, the Arrival and the Dream," a remarkable narrative from *Daily Horoscope*, is about a woman traveling through the Italian Alps. The journey itself seems nearly arbitrary, purposeless: "Journeys are the despair before discovery, / you hope, wondering if this one ends" (*DH* 64). Addressed in the second person as if by her own demonic inner voice, the woman arrives at a hotel, but in the poem's dream logic nothing connects. She even writes "a letter in a language" she doesn't understand (*DH* 64). The rarefied beauty at which she has arrived, the sublime, is uninhabitable.

> Emptying your pockets on the dresser, notice
> how carefully you put down all the useless keys
> and currency you've brought from home, so terrified
> of scratching the patina of the varnished wood
> that innocently reflects the lamp, your hand, the curtains,
> and the badly painted cherubs on the ceiling
> who ignore you. Light a cigarette and watch
> the lazy smoke creep up and tickle them
> to no effect and realize you don't
> belong here in their world where everything
> is much too good for you, and though the angels
> will say nothing, they watch everything you do. (*DH* 64)

You don't belong. These three words recur in Gioia's work—most conspicuously in his latest book, which I'll delay discussing till the end of my essay. Gioia's theme of unbelonging—the exiled self—can be understood biographically, of course, in the way a working-class kid might feel at Harvard or Stanford or for that matter in the White House. But, while I do think those three words, *you don't belong*, are the psychic key to all of Gioia's work, I should also point out how he dramatizes them, turns them into something other than mere confessionalism. Like Eliot he transmutes the private into lines of broader psychological significance.

The lines you've just read are also Catholic. There's the displacing guilt of being watched by angels, the apartness from art's cherubic bliss. For Gioia Catholicism has been a complex inheritance. On the one hand it is a house for the dispossessed, a home in which one is never fully at home. It's also a cultural tradition, connecting his Mexican and Italian roots to Rome, putting his languages in one basket, as it were. Here I pause to connect my beginning with my end. To understand Gioia's first book, I quote from his essay "The Catholic Writer Today":

> Catholic writers tend to see humanity struggling in a fallen world. They combine a longing for grace and redemption with a deep sense of human imperfection and sin. Evil exists, but the physical world is not evil. Nature is sacramental, shimmering with signs of sacred things. Indeed, all reality is mysteriously charged with the invisible presence of God. Catholics perceive suffering as redemptive, at least when borne in emulation of Christ's passion and death. Catholics also generally take the long view of things—looking back to the time of Christ and the Caesars while also gazing forward into eternity. (The Latinity of the pre-Vatican II Church sustained a meaningful continuity with the ancient Roman world, reaching even into working-class Los Angeles in the 1960s, where I was raised and educated.) (*CW* 20)

Even in poems that have nothing overtly to do with Catholic subject matter, Gioia depicts a fallen world and the suffering of the individual desiring grace, which might also be understood as a sort of unity of being.

One further point. Because Gioia is also a Westerner, a city boy who grew up without access to sublime and relatively unspoiled nature, the natural world remains a saving presence in itself. It is evidence of God. Gioia is a California Catholic who has read and understood the nature poems of Robinson Jeffers and others, has read praise of nature in poets like Gerard Manley Hopkins. His notion that "all reality is mysteriously charged with the invisible presence of God" makes him on the whole less eager to transcend the body, more willing to admit immersion in the world as a way of being.

This grief with this unbelonging, this schism, this inner exile—both forces are at work in Gioia. The sexual histories of his characters always have something secret and illicit about them. The first book contains "My Secret Life," a poem in which the words of a Victorian pornographer morph into another of those daimonic second-person narrators:

> No other details of your life survive,
>   and so your secret will be kept
> forever. Now you are only what you wanted
>   to be: a scholar of seduction,
> certainly more the antiquarian than lover,
>   and these pages catalogue a life's
> accumulation of encounters with the same obsessiveness
>   an eccentric would bestow
> on a collection of exotic stamps: clipped,
>   soaked, separated, and arranged
> by year and origin neatly in an album
>   until it is almost unbelievable
> that every one could bring a human message. (*DH* 50)

That message might be love, but can a pornographer say it? The title poem of *Daily Horoscope* turns the second person into the hectoring voice of the astrologer, those newspaper columns in which we mirror meaning for our lives. Another lovely lyric, "Cuckoos," takes up the folklore in which the birds are emblems of betrayal but points out that "the Chinese took their call / to mean *Pu ju kuei, pu ju kuei— / Come home again, you must come home again*" (*DH* 70).

Where would that home be, and could he ever belong in it? The book's final poem, "Sunday Night in Santa Rosa," is set where Gioia would eventually come to live, at least temporarily, in a house on a hill in Northern California. But the poem is not restful. It's about a carnival packing itself up to hit the road again:

Off in a trailer by the parking lot
the radio predicts tomorrow's weather
while a clown stares in a dresser mirror,
takes out a box, and peels away his face. (*DH* 87)

Gioia's second book, *The Gods of Winter*, appeared in 1991. In the five years between these two books, he had faced the greatest crisis of his private life—the death of his first-born son, Michael Jasper, of sudden infant death syndrome at only four months. As Dana had comforted me when my older brother died in 1979, I found myself trying to offer solace to a friend who was staring into the abyss. Many friends tried to comfort Dana and Mary. But there is no solace and there is no comfort in the face of a child's death. I mention this because it relates to my theme of exile. Gioia's position is no intellectual exercise. It is born of raw feeling and trauma and grief. This awareness of loss, even extinction, has made him the poet and critic he is, a patron of the unrecognized, the unseen, and a poet who knows all about the unsaid.

Two short poems in the second book stand at the poles of his life. The opening "Prayer" comes from the Catholic as well as the grieving father, addressing God in metaphors:

Seducer, healer, deity or thief,
I will see you soon enough—
in the shadow of the rainfall,

in the brief violet darkening a sunset—
but until then I pray watch over him
as a mountain guards its covert ore

and the harsh falcon its flightless young. (*GW* 3)

That harsh falcon could of course come from Jeffers or Hopkins, secular and Catholic at the same time.

Another short poem "Money" is in freer verse and is in fact adapted from the prose of his essay "Business and Poetry." "Money" gets a laugh in readings and represents Gioia's rueful take on pecuniary realities. But just like "Prayer" it is a list poem, a series of metaphors or slang terms, using as its epigraph a metaphor from Wallace Stevens: "Money is a kind of poetry." It's one of several Gioia poems in which the efficacy of language itself is challenged. Poetry and prayer inhabit a realm apart from the man of action who effects change in the world. Gioia had by now a reputation as a businessman poet, often compared to Stevens, or to figures like James Dickey or A. R. Ammons. People in my own profession, teaching, look down their noses at the business world, and Gioia bore a lot of criticism for his chosen life. But I also know the choices he had made were becoming worrisome to him. The privilege of independence he had earned with no small measure of courage allowed him to be the writer he wanted to be, but it was also killing him, and he knew it. His own mother could see it too and would eventually advise him to quit business and strike out on his own.

These personal details may cast some light on the struggles of the poems, the effort to reconcile public and private realms made more difficult by the elder son's responsible nature. Two long narrative poems in *The Gods of Winter*, dramatic monologues in the voices of very different personae, emerge ironically from that nature. "Counting the Children" is in the voice of an accountant, Mr. Choi, who must tally the estate of a deceased old woman, a collector of dolls. Choi is the responsible man of business, but also a kind of artist: "And though you won't believe that an accountant / Can have a vision, I will tell you mine" (*GW* 17). His vision is of childhood, of individual nature. The weird nonlives of the dolls he has had to count have given him nightmares; he feels their contempt for our fragile humanity—again like that traveler under the ceiling cherubs, the transcendent mocking the ordinary. The second monologue chills in another way. "Homecoming" is in the voice of a mass murderer driven to hatred by the love of the woman who raised him. Her moral righteousness served only to underline his essential illegitimacy.

> But as I stood there gloating, gradually
> the darkness and the walls closed in again.
> Sensing the power melting from my arms,

I realized the energy I felt
was just adrenaline—the phoney high
that violence unleashes in your blood.
I saw her body lying on the floor
and knew that we would always be together.
All I could do was wait for the police.
I had come home, and there was no escape. (*GW* 52)

The desire for arrival has a dark side. The idealism of a killer matches the idealism of a world that would correct his nature.

The Gods of Winter contains some of Gioia's most soulful lyrics about grief, including the title poem and "Planting a Sequoia." It also contains "Rough Country," which I cited in my opening, and his gorgeous poem about belonging, or nearly belonging, "Becoming a Redwood":

Stand in a field long enough, and the sounds
start up again. The crickets, the invisible
toad who claims that change is possible,

And all the other life too small to name.
First one, then another, until innumerable
they merge into the single voice of a summer hill. (*GW* 55)

Like his first collection, both varied and accomplished, offering poems in rhyme and meter as well as free and blank verse, *The Gods of Winter* confirmed Gioia's reputation, as they say, yet was relatively ignored in establishment circles, where he was dismissed unjustly as a formalist conservative, the devil who had dared to criticize the creative-writing programs. *The Gods of Winter*, it should be said, fared very well in England as a Choice of the Poetry Book Society, which in turn gave Gioia opportunities to work for the BBC and cemented several friendships abroad.

Gioia's third book, *Interrogations at Noon*, won the official outsider's literary prize, the American Book Award, signaling that he might not be ignorable as a poet much longer. Coming a decade after his second book, the new collection also demonstrated the toll his busy life exacted on his creativity—it simply took him longer to finish enough good poems to make a collection because, having left business in 1992, he was so busy working as a freelance writer and editor. The book contains more translations, song lyrics, and operatic arias than earlier collections, and though these first-rate pieces are by no means padding, a careful reader will wonder why there are fewer new poems on offer—the one big dramatic monologue is from his superb translation of Seneca's *The Madness of Hercules*. "The world does not need words," says Gioia's opening, and the poet in this volume is certainly more austere and self-critical. The dry noon of mid-life interrogation makes the book feel chastened, as if trying to suss out where to go next. Among the masterpieces of the book, I would single out his blank-verse lyric, "Metamorphosis," the only poem I have space to give you in its entirety:

> There were a few, the old ones promised us,
> Who could escape. A few who once, when trapped
> At the extremes of violence, reached out
> Beyond the rapist's hand or sudden blade.
>
> Their fingers branched and blossomed. Or they leapt
> Unthinking from the heavy earth to fly
> With voices—ever softer—that became
> The admonitions of the nightingale.
> They proved, like cornered Daphne twisting free,
> There were a few whom even the great gods
> Could not destroy.
>
> And you, my gentle ghost,
> Did you break free before the cold hand clutched?
> Did you escape into the lucid air
> Or burrow secretly among the dark
> Expectant roots, to rise again with them
> As the unknown companion of our spring?

> I'll never know, my changeling, where you've gone,
> And so I'll praise you—flower, bird, and tree—
> My nightingale awake among the thorns,
> My laurel tree that marks a god's defeat,
> My blossom bending on the water's edge,
> Forever lost within your inward gaze. (*IN* 17)

The language here is simply beautiful, and that's where I want to leave, momentarily, my consideration of Gioia as a poet, and turn to other things.

Criticism, Translations, and Libretti

> "I was attracted to poetry long before I ever thought of writing it."
>
> —Dana Gioia, *Can Poetry Matter?*

Of course, Dana Gioia is more famous as a critic and public servant than as a poet, but I wanted to set aside that fame—or infamy as some would have it—to consider the work of most importance to him. Now that I have begun to do so—there's still one more book of poems to go—I'd like to look briefly at the larger picture. The private grief of the poet is one thing, the public utterance of the critic quite another, but both are possible because of Gioia's outsider stance, his privilege of apartness.

The first criticism I saw from Dana came in his book reviews for Stanford literary magazines, then for the *Hudson Review*. These reviews astonished me, educating me about poets I had never heard of. He taught me how to read poets as different as Radcliffe Squires, Jared Carter, and Ted Kooser, and reminded me of German and Italian poets and obscure Californians, regional poets, and poets with eccentric lives. As a West Coast boy whose upbringing was more prosperous but also more provincial than Gioia's, I needed instruction badly, and it was Dana's criticism more than anyone else's that gave it to me. He's not a close reader like Helen Vendler—she lodges that complaint against him in her *Paris Review* interview. No, Gioia's criticism works outside accepted academic modes in two very different ways. On the one hand we have his essays of sociological diagnosis, standing at a distance from the literary world and examining it in the context of a culture the academy often fails to see, let alone acknowledge—the culture of people who are not poets and professors. On the other hand, we have appreciations of neglected masters. Here Gioia is not only the protector of the uncanonical, but a teacher of remedial reading. Do you think anti-populist modernism has swept the field? Gioia responds with a lengthy defense of Longfellow. Are you sure the long poem is a measure of magnitude? Gioia tells you about Samuel Menashe, the great bohemian master of mind-expanding miniatures. Among the California writers he has reminded us to read are such utterly different figures as Kenneth Rexroth, Jack Spicer, and Kay Ryan. Critics who label Gioia a conservative have neglected to notice how broad-minded his tastes really are. No other writer of our time has devoted so much energy, so many felled trees and pots of ink to resurrecting poets the academy assumed were safely dead or just invisible.

Try an experiment. Look at the tables of contents of every book of criticism devoted to modern or contemporary poetry, and you will see something curious. The same poets get discussed over and over again, as if we really needed another essay on Bishop or Lowell or Ashbery or Graham. Now look at Gioia's collections of critical prose and you will see how far outside the kingdom he has walked, and how clearly he has seen the fields around the castle. When Gioia does write about a canonical poet—Robert Frost or T. S. Eliot, for example—it is because he has something fresh to say about the work or the life. Gioia's essays are among the very few that make us better and broader readers. He leaves the close reading to us, trusts our intelligence, and simply reminds us to take a look at figures we might have missed in our busy lives.

His most controversial essay remains "Can Poetry Matter?" which caused much consternation on its appearance in the *Atlantic Monthly*. For one thing, people in my profession—and I do teach creative writing as well as literature courses—felt assaulted. They *were*, of course, but criticism needn't be felt so personally, and the attack was delivered with such reasonable civility that it hardly constituted terrorism. Gioia never said there was no such thing as a useful creative-writing class—after all, he had studied with Miss Bishop at Harvard, which is a lot more creative writing than I ever got. Instead, he pointed out an obvious truth—that people in a particular job begin to act as a group, sharing particular assumptions, protecting their own and one another's interests. This is simply true. I see it whenever I look in at MFA programs or wonder about new anthologies. The cronyism is still there, still self-protective, still more about keeping the job and publishing than promoting great poetry.

While it is statistically true that poetry *matters* a great deal in America right now, with more money and publicity to back it up than ever before, it is equally true that the contents of most magazines and books of poetry are spectacularly dull. I am one reader who finds far more poetry in a good novel than in most contemporary poems. This is more than a grouse. It is a crisis for the art, and the smug response of many poets to Gioia's criticism does them no honor. I have met writers with MFA degrees who do not know the history of their art and do not understand the rudiments of traditional techniques like meter. Their education in self-worth has, frankly, been a sham. They have paid poets to tell them they are wonderful, which is not the most valuable lesson for an artist to learn.

"Can Poetry Matter?" was the title essay of Gioia's first critical collection, published in 1992. The book had something to infuriate everyone: the essay "Business and Poetry," reminding us that there was more than one way to make a living; a skillful attack on "The Successful Career of Robert Bly"; a piece called "Notes on the New Formalism," which was a nonpolemical look at forgotten techniques; and essays on regional poets unknown to the arbiters of taste. One of them, Ted Kooser, has since been named Poet Laureate and won the Pulitzer Prize, a fate befalling still another of Gioia's "discoveries," Kay Ryan. When Gioia was asked to judge a first-book contest in 1999, he chose an unknown young poet from Georgia named A. E. Stallings.

Each of Gioia's essay collections, including *Disappearing Ink: Poetry at the End of Print Culture* (2004) and *The Barrier of a Common Language: Essays on Contemporary British Poetry* (2003), contains work that is prophetic, taking the long view, and useful in what it teaches about reading. Gioia the critic translates or carries over poetry from its academic ghetto to the common reader. He anticipated the connections between poetry and such popular phenomena as rap before they were taken up in the universities. In short it is impossible for me to convey how much good he has done for the arts in America, and it surprises me how slowly and grudgingly some American artists will admit it.

Gioia's devotion to the modernists as well as the classics shows in his work as a translator from Italian, German, Latin, and other languages. He is simply one of the best verse translators we have at work today. And he translates in other ways, too, in his work with composers and musicians. His original opera libretti, including *Nosferatu* and *Tony Caruso's Final Broadcast*, are masterpieces of modern verse drama. No contemporary poet has taken a deeper interest in the genre of the art song or has done more to promote the work of contemporary classical and jazz composers.

My discussion of these activities leaves much out, of course, but it also explains why we had to wait more than a decade for a new collection of poems. In his six years running the NEA, Gioia surely wondered whether he would ever write poetry again. But the muse did not desert him. Poetry came back, haltingly at first, and the new book proves that, while he may feel exhausted by his battles, he can still write like an angel.

The Inner Exile and the World

> Now you are twenty-one.
> Finally, it makes sense
> that you have moved away
> into your own afterlife.
> —Dana Gioia, "Majority"

Gioia is the sort of poet who would rescue populism from the charge of stupidity. He has always been a reader of the popular, including science fiction and ghost stories, and his poems frequently touch on the supernatural, being set in graveyards, or offering prayers or otherwise keeping that Catholic eye on the afterlife. In some ways the most remarkable poem in his new book, *Pity the Beautiful* (2013), is the long dramatic narrative at its center, "Haunted." A classic ghost story, its source is the psychic schism I mentioned earlier, both a class division and an inner one, a divided soul.

A young man is in love with a rich, spoiled, and callous young woman named Mara. They visit her family's sumptuous home in the Berkshires and have the place to themselves for their dining and love-making—the Massachusetts setting also suggests they could be students at Harvard, or otherwise denizens of economic privilege. The speaker is clearly an outsider, appreciative of all that money buys, hopeful for his love life, but uncertain how to behave among such glamour. After a spat with his girlfriend, he wanders off alone in the cold palatial house, which is very much a gothic movie set. In the library he reads Shakespeare's sonnets: "What is your substance, whereof are you made, / That millions of strange shadows on you tend?" And then, of course, he discovers that he is not alone. Another woman is there, a ghost:

> We stood there face to face, inches apart.
> Her pale skin shined like a window catching sunlight,
> both bright and clear, but chilling to the touch.
> She stared at me with undisguised contempt,
> and then she whispered, almost in a hiss,
> "You don't belong here. No, you don't belong here."
> She slowly reached to touch me, and I ran
> leaving behind both Shakespeare and my shoes. (*PB* 41)

The language here is simple and clear, serving the story more than luxuriating in the rich textures of sound we might get from a poet like Anthony Hecht. But you can see this is the ghost that has haunted Gioia all his life—the voice that sees him and knows he does not belong, the judging voice that drives him and finds him wanting. The poem even whips up the sort of surprise ending we might find in popular fiction, and there again it stands outside the kind of writing usually found in contemporary poetry magazines. Thankfully, the *Hudson Review* has always saved a place for narrative verse, and that is where "Haunted" first appeared.

Now in his senior years, Gioia has not escaped these hauntings, these real and imagined presences, but *Pity the Beautiful* contains poems suggesting he may be ready to let them go. To be sure, some works in this collection are very dark, even chilling, like the masterly "Special Treatments Ward," one of the best things he has written in years. "So this is where the children come to die, / hidden on the hospital's highest floor" (*PB* 29). I can hardly bear to read the rest of this painfully honest poem.

Still *Gioia* does mean *joy*. He's a man with much to be thankful for, including his wife, Mary, and his two living sons. His "Prayer at Winter Solstice" is a praise poem, and "Majority," the beautiful lyric closing the book, finds new meaning in Michael Jasper's early death—how death resembles other ways of maturing and moving on. The book's title poem has been compared by Bruce Bawer to Frost's "Provide, Provide," and it may be that a more resilient stance has arrived in Gioia's poetry. After all he has his Catholic continuity, his belonging among the exiles. And one hopes he is done with public service, ready at last to let others take the heat and acknowledge his own gifts. In his essay "The Catholic Writer Today," he maintains that "Nature is sacramental, shimmering with signs of sacred things" (C*W* 20). It may be something else, of course—just nature, a meaning of its own—but how astonishing it is, this world we are given to see, however briefly and however much it hurts us. We don't need to feel belonging in order to see the blessings where they are, the shimmering gifts, the world's beautiful otherness, tongues in the trees, books in the running brooks, and sermons in stones. Among these gifts I would number the works of Dana Gioia.

SELECTED BIBLIOGRAPHY

POETRY

Daily Horoscope. St. Paul, MN: Graywolf Press, 1986.

The Gods of Winter. St. Paul, MN: Graywolf Press, 1991; York, UK: Peterloo Poets, 1991.

Interrogations at Noon. St. Paul, MN: Graywolf Press, 2001.

Pity the Beautiful. Minneapolis: Graywolf Press, 2012.

99 Poems: New and Selected. Minneapolis: Graywolf Press, 2016.

Meet Me at the Lighthouse. Minneapolis: Graywolf Press, 2023.

CRITICAL COLLECTIONS

Can Poetry Matter?: Essays on Poetry and American Culture. St. Paul, MN: Graywolf Press, 1992. [Revised Tenth Anniversary Ed., 2002]

Barrier of a Common Language: Essays on Contemporary British Poetry. Ann Arbor: University of Michigan Press, 2003.

Disappearing Ink: Poetry at the End of Print Culture. St. Paul, MN: Graywolf Press, 2004.

The Catholic Writer Today: And Other Essays. Belmont, NC: Wiseblood Books, 2019.

Studying with Miss Bishop: Memoirs from a Young Writer's Life. Philadelphia: Paul Dry Books, 2021.

Christianity and Poetry. Menomonee Falls, WI: Wiseblood Books, 2024.

Poetry as Enchantment. Philadelphia: Paul Dry Books, 2024.

Weep, Shudder, Die. Philadelphia: Paul Dry Books, 2024.

TRANSLATIONS AND LIBRETTI

Montale, Eugenio. *Mottetti: Poems of Love*. St. Paul, MN: Graywolf Press, 1990.

Nosferatu. St. Paul, MN: Graywolf Press 2001.

Seneca. *Seneca: The Madness of Hercules*. Translated with introduction by Gioia. Menomonee Falls, WI: Wiseblood Books, 2023.

CONTRIBUTORS

NED BALBO is the author of six books, including *The Cylburn Touch-Me-Nots* (New Criterion Poetry Prize winner), *3 Nights of the Perseids* (Richard Wilbur Award), and *The Trials of Edgar Poe and Other Poems* (Donald Justice Prize and the Poets' Prize). He received a 2017 NEA fellowship for his translation of Paul Valéry. He has been a visiting associate professor at Iowa State University's MFA program.

MATTHEW BRENNAN, PhD, is the author of *The Colosseum Critical. Introduction to Dana Gioia* and *Dana Gioia: A Critical Introduction*. His most recent books are *The End of the Road* (2023) and *Snow in New York: New and Selected Poems* (2021). He retired as professor emeritus of English at Indiana State University.

CHRISTOPHER CLAUSEN, PhD, was a professor of English at Penn State University for several decades. His books of criticism include *Faded Mosaic: The Emergence of Post-Cultural America*; *The Place of Poetry: Two Centuries of an Art in Crisis*; and *The Moral Imagination: Essays on Literature and Ethics*.

ROXANA ELENA DONCU completed her PhD in cultural and literary studies at the University of Bucharest and is a university lecturer in the city. She is a scholar on American and European authors. She has translated more than fifteen books from Russian, English, and German.

JACK FOLEY has published fifteen books of poetry, five books of criticism, and the two-volume *Visions and Affiliations: A California Literary Time Line, Poets & Poetry*, a history of California poetry from 1940 to 2005. His most recent books include *When Sleep Comes: Shillelagh Songs* (2020) and *Riverrun* (2017). He discusses Gioia in *The "Fallen Western Star" Wars: A Debate about Literary California* (2001).

JOSHUA HREN, PhD, is founder of Wiseblood Books and co-founder of the MFA in creative writing program at the University of St. Thomas,

Houston. He is the author of eight books, including two story collections, *This Is Our Exile* and *In the Wine Press*; the novels *Infinite Regress* and *Blue Walls Falling Down*; *How to Read (and Write) Like a Catholic*; and *Contemplative Realism*.

HILTON KRAMER was the founding editor of *The New Criterion*. He was the chief art critic of the *New York Times* from 1973 to 1982. From 1987 until 2006, he was the art critic for the *New York Observer*. He was the author of *The Triumph of Modernism: The Art World, 1985–2005*; *The Revenge of the Philistines: Art and Culture, 1972–1984*; and *The Twilight of the Intellectuals: Culture and Politics in the Era of the Cold War*.

SHIRLEY GEOK-LIN LIM, PhD, is professor emerita in the English department and former chair of women's studies at the University of California, Santa Barbara. She was both the first woman and the first Asian person to be awarded the Commonwealth Poetry Prize. She won the American Book Award as editor of *The Forbidden Stitch: An Asian American Women's Anthology* (1989) and for her memoir, *Among the White Moon Faces* (1997). She is the author of eleven poetry collections, three novels, *The Shirley Lim Collection*, three books of short stories, and two books of criticism. She was born and raised in Malaysia.

APRIL LINDNER, PhD, is the author of two books of poetry, *Skin*, which won Walt McDonald First Book Prize, and *This Bed Our Bodies Shaped*. She is the author of a critical monograph, *Dana Gioia*, in the Boise State University Western Writers Series. She has published three young adult novels. She teaches at Saint Joseph's University in Philadelphia.

FRANZ LINK was the professor of American Literature at the University of Freiburg. He was the co-editor of Germany's *Yearbook of Literary Scholarship*. Among his many publications, Link was best known for his comprehensive, two-volume history of American poetry, *Make it New: US-amerikanische Lyrik des 20. Jahrhunderts* (1996).

SAMUEL MAIO, PhD, is professor emeritus of English and comparative at San José State University, where was director of creative writing.

His poetry collections include *The Burning of Los Angeles*. His criticism includes *Creating Another Self: Voice in Modern American Personal Poetry*. He is also editor of *Dramatic Monologues: A Contemporary Anthology*.

DAVID MASON, PhD, is the former poet laureate of Colorado and author of eight books of poetry including *The Country I Remember*, *Sea Salt*, and *Ludlow*, which won the Colorado Book Award. He has written a memoir and four essay collections, including *Voices, Places* (2018). His writing has appeared in the *New Yorker*, *Harper's*, the *Times Literary Supplement*, *Poetry*, and the *Hudson Review*. He lives in Tasmania.

JANET MCCANN, PhD, is professor emerita of English at Texas A&M University, where she taught for more than forty-five years. Her poetry collections include *The Crone at the Casino* (2015), *Pascal Goes to the Races* (2004), and *Looking for Buddha in the Barbed-Wire Garden* (1996). She received a National Endowment for the Arts fellowship.

ROBERT MCPHILLIPS, PhD, taught literature for many years at Iona College. He was the author of *The New Formalism: A Critical Introduction*. In addition to his essays on Gioia, he wrote "What's New About the New Formalism," which was published in *Expansive Poetry*, and "Reading the New Formalists," in *Poetry after Modernism*.

LESLIE MONSOUR is the author of the full-length poetry collection *The Alarming Beauty of the Sky* (2005) and several chapbooks. Her poetry is included in *New Formalist Poets of the American West* and *A Formal Feeling Comes: Poems in Form by Contemporary Women*. She has written essays on Rhina Espaillat, Richard Wilbur, and other formal poets.

WILLIAM OXLEY was a poet, critic, and editor. In 1985 he and his wife Patricia Oxley co-founded *Acumen*, a British journal of poetry and criticism. Oxley published two dozen volumes of verse, which were gathered in *Collected and New Poems* (2014). He also wrote fifteen books of prose, most notably *Woking Backwards, A Poet's Notebook* (2008).

JON PARRISH PEEDE is the president of Ashland University. He is the former chairman of the National Endowment for the Humanities. Peede previously served as literature grants director at the National Endowment for the Arts. He is co-editor of *Inside the Church of Flannery O'Connor: Sacrament, Sacramental, and the Sacred in Her Fiction*.

ANNE STEVENSON was the author of numerous collections of poetry, including *It Looks So Simple from a Distance* (2010), *Selected Poems* (2008), *Stone Milk* (2007), and *Poems 1955–2005* (2006). Her critical works include a biography of Sylvia Plath, *Bitter Fame*; *Five Looks at Elizabeth Bishop*; and *Between the Iceberg and the Ship: Selected Essays*.

KEVIN WALZER, PhD, is the author of *The Ghost of Tradition: Expansive Poetry and Postmodernism* (Story Line, 1998). He is also a founder of WordTech Communications, a publishing house that has released more than forty books. In addition to three books of literary criticism, Walzer has published poetry in *Connecticut Review*, *Poetry*, and other journals.

JAMES MATTHEW WILSON, PhD, is Cullen Foundation Chair in English Literature and the founding director of the MFA program in creative writing at the University of Saint Thomas, Houston. His books include *The Vision of the Soul: Truth, Goodness, and Beauty in the Western Tradition*; *The Fortunes of Poetry in an Age of Unmaking*; and a monograph, *The Catholic Imagination in Modern American Poetry*. He is poetry editor of *Modern Age* and series editor of Colosseum Books.

JOHN ZHENG, PhD, is professor of English and chair of the Mississippi Valley State University department of English & Foreign Languages. He is the editor of six books, including *The Other World of Richard Wright* and *Conversations with Dana Gioia* (2021). Publishing under the name Jianqing Zheng, he is the author of the poetry collection *The Dog Years of Reeducation* (2023) and *A Way of Looking* (2021), which won the Gerald Cable Book Award. A native of China, he edits the *Journal of Ethnic American Literature*.

ACKNOWLEDGMENTS AND PERMISSIONS

Ned Balbo, "Beloved Communities: On *Meet Me at the Lighthouse*," was excerpted from "Beloved Communities, Lasting Divisions: Poets on Country, Culture, and Kinship," in *Literary Matters* 15/3 (Spring 2023) https://www.literarymatters.org/. It is reprinted with permission.

Matthew Brennan, "The Poet as Critic and Public Intellectual," is expanded from "Dana Gioia: Thc Poet as the Puhlic Intellectual," *South Carolina Review* (Spring 2003). It is printed with permission of the author.

Christopher Clausen, "Culture and the Subculture," was first published in *Commentary* 95/2 (February 1993): 75–76. It is reprinted with permission.

Roxana Elena Doncu, "Naming and Taming the Truth: Dana Gioia's Transformative Poetry," was first published in *American, British and Canadian Studies* 36/1 (June 2021): 26–48. This work is reprinted under the Creative Commons Attribution-NonCommercial-No Derivatives 4.0 International License.

Jack Foley, "The Achievement of Dana Gioia," was first published in *The Dancer and the Dance: A Book of Distinctions, Poetry in the New Century* (Los Angeles: Red Hen Press, 2008), 150–56. It is reprinted with permission.

Joshua Hren, "Climbing to God on 'The Burning Ladder': Dana Gioia's *Via Negativa*," was first published in *Religion and the Arts* 23/1–2 (2019): 124–41. It is reprinted with permission.

Hilton Kramer, "Poetry & the Silencing of Art," was first published in the *New Criterion* (February 1993): 4–9. It is reprinted with permission.

Shirley Geok-lin Lim, "The Turn in Dana Gioia's Meet Me at the Lighthouse," was first published in the Journal of Ethnic American Literature (2023): 5–21. It is reprinted with permission.

April Lindner, "Poems of Exile and Loss: *Daily Horoscope*," was excerpted from her monograph *Dana Gioia* (Boise: Western Writers Series, Boise State University, 2003), 16–35. It is reprinted with permission.

Franz Link, "Dana Gioia: Critic and Poet of the New Formalism," was first published in *Symbolism* (2001): 207–28. It is reprinted with permission.

Samuel Maio, "Dana Gioia's Dramatic Monologues," was first published in the *Formalist* 13/1 (2002): 63–72. This revised and expanded version is reprinted with permission.

David Mason, "The State of Letters: The Inner Exile of Dana Gioia," was first published in the *Sewanee Review* 123/1 (2015): 133–46. It is reprinted with permission.

Janet McCann, "Dana Gioia: A Contemporary Metaphysics," was first published in *Renascence* 61/3 (2009): 193–205. It is reprinted with permission.

Robert McPhillips, "Dana Gioia and Visionary Realism," was first published in *Dana Gioia: A Descriptive Bibliography with Critical Essays*, edited by Jack W. C. Hagstrom and Bill Morgan (Jackson: Parrish House, 2002), 259–81. It is reprinted with permission.

Leslie Monsour, "*On Interrogations at Noon*," was first published as "O Dark, Dark, Dark, amid the Blaze of Noon: The Poetry of Dana Gioia," *Able Muse* (Winter 2002) at AbleMuse.com. It is reprinted with permission.

William Oxley, "The First Shall Be Last," a review of *Interrogations at Noon*, was first published in *Acumen* 41 (Sept. 2001): 101-4. It is reprinted with permission.

Anne Stevenson, "On *The Gods of Winter*," was first published in *Poetry Wales* 27/4 (April 1992). It is included in her essay collection *Between the Iceberg and the Ship: Selected Essays* (Ann Arbor: University of Michigan Press, 1998), 156–58. It is reprinted with permission.

Kevin Walzer, "Dana Gioia and Expansive Poetry," was first published in *Italian Americana* 16/1 (Winter 1998): 24–40. It is reprinted with permission.

James Matthew Wilson, "In Christ-Haunted California: Dana Gioia's *99 Poems*," was first published in *The Catholic World Report*, April 26, 2016. It is reprinted with permission.

John Zheng, "The Art of Story-Telling: Dana Gioia's 'Ballad of Jesús Ortiz,'" was first published in *Valley Voices* 18/2 (Fall 2018): 117–22. It is reprinted with permission.

INDEX